A

Destiny

is

Sworn

Rhianwen Roberts

ISBN 0-9679844-3-2
Library of Congress Catalog Card No. 00-112117

Cover by Brent Jeffrey Thomas
The Coat of Arms of the Men of Eden

Farolito Press
P.O. Box 60003
Grand Junction, Colorado 81506

Manufactured in the United States of America
Pyramid Printing and Copy Center
Grand Junction, Colorado
www.pyramidprinting.com

O diengyd, ath welif;
O'th ryledir, ath gwynif:
Na choll wyneb gwr ar gnif.

If thou escape, I shall see thee again;
If thou art slain, I shall lament thee:
Lose not the honor of a warrior, though thou suffer for it.

Llywarch Hen (Welsh poet-king: 9th Century)

Contents

Author's Foreword
Genealogical Table
Map
List of Chief Characters

AUTHOR'S FOREWORD

This is the story of a rebellion which took place in the small country of Wales six hundred years ago. It was led by a man known to the English speaking world as Owen Glendower. Being Welsh I was taught to call him Owain Glyndwr (glinnDOOHR) or Glyn Dwr. It is the first of these two forms that I use in this book.

His rebellion seems significant to me on two counts; it was surely one of the first national risings in European history. It also marked the emergence of the Tudors, who interestingly enough were cousins of Glyndwr and played a prominent part in his rebellion. They had in fact been involved in litigation and an insurrection of their own in the previous century.

The question then arises: if Glyndwr's rebellion had not occurred would there ever have been a Tudor dynasty? For all its high ideals, the uprising left a bitter legacy of feud among the Welsh families, and many fled the land at that time to escape not only the severe penal laws but the vengeance of their enemies. One of these fugitives, if has been said, was Meredith ap Tudor's son Owain, the Owen Tudor known to history as the grandfather of Henry VII of England.

In Welsh mythology 'to swear a destiny' on anyone was to condemn him—or her—to a fate as inevitable and irreversible as time or tide. It is for this reason that I have entitled this novel: A DESTINY IS SWORN.

THE MEN OF EDEN

descendants of Ednyved Vychan, lord of Criccieth
Chief Counselor of Llywelyn the Great,
Prince of Wales: 1200-1240 A.D.

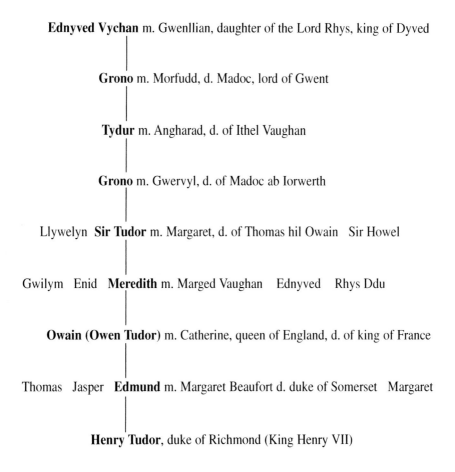

Ednyved Vychan m. Gwenllian, daughter of the Lord Rhys, king of Dyved

Grono m. Morfudd, d. Madoc, lord of Gwent

Tydur m. Angharad, d. of Ithel Vaughan

Grono m. Gwervyl, d. of Madoc ab Iorwerth

Llywelyn **Sir Tudor** m. Margaret, d. of Thomas hil Owain   Sir Howel

Gwilym   Enid   **Meredith** m. Marged Vaughan   Ednyved   Rhys Ddu

Owain (Owen Tudor) m. Catherine, queen of England, d. of king of France

Thomas   Jasper   **Edmund** m. Margaret Beaufort d. duke of Somerset   Margaret

Henry Tudor, duke of Richmond (King Henry VII)

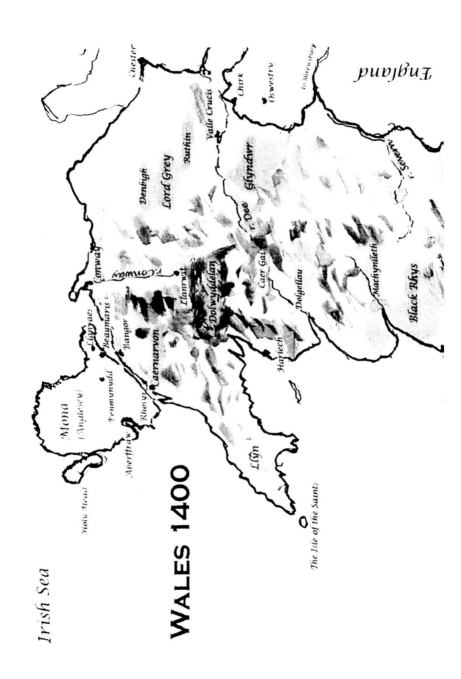

Irish Sea

Chester

England

to Shrewsbury

Oswestry

Chirk

Valle Crucis

Ruthin

Lord Grey

Denbigh

Glyndwr

r. Dee

Severn

Conway

Ti Corwen

Llanrwst

Caer Gai

Machynlleth

Dolwyddelan

Dolgellau

Black Rhys

Llanfaes

Beaumaris

Bangor

Harlech

Mona
(Anglesey)

Penmynydd

Rhosyr

Caernarvon

Holy Head

Aberffraw

Lŷn

WALES 1400

The Isle of the Saints

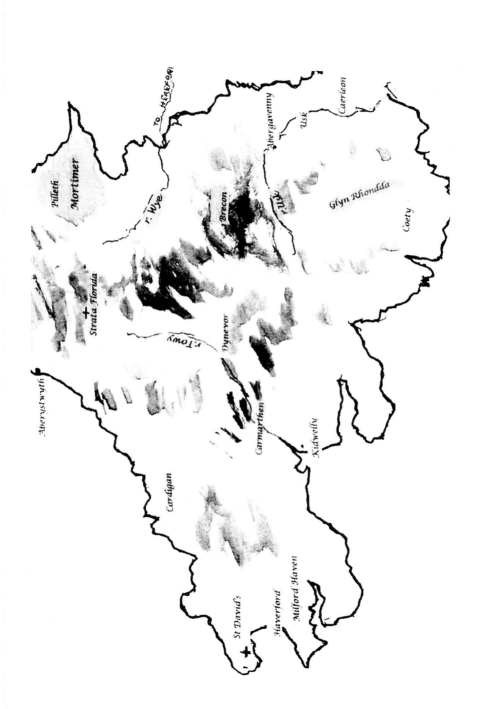

CHIEF CHARACTERS

THE CHILDREN OF **SIR TUDOR AP* GRONO** OF THE ISLE OF MONA.

Meredith (meh-RED-th), the Chieftain of the Men of Eden and master of Penmynydd (pen-MUNN-ith), m. to Marged Vaughan. Their son was Owain ap Meredith.

Gwilym (GWILL-im) master of Trecastell m. to Eilian of Nantanog.

Rhys Ddu (Reece Thee) m. Eva, the daughter of Red Iwan.

Ednyved (ed-NUV-ed)—familiar form Eden (EDD-enn) master of the Old Hall, m. to Annes (ANN-ess).

Enid, m. to Einion (INE-yon) ab Ithel, Constable of Dolwyddelan (doll-with-ELL-an) castle.

OTHER ISLANDERS:

Father Conan, the priest of Penmynydd.
Mam Indeg, his wife.
Gerallt, their elder son; Eden's foster-brother and the steward of the Old Hall.
Mererid (meh-REH-rid) their daughter.
Alun (ALeen), younger brother of Gerallt and Mererid.
Sioned (SHON-ed), Gerallt's wife.
Robyn ap Traphern, Eden's foster son, the nephew of the outlaw David ap Jenkin.
Mabon, the housebard of the Old Hall.
Meredith ap Kenvric, Sheriff of Mona.
Joanna Beaupine, his wife.
Annes (ANNess), their daughter, Eden's wife.
Elianor (ell-YAHN-or), the lady of Dyngannan (dunn-GANN-an).
Andras, her son.
Em of Tregele, the wife of Andras.

*ap is a shortened form of *mab* or *map*. It is cognate of Irish *mac*, meaning *son of.*

Chief Characters *(cont.)*

Owain Glyndwr (Owen glinn-DOOHR), the Welsh leader.
Margaret Hanmer, his wife; daughter of Sir David Hanmer of Hanmer.
John Hanmer, his brother-in-law.
Robert Puleston, his brother-in-law, m. to Glyndwr's sister Lowri.
Black Rhys of Ceredigion (kehreh-DIG-yon), a Glyndwr supporter.
Henry Don of Kidwelly, a Glyndwr supporter.
Cadwgan (cah-DOO-gan) of **Glyn Rhondda**, a Glyndwr supporter.
Master Walter Brut, the Lollard. A Glyndwr supporter.
Howel Vaughan of Mathebrud (math-EBB-reed), the head of the Men of
    Ithon; a Glyndwr supporter and brother-in-law to Meredith ap Tudor.
Olwen, wife of Howel Vaughan.
*****Red Iwan (YEWann)**, of the Great Strand, governor of Caernarvon. His
    first wife was Eluned (ell-LEEN-ed) Sir Tudor's sister.
Madoc, their older son.
Huw, their younger son.
Eva, their daugher, m. to Rys Ddu of Mona.

*His name was actually **Ieuan ap Maredudd**. Iwan, another of the Welsh
forms of John, seemed to me a simpler alternative for non-Welsh speaking
readers.

A Destiny is Sworn

Book One

The Island

PROLOGUE

In ancient times it was said to be one of the Three Islands of the Dead. The Irish called it Conaing's Swamp. It was here that the Druids made their last stand against the Romans under Suetonius Paulinus. Branwen, the ill-fated Queen of Ireland, lay buried in her four-sided grave in one of its grey fields. Here came St Cybi the Swarthy, the grandson of Geraint ab Erbin, who was with Arthur the seven Easters, five Christmasses, and the one Pentecost he held court at Caerleon, the City of the Legions, to drive out the pagans and establish his great house. In the time of the princes it became the chief seat of the Lords of Gwynedd. The years grew rich there with poetry and song.

> *There is a host in Rhosfair*
> *there is drinking, there are golden bells.*
> *There comes my Lord Llywelyn and tall warriors*
> *follow him,*
> *a thousand, a host in green and white.*

Such was the island called by the Saxon Anglesey, but known to the Welshman as Môn, Mam Cymru—Mona, Mother of Wales.

Towards the end of the twelfth century Ednyved Vychan* was a young warrior in the Lord Llywelyn's retinue. When no more than seventeen he led a force of Welsh troops against Earl Ranulf of Chester and defeated him. To the three knights he slew in that battle he owed his coat-of-arms: gules, a chevron between three Englishmen's heads proper couped. By the year 1215 he was the chief counselor and commander of Llywelyn the Great* and had to wife Gwenllian, the daughter of the Lord Rhys, King of Dyved.

*Ednyved Vychan-See Note 1
*Llywelyn Fawr (Llywelyn ap Iorwerth). In 1202 he was the ruler of Gwynedd (North-West Wales). By 1240, when he died, he had united most of Wales under his rule. His grandson Llywelyn ap Gruffydd, known as Llywelyn the Last, was recognized by most of the contemporary Welsh rulers as Prince of Wales.

It was to this warrior-statesman that his descendants owed the name by which they became known: The Men of Eden *(Wyrion Eden)*. Distinguished by their exceptional prowess in battle they formed a class apart; they accumulated much wealth and property, they were freed from all dues to the Crown, and their only obligation was one of military service.

Then in 1282 the death of Llywelyn the Last in a skirmish with a band of English soldiers near the border led to the seizure of his lands by King Edward the First of England and things were no longer as they once had been. A chain of castles was raised around the country to keep the native population in check. Walled towns were built and Englishmen given franchises by the King's charter to settle in them. Another system of government was introduced, but this new order was ill-understood by the Welsh who clung to their old laws and traditions and found it difficult to acknowledge the authority of a foreign power they had so long resisted, feared and hated. Unrest spread as the official tyranny grew. During the next two reigns the courts fell into confusion, the laws became a mockery, and corruption was rife. Dark words broke over the lips of men. Horror-striking bards preached in firelit glades and men with axes and knives gathered in mountain glens. Scattered uprisings of varying force were constantly being put down. One of these was that of Sir Tudor ap Grono.

Sir Tudor was a great-great-grandson of Ednyved Vychan and already had the reputation of being a turbulent man. Years earlier he had abducted and married one of the greatest heiresses in Wales, the young widow of the lord of Mawddwy, a man with whom in the past he had often been in contention. Far off to the north, in the Valley of the Conway, the bride declared proudly that hers had been a wedding of personal bestowal, and it was not hard to believe, for Sir Tudor was a man of great personal beauty and charm. At the same time he knew how to breathe scorn. His smile could sting like a nettle. He refused to depart from his path by a step to mollify his wife's outraged kinsmen. Hence he denied himself the support of some powerful chieftains in his conflict with the overlords. As it was he caused trouble enough.

The kings of England and France were once more at war when Sir Tudor unleashed his force of Welsh rebels upon the hundreds of Gwynedd. Baggage trains were pillaged and garrison towns attacked. One summer morning the townsfolk of Rhuddlan were harvesting grain when Sir Tudor's men fell upon them. The rebels broke skulls and burned the crops. The reapers fled back to the town in panic. They climbed on the walls and displayed the banners of King Edward and his son the Black Prince, but to no end. The Welsh only jeered and hurled filth. The assault went on all day. Then it was Vespers. Through the waning light the town cattle came ambling from their pasture homeward, lowing and chasing the gnats with their dung-scabbed tails. Only then did the besiegers desist, driving the herd before them into the forests and glens. There, as long as the supply lasted, the call that went up was: "Tripes, broth, hot ribs of beef!" Everyone with a wild leek in his bonnet was bidden to the feasting: beggars, orphans, old folk, poor widows, traveling minstrels and friars might have their meat, roast, sod or fried, and nothing to pay, all was free.

Such the merry doings of those days—days when it was told that the lives of crooked sheriffs* and king's attorneys did not amount to a black fig in those parts. It was a worthy if violent piece of brigandage no doubt, but as so often befalls those who rise up against the tyranny of the powerful, it was ill-fated. The rebels were crushed in the end and Sir Tudor's lands and manors this side of the straits of Menai laid forfeit for treason each one. He was compelled to retire to the only estate that was left to him, the ancient settlement of the fathers on the Isle of Mona.

Adversity, the sages tell us, comes with instruction in its hand. All very well to say. In defeat, Sir Tudor, that lordly dispenser of roast beef, did not change his ways. He continued to hold sumptuous feasts, took it upon himself to settle the grievances of his tribesmen and tenants, and generally flouted authority. Nonetheless, tragedy dogged him. A few years after he had taken up residence at the Old Hall, his eldest and favorite son Grono was killed in a fall from a horse, and one black and blowing October night in the following year, his wife, a woman worn out by childbearing and the hazards of the years, died in giving birth to his youngest. That same night the priest, Father Conan, brought the new-christened baby home to his wife Mam Indeg at the church-farm at nearby Penmynydd.

"What name has been given the mite?" she asked as she laid him in the crib beside her own baby son Gerallt,

"Ednyved."

---

* sheriff: under Norman law a sheriff *(shire reeve)* was the chief administrator of the king in shire or county.

"God's welcome to you, my little Eden," said Mam Indeg. "May you be happy."

And she blessed his red, peevish, wrinkled brow three times with the figure of the Cross.

During the remaining years of his father's life, Eden saw him but rarely. Twice or three times after he had turned his seventh birthday he was dressed in his best blue tunic with the little golden petrels inwoven. Shoes that plucked his toes and made him walk like a hen were put on his feet, a blue cap with a pheasant's feather caught in the brooch was set on his head, and thus adorned he was borne to a torchlit hall somewhere at the bounds of the earth where he was kissed and blessed by one he took to be no less than a hundred: a chieftain in a dark silken gown, with a gold thread in his hair and a silvery beard like a river, who used to ask him how old he was, and whether he was a good boy, and then send him to sit at the children's board among brats who mystified him beyond words by calling him 'Uncle'.

And there he would sit, peering at the Chieftain through the painted wooden columns like a young deer in a thicket. Could it be that he was the son of one of so strange and ancient an aspect, he asked himself? No, the thought was incredible to him.

His home was the house and farm next to the church at Penmynydd. Father Conan was his father, Gerallt was his brother, and his mother was Mam Indeg. She was the baseborn daughter of a scion of the mighty Welsh border house of the Trevors, but this was no big matter. She got the man she loved. She was happy. Is more necessary?

She was, besides that, a bewitching teller of tales. Say it was a dark rush-peeling winter's night and the priest-father was out on a mission to some lonely croft—ah, the tales she told her lads then! From her lips they learned how the boulders on the haunted mound had been borne there long ages before by a giantess in her apron; and how the wizard Gwydion had called out of the flowers of the field and forest that maiden unto whom there was never one in this mortal world to be compared in beauty and grace; and how Hu the Mighty and his big bull buffaloes had checked the ravages of the Flood and the devastating cocodryllus.

For some reason the boys marked that she did not relate these stories when Father Conan was near. It was always Jesus, Mary and the holy saints then.

Meanwhile Sir Tudor fell sick. The island went to prayers. Sleeping in his bed of rushes under the mouse-riddled thatch one January night, Eden was awakened by Father Conan. Mam Indeg was weeping.

"Och, joy of my heart!" she said.

An icy rain was blowing in shuddering gusts about them as they rode to the Old Hall. Keening phantoms met the lad's gaze there, their shadows swaying eerily along the wooden posts glassed by firelight. A pretty young woman crushed him to her bosom, sobbing: "Little brother, do you know who I am? I am your sister Enid." She took him by the hand and led him into the death-chamber. The dying man was lying in his bed with his eyes closed, the breath coming and going harshly between his hanging lips. At his bedside knelt three men, lost in a fervor of prayer. They were Eden's grown brothers, likewise strangers to him at the time. Their names were Meredith, Gwilym, and Rhys Ddu.

"Look, father," said Enid, her lips whispering into the dying chieftain's ear. "See who is here."

At that the old man opened his eyes, already clouded with dreams not of this world. He turned his head ever so slightly to look at the boy who knelt to kiss his clammy waxen hand.

"Huw," he breathed in a hoarse whisper, taking him for a cousin of his, dead of a fever at the age of ten.

"What are you about?" growled one of the men kneeling at the bedside to Enid. "Can you not see that our father is travelling? Leave him be."

This was Eden's eldest brother Meredith. Upon Sir Tudor's death he was the man who now became the Chieftain of that faction known in the land as The Men of Eden.

There was no question of it from that hour. Until then Meredith had lived with his wife Marged Vaughan across the sea-river of the Menai, at her ancestral hall of Mathebrud in Nantconway. He and Sir Tudor had not got on well together—every encounter had seemed to end in a battle of words. Big, black-fleeced, blue-eyed, stern-browed and limping— he had been crippled during his father's uprising—he now made his home at Penmynydd. No one had lived in the hall since the death of Grono, the favorite son. Everything smelt of neglect. The nettles were high in the courtyard, and the sagging roofs gaped with holes.

The new Chieftain did not waste a moment. He rebuilt the hall and houses, ploughed up the yards, had hard stone hauled in for paving, erected fencing and had his eye, it seemed, on all things. It was not long before it fell upon his youngest brother.

Eden was now eleven. From the priest-father he had learned his catechism, his Aelius Donatus, and he knew how to read and write and pipe a tune; but Father Conan had a large parish, and so the boy was left for much of the time in the care of Mam Indeg, who spoilt him and let him run about the turbary with her own son Gerallt, the two of them as wild as wasps. A good reason for priests not to have wives, the Chieftain decided. But there, it was his uncle Sir Howel, the Archdeacon of Mona, who had placed Father Conan where he was. Who can alter the weather?

Meredith bestirred himself. He plucked his youngest brother away from Mam Indeg's nest, and to the boy's great alarm and dismay delivered him up to the monks at the Abbey of Llanvaes, the great house of the Minorites on the island. Eden was left there for four years. At the end of that time, he was led brimful of excitement to the Old Hall and installed there as master. His long crow-black locks were trimmed by the Chieftain with the ceremonial shears with the silver loops, he was put to sit in the highseat and his three brothers acted as servers. All the familiar faces were there, saving only that of Mam Indeg who was at home with a sick baby—a little girl named Mererid.

Eden felt aglow. Everything shone in the torchlight—the shields and weapons had been new-painted and burnished, and the fumes of the wine rose to his head and made it swim pleasantly. He looked down the hall and directed his proud and beaming glance at the children's board. Now he was a man.

Among the guests at that memorable feast were two merry youths, David and Trahern, sons of Jenkin of Welsh Maelor, a border chieftain who had supported Tudor in the time of his troubles. Eden took an instant liking to them. Next year when, as a part of his training in arms, he went about the land shooting matches and masteries at the halls and practice grounds of other chieftains, they bore him company. One day they arrived at the hall of the Trevors. They were given a good welcome there—the lord Rhisiart was a brother of Mam Indeg's father Lewis—but it was not by reason of the chieftain's bounty that Eden stayed on at the hall as long as he did. Angharad, the daughter of the house, was a beauty. From the moment he saw her, he knew that no other girl would content him. She and she alone must be his wife. She had hair of a darkness to beggar the rooks, the merriest laugh in the world, and her kisses made him lose sense. By the end of the summer when they parted, both were madly in love. They wept, exchanged rings, and swore to be faithful to each other.

Once home on the island Eden lost no time in beating a path to the Chieftain's door with his tale. Meredith, who had no great love for the Trevors, heard him out and said no. He had another match in mind— Annes, a young and virtuous widow, who dwelt with her father, the Sheriff of Mona, in the King's town of Beaumaris. Eden liked Annes well enough—she was a good lady, gentle and kind—but she was seven years older than he was least and had a disagreeable mother. Besides, he loved somebody else.

"If I cannot have her I will die."

"Nonsense. You are not yet turned of seventeen. You will not die."

One week, two weeks, three weeks passed. Eden's seventeenth birthday came and went. The Chieftain remained inflexible. To make matters worse, it was much about this time that their brother Rhys Ddu, the seafarer, stole away and married his first cousin Eva, thus bringing them under the ban of the Church. Such shame and disgrace had not been visited on the house in time of mind—even that lusty galliard Sir Tudor had been free of the stigma of incest. It put the Chieftain's patience and philosophy severely to the proof.

"Who will have you now, little brother?" he mused, savagely smiling, as he contemplated the youth's pale face with its new-springing beard and red eyes of unsleeping. "Perhaps one of those fisher-maids down at the saltings? Or Long Bet the Leech?—she is a widow now they tell me."

"I shall run away with her."

"Who? Long Bet?" the Chieftain roared.

Aye, God alone knows it was not the work of an hour winning Meredith over to the charms of the fair Angharad. And yet, in the end he succumbed. Love is irresistible, as the poets tell it. It spins the giddy wheels of May. It lights the fires that illumine the saints in Heaven. Less fanciful folk maintained, however, that it was the birth of his first son at

Epiphany that finally brought the Chieftain to a submission, that all unwonted and joyous event having gladdened his heart immeasurably.

"So she's really a prize, eh?"

"She would destroy the sun shining, Meredith."

"Ach you. You have begun to screech in my ears like an old wheel truly. Enough. So be it then. Be off with you and if you find her as you left her—well, we shall see what we shall see. You may have to answer some awkward questions yonder this time, mind you. Rhys and Eva, eh? John Trevor is the Bishop of St Asaph. Have you given some thought to that?"

"No, not a scraping of one. But it's not him I am bent on wooing, although he has very fine red hair, it's said."

"Don't be flippant. You may find yourself wooing him nonetheless. And he's no mean dialectician, it seems."

"What does love have to do with dialectics?"

"That I cannot say. You may be on your way to finding out. Tell me when you return. By the way, set nothing down in writing. Weigh your words with care, make no promises, swear no oaths."

"I swear."

"And be back to lead the first mowing. You owe us that spectacle."

"You have my word."

Bang the timbrels! Put out the flags! So exulting and triumphing, Eden set forth in the young of the day for the township of the Trevors, wearing a new dove-grey mantle and tunic of fine Flemish cloth, and riding a willow-grey steed four winters old. No more than a week later he was brought back to the island on a litter, his fine clothes torn and stained, with a gashed head and a broken heart.

2

One summer's night, in the year 1394, in the province of Ceredigion in the west of Wales, in a great clearing as of a river plain in the deep middle of a forest, Black Rhys, the territorial lord of those parts, shagbrowed and burly, was sitting in his huge high-raftered hall drinking a bowl of metheglin,* the juice of sabbats, when there came a blast of horns outside in the darkness and the booming blows of the gate-hammers.

*An old Welsh variety of mead.

"By the Lord," he exclaimed, "who can be coming here at this ungodly hour? Fiends? Bolols? Witches?"

His wife, the lady Madlan, who was nodding over a pile of swaddling bands and baby clothes, came awake with a start.

"Witches?"

"Sit where you are, dear lady. Do not excite yourself in your condition," he said, reeling up and hastening out to the courtyard. Moments later he returned, leading in at the head of a boisterous troop a tall broad-shouldered man with hair and beard of gold-tawny color, in a dark furred mantle.

"Look who is here, Madlan."

Peering at the newcomer striding towards her through the smoky light, it was with ill-concealed dismay that the lady now recognized a man, who of all chieftains in the land, must have been the wealthiest and most powerful. He was Owain ap Griffith Vychan, the Lord of the Vale of the Divine Water, a patrimony so ancient and storied that it had given him the name by which he was best known to his countrymen, that of Glyndwr.* Madlan herself was a lady of proud descent. The blood of the old Kings of South Wales ran in her veins. On the distaff side she claimed descent from the family of the blessed Nonnita, the mother of the patron saint of her countrymen, St. David the Water-drinker. The dear knows that under different circumstances she would have run herself into a coil to make this man welcome. But now she could barely find it in herself to marshal a smile as he embraced and greeted her with a burst of chivalrous gallantry. Why did people have to arrive at such an hour? She was in the eight month of her pregnancy—the little one was kicking so much she could no longer bring herself to sleep at night. Of a necessity she could not attend to the housekeeping as she used to—the flagstones of the great hall were littered with scraps of food, nutshells, children's playthings, God knows what else. She was so worn out and tired.

"And what brings you to these parts, my soul?" asked Black Rhys.

"I was at the Abbey awaiting these kinsmen of mine when it occurred to me that since you were not too far away I might as well call on you, too."

Owain Glyndwr paused and eyed his host with a roguish smile.

"I have been to London to see the King."

*Owain Glyndwr—See Note 2

"Do you hear that, Madlan? Our friend has been to London to see the King. What matter took you there? Shall I venture a guess? You have an unpleasant neighbor, Lord Reginald Grey by name, who covets some land of yours. So what did King Richard say?"

"He declared in my favor."

"Give God the glory. And Grey, how did he take it?"

"Imagine."

"Well, aye."

"The last that was seen of him at Westminster he was hurrying down a dark passageway like an ague in a gullet. Come away with us, eh, my pet? Rejoicings are in order."

They did not delay. At earliest light on the following day the cavalcade was on its way through forest and rock-and-river glen to the Welsh border and Glyndwr's great hall of Sycharth where a feast was being made ready against his return.

For five days the feasting went on, with games and sports by day and torchlight revelry at night. Glowing with vitality and good humor, the host moved among his guests. One evening he came to a halt, with an approving grin, before a lovely fresh-hued face, a slender form in a gown of white-flowered silk worked with threads of gold.

"God preserve you in your beauty, fair flower of the Trevors," he said with a glance at her wife's cap and golden rings. "But how is this? Married? And to whom?" he asked, with a sly wink at her husband, the Keeper and Master Forester of Chirkeland, a young black-jawed Welshman with half-shut laughing eyes. "I thought I heard someone tell me once that you might wed my kinsman, young Ednyved of Mona."

"Truly?" she marveled, blushing to the bone. "And what else did you hear?"

"Scraps of garbled tales, puzzling rumors. Hostile occasions, ambush by night, stolen horses and a deal of devious verbiage, great dissertations de legibus—is that enough?"

"More than enough, my lord Owain," she smiled.

"It is not a faction to come to a grapple with."

"It is unforgiving you mean."

"Sir Tudor was so certainly. You must know that he abducted my mother's sister. My parents did not attend the wedding. Neither did your kinfolk for the matter of that. We were never forgiven that slight. When I heard that the youngster had been your way a-wooing, I thought—well,

God be praised, the thaw begins. Then, to be sure, that rogue Rhys Ddu must elope with the beauteous Eva, eh? Bad."

"Especially as my uncle is a bishop."

"Aye, indeed, fair lady. I parted from him at Westminster not a month since and he was still fulminating."

Glyndwr let his mind run back briefly over that encounter with the companion of his boyhood. What a merry fellow he had been of old, the reverend lord John! And now, look at him—as flamy-eyed as he was flamy-haired. Stern his voice, deep from the chest:

"Terrible, terrible! Have you heard what has happened? Those scapegrace curs, the sons of Jenkin of Welsh Maelor have slain Simon Thelwall, my sister's son. Cold-blooded murder, my dear Owain. You remember them, sure, those courtship attendants Ednyved ap Tudor brought with him when he made suit for my niece's hand in marriage?"

"They did not come my way, you know."

"What a blessing they did not! Did you hear what they did to my brother's fine hall? Dear my fathers, talk about a *boloch!**   Plates and cups flying, tables and benches and a tapestry the women made of the Wedding at Cana torn off the wall, ripped and besmutched, all but ruined."

"And what occasioned the fray, say you?"

"Aye, Simon it may be spoke rashly, a proud and headstrong youth, God rest him, but let us not forget that he was a good son of Holy Church for all that. Think of it, my friend. Rhys ap Tudor has seduced and wed his first cousin. His own aunt's daughter. Wicked. The ban of the Church is upon them. Well, they are aye a pack of lawless men, given to violence and wanton play, you know that. I said as much to my brother from the outset but he liked Tudor's whelp well enough then as it seems did my niece."

"And Jenkin's sons, what has become of them?"

"The older one is dead. They say the other's an outlaw in Ireland somewhere."

Simon Thelwall! Glyndwr had an image of a big young man with bristling blond hair and bold staring yellow-hazel eyes. The Thelwalls had come into Ruthin with the forebears of Lord Grey, Glyndwr's arch-enemy. Only to think of that was enough to set his teeth on edge. Away, was this the time to dwell upon such things?

*boloch—uproar.

"And what has happened to Ednyved, do you know?" he asked the Bishop's niece.

"He is newly married to a widow, I hear. Annes, the daughter of the Sheriff of Mona?"

"Ah, he is married into riches then. Are you happy?"

She rested her hand tenderly upon that of her husband.

"Yes, I am," she said. "My kinsman used him badly. I am sure I wish him a good marriage." She added softly: "As is mine."

But now Glyndwr's wife, Margaret Hanmer, was beckoning him away. "Iolo is going to read his poem to us," she said. At that he sat down in quiet amidst the throng to hear the old bard, Iolo Goch, recite for the first time his long ode extolling the wonders of Sycharth: its bridge with the gate for a hundred loads, its herons and peacocks, its girdle of golden water, its lofts where travelling poets slept, its tiled roof, its bountiful chieftain, its gracious lady.

> *Bragget he keeps, bread white of look,*
> *And, bless the mark, a bustling cook.*
> *His mansion is the minstrel's home,*
> *You'll find them there whene'er you come.*
> *Of all her sex his wife's the best;*
> *The household through her care is blest;*
> *She's scion of a knightly tree,*
> *She's dignified, she's kind, she's free.*
> *Her bairns approach me, pair by pair,*
> *O, what a nest of chieftains fair!*

And the birds settled in the trees. Swans glistened like pearls on the darkening water. Far off in the west a red sun was setting in the sea.

3

With the passage of the seasons Meredith ap Tudor had mellowed. The years since that ugly brawl and business with the Trevors had not been unkind to him. His affairs were thriving, his son Owain was bright and bonny, albeit woefully spoil—he would have to do something about that one of these days for sure—and Eden was married to the fine young woman the Chieftain had had in mind for him in the first place..

And then it was 1399. An awesome time began. From one end of Wales to the other the shoulder bones of goats and the livers of rams were being examined for signs. On the druid isle the vapors of prophecy thickened. Owls screeched in belfries, cattle lowed in the middle of the night, white women were seen walking the waves, and as Eden hastened to note, his mother-in-law, Joanna Beaupine, having taken with an ague to her bed, where she remained in daily expectation of death, recovered her health. In a word, wherever one looked there were bad omens.

The world was coming to an end, it was decided. And so in a sense it did.

1
POOR RICHARD WAS TOO TRUSTING (1399-1400)

l

Nobody well knew how it all began. Something perhaps had been heard of the great tournament at Coventry in 1398 where—to the stupefaction and dismay of their countrymen—King Richard the Second had thrown down his marshal's staff and banished his cousin Henry Bolingbroke, the Duke of Lancaster, from England. Still, this life that moved in the disorders of people outside their borders seemed remote to the men of Wales at first. It could just as well have been happening in France; in other words, at the bounds of the earth and the desolate mountains.

And then early the next summer King Richard left his shores to settle a dispute in Ireland and the air grew heavy with Fate. In July the banished Duke landed at Ravenspur in Yorkshire where he was met by the Earl of Northumberland and his son Hotspur. Within two months he was in full possession of London and king in all but name. Meanwhile, the Earl of Salisbury, one of the few English nobles still loyal to Richard, rallied his supporters about him and rode westward along the northern coast of Wales to the garrison town of Conway, where he established himself at the castle, one of the most impregnable of fortresses. Once there, he summoned the chieftains of the surrounding countryside to gather to his side with as many men as they could muster.

From the Isle of Mona came Rhys Ddu and his brother Eden at the head of seven score bowmen. They were met at the castle by the Sheriff of Caernarvonshire, a long-boned soldier with a lopsided nose, who was known to the Welsh of the region as the Siri Mawr.*

"Greetings, sons of Tudor," he said. "But how is it that I see only two of you?"

"Our brothers are out at grass," said Eden.

"Gwilym is on pilgrimage," Rhys Ddu explained, "and Meredith, as you know, no longer practices the art of war."

"Aye, more's the pity. Why are you smiling, Eden? Your chieftain was a notable warrior once upon a time."

---

*Siri Mawr: the Great or High Sheriff. He had precedence over the other sheriffs of the region.

"How long ago is once upon a time, Sir Siri?"

They entered a large hall, stony and bleak as a quarry. John Massey, the Constable of Conway, stood staring down at the flagstones at his feet as though into an abyss. As for the Earl, it was plain that he was beside himself with anguish. Bluish folds hung under his eyes, and the skin about his nose and mouth, quivering with emotion, looked as grey as chalk as he paced up and down, speaking of the atrocities that were being perpetrated in England, where Richard's followers were being hunted down and slaughtered. He assured his listeners, in the meantime, that the King was on his way back from Ireland, and that he was counting on his loyal subjects, the Welsh, whom he had so stoutly defended in the past against the greed and despite of his lords, to stand by him.

The Welsh captains gave the Earl their word and remained with him awaiting the King's arrival. The town and castle swarmed with armed troops. Games and sham fights were got up to keep them busy. But the days passed, one after the other, and the army grew restive. When comes King Richard, the cry went up, and where are the wages we were promised? The older men grumbled, thinking of their wives and children laboring alone on their crofts, while the younger men fell foul of the townsfolk. brawling and roistering.

"But these folk here treat us like scum," they protested when they were haled before their betters. "They lock away their daughters and won't trust us for the worth of a penny. Let's go home, chieftains."

At last, one September day, Rhys Ddu and Eden appeared before the Earl to tell him that they could no longer detain their soldiery. Among the other captains of troops who accompanied them was their brother the Chieftain's, brother-in-law, Howel Vaughan of Mathebrud, the pride of the Men of Ithon, and a notorious hawk of the bower.

The Earl was bitter.

"Have you no power over your people at all?"

"Not at this time of year," Rhys Ddu told him. "Even in their darkest hour of trial our princes were hard put getting men out of the fields at this season. Sure, a law had to be passed: No battles at harvest-time."

"I am not interested in your laws," the Earl said sharply. "But as to hours of trial, what then do you call this?"

He stopped, looking at the faces of the men before him with a dull, simmering irritation. He fixed his gaze on Rhys Ddu. He saw a handsome man, not tall, but well-built, swarthy as an infidel, with wolf-white teeth. A ruby glistened in one of his earlobes like a bright gout of blood. His younger brother was taller, leaner, with a pale skin and a childlike smile. His right eye, dark-brown and melancholy, strayed outward noticeably, and this gave him a dreamy, rather absent look, as though he were gleaning messages out of the air. A mooncalf, the Earl decided.

"You are the sons of Sir Tudor ap Grono, are you not?" he said then. "May I remind you that it was not too long ago that a kinsman of yours was given proof of King Richard's benevolence towards him and the Welsh. Come, you must know of whom I speak," he frowned, seeing them dumbly stare. "The Lord de Glendower. King Richard took his side against Lord Reginald de Grey in a landsuit."

Eden knit his brows.

"The Lord de Glendower?" he asked innocently. "Who would that be then?"

"Sure, you know that," the Siri Mawr told him. "Owain Glyndwr."

"Good luck to him," said Rhys Ddu, "but what does that landsuit have to do with us? It's true we are kinsmen, my lord Earl, but our houses have been at odds for I do not know how many years now."

"Fifty perhaps," the Siri Mawr suggested.

"Since the marriage of our parents in fact," Rhys Ddu observed.

"If it was a marriage," said Eden, grinning.

"Do you know what you are saying?" Rhys Ddu asked.

Some of the other Welsh captains started laughing.

"O, shame and despair of your tribe!" Howel Vaughan of Mathebrud exclaimed. "Are you following this, lord? The father bore the mother away by the strong hand, you see."

"She was consenting, Howel," Rhys Ddu argued.

"The law still adjudges it rape, you old pirate."

The Earl's lip twitched convulsively. These Welsh jesters with their goatskin battalions can bicker and banter about their trumpery feuds and debaucheries and Richard, their defender and savior, out there in his agony somewhere—but where? Ah, that he come!

He gave his hand an impatient flourish. "Let this be on the bye," he said, swallowing back the bile that was souring his tongue. "What I want to tell you is this. I know Henry of Lancaster. He is a vindictive man. If he wins power it will go hard for King Richard's friends. And Lord

Grey of Ruthin, that enemy of your kinsman, is the Duke's boon companion. He is at his side in Chester even now. Does that mean nothing to you?"

"I am sorry, lord," said Rhys Ddu. "Our men have yet to receive a day's wages and are in want of food. Shout and bully as we will, there is no holding them here another night. 'Tis pity of it."

Salisbury gave a harsh laugh.

"Aye," he said. "'Tis pity of it."

"I am glad that I am not in that old fellow's skin," Howel Vaughan said as they left the castle. "I would not change places with him for the world. Come home with me, eh, sons of Tudor? 'Meat's in pot and pot's on fire,' as my big Olwen says."

Rhys Ddu begged his excuses, but Eden had no pressing errand that drew him homeward, so he rode up the valley of the Conway to Mathebrud—a hall where he had always enjoyed a good time, but where his eldest brother, the Chieftain, never went if he could possibly help it. Dusk was falling when they came within sight of the timbered palisade hung about with the decaying carcasses of blood crows and weasels. Howel's wife Olwen, a large woman with berry-bright cheeks and a great shouting laugh, came out to meet them.

"Where is King Richard?"

"I asked him come sup with us," Howel told her, "but he was trysted elsewhere."

"So you have brought me Eden in his stead and I find I am no less rich. Let me feast my eyes on you, little brother. What a handsome cuirass!"

"Some day he may find a use for it."

"A gift from my wife, Olwen."

"Annes was sick and tired of seeing the wall-eyed nonny lolling about the Old Hall reading pictures in the fire with Mabon of the Silver Harp," said Howel. "After all, her first husband was a belted knight, think of it."

"You think of it, Howel," said Eden. "I am hungry."

"Come along then, my dear. Meat's in pot and pot's on fire. . . ."

"I have already recited that canticle, wife," said Howel, and he led Eden into the hall and up to the long hearth where Davydd Vaughan, the aged chieftain his father, sat spitted like a red demon on a glowing shaft of firelight. Nodding in a drowse, the head, shield and defender of the

Men of Ithon, gave a start as he heard someone greeting him, and peered hard at Eden for several moments before sinking back again with a little laugh into his cushions.

"Bless my soul, I took you for your father," he said, as if he had been delivered of a dread apparition.

"He wanders these days," Olwen told Eden softly.

"But not far enough," Howel muttered in his turn.

Two evenings later the captains were taking their ease in the hall after a day on the river with their fishing spears and nets, when horsemen came riding out of the forest. A helmeted man in a red mantle blotted with sea-ravens hurried across the threshold. It was the Siri Mawr's nephew, Tango of the Bay of the White Stones, one of the handsomest of youths, and a grandson of that celebrated warrior, Sir Howel of the Battleaxe, the captor of the French King at the Battle of Poitiers.

"Richard's there," he told them breathlessly.

"At Conway?"

Tango nodded.

"His army abandoned him when they landed at Pembroke, it's said. All his knights and loyal liegemen. He has ridden north here all alone. Not a soul with him."

He spat on the ground and crossed himself.

"God save us from such friends! They say the Earl of Northumberland and the Archbishop of Canterbury are come to meet him." He gazed at the other two with his great blue eyes like sapphires, then ventured hesitantly: "Nothing can be done now, I suppose?"

Howel burst out laughing.

"Good God, my dear Tango! What would you have us do? Attack Northumberland and the Archbishop? And that whole great army? Little us? Come, it's over. We can do no more. Besides, it's not our quarrel, is it?"

Nonetheless, the curiosity of the three captains had been quickened. On the following morning they rode to Conway.

Crowds were there, drawn by the news of the great parley. In the meadows on the south side of the walls, the press of folk was so great that the three horsemen had to dismount and elbow their way through. Around the parish church stood a buzzing group of onlookers, held back a spear's length from the doors by a row of soldiers armed to the scalp. The King and Northumberland were inside with the Archbishop, it seemed, swearing oaths of undying friendship over the Host. Taking advantage of this portentous moment, hawkers and peddlars were out in strength, threading their way through the mob, shouting their wares. The wealthy women had donned their jewelry, and gaudy young bloods in plumed bonnets and piked shoes trod like roosters amid the throng, striking poses and furtively eyeing the tittering maids.

"You would think a fair was going on," said Eden.

"Or an execution," said Howel, then gave a whistle.

Following his gaze, Eden and Tango found themselves looking at Alison Massey, the wife of the Constable of Conway, who was standing with some of the other ladies of the town on a mound nearby. She was a slender, pale-cheeked woman with the face of a sulky handsome boy, a petulant mouth, and eyes that were perhaps too narrow and arrogant for Eden's taste, although Howel was quite enchanted.

"Bonjour," he said, doffing his crimson cap and louting low. She gave a haughty little toss to her head and turned with some laughing remark to her companions.

"She is too skinny," said Tango.

"Be on your guard, Howel," Eden cautioned. "That is John Massey's lady."

"You don't have to tell me that," he said, grinning in a trance and looking at her with his very fine dark-lashed grey eyes alight with sudden desire, "for we have already met."

"When we were in the castle a while ago?"

"Are you jesting? And the place swarming with soldiers? Sure, you must know the old John would have that lovely pet of his locked away then." He paused, glancing at them slily. "Shall I tell you when?"

"I am almost afraid to ask," said Tango. "Was it when you were in prison last year?"

"Ah, you heard about that then?"

"Who did not? As it happens, my she-comrade told me. 'Tango', she said 'you will never believe this, but Howel Vaughan has been put in prison for adulterous intercourse with the wife of Morgan the Interpreter.'"

"Your she-comrade has been very cruel to me lately. Can it be because I told her that her kiss is like the bite of a tench?"

"Go on with your story, Howel."

"Utter childishness. Bundling, that's all we were doing, an old and honorable custom in this land. We were having a talking time together in the hay. It's a pity for her, wedded to such a man. Did you know that the lawyers of Caernarvon call him Morgan the Abstruse? She might as well be married to a foreigner for what she can understand of his jabber. It was Holy Innocents' Day, as I recall."

"You must, I dare say, have been discussing King Herod," Eden suggested.

"You mock me, son of Tudor, but as God is my witness I was as innocent of sin this time as the holy babes themselves. What the Abstruse One said to the ecclesiastical court was rubbish. The offscourings of a filthy mind. Dada was shocked to the very quick of him, of course. 'Let the lewd liver stew in prison for a while,' says he, the end in view, to be sure, being my humiliation and correction. Not that I could complain. They put me in the Queen's Tower, a pleasant little room looking out on the water and the shipping. Alison used to bring me my daily dole of black bread and horsebeans, an old woman along of her. 'God give you good day, sir,' she'd say. 'May God repay you the kindness of that greeting, madame,' I'd say. We could come to no more fruitful result than that, the crone being there. But ah, the glances that she sent me, lads! They bade fair to melt me like a fire in a candle."

"Out with you, Howel, for the prowling tomcat that you are!" Tango shouted laughing.

Almost simultaneously another voice rang out: "The King! The King!" and the crowd surged forward.

Mounted on a white palfrey, Richard was moving slowly towards the town along the path leading from the church, flanked by the Earl of Northumberland and the Archbishop of Canterbury. "Vivat Rex!" someone shouted. Others stared at the King in amazed silence. Was this the golden monarch who had so loved to peacock it in the world's eye? Ah, what mortal seed all earthly splendor rests upon! Bareheaded and dressed in a plain black gown, his face rough in a stubble of grey beard, this man looked as haggard and beaten out as a palmer home from a long and harrowing pilgrimage to the Holy Land. Only the twisting bitterness of the smile that bent the royal lip belied thoughts of holy simplicity. And as he drew near the three Welsh chieftains, Eden was startled by a glimpse of eyes that blazed out of the King's face with such a helpless animal fury that a pang of pity ran through him, as sharp as the stab of a knife.

"God's my life," he thought, "he rides to his death."

And it was as if something were growing in the air about the young islander in those moments, something that was cold and made dark his breath.

Then the King had passed, and the crowd went scattering, and Eden's eyes were opened once again to the bright life of that September morning. He was intensely aware of everything suddenly. How warm it was! The leaves hung still on the trees, and they moved a little in the soft breeze that blew now and then off the waters. The sea moved gently against the rocks and he looked away in the direction of Mona and thought of Annes and the Old Hall—his happy brood.

"And what will happen to him now, I wonder?" Tango mused.

"As to that," said Howel, "it is no longer our concern, thank God. Away with them for the ugly pack of knaves that they are! Let them wrangle to the death over the shoddy trappings of their power, it's nothing to me. I have what's better than any crown."

"What's that, you rip?" asked Tango.

"The power to make unhappy wives forget their woes," Howel replied.

"And mine will be unhappy if I am not home soon," Eden said. "Farewell and God speed, chieftains."

The other two in their turn blessed him on his way, then they rode to a nearby tavern. There Howel bought a flask of wine of Rhenish which he sent off in custody of a potboy as a gift for the Constable's lady. Some little while after, the lad returned, wine dripping from his hair like rain from a thatch, and smiling sheepishly.

"You have lost her, Howel," said Tango.

"Say you so, my friend?" grinned his companion. "Make me a wager."

And the eyes of Howel Vaughan were sparkling with dreams of Heaven, and like enough were still doing so later that day, yes, perhaps in that selfsame moment when, amidst the wild spinneys and crags of Rhos, the forces of Henry Bolingbroke, the Duke of Lancaster, descended like a flock of kites upon the King's troop, and Richard found himself staring all at once into the very maw of Hell.

Early the next spring Meredith ap Tudor, the Chieftain of the Men of Eden, put his son Owain out to foster in the house of Father Mathau, a learned priest and dominus of spotless life, who dwelt beyond the waters of the sea-river in the ancient royal vill of Llanrwst in the valley of the Conway, not far from Mathebrud, the hall of the Vaughans. The Chieftain had been in two minds about it for some time. The boy was spoilt and precocious—he defied his father and ran to take refuge behind his mother's skirts whenever threatened with a whipping. And Marged Vaughan always flew to her brat's defense, of course. Five daughters, the eldest of whom was already a wedded wife, had been born in the house before their brother Owain had first seen the light of day—there was the whole story in a nutshell.

Meredith announced his decision to his wife one evening while they were at meat. They were sharing the same trencher and when he spoke she almost ran the ivory-handled little knife she used for cutting food into his thumb. She stared at him in disbelief for the first few moments, and then as it broke in on her what he had said, she was filled with a cold impotent rage against this man who could so ride roughshod over her feelings.

"Nantconway? Llanrwst?" she cried in stupefaction, as if saying the Valley of Grief in the Uplands of Hell. "Are you serious?"

"Do you see me laughing? Of course I am serious."

"Forgive me if I appear dull of wit," she said with biting coldness then, "but you have so astounded me. I wonder why you have not spoken of this to me before? Do I count for nothing in this house? Am I not the child's mother?"

Her eyes glowed.

"Heart alive, man, why Father Mathau? Why not our own good priest? Tudor, your own father, thought well enough of Father Conan to put your little brother Eden out to foster under his roof, did he not?"

"I am trying to be patient with you, Marged," her husband informed her in tones of quiet menace, "but you are putting me hardly to the test. Must I remind you that Tudor was beyond thought at the time? My mother, God rest her, was at point of death. She was being given the last sacraments while they were rolling Eden in the trough. A woman with milk had to be found. Mam Indeg met the need."

"And a good mother she proved to him, I don't think you will deny it. She has bred up all her children to be a credit to her and Father Conan. A loving hearth," she said, her lip beginning to quiver. "Only look at Gerallt, their first born. Is he not as dear to you as a son?"

The Chieftain raked his brow with weary fingers.

"I cannot understand you, Meredith."

He lost patience.

"Why don't you put hooks in your jaws then?" he said.

Marged's eye fell on her two youngest daughters, Gwladys and Regin, twelve and thirteen years of age respectively. They were sitting in the middle of the floor with Mererid, the priest's daughter, and little Owain, playing at knuckle-bones with walnuts, but it was at once apparent to the Chieftain's lady from the aimless movements of their fingers and the unshifting drop of their heads and shoulders that they had only half a mind on what they were doing.

"Can you find no more useful employment?" she snapped at them. "Go from here. And take that walnut out of your brother's mouth before he breaks a tooth on it."

The children entered the kitchen. Megan, the serving woman who had been with Marged Vaughan longest, having come out of Nantconway with the mistress and her husband when they had first taken up residence on the island, was sitting on the highbacked oaken settle, stitching upon an altar cloth. She looked up when they came in, then set her work aside and went to the door, peeping. The two of them were sitting there civilly enough. Perhaps a thought too civilly. Aye, the hush before the storm, as the saying is. "I wonder if he likes my venison pasties," she mused "The dear knows that Meredith ap Tudor is a difficult man to feed. That time I baked those doucettes, half the afternoon toiling. . . ."

"Are they throwing things yet, Megan?" Mererid asked.

In stern astonishment Megan turned and saw the priest's daughter watching her, the freckles on her pert nose pinched in wrinkles of hilarity. The Chieftain's daughters exploded into a fit of mirth, burying their faces in their aprons. "Hush, shame on you!" Megan exclaimed in alarm. "Stop it at once! Stop it, I say! Marged Vaughan will have you in a convent, if she hears. And you, too, naughty lad," she warned the merrily squealing boy.

"No, no, I am not for the convent," he gasped. "I am to go to Father

Mathau."

Megan paused, interested.:

"The holy man of Llanrwst?"

"So says the Old Hand."

Megan stiffened with horror anew. "The Old Hand? Is that what you are calling your lord and father, you naughty boy?" she demanded sternly as she hastily closed the door.

Marged Vaughan glanced over at it absently, hearing childish laughter from afar, as it were from Elfinland. She was trying to follow the devious turns and dodges of her husband's mind. She knew that he held Father Conan in the highest esteem; therefore, it had to be the priest's wife who was at the root of the trouble.

"You have never forgiven Indeg for being a daughter of the Trevors, have you?"

"Daughter?"

"Yes. Daughter. Are you sneering? You know full well that if her father, Lewis Trevor, had not been gored to death by a bull before he could marry his betrothed sweetheart, Indeg would have been the equal of any highborn maid in this land."

"Aye," he smiled, picking about in the food for a piece of meat that was not smothered in pastry, "and if Lewis Trevor, God sanctify his bones, had not got his betrothed sweetheart with child before wrestling with that bull, their daughter Indeg would not have been given in marriage to a wandering scholar, would she? And we would then have been spared the presence of that Mother of Fantasy in our domain."

Another retort began to turn itself about her tongue, then she thought better of it and knit her brows, puzzling. After a few moments Meredith cast her a sidelong glance. A fit of the sulks now, he concluded.

"Megan certainly has a rare talent for ruining good beef," he observed.

She snatched up the trencher and flung it across the hall.

"Let the dogs have it then!" she exclaimed bitterly.

Meredith stared at her, his eyes opened wide.

"Whatever has come over you?" he asked. "Once upon a time you used to be a sensible, sagacious woman, but these days you seem witless. What can it be, I wonder?" He eyed her a moment longer, then wiped his hands in the skirt of his tunic. "Perhaps," he concluded gravely, "it's your age."

She rose and swept out of the hall, her skirts hissing at her heels like a covey of quail.

Scowling, Meredith watched the dogs gobbling up the strewn remnants of the meal. Women! Still he should not have said that about her age—that had been ill done in him. Now she would not talk to him for days. After a short while he rose and went after her into the kitchen. Everyone was sitting there as though under the spell of an enchanter. Marged was stitching upon a long piece of cloth with Megan. Some sacred stole pontifical, no doubt. He gazed down upon her bended head, the white curve of her cheek, the stern set of her lips, the hostile glitter of her lowered eyes—ah, have it so then! He caught his children and the priest's daughter eyeing him with slily amused looks, frowned forbiddingly, and said to Megan:

"Thank you for those beef fritters. Never have I tasted the like."

The woman glanced at him hesitantly, not knowing whether he was in earnest or jesting. But Marged Vaughan did not raise her head until he had wished all goodnight. Only then did she deign to look after him as his big limping bulk went stooping through the doorway into the yard.

"And what you do not seem to realize, you clever head," she longed to jeer in the heels of him, "is that if Lewis Trevor had not got his betrothed sweetheart with child before wrestling that bull there would not even have been a Mam Indeg."

But then she would have had to laugh. And laughter would have tempered her wrath. And naturally, she was still too angry for that.

So it was that at first light on a morning a week later, among tears and lamentations enough to float a ship of exiles, to use the Chieftain's own expression, the father rode away with his white-faced, seven-year old son Owain to Nantconway. For company, he took along with him Gerallt ap Conan, the priest's son. A tall full-bodied young man with murrey-brown hair and dimpled cheeks, he dwelt with his wife Sioned and his foster brother Eden at the Old Hall, where he was steward.

They arrived in Llanrwst two evening later. They saw the boy settled with his cousin Elise, the son of Howel Vaughan, in the house of Father Mathau, and then they rode to Mathebrud.

It was a stormy night. The sky was black and it rained heavily. The hall was as full of smoke as though all the witches in Gwynedd were coughing and spitting down the vents. Meredith could not sleep. Not only was the smoke eating his eyes out, but his game leg ached and throbbed.

"It knows this accursed hall," he told Gerallt. "I thought I had laid the axe at the root of my old life, but indeed it is still breathing here, waiting to leap up and ambush me."

More years than he cared to remember had passed since he had been brought to Mathebrud in convoy of his mother and a few spearmen, the barb of an arrow fastened in his knee. That must have been the worst night of his life. Well he remembered it—the nightmare ride through the forest, the gloomy high-raftered hall; the prayers and incantations; the cauldron boiling over the roaring logs; the trestle table lighted with firebrands; his body stretched out on the blood-soaked winnowing sheet; the great hacking oaths tearing his chest—his mother, her cool hand on his brow, her voice, soothing, crooning.

What wonder that the old master here shrank from him as from some hellish phantasm. "Tudor shall not bring blood upon my house," he was said to have declared in the course of those troubles. "Poor Davydd," thought the Chieftain, looking through half-closed lids at his father-in-law where he sat, head a-drop, wrapped up in his time-sabled sheep-fleeces at the other side of the hearth, snoring with a sound as if hot fat were bubbling inside him.

As always Meredith could not wait to get away.

"You are leaving already?" Olwen protested the next morning. "We hardly see you and you are gone."

"I owe it to the old gentleman," Meredith jested. "I have troubled him with my presence enough."

"What sort of talk is that?" Howel Vaughan demanded. "You owe my father nothing."

" I owe him my wife," Meredith said. "So I am eternally in his debt. And but for her, you know, I would not be here today."

They thought he was speaking of the time when Marged had helped nurse him back to health, but Gerallt knew better. He caught the Chieftain's eye and looked down at his fingernails, smiling.

They rode back at an easy pace along the ancient beaten forest paths. Towards noon they reached the point where they had crossed the river on their journey to Llanrwst the day before, only to find that during the night the bridge had been swept away in the storm and the waters were now unfordable.

"I know another way further up," said Meredith, and wheeled his horse westward through the dripping trees.

When they had ridden a few miles they came out on a wide grassland. Hills veiled in a misty rain loomed up behind and heaps of stone lay scattered about among the ferns and rushes.

"This must have been a dwelling place once," Gerallt said.

"Yes," said Meredith, "this was Caerhun."

Tudor's hall! Gerallt caught his breath and crossed himself. It was a few moments before he could speak.

"You were born here, Meredith."

"I was born here."

Amazed, Gerallt looked about him. Here had been held that wedding feast of fabulous duration he had heard of so often during his childhood. Mabon, the bard, had won the bag of the silver harp here of old—that harp that still stood beside the hearthrock in the Old Hall in Mona. Wild ponies used to come down here in snowy weather to be fed horsebread and hay at the gates. At Christmastide three hundred fat geese used to be given by the lord of the hall to the crofters of the region.

And now there was only this silence—the faint crackle of softly falling rain in the grass, the small kick of a rabbit in the brush, the cry of a lapwing somewhere far off in the hills.

"It's sad," said Gerallt.

"It's life," said the Chieftain.

They rode on. And that day no more was said on the subject.

On their return to the island they went to the king's town of Beaumaris to get some bags of seed corn. While Gerallt saw to the purchases, the Chieftain called upon his namesake, Meredith ap Kenvric.

He enjoyed his company. Certainly he had known no other like him. Apart from the fact that he was the richest merchant in Beaumaris, he was also the Sheriff of Mona. Besides that, he was Eden's father-in-law. But better than all this where the Chieftain was concerned was that he was a man of mystery.

He hoarded his confidences as a magician his formulas. What of his father Kenvric, for instance? The story the son had given out was that he had been a nobleman of Gwent who had lost his inheritances through falling foul of the English. It was plausible. God alone knows it was no new story in this land. Maybe he was even in descent from St Brychan as he claimed, although Mabon, the bard and pedigree man at the Old Hall, doubted it.

"You had best take that tale with a pinch of salt, Meredith," he had told the Chieftain, when the subject of Eden's marriage with the merchant-sheriff's daughter Annes had been under discussion.

"Aye, and buy that pinch from him, too," had been Meredith's reply. "For if I'm not mistaken the son of Kenvric owns the salt pit this side of the cell of Basingwerk."

But how from being plucked out of the gutter by Nicolas Beaupine, the wealthiest dealer in armories in the palatinate of Chester, this same Kenvric had risen over the course of the years to become his benefactor's partner—it was there that the real mysteries began to gather. And married off his son and heir to Nicolas's daughter to seal the bargain, naturally.

What could account for such a prodigy? The Chieftain had heard sagacious old men, of good credit, suggest that Kenvric had employed enchantments to gain his ends. But he, for his own part, was unwilling to draw the fine thread of his conjecture through stuff so flimsy. What alone in the end could be safely asserted, perhaps, was that at the death of the two merchants the son of Kenvric had been left the master of a flourishing house, and that in due course he had arrived at Beaumaris with his wife Joanna and opened up another house on the quay next the castle.

There it was that the Chieftain rode that day. He found the merchant sitting alone in the dark and yawning depths of his warehouse. Robed against the damp chill March air in blood-red velvet furred with crestigray, the point of his curving hawk's beak finding confederacy in the twinklings of the blue crystal stones of his crucifix, he was huddled over his candlelit counting board, fingering through some jewels.

"You are the image of a miser gloating over his hoard, my friend," the Chieftain observed with amusement.

The merchant looked up.

"God give you good day, it's the business, chieftain, it's the business. There's a story going the rounds that Henry of Lancaster is going to marry King Richard's widow, the French princess."

The Chieftain raised his brows.

"Already the widow of one king? And so soon to wed another? How old is she now, say you?"

"Oh, eight or nine, I daresay. But you know how it is with these marriages of state. I thought at first I would send her a doll, but perhaps it would be wiser to send her one of these jewels. This new monarch might not take it kindly if I sent his bride a poppet. And he's a very angry, short-tempered man, they say. A proper furibundal fellow."

"Capable of having murdered Richard, perhaps?"

The merchant was guarded, peering around him at the bales. He lowered his voice and bent forward.

"Is that your thought?"

"Well, if he did not murder him, it was certainly most convenient that Richard breathed out his soul when he did."

"Aye," the Sheriff of Mona nodded.

Tall and gaunt of frame, his hard penetrating eyes gleaming like chips of shale in the yellow bones of his face, he put the Chieftain in mind of nothing so much at that moment as the picture of Death leading the estates on the wall of the crypt at the nearby Abbey of the Minorites at Llanvaes. What had Eden said about him once? "The in-law was born speculating as the rest of us are born bawling."

"But there you are," the merchant went on presently. "poor Richard was too trusting. To have left his kingdom when he did. And then on returning to have let himself be duped into captivity by cousin Henry's promises that he had no treasonable intent—to have entrusted his life in those ungentle hands—well, it was folly."

"Sooner to go than the tree and herb that stood so dumbly at his passing."

"Faith, aye."

Sighing, the merchant locked away his jewels and conducted the Chieftain up a flight of stairs to a chamber dressed with cloth of arras, with five windows looking out upon the sea-river; and an escutcheoned fireplace enlivened with a merry blaze, before which the two men now sat, legs outstretched, with cups of wine at hand to kindle the blood.

"If only Richard had stayed at Conway, eh? He had friends there. He could have held that castle against all assaults."

The Chieftain smiled.

"What are you doing, my friend? Looking for last year's snow?"

The merchant narrowed his eyes at him thoughtfully, and then nodded.

"You are right, of course," he said. "There is no looking back. That's fruitless pain. It's Henry of Lancaster we have to deal with now. Son of that old warhorse, John of Gaunt. Bred up to arms as it were at mother's teat. God save us, I'm afraid he is no friend of ours, the Welsh."

"How do you say that?"

"Only look at the paste of men he is appointing to govern us. The Earl of Northumberland's son, him the English call Hotspur, is our new Chief Justice. And that misbirth, Grey of Ruthin, is now Chief Lord of our Marches. Oh, by the way," he paused, "did you know that a cousin of yours is in some strait on his account this season?"

The Chieftain considered this for a few moments, then asked: "Are you talking of Owain Glyndwr?"

"Yes, I am. So you have heard of it already?"

"The Earl of Salisbury touched on the matter when Eden and Rhys were at Conway last summer," Meredith replied. "Would the trouble have something to do with the disputed land at Croesau?"

"Blood o' my body, you're on your toes today, son of Tudor. Aye, that old, old land-suit. Who would have thought that Grey would have been supping all these years on the distilled essence of those sour grapes of his, eh? Well, his moment has arrived. Richard could not suffer him. Now he shines conspicuously at the English court. Sits next below King Henry at table. Glyndwr will lose his land."

"How can you be sure?"

"You have yet to hear the end of the story. Your cousin went to Westminster a while ago to plead his case. King Henry refused him a hearing. He received the Bishop of St Asaph, however. An old friend of Glyndwr's, I believe. The reverend lord Trevor."

"But what names you are resurrecting, son of Kenvric, what names! Say on."

"I'm told he put Glyndwr's case most fairly, but to no end. Do you know what the King did? Snapped his fingers under the Bishop's nose. 'That for Glendower!' says he. 'The Devil fetch him and his race of barefoot knaves!'"

"Go home, is it the truth he said such a thing?"

"So I'm told. And where there's smoke there's fire, as the byword has it. Do you want my opinion?" he went on to observe portentously. "I fear the days of peace are over. I seem to hear the baying of the hounds of war upon the wind. . . ."

He stopped, his eyes staring beyond the Chieftain's shoulder. There was a womanly rustle of skirts, the whiff of musk. Meredith rose to face Joanna Beaupine. Heavens, where do they get their hats? Bagpipes of Chirk! She returned his greeting with courteous indifference, her ice-blue glance was chilling.

"How is my daughter Annes?"

"Radiant," the Chieftain replied gallantly.

"I am glad to hear it. The last time she came here I fancied I saw a corpse walking in."

She turned towards her husband.

"A courier awaits you."

The merchant flinched noticeably. A thin smile, replete with scorn, passed over his wife's lips.

"Be of good cheer, husband," she said. "The price of wool has not gone down."

Of the four halls which Tudor's sons inhabited in the heart of the island, that of Gwredog was by far the oldest. It had been first built by men out of the land of the Gododdin* who had come into Wales with their leader Marr at the behest of Rhodri Mawr to help him in his war against the Vikings. Since that time the Old Hall, as it was known, had been rebuilt more than once, but the signs of that Northern tribe the Romans had called the Ottadini could still be seen, hewn into the stone of the great hearthrock.

No one could interpret them, not even Mabon, the old housebard. One thing alone was certain; they marked this spot as the first settlement of the fathers in Wales.

The youngest son inherited according to custom. Hence it followed that Eden was now master here, as his father before him.

It was late in the day of their visit to Beaumaris when Meredith and Gerallt came within sight of the Old Hall. From afar in the grey twilight, through which the rain was still drizzling, the white thatched houses huddled on the bleak slope looked like the heads of old men nodding in

---

*The Gododdin: In Celtic Britain the Gododdin was a tribe that once lived in what would later be known as Strathclyde and Cumberland. The capital of their territory was Edinburgh.

sleep. They rode across the grassland threaded by turfbanks towards the walls. The cows were returning from the byre to the fields. The two men drew rein, to let them amble past. Involuntarily, the Chieftain found himself looking at the shield hanging over the gates—three lopped-off Englishmen's heads, who would have guessed? It was scarred and pitted beyond recognition.

"My ancestor put in a hard day's fighting against Earl Ranulf of Chester to earn that shield of honor," he observed.

"It's the lads," Gerallt explained. "They use it as a target. We can replace it."

"Don't," said Meredith, and they rode into the courtyard.

Sioned, Gerallt's wife, appeared in the byre doorway. A small lad peeped out from behind her skirts, then whooping with delight, came skipping and hopping over the puddles.

"Heyday, Gwyn!" Gerallt laughed, and caught him up in his arms.

"Look at that hair," Meredith smiled, twining one of the boy's red-gold curls about a finger.

"Mam Indeg calls it the badge of the Trevors," Sioned said proudly.

"Oh, Mam Indeg, to be sure," said Meredith.

"Things are well with you, Chieftain?" Sioned asked, exchanging amused glances with her husband.

"Praise be."

In the hall the only light was from the blaze on the great hearth. Six or seven figures sat clustered about it, their faces glowing like fire-berries against the dark. "Where are all of you? Faith, it's like a cavern of the Underworld here, goblins and elf-folk," Meredith exclaimed, thinking with renewed pleasure of his hall at Penmynydd, so lightsome and floored with tile—it's louvre and new fireplace with the size of a ship in its mantel.

Eden came towards him, grinning.

"Give God the glory, is it you, brother? How is it that you are honoring us with a visit? Ah, I see the color of the wind. You are afraid to go home and face Marged Vaughan. Why did you have to send young Owain so far away? You ought to have followed your wife's advice, Meredith."

"Why ought I? I asked for none."

"That's bad luck then," Eden observed. "Sure, you know what they say—a wife's advice unasked for is auspicious."

"More omens," the Chieftain grunted.

He looked over at Annes, who sat spinning in her sewing chair, and smilingly bowed his head to her.

"Greetings, sweet sister."

Grave and tender presence. She's too good for the knave, he thought. What a pity she has such trouble bearing children.

"I saw your father today."

"How was he?"

"Foreboding. He seems to think there will be war."

She glanced up at him and gave a bemused smile.

"Oh, Meredith, surely not. Where? Between whom?"

"The King of England for one."

"Him. And who else?" Eden asked with sudden interest.

"Who knows? Maybe he will take up the cause of his fathers and invade France," said Meredith, and he turned his gaze upon a snub-nosed black-haired boy who was sitting at the other side of the hearth, putting new strings to a hand harp under the watchful eye of the housebard.

"How is your apprentice, Mabon?"

"Well, he can string a harp, as you see."

"And play it, I trust."

"How not?"

"What else do you know, Robyn?" the Chieftain asked, and stood in sober earnestness while the boy bashfully recited his skills.

"And do you know the rolls of the genealogies?"

"Those of this house I know, Chieftain."

"Excellent. You could not possibly begin with a better. But now you must go on to learn the rolls of all the other houses, too."

Eden laughed.

"Turf shoddy and whitestone castle, one and all, aye."

The boy looked from one to the other with solemn wondering eyes, puzzled to know if they were jesting or no.

"Commit them to heart," the Chieftain told him then. "In this land where every freeman claims descent from Brutus and the Trojans, it will hardly fail to purchase you a night's lodging in time of need. I am serious. And after all, what will it cost you to humor the poor knaves, eh? You will know something that they do not know, will you not, lad? That as a bard you are liege to a suzerainty older than kings."

From his chair, the old man who had been dozing, heard through some dream of his the rustling of the rain upon the roof and the faint distant pleading of the wind in the trees and after a while realized what it was that had awakened him. His hands. The hands of Mabon of the Silver Harp. Aching and knotted with gouts in the joints. He opened them, flexing and unflexing his fingers. What's the use? A harper's hands are a dignity greater than his life, he told himself. So it is written down in the laws of King Howel the Good. Of course, I am better than a mere harper, he thought. Once my proficiency in the bardic joust was such that men scarce dared to venture out of doors for fear of being hit in the head by a chiming consonant. Once.

He sighed and bending down stiffly over the hearth stirred up the embers of the fire. The boy moved in his bed of straw nearby.

"Shall I put some more peat on it for you, Mabon?"

"Sticks would be better. I don't like peat smoke. It stains the skin and the dear knows mine is yellow enough already. Why are you not sleeping?"

"I can't, Mabon. There is such a ringaround of things in my head."

"That's an old man's game, my dear," the bard smiled.

"Well, perhaps it's old I am," the boy said reflectively. "When I was born Sibli says that she bathed me in a solution of foxglove juice on the sly. She was so frightened that I might be a fairy changeling when she first saw me, you see. There was such an ugly and ancient look on me, she says. She feels sure I have lived on this earth before."

"What a crock of tripes!"

Laughter crackled like kindling in the depths of the bard's scriptural beard.

"The shrivel-faced old turnip! She thinks all men are devils, if the truth be known."

"Why would that be, Mabon?"

"Who knows? Maybe because she failed to snare one of us."

He puckered his brows in thought.

"Women are curious creatures, Robyn," he went on in a little. "They are so wrapped up in their one miracle, they can see no other. They are born to breed. Everything must take its color from that. If they are denied that one miracle of theirs for some reason—it may be because they are ugly, diseased or dowerless—something goes awry within them. Twisted and strange. Cracked and dripping venom. Like that gravelly-throated old crow yonder. Pay her no heed, my little one. You well know who and what you are."

"A bastard."

"That was not my meaning. The foster-son of the master of the Old Hall is who you are. As to being misbegotten, there's no shame in that, either, in our land. Prince Howel, the son of Owain Gwynedd, one of the greatest of our rulers, he was a natural child."

"And he was a poet."

"An enchanting poet."

Robyn gazed dreamily into the fire. He was ten and had never known his father. When Eden, but a beardless youth himself then, had become master of the Old Hall, youths in gay woven cloaks, with spears, in cordwain shoes with bright buckles had ridden here to celebrate the occasion. Among them had been Robyn's father Trahern, a son of Jenkin of Welsh Maelor, a border chieftain. In the course of his stay here he had made one of the maids of the hall pregnant. Sometime after that he was slain in a brawl, far off to the east. A brother of his had fled the country at that time. He was in Ireland, it was said, somewhere beyond the Pale, a fugitive in the household of some Irish chief.

So it was that for Robyn this house was the place where all things in this world had their beginning: the Old Hall, with its painted wooden posts hung with weapons, its clay floor worn down with age and the feet of the generations , its long hearth roaring against the dark, the strange markings on the hearthrock—ah, if he could only riddle out their meaning. He longed to know who those men were who had set them there.

"What were they like, Mabon, think you? The chiefs of the Gododdin?"

The old bard in his turn then fell to musing.

"They were the descendants of Eiddin. He was the founder of Caer Eiddin, that citadel of the North which the English call Edinburgh. They rode against Edwin and his Saxons those men—*they were familiar with laughter, their shields were gold-patterned, their swords rang out in the hearts of mothers.* Owain of the Three Hundred Ravens was one of them. Their bards were Aneirin and Cian of the Wheatsong, yes, children of the wind and flame they were. . . ."

The old man's voice crumbled away and fell into a soft whisper. He was quiet a while, reflecting.

"Tudor had some of that quality," he went on then. "He was a magical man. But his sons—ah, I don't know. They are not as he was. Meredith's worthy enough, but what in truth is he more than a farmer? Gwilym's a monk at heart, Eden, bless him, is such a child. Rhys Ddu perhaps."

"They say Rhys Ddu is a pirate."

"They say many things about Rhys Ddu. But a pirate? Where did you hear that? True, his wife Eva is pranked up in jewels and finery enough."

"She's beautiful, isn't she?"

"She's a temptress." The housebard's voice was fierce suddenly, his eye censorious. "She lured Rhys Ddu away from the bosom of Holy Church. She's his first cousin, you know. The curse of the clergy is upon them." He crossed himself. "The worry and woe she has brought on this proud house! Ach, but what am I about, jangling on so before an innocent? Sleep now, lad. Enough talk."

Robyn curled up once more in the straw next the hearth. He lay there with his cheek in his hand, yawning, blinking into the heart of the log that licked and flamed amid the red ashes. He looked back over what Mabon had told him, searching his words, but suddenly a phrase, something someone else had told him earlier on, came to chase all thought of that away.

"You are liege to a suzerainty older than kings," he murmured within himself, and the sticks burnt and crackled and seemed to breathe back the words in his ears. They burnt into his skull like letters of fire.

And the night grew mythic behind.

2

THE DROWNING OF THE HARVEST (1400)

1

On the Feast of St John that year, Eden and Gerallt went to Croes Gwion* with their longbows to try their skill at the butts—Croes Gwion, that ancient moorish village with its pothouse, its cluster of hovels, its stone cross, its clacketing windmill, its salty leas, its rushy hills. As a rule it was as quiet there as the grave—an old woman cackling to keep herself company, maybe, or a boy watering a donkey at the village trough. But that day crowds were there, so many entertainments were being enacted for their pleasure at the same time. Robert Crossetes, the constable of Beaumaris, was presiding as marshal over a friendly joust in a nearby field. A Lollard was preaching at the market cross. Tables with fruit, fish, hot pasties and drink had been set up. Girls were flirting with the revelers ranged along the ale benches. Boys were cockfighting and playing ball. Hawkers and vendors were in full voice, and cows with calves were lowing in their pens.

Eden and Gerallt were walking across the marketplace towards the archery meadow when a familiar voice hailed them. A woman, all in yellow and green, like a hill primrose, was standing at the edge of the crowd listening to the Lollard. It was Gwennan, the lady of Croes Gwion, the sister of Tango of the Bay of the White Stones, and one of the beauties of the isle.

Swinging her supple hams she came towards them, flanked by her husband Ivor's young stepbrothers, two hobbledehoys named Tomas and Sianco.

"You should hear what that Lollard is saying, Eden," said Tomas, showing the gaps in his teeth in hissing horror.

"And what is he saying then?"

"They are burning men of his sect in England."

"Burning them alive!" breathed calf-eyed Sianco.

Gwennan shrugged her shoulders.

"Come you, had I to listen to dreary old crabs like that preaching day in and day out I would be for burning them, too."

*Croes Gwion—Gwion's Cross

She turned and looked at Eden with her great, beautiful, goose-gray eyes.

"Ivor has gone to Rome for the Great Pardon."

"That is what I hear," Eden said. "And Caradoc of Penhesgin, too."

"Aye," she sighed. "Caradoc, too."

Gerallt and Eden tried not to look at one another. There was nobody could guess what burden of sin had drawn Ivor's feet as far away as the Holy City. Caradoc's admitted of no such doubt.

"Pope Benedict has proclaimed Jubilee, Ivor told me. I think I will go to Rome on pilgrimage."

"It's Pope Boniface you mean, Gwennan."

"Do I? By my hand, I could have sworn Ivor said Benedict."

"Benedict is Pope in Avignon."

"Where is that?"

"France."

She knit her brows in bewilderment.

"There are two Popes then?"

"Pope and Anti-Pope, depending which side you are on."

"Pendragon's beard, how confusing!"

"Goodnight," Eden muttered on the sly, "maybe the two of them will end their journey at Avignon and the whole pilgrimage will have been for nothing."

"Oh, I would not go so far as to say that, my heart," murmured Gerallt.

"Hi, what's to do?" one of the boys exclaimed suddenly.

There was the clatter of hooves and Robert Crossetes, the constable of Beuamaris, came riding up at the head of a small band of men-at-arms.

"Can the tilt be over so soon?" Eden puzzled.

A grey friar at his elbow said: "He has come to arrest the Lollard. Did you not hear him? He has been damning the King of England as a homicide."

"Lord Jesus Christ preserve us!" A piercing yell broke out. In the next moment the marketplace was in an uproar. A brawl blew up, centering around the market cross where Robert Crossetes was bellowing threat and sawing the air with his sword. From all sides crofters and revelers came running. Seizing Gwennan by the arm, Gerallt hurried her away to the shelter of the village alehouse.

"Tomas, Sianco, the lads!" she screeched. "Save them!"

Standing on a bench already copiously splattered with the droppings of hens that had flown squawking upwards to the ridge of the thatch, Gwennan anxiously watched Gerallt elbowing his way through the milling crowd towards Tomas and Sianco. She saw him dragging them away and groaned when she saw that Sianco's best holiday tunic had been half torn off his back. Eden, in the meantime, had run with the grey friar to rescue the Lollard, but he could make little head against the seething mob. Fists were flying around him, gobbets of blood. The smith of Dragon, a grey giant of a man, hairy as a wolf, had torn one of the timbers out of the tribal bathhouse and was laying about him with a will.

"The swine have killed Cochyn!" a man roared. "They have killed our dear old Fool!"

Eden had a sense of a wall heaving up before him, a wall of thirst-maddened oxen on the move—eyes bulging with murderously yellow bile; hot smells of sweat, dung and hay. A hard blow caught him in the ribs and all at once he was overthrown and trodden underfoot. Somehow he managed to roll under a wagon out of reach of the trampling feet, and he lay there, heart alive, he did not know how long: salt tears blinding his eyes, his head humming like a swamp. The first he knew after that was wiping his eyes and seeing the body of the Fool of Croes Gwion lying in its blood in the straw a few yards away from him. Another body lay hardby, that of the constable of Beaumaris. His head was cloven in two and the bloody jelly of one of his eyes hung in his moustache, dribbling into his ferociously bared teeth. It was clear that Robert Crossetes, too, had departed this merry life.

At last, seeing his way clear, Eden ducked out of his cover and ran to the alehouse where Gerallt and the others beckoned him.

"You are bleeding, my friend," Gwennan said. "Your face is covered with blood."

"Away!"

They quickly untethered their mounts and rode a mile along a cobbled track running between high earthen banks sprinkled with seagulls until they reached the sod castle of the lords of Croes Gwion.

"Wait here!" said Gwennan, when they entered the courtyard.

She darted inside. Eden went to the well and washed the blood from his face with the skirt of his mantle. After a while he said with a pained grimace:

"I am aching and sore, lads. What is your lady sister doing in there?"

"Tasking the women to clean up a bit, belike," said Tomas with his gappy grin.

Belike indeed, Gerallt thought, when at last they were bidden enter. For sure it was a dirty place just as Sioned had told him—the crumbling plaster of the walls furred with enough soot and cobwebs to put a dead man to the sneeze, new straw over old on the floor, the air reeking of peat smoke and goat piddle.

"They killed him?" Gwennan asked. "The constable yonder?"

"Aye," Eden replied. "I doubt any man could look more dead than Robert Crossetes."

Gwennan flung herself into a chair and kicked up her heels with laughter.

"Holy St Cybi, I can't believe it. Nothing exciting ever happens around here, except it is a cow running a bull. Well, why are you standing around all agape, you idle wenches? Set the table! And you two losels," she said to Tomas and Sianco. "Red wine! Tudor's son has lost blood today. We must restore it."

While the youths tripped over themselves in their hurry to serve, a snowy white linen cloth was spread over the greasy board and the guests sat down. A pile of the hardest hard bread in the world and two messes of stewed puffin were set before them. Gerallt looked at his dole of purple meat in dismay, but marveled at the plate upon which it was served. Although dinted and badly tarnished, it was exquisitely chased and was obviously costly. Meanwhile the lovely Gwennan sat down on a joint stool and began to sing stanzas on the harp for their entertainment. Her voice was quite pleasing but the songs she sang were full of mawkish lament.

A dying wood pigeon, thought Gerallt, but at his side Eden was enrapt. In the glow of her hell-black hearth, a wan light falling on her from a grimy crevice, in her hill-primrose garments, with her golden hair and her charming face upturned in poignant song, she seemed to the master of the Old Hall irreproachably pure and sweet.

"Look, Gerallt," he murmured, one lively dark eye sparkling with amusement—the other as usual was leading its own somber and independent life. "An angel in the devil's redoubt."

"What are you two whispering about?"

"We were saying that you look like a fallen angel, Gwennan."

"God repay you for those pretty words, my lord Ednyved."

It takes a long time to chew bad meat, but at last with an inward sigh of relief, Gerallt succeeded in forcing the last mouthful down.

"Give you thanks, Gwennan," he said, "but I think I will be going now. They will have heard of the affray at the Old Hall and will be worrying."

His foster brother rose at the same time, designing to go with him. Gwennan hastened towards him, her gown rustling like wings in the straw.

"Wait a while, Eden," she said. "There are some sheep fells in the loft here. Ivor and I have been wondering this long while whether your father-in-law, the son of Kenvric, would have some use for them."

Gerallt stared at her in frowning perplexity, but his foster-brother nodded at him smilingly.

"Go to, Gerallt," he said. "I will not be long."

Once his foster brother had gone, he followed the mistress of the hall up a flight of creaking stairs into a dusty loft where rows of fleeced hides were hanging like the mosses that drape ancient trees in sunless river gorges. Eden looked at them and then at Gwennan and burst out laughing—so filthy and rotten as they were.

"You must be jesting, sweet sister."

"Aye, I am. It's a talk I want with you. I think I am going mad, Eden. I cannot talk with Tomas and Sianco, they are so simple of wit. In all conscience, how could I confide in them? How long does it take to go to Rome and back?"

"On foot? A year, I'm told."

"Mary and Joseph, as long as that even? A year! What am I to do with myself? True God, I do not know how I shall find the strength to carry me through so many days. I yearn for him, my friend, do you understand that? Caradoc, my bright falcon."

Her eyes began to fill with tears, her shoulders shook.

"But what am I about?" she sniffed then. "Forgive me, chieftain, I am keeping you. Have pity on a poor woman's weakness."

There was but one answer that a freeman of the highest degree of dignity could give to that.

It was late when he arrived home. He was rather hoping folk would be in their beds but, of course, that was idle dreaming. It was midsummer night. Every village on the island was wakerife and alight. The very stars looked like sparks scattered from the scores of fires. On the slope where the Old Hall stood, Gerallt and a throng were busy about a great blaze, dancing and singing and leaping over the flames.

Three women remained within: Annes, Sioned, and the aged virgin Sibli.

"Here he is at last," said Sioned.

"Eden," said Annes. "How are you? Are you hurt?"

"Whisht, no. I was stunned for a space, no more."

"They killed the constable," said Sibli. "What a dreadful, dreadful thing! And on St John's Day. It bodes ill for the crops."

"How is Gwennan?" asked Annes.

"Aye, Gwennan. She is missing Ivor."

Silence from the three.

"Were the sheep fells any good?" asked Annes.

"No, not very good."

"I never knew Ivor of Croes Gwion raised sheep," said Sioned.

"It seems to me his father used to," said Sibli.

"They might well have been his," Eden observed. "They must certainly have been very old. Well, I won't lie, those sheep fells were only an excuse. She just wanted to talk, she is so lonely there, only those two lumps to keep her company. She wanted my advice."

"God help her then," said Sioned.

"About what, pray?" asked Annes.

"All manner of things. She seems to be at a complete loss what to do with herself."

"Perhaps," said Annes, with a sudden edge of sharpness to her voice, "she should have gone to Rome with her husband and her lover."

Eden stared at her, startled. Had those words come out of that mouth?

"Now I remember," said Sibli, peering squintingly into the hearth-smoke. "They came down with the scab and the red water, those sheep of Croes Gwion. The whole flock had to be destroyed."

Two days later Eden went to the garrison town of Beaumaris to attend an inquiry into the constable's death. As he was leaving the castle, Sipyn Torgoch, a grizzled, bowlegged seaman in Rhys Ddu's service, came up to him and told him that his brother awaited him at the Abbey of Llanvaes.

Founded and built by Llywelyn the Great in memory of his wife, the Lady Siwan, the great house of the Minorites on the island lay a mile or so north of Beaumaris, some little way inland from the sea. Eden knew it well. His ancestor and namesake, Ednyved Vychan, was buried there. The tombs of Sir Tudor and his wife lay in the warrior statesman's chantry chapel. There, in one of a frame of four wooden houses, thatched with reeds and straw, which stood against a mud wall facing the cloisters, Eden himself had spent four years of his boyhood. He shivered still, thinking of those winter nights—gusts of sea air blowing, cold from the gullets of the drowned.

Rhys Ddu was in the Abbot's parlor. Several other men were gathered there with him, but Eden had time enough only to cast them a cursory glance before his brother demanded:

"Well, what happened?"

"No malfeasance on the part of any man living could be proven by inquisition."

There was a silence, then everyone started laughing.

"By the gallows," Rhys Ddu grinned, "what a Sheriff!"

"Dickon Lescrop, the sergeant at arms, claimed the Fool of Croes Gwion slew Robert Crossetes."

"And, of course, Cochyn is no longer in a position to answer for himself."

"If ever he was, God rest his innocent soul," said the Father Abbot, crossing himself.

"Was aught said of the Lollard?" asked Rhys Ddu.

"Only that he had disappeared. . . ." Eden began.

And then he stopped and stared.

"Goodnight!"

"I wish you a blessing, son of Tudor."

"Glory be!" Eden laughed, wondering how on earth he could have formed an image in his mind of a fiery religious, his two eyes boiling in his head like cockles in a black-bottomed pot, when all the time he had been none other than the man in cloth of russet he now saw—his broad face stained to the hue of a nut by wind and sun, his slow humorous mouth turning from moment to moment in a wide and honest smile.

Master Walter Brut was his name. Only a few months earlier, while a lay priest in the diocese of Hereford, where he had been born and bred up and where his wife Alice still lived, he had been put on trial before the ecclesiastical consistory.

"For what?" Eden asked.

"For carrying the bell for the simple life."

"But then these Little Brothers must be heretics, too," he remarked, with a glance of affectionate mockery at the Father Abbot Anianus, whose kindly patriarchal face was sewn with innumerable brown wrinkles.

"Good, good, my dear," the old priest grinned, supporting his comfortable little potbelly with hands as raw and rough as a washerwoman's. "Our Father in Heaven must be well pleased with you. For sure he has graced you with a tongue as sweet as the honey of a virgin swarm."

"True, there is more to Lollardry than that," Master Brut observed.

"Aye," the Abbot nodded. "I am not unfamiliar with the treatises of John Wycliffe. But enough of that now. You are but now come from our Marches, it seems. There are great disturbances there, we are told."

"It is a tinder box," said the Lollard. "You have heard perhaps that the ban of outlawry is now on the head of the Keeper and Master Forester of Chirkeland?"

Eden gave a start of surprise.

"Griffith ap Davydd, the lord of Bryn Cyffo?"

"Aye," said the Lollard. "Do you know him?"

"Say rather that I know *of* him," the young islander replied with a wry smile. "I was once bound by pledge to the lady he married."

"Troth was broken?"

"It was a secret troth-plight. We were all too young then, she and I."

"Nonetheless. . . ."

"My own marriage must bear the blame for that breach of faith, I fear," Rhys Ddu broke in. "Maybe you have not heard, Master Walter, that my wife Eva and I are first cousins, but I must marvel at it if you have not. I thought it all over North Wales like the smell of fire. But while we await a plenary remission for our sins, tell us more about the Keeper. Why has he been outlawed?"

"He has been raiding the studs and lands of Lord Grey and distributing the booty among the poor and oppressed of the region."*

"God preserve him!" said the Abbot.

"Where is the Keeper now?" Rhys Ddu asked.

"In hiding. Nobody knows where."

"In Glyndwr's lordship perhaps."

"It is not unlikely."

Eden was no longer listening. Angharad Trevor. He could still remember the agony he had once suffered on her account. He had thought he must die of it. A youth of seventeen. A whole night he had spent abased on the stone flags before the shrine of the love-saint, Dwynwen, on her islet of sighs, begging to be rid of his passion. Surely he had been much to be pitied. Laughable he had been without question.

But the years had passed. He had grown older, it was to be hoped wiser. At last he had put her out of his mind. He had married Annes. He was happy.

And then, only a few moments before, something had trembled close at his heart. Strange.

A word about Rhys Ddu's wife Eva.

Her mother, Eluned, Sir Tudor's youngest sister, had died when Eva was less than a year old; hence she had no memory of her. But throughout her childhood the little girl had felt that her mother must have been a goddess walking this earth—everyone spoke of her with such awe. "Would that the lady were here now. She would know what to do." "How beautiful she was! When she entered Bangor cathedral, half the congregation turned their backs on the pure body of God to stare."

Red Iwan, Eva's father, had been an overgrown boy of twenty-five when his wife died. His abounding innocence and tender simplicity of heart had ill-prepared him to withstand a grief so overpowering. At first he retired to a monastery, determined to renounce the world. Then, as though possessed by a demon, he ran to the opposite extremity and gave himself up to a life of merry disport and luxury, squandering his own fortune in the process, as in later years that of his second wife, Pia of

*See Note 3

Nanmor, a piously submissive lady of ample proportions whose soft mournful face and manner her stepdaughter Eva would liken to that of a devout ewe.

At sixteen Eva was given in marriage to Llywelyn of Trewalchmai, a chieftain of Mona. Although he was elderly, and indeed had already buried two wives, the match was considered a good one where Eva was concerned, for she brought her husband next to no dowry apart from her virtue—and even that was open to question to go on the whisperings of the gossip-mills and certain of the bride's middle-aged stepchildren— while Llywelyn, besides being of the best lineage, was a wealthy man. As it fortuned he was also a likable and indulgent old chieftain and his young wife grew to feel a real affection for him, even if, as she once declared in the horrified hearing of Sibli at the Old Hall, he had been good for little but to tickle her with his beard.

Alas, life is but grass. A year after the wedding Eva's husband was stricken by a fit of apoplexy after a hearty repast and gave up the ghost within hours. The widow retired to a nunnery on the western shores of the island for three months. At the end of this period Rhys Ddu, the sea-captain, arrived in his ship at the port of the convent to bear her back home around the peninsula of Llyn to her father's hall at the Great Strand. She never got there.

Red Iwan was beside himself. Sparing neither whip nor horses he rode with Eva's brothers, Madoc and Huw, to Mona to see Meredith ap Tudor, the Chieftain. Eden happened to call at Penmynydd soon after their arrival. Sweated horses were snorting and champing the earth in the courtyard; inside the hall the women were treading lightly as though on eggs. Meredith was silent. Eva's brothers were pale and grim. Red Iwan's face was the color of his hair.

"By God's tooth!" he was shouting. "You must disown him!"

Eden stood a while to listen, then rode homeward with the tidings.

"It's the Last Trump, boys You had best get beads and Book ready," he jested, blissfully unaware then of the consequences that the scandalous elopement would have upon his own nuptial designs.

During the year that followed—a year which saw Eden spurned, wronged, scarred and, as he was to say, age unseasonably—the voyagings of the errant lovers, Rhys Ddu and Eva, carried them from the commodities and delights of High Kinsella in Ireland to the pageants and festivities of the court of Jean 1V de Montfort in Brittany. Then they returned to Wales. As soon as he heard they were in the land, Meredith summoned them home and they arrived on the island at the beginning of Advent.

It was a ringingly cold night and Eden and his household were huddled together in a sleepy torpor about the hearth at the Old Hall, when the hounds began to give tongue, there came the muffled sound of hoofbeats, shouts, horns, and almost before folk could look at one another and say: "No, can it be?" the amorous delinquents had burst in upon them and the night was roaring in the fire.

Rhys Ddu's eyes shone like jewels. Eva looked radiant and bewitchingly beautiful. She drew an ice-cold fingertip over the scar that ran aslant across Eden's forehead.

"Was it the Trevors' English kinsman, Simon Thelwall, who did that to you, little brother?"

"It was the wildest free-for-all."

"What was so provoking? Was my honor flouted?"

Eden smiled and was evasive.

At Easter that year Simon Thelwall was slain in an ambush near the Welsh border. Eden's courtship attendants, the two sons of Jenkin of Welsh Maelor, were held responsible for his death. Trahern, the older of the brothers, was slain a day later. David, the younger, escaped and fled into Ireland.

Thenceforward, prudent men in Wales were very careful before they uttered slanders about Rhys Ddu and his lady.

Vain, vindictive and arrogant as she was, there were however certain sides of Eva's nature for which one could only have respect. She had a rich sense of humor, a passionate loyalty to those she loved, and the courage of a lioness.

She could also be generous to a fault. As for example: early in the year she had lent some of her best plate to the lady Gwennan of Croes Gwion, who was preparing a feast for a crowd of kinfolk and holy monks against the departure of her husband Ivor for Rome and the Great Pardon. Eva had since sent for the return of the plate, but to no avail.

Then in July Rhys Ddu and Eden received orders to join an army being assembled at Chester, for some punitive expedition of the King's into Scotland.

"It's war," Eden declared. "The in-law foresaw it. What a prognosticator!"

Rhys Ddu was less impressed. He did not think this campaign was going to amount to much more than a brazen clash and show of arms; nonetheless, as leader of the island archers, he decided to hold a feast for his fellows before they took their leave of their dear ones.

"By the way," he said to Eva, "where is that plate I brought you from Venice? It seems to me that I have not seen it in an age of days."

Blushing guiltily, she told him. He stared at her in angry wonder.

"Is this the care you have for my gifts? For pity's sake, Eva, that woman will have the dogs eating off that plate. When were you at Croes Gwion last?"

"Heavens, I can't remember when! Last Michaelmas was it? When Tango and Llio and all the family from the Bay of the White Stones were there? Well, everybody knows that Gwennan has no hand for housekeeping."

"The housekeeping has gone from bad to worse, lady. Go see for yourself. Besides, you will never get that plate back else."

"I shall go there, I promise you, my sweet. After the morrow mass."

That same morning Eden went to Caernarvon to get the initial wages for the troops. The first person he met, striding the halls of the castle in a dignified and impressive manner, was Eva's father, Red Iwan. He had not seen him in what seemed an age of days, but the two kinsmen were at once on the same comradely footing as of old. Richly appareled in a robe of dark blue velvet with ermine facings, Red Iwan was outwardly as affable as he had ever been, and seemed unchanged in appearance, save that he had begun to dye his fading hair and beard with henna.

"Greetings, old herring!" Eden said. "How grand you look!"

"I hear Meredith has put little Owain out to foster."

"Aye, to Father Mathau of Llanrwst."

"I was surprised when I heard of it. A rustic like that."

"A rustic who was once the pride of Alba Domus, however. As a boy it's said that he sat at the feet of the Anchorite himself."

"Sitting is not learning," Red Iwan scoffed genially. "A simpleton could sit at the foot of the Apostle Paul and be none the wiser. I cannot understand Meredith."

"You are not the only one," Eden observed. "No more can Marged Vaughan."

"I like Marged," Red Iwan said. "She and I have much in common. How is the Rose of Mathebrud these days?"

"Still blooming. But what of you, kinsman? Why are you here today? Are you for Scotland too?"

Red Iwan laughed.

"Haven't you heard?" he said. "I am now governor of Caernarvon."

Eden was astounded.

"Go home! I can't believe it!" he exclaimed. "Whatever can you have done to win the favor of the King of England?"

"I cannot tell you that, lad," Red Iwan replied, "unless it is that my father served under his at the Battle of Poitiers."

"Well, everyone but Tudor seems to have been fighting there for sure," Eden said. And with any suspicion of treachery far from his mind (would it not have been a kindly thought on the part of our Creator to set a Judas mark on the face of those who plan to betray us? he would ask himself later) he rode home in great amusement to think of this honor which had been bestowed upon Red Iwan from on high.

Once back in the Old Hall, however, his winning vein swiftly gave way to feelings of sadness and unease. He was leaving his homeland for the first time, and all his housefolk looked so down in the mouth and forlorn. Sibli was on her knees when he entered, running her beads through her gnarled fingers, and Annes glanced at him with an absent, puzzled look, almost as though he were a stranger, but her cheeks were wet, he saw, and the faintest of smiles hovered over her lips like the shadow of an unseen wound.

"Dear Annes," he said to her gently. "I beg you not to take on so. It is not the end of the world. I shall come back, I promise you."

"There is food for you on the board," she told him in a small, strained voice.

As he began to eat his manchet of bread and cheese, Gerallt sat down beside him. He was quiet a moment, then he leaned close to Eden and murmured: "Eva has been here."

"Good luck to her, what did she want?"

"She has found out about you and the lady of Croes Gwion."

Eden was speechless. He stared at his foster-brother in horror.

"I only came in as Eva was leaving. She wanted Annes to go down with her to Croes Gwion and confront Gwennan."

"May God pluck out her tongue, the mischievous bitch, how did she learn of it? Who told her?"

"I have no idea. Ask her."

"Yes, ask her—the viper!"

The feast was held at Rhys Ddu's on the following day, a Wednesday in the evening. Geese, ducks and hens had been decapitated and a large hog slaughtered. Only Gwilym ap Tudor, the master of Trecastell, seemed to remember that this was a fast day. He was a rare man, the most formal and dignified of Tudor's sons. He had been raised at Bangor, in the house of his uncle, Sir Howel ap Grono, the Archdeacon of Mona, and had been intended for the church. But in the heyday of his blood he had made Eilian of Nantanog pregnant and had done the honorable thing. She was a pallid uninteresting creature, but he was very kind to her.

"Are you fasting?" he said to Eden with a smile on seeing how his youngest brother was picking at the food on his plate.

He was surprised at the smoldering glance he received in return.

At last Eva rose and went out to the kitchen. Eden followed her. She looked at him in astonishment.

"How is this?" she asked. "Have you come to help the serving women scour the crocks?"

"It's you I've come to scour, lady."

"Out!"

The maids scattered like butterflies. Menace was in Eva's eye and voice.

"Explain yourself!"

"You explain yourself, sister! Where did you unearth this filth about the lady of Croes Gwion and me?"

"Filth?"

Eva's lip curled disdainfully.

"I am glad you know enough to call it by its true name."

"Where I ask you?"

"Where? Do you really want to know where?"

And she stood gazing at him in silence for a moment at that, with a mocking smile that sharpened the malicious gleam in her eyes. And suddenly, at that look, Eden was half wishing he had not asked her where, for it seemed to him that he knew it already.

"Hazard a guess, little brother."

He stared at her, stunned, and she stared at him. The smile was breaking into a grin even as he watched; the eyes were narrowing down into glimmering slits; the wondrously long and sable eyelashes were flickering with spite. Plainly the lady was beginning to enjoy herself. It was a moment of triumph. She had to savor it for a while, before going on with her tale. Holy Mother, what a story she told him then! Why had she lent Gwennan that wretched plate? Where was ever plate more fateful than that? Sure, she had found it the worse for wear and sure, being Eva, she had given her tongue free rein, calling up Gwennan's sloth and slopwork into that lovely dreaming face until up with that lady in her turn, all fire and spit. Insult begets insult, aye, by the devils. So Eva sneered: "You are wearing such a pretty gown today, Gwennan, but I'll go bail your shift's as dirty as a hag's washclout." And Gwennan flashed back: "Well, dirty as it is, yon Ednyved seems to prefer it to his wife's snowy white nightrail. . . .Lying am I? May God curse me and demons tear the tongue out of my head with red-hot hooks if I am lying. Ask that wanton fellow over at the Old Hall if I am lying. If he says that I am I will send for the priest with the Book of the Gospels. By the body of the Virgin, I will swear to it at the altar, and on your brother-in-law's privy members if Holy Church so decrees. . . ."—Aye, everything was brought out in the open at last, like the sheep fells of Croes Gwion, Eden reflected miserably, breeding their maggots in darkness for a season before sending them forth on the wing in all their full-blown glory to kiss the summer sunlight.

"And it was no lie, either," Eva said scornfully. "One look at your face is enough."

Eden leaned back against a table, pressing down hard upon his hands.

"In the name of charity," he said hoarsely. "why did you have to tell Annes?"

"I was hoping to use that plate tonight. Do you know that Rhys brought it here from Venice? It is priceless. And she has ruined it, the slovenly cow!"

"A pox on you and your shitten plate!"

Eva fell back, as if struck in the face.

"What do you say?" she cried, her voice trembling with fury. "How dare you!"

"How dare he what?" another voice broke in.

Rhys Ddu stood in the doorway, frowning.

"Rhys!" Eva flung at him wildly. "Know that since your brother followed me in here I have had nothing out of his mouth but the vilest incivilities."

"Sure your shouting has been enough to raise the dead."

"Lord save us, aye," said the Chieftain, who now put in an appearance in the doorway with a flock of guests peering over his shoulders. "What's to do here?"

Flushing darkly, Eden made a brusque gesture.

"Enough! These are private matters."

Eva gave a harsh laugh.

"Private?" she jeered. "Come, how is it that you are grown so shy and sparing of words so suddenly? You need have no secrets from us, my dear. We are all of us friends and kinfolk here; your welfare is as our own. And God knows we have had little amusement here tonight. Charm us with some more of your honey words, sir. Beguile us with the tale of your amorous trysts."

"Have done now, I say!"

"Adulterer! Whoremonger!"

"For the love of Heaven, shut your mouth!" the Chieftain exploded furiously. "Get these children out of here! Where are the women who should be watching over them?" He kicked the door shut behind him. "This is quite an accusation you are making, Eva," he glared in hot anger. "Are you out of your senses?"

"I am not" Eva said, calm now and smiling. "Your brother has besmirched the bed of a married man."

"Whose?"

"Ivor of Croes Gwion"

"Eden?"

"Aye, it is so."

A dark, ugly growl came from Rhys Ddu.

"Go from my hall!"

"With pleasure."

"We shall all go," said Meredith. "Enough's been said here tonight, I warrant, to serve the wantonness of every carping tongue on this island for a year and a day. You must be leaving at first light besides."

"I am not leaving," said Eden.

"Be sure you are not," said the Chieftain "You will have to pay your scot and lot like the rest of us."

"I shall need another deputy," said Rhys Ddu.

"Take Gwilym," Eden told him bitterly. "He can preach to the troops."

So that's how it was. Eden left his brother's hall with his thoughts in a furious jumble. Not a word did he get from Annes all the way home, but when he sought to help her dismount at the horseblock, she struck his hand aside. Tears were streaming down her cheeks.

"O, such doings!" she cried wrathfully.

And she ran before him into the hall, slammed the door of the bedchamber and slid the bolt.

Misery. Throughout the days that followed, it seemed to Eden as though a death watch were being held at the Old Hall. An uncanny silence reigned over hearth and byre, and whenever he sought to break it with a light remark the women looked him over like a scabby horse. They were all in league against him on the side of the mistress, and as the hours dragged by and he sat mumbling over his psalter as the priest-father had charged him to do, it almost seemed to him in the wretchedness of his spirit that he could see nothing but a grey dreary vista of days reaching away before him as upon the eve of an unending Lent. Lord, he thought, what trials and tribulations art Thou visiting upon the head of this humble servant of Thine for this foolish unguarded straying of his appetites. Have mercy upon me! Engage me in some more fruitful endeavor!

And in a manner of speaking, one might say that so He did. For even as Tudor's youngest son was passing his time in this manner, grouching over his penitential bread and water like an old dog over his fleas, two events, the one following on the other with breath-catching rapidity, came his way. The first of these struck him as the least calamitous at the outset: His kinsman, Owain Glyndwr, the Lord of the Vale of the Divine Water, had not responded to the King of England's recent call to arms.

What was not commonly known then was that Lord Grey in his capacity as Chief Lord of the Marches had purposely withheld the summons from his hated Welsh neighbor in order to further antagonize the King against him. The devil knows how well and dreadfully he was fated to succeed. Howbeit, the folk at the Old Hall were still trying to absorb these tidings when the second shock reached them.

Early one August morning Meredith rode into the yard of the Old Hall with some of his men. They were armed at all points and the Chieftain was white in the face with anger and worry.

"Get your gear!" he told Gerallt and Eden curtly. "Red Iwan and his ruffians have set upon Father Mathau of Llanrwst and brutally wounded him."

Annes' hands flew to her throat in dismay: "The children!"

"The lads, thank God, are unharmed," Meredith reassured her grimly.

Eden could not get over it.

"Red Iwan has attacked Father Mathau?"

"Is this the time to stand about like a fool marveling?" the Chieftain snarled. "Whip to it!"

Without another word, Eden and his foster brother hastened to obey him, and giving their bridles the slack rode through the summer rain to Nantconway and Mathebrud, arriving there not long before nightfall.

With her rough farmer's walk, her heavy flannel skirts hitched up to her knees, Olwen came to meet them surrounded by a babbling crowd of peasants, striding across the courtyard as if she had some great project in mind, her heavy clogs ringing out firmly over the stones, sloshing through the yellow mud. "Stand back there, Welshmen, you are breathing me! God bless you, Meredith, for having come so swiftly. Eden, is it you? I thought you gone into Scotland with the others."

"It's a long story, Olwen."

"It's not so long," Meredith observed drily. "But it can bear being buried in the bog with the butter for a while. Well, bless my breeches, look who is here!"

His face broke into the first grin of the day as he watched a slightly-stooped, big-boned man with humorous eyebags making his way towards them, silver spurs jingling. It was the Chieftain's brother-in-law, Einion ap Ithel, the constable of Dolwyddelan castle. He embraced the brothers with a hearty kiss that smacked of horses and leather.

"I wish you a blessing, Einion, how is my sister Enid?"

"As beautiful as ever. And you, brother?"

"As you see. Still hobbling around. How many men do you have at the castle?"

"A handful merely. This Scottish campaign of the King's has thinned us out somewhat."

"Kinsmen, you are wet," said Olwen. "You must come in and dry yourselves. I have the long fires going and meat's in pot."

"Lady, who is thinking of eating now? We are for Llanrwst to see Father Mathau."

"Wait then. Einion and I will go with you. What is wrong with Red Iwan, Meredith? Has he gone quite mad?"

At Llanrwst they found the priest in his bed, attended by an ancient handmaiden who filled the air with joyful tremors upon seeing them. "The saints be praised, chieftains, that they have brought you here with such good speed to avenge this wicked act!" They kissed Father Mathau's hand and asked him how he was feeling. Judging by the news they had received they had looked to find him at death's door, but although he was very pale, it was at once apparent to them that the wound was not deadly and that he stood every chance of recovering. After chiding his old nurse with benevolent sweetness for her vengeful attitude, he turned towards them his rough grey peasant's head, ennobled by meditation and fasting, and began to tell them an astonishing tale.

During a thunderstorm a week earlier, a young woman had come to his door begging shelter from the rain. She told him that her name was Genilles, that she was the daughter of Ricca, the steward of Red Iwan's manor at the Great Strand, and that she was on pilgrimage to the shrine of St Gwenfrewi at Holywell. The priest asked her inside, told his charges, the Chieftain's son Owain and Elise of Mathebrud, to set up a pallet for her in the fireroom while he boiled her some gruel.

"Why are you going to Holywell, my child?" he asked her "Are your nerves impaired?"

"I have fits of the trembling, Father," she replied.

"Who does that remind you of, eh?" Olwen broke in with sarcasm.

"Red Iwan's wife," said Einion.

"Pia of Nanmor, aye. Do you know that she herself went on pilgrimage to Holywell last year? Is it not curious? No doubt if Pia suffered from the falling sickness that slut Genilles would have been beating a path to the shrine of St Tegla."

"Olwen, my dear child," said the priest, shaking his head with a reproachful smile.

In the middle of the night Genilles came scratching at the priest's door. She wailed that she was in great trouble of soul. Father Mathau donned his cassock and hastened to give her succor. What was his astonishment upon entering the fireroom to find that his guest was half naked and that blood was flowing from her loins. Worse was to follow as she fell upon him convulsively, clawed his face and fell to screaming: "Rape! rape!" And before the astounded priest could get his breath, she was out through the door and running down the ancient sleeping lanes of Llanrwst, rousing all the folk with her wild shrieks.

"Your priest is a lustful devil!" she yelled as they sped towards her with firebrands. "See!" And she held bloody hands towards them. "He has ravished me!"

Confusion reigned. Folk kept running into one another in the darkness; the tribal bull took fright and broke out of his pen, charging among the wooden fences and the thatched cottages. Some men ran to the priest's house to find out the reason for the woman's wild assertions. Olwen came from Mathebrud. But as for the woman herself, when men went looking for her she was nowhere to be found.

On the Sunday the next following the lady of the hall and the villagers were leaving the church after the morrow mass. Olwen stared. Armed horsemen were breaking out of the forest, a tongue of flame traveling to the fore: Red Iwan's beard. Catching sight of the priest, the governor of Caernarvon gave a warlike whoop, and putting his horse to the gallop, rode down upon him at the head of his troop, tearing through the crowd with his spear crouched and roaring: "You stoat in a surplice! Rape the daughter of my steward, will you!"

The terrified villagers scattered in all directions. Only Olwen held her ground. Shocked at first, she drew herself like the bolt of a leveled crossbow directly. Mailed and belted men with weapons! The priest! The children! Rage took her. Like a maddened she-bear defending her cubs she flung herself in the path of Red Iwan's horse, and clutching convulsively at his saddlebow with one hand, fell to striking the rider so hard with the other that the spear was deflected in its flight, wounding the priest in the shoulder instead of the breast. "Get out of here, you damned woman!" Red Iwan bellowed at her. "I have no quarrel with you." But Olwen had served her turn. In the next moment, taking heart at her boldness, the men of Llanrwst snatched up pitchforks, staves and mattocks, and came running back. Raising a roar of "Kill them!" the crowd struck out at the horsemen, belaboring them and their mounts, until seeing that they were outnumbered, they wheeled their horses about and rode away.

"With their tails between their legs, sure," Olwen scoffed. "Like the cowardly pack of curs that they were."

"Aye," said Father Mathau. "I owe my life to this brave woman, God bless her."

"By my soul," Meredith laughed, giving her a great hug, "you are a wonderful old filly. Boudicca in her war chariots could have done no better."

"I will list you in my company whenever you choose, Olwen," Einion grinned. "Only say the word. Should you ever tire of Howel Vaughan and his naughty capers, come to my castle and I will make you my sergeant-at-arms."

"Oh, lol, how you talk! What was I supposed to do, eh? Let the brute slaughter our beloved Father Mathau and do injury, Heaven help us, to our little ones? If I'd had a weapon handy, believe me, I would have dealt with the scum worse."

"It's as well that you did not, Olwen," said Einion. "Red Iwan is cock o'the walk at Caernarvon now. He enjoys the favor of the King of England. And you have already been given one example too many of how rogues like this will abuse their power."

"And yet, my sons, I still fail to understand how he came to do such a thing," Father Mathau said with a perplexed frown.

"That is what we purpose to find out, reverend sir," said Meredith. "We ride to earth the fox in the morning."

They set out at earliest light, pausing at Dolwyddelan castle on the way to pick up more men-at-arms. They reached Red Iwan's estate on the Great Strand on the following day, having ridden through the night. From afar the black timbered hall with its houses seemed deserted, standing out like a flock of motionless rooks against the silvery fields of barley and the gleaming sea beyond. "I think your fox might have given us the slip, brother," said Einion, and Meredith grunted disgustedly. Then, as they rode through the gates into the yard, the hounds began to bay and a horseboy came out of the stables. At sight of the men he stopped, his eyes wide with fright.

"Where is your master, gog?" Einion asked him sternly.

The boy pointed to the bakehouse and the men went in. Pia, the lady of the hall, was standing in the midst of her women rolling dough in a trough, but as soon as they entered she began to shake and tremble from her matronly jowls to her feet as though in the toils of a palsy. Taking a few steps towards them in a cloud of flour dust, she tottered and tried to speak.

"Where is your husband?" Meredith asked her in a voice of thunder.

Pia swooned. The men picked her up and carried her into the fireroom of the hall where they laid her down on the great settle and tried to force some water between her chattering teeth, while Einion, his broad freckled face drawn in kindly lines, knelt beside her rubbing her hands and now and again patting her cheeks.

"Come now, woman, don't be silly," said Meredith. "No one is going to harm you. Where is Iwan?"

"At Caernarvon."

"Of course. Why do I ask?"

The Chieftain stretched his leathery, sun-blackened neck and stared at her searchingly.

"Tell me, lady," he asked then, "is it possible that your lord and master hates me?"

"Hates you?" sighed Pia, still trembling agitatedly. "Hates you? Oh, heavens, how can you think such a thing? It's true that you have hurt him deeply at times."

"How have I hurt him?"

A word spoken out of turn, the order of precedence at table not strictly observed, an imagined slight—the Chieftain listened to the recital of his offenses against Red Iwan in silence, now and again rubbing his brows as though to rid them of an itch, until he heard Pia say: "And then it was understood that little Owain, your son, would be put out to foster here."

Meredith stiffened and stared at her frowningly.

"Understood? When?"

"Years ago. When my lord's first wife was still alive and mistress here. Eluned, your father's sister of blessed memory. It was understood then that your heir would be put out to foster here."

"Lady," said Meredith drily. "I had no heir in those days."

"You have one now. Iwan thought for sure he would be fostered here. He would sit here and talk about it—he and the lads. Wait till little Owain comes. Won't we show him the good times? Show him where the dwarf falcon nests and the wild horses graze. Iwan loves children so-

so soft his heart. And now this! Och, it has wounded him to the very quick of him."

"This is monstrous!" Meredith exploded. "The favors I have done your Iwan in his day! But those he will forget, aye. While a stupid and groundless grudge such as this he will carry with him to the grave! And to try to kill an innocent priest on account of it!"

"Innocent? What are you saying?"

Pia began to tremble even more, if that was possible, than she was doing already, and raising her voice to a shrill and nervous pitch, went on to tell the men of the terrible shock received by all under Red Iwan's roof at the outrage done to their steward's daughter by Father Mathau. "O, sweet Jesus! Genilles, that sweet pure maid . . . so chaste and biddable. Her pretty voice like a sanctus bell. Heavens! O, fearful! They found her in a ditch . . . shaking . . . bad nerves like me . . . could not talk. Naked. Only a cloak to cover her . . . Bleeding and covered with mud. That old man there . . . that priest out of hell . . . . Ricca, her father, went out of his mind when he saw her. Howling . . . like a wild dog . . . made me, o, made me . . . . And Iwan! His face! Did you but see it? White . . . white. . . . 'What is wrong with Meredith ap Tudor?' says he. 'Is he a stone-blind donkey to put his son out to foster to such a priest? Nay, no priest. A fiend. A toad of blasphemy. He shall not escape us. No, no, he shall not escape us!' . . . Och, the scratches on her thighs! Poor child . . . made me ill. That vile old man . . . lustful beast clawing. Did you but see them, those scratches? Yes, yes, see them! . . ."

"Yes, yes, see them!" the Chieftain broke in savagely. "I would like to see those scratches very much. But where is she then, our poor ravished Genilles? I see her nowhere. Where can she be, I wonder? Is it possible that is at Caernarvon, too?"

"Physician there . . . help for her . . . healing salves . . . ghostly comfort. . . . Ah, what are you doing?" she shrieked, seeing the Chieftain snatch up an axe from a pile of kindling near the fire.

"Christ's curse on the scoundrel!" Meredith exclaimed, burying the axe with a crash in one of the oaken crucks.

"Show that to your Iwan when he returns," he told the terrified lady. "Tell him that I set it there now as a mark of the blood that lies between our houses."

She sat there staring at it long after the sound of hooves had died away in the distance.

Vengeance is sweet to the heart of a freeman, it's said, but the Chieftain and his companions saw that whether they liked it or not, it would have been a bad thing, placed as they then were, to have taken harsher measures. The Bishop of Bangor, the lord John Swaffham, had recently died, and the Chief Justice was gone with the warchiefs into Scotland. There was no one therefore to whom an appeal could be made and for the moment the advantage was clearly on Red Iwan's side.

"Was there ever such an understanding, Meredith?" Einion asked as they rode along. "About the fostering I mean."

"In Aunt Eluned's time," his brother-in-law replied, "many words were spoken and promises made that are now dust on the wind. So much has changed since those days. So much."

The Chieftain paused and sighed.

"It's hard to believe, but Red Iwan was a likely fellow once."

"So there could have been an understanding?"

"Good God, Einion," Meredith exclaimed hotly. "Do you think I would put my son out to foster in the house of that fool and debauchee?"

Einion and Eden exchanged glances and were silent. They rode to Dolwyddelan.

Eden had always been fond of the place. Lost to time and the great world as it seemed in its mountain meadow, the white-towered castle on its crag was still garrisoned solely by Welsh men-at-arms as in the days of Llywelyn the Great, who had built it. It was wild country thereabouts. Wolves lurked in the forests and outlaws in the solitudes beyond. Einion's chief task as castellan, indeed, was to protect the crofts and villages of the region from their depredations and to hunt them down whenever possible. But that evening, descending into the river valley from the high passes, nothing could have looked more peaceful and free from danger. There was a smell of earth, trees and flowers, and a vesper hush lay on things: just the whispering of the wind along the darkening sweep of the meadows, the rippling song of the green hill torrents, and of the river where the drinking cattle stood lazily swishing their tails. Two old women in black, gathering rushes on the bank, straightened up and watched the chieftains as they came, kneading the small of their backs with their knuckle-bones.

Einion unslung his horn and blew it, and from the roof of the keep where helmets gleamed, there came an answering call. Enid, Tudor's daughter, the lady of the castle, came out and walked down the path winding amidst the dripping oaks and hazels to meet them. She was breathing with excitement. "There is a minstrel inside, newly come from the border country," she said. "He brings us tidings. Lord Grey has entered Owain Glyndwr's estate at Croesau and seized it on orders of the King."

"Mother of God!"

If she had thrown a pail of cold water over them they could not have been more startled.

"Croesau," the Chieftain murmured. "It is even as our Sheriff said."

"When did this happen, my dear?" Einion asked.

"A few days ago. A week perhaps."

The men looked at one another, then followed her up the hillside into the great hall. After washing and changing, they sat down at the hearth to eat, with their platters of food on their knees. Einion backoned to the minstrel, who was sitting with a group of soldiers at the gameboard, and he came over. He was a thin brown sinewy man. The marks of the road and the weather were upon him as upon a thousand others. He related that he had been bound for Glyndwr's hall of Sycharth when he had been turned westward and away by the news that Grey in company of Earl Talbot of Chirk had descended upon it, taken everyone he had found there captive, and thrown them into his prison at Ruthin.

"What!" Einion exclaimed. "He attacked Sycharth, too?"

"The Keeper of Chirkeland was in hiding there, it seems. He has been raiding Grey's manor, stealing his horses and cattle."

"Aye, we have heard that tale," the castellan nodded. "What of Glyndwr?"

"As it fortuned, the Lord Owain was not there at the time. It's said he and his family were at his other hall in the Glens of Dee."

"As it fortuned, indeed," Einion nodded.

The minstrel returned to the gameboard. For a few moments the kinsmen were quiet, staring into the fire, musing.

"This has come about most timely, it seems to me," the castellan said at last.

"How do you mean?"

"Red Iwan's murderous caper," Einion replied. "Do you think he knew that this attack on Croesau was portending? Was he trying to connect you with Glyndwr's troubles in some way?"

"But that's absurd, lad. We have had no dealings with our cousin's house in years."

"Ah, but they are not aware of that beyond our Marches, are they? There they have as little knowledge of the ways and usages of our people as though we lived in Tartary. How should they know about our feuds and follies? Think of it. Red Iwan is governor of Caernarvon. He has the King of England's ear. Sure, he wanted you to ride upon his manor yesterday, did he not? He provoked you into it, did he not?"

Curses mingled softly with the Chieftain's breath.

"God's one Son, but he was looking for worse from me. He was counting on a raid."

"Attack his hall and burn it down. Look, dread King, kinsmen of the lawless Glendowrdy have burnt my fields and houses."

Enid was shocked.

"And poor Pia there."

"All the helpless womenfolk, aye. The sacrificial sheep. He wanted to get back at you about that matter of the fostering. That devilish snub. Get rid of the offending priest and at the same time avenge himself upon you by bringing the King of England's wrath down upon your head. I think that is what men mean when they talk about killing two birds with one stone."

"Only this fellow is a cunning old bird," Meredith croaked sardonically. "He is not ready to be netted yet."

The castellan cast him a droll look over the rim of his alepot.

"And when will he be ready, say you?"

"Ready?"

The Chieftain paused a moment, smiling craftily.

"As it is written down in the Book of Cynog," he said then. " 'Take upon thyself no mischief not originating with thee and be not quick-handed in a multitude.' When I forget that advice I may be ready. But I doubt it."

"Ah, there speaks the justiciar. The model of caution. But there is a power not all your laws and bywords can withstand, isn't there?"

"Are you speaking of God?"

"I was thinking of Fate."

"Old pagan," the Chieftain said.

He shook his head and laughed.

"I don't believe in Fate, Einion. I am a very sensible man. No nonsense."

"Aye, my Meredith," his brother-in-law agreed. "What a pity the rest of us are not."

Something untoward was happening in the Vale of the Divine Water throughout the waning days of that summer. At Owain Glyndwr's hall overlooking the river Dee the fires burned far into the night. Against the vast outreaching dark, the sky over the roofs glowed like a portent.

Like a swarm of wild bees flying to the refuge of its nest in the path of a storm, people kept pouring in along the road that led to its gates. Many of them were homeless, their crofts and homesteads put to the torch by Lord Grey of Ruthin. Some were itinerants—mendicant friars, minstrels and vagabonds. They camped out in the woods and water-meadows and waited.

Owain Glyndwr's lady, Margaret Hanmer, grew worried, watching them. How are all these folk to be fed, she wondered?

And every day room had to be found for more guests: the English outlaw John Astwick and his band; the Dean of St Asaph and his nephews, the Kyffins; Madoc of Eyton and his brothers; the Prophet of Ffinnant, a seer so hideous that he was sometimes called the Scab, the bard Griffith Llwyd; and numerous tribal elders with impressive beards and fire-speckled legs, and memories so long—as Glyndwr's brother-in-law, John Hanmer jested—that they still nestled blinking beside the fires of the holy Druids.

And then, at Bartholomewtide, in the midst of a tumult of horns, potbangings and cheers, two soldiers rode in at the head of a warband. They were the half-brothers, Rhys Gethin and Howel Coetmor, two of the most renowned warriors in Wales.

They were admitted into a hall as bright and lively as a marketplace. Glyndwr was sitting in the center of the main floor beside his old friend, the Abbot of Valle Crucis. Across his knees lay the sacred sword of St Eliseg, which had been brought to him that day from the Abbey in the gorges of the Dee. He was wearing a leaf-brown damask gown, and with his tawny hair and beard looked like nothing so much as a genial cat-lion. Only under the bushy patriarchal brows the large greenish sea-grey eyes were strange—their glance at once penetrating and aloof.

"Whence come these warriors, so soiled and battleworn?"

"From Northumberland, lord."

"You have deserted the King's army?" he asked them in mock amazement.

"We have deserted the Usurper's army, o, great one," replied Rhys Gethin, the older of the two brothers.

"Ah, the Usurper, do you mark that, Father Abbot?"

"His boonfellow Grey is with him now in the castle of the Percies. We heard that the Keeper of Chirkeland had been seized and thrown into the prison at Ruthin."

"Aye," said Glyndwr, his eyes suddenly hardening, "and many another innocent along with him."

He looked down at the sword across his knees and drew a finger along the rib of the blade. His blood tingled fierily. In that golden hall, with its minstrel gallery and its blaze of lights, his thoughts went out in that moment, as so often in the course of the last days, to the foul hellborn darkness of that dungeon where the victims of Grey's tyranny lay, and he knew that he—a man in his middle years, a Welsh chieftain of affluent means and princely descent, one whose life had been devoted to cultivating the arts of peace—was now being drawn forward with all the inevitability of Fate towards the irreversible act—the undreamed-of encounter.

"Those carvings on the hilt . . ." he said to the Abbot.

"A lion and a lamb."

"Lying down together in peace and amity," Glyndwr said with a wry smile.

He took the sword by the blade and held it outward before him, letting the light play on the heavily-embossed handgrip and pommel.

And then, suddenly, Rhys Gethin stepped forward. He dropped down on one knee and kissed it.

Autumn days, gracious and golden.

So they would forever smile in Eden's memory. After the summer rains the weather set in hot and bright. The corn came to heavy ear and was cut, a sea of grain to outglare the sun. On the island the work went forward from day to day, and in the evening when the scents of the earth thickened in the blue twilight, and the breeze blew softly over the mown meadows from the sea, the master sat in his place in the Old Hall with his shoulders aching and a pleasant weariness lapping over his body in warm waves, and thinking—well maybe things are not sorting out so badly after all.

As long as the weather held, the harvest would be a good one, everyone was agreed. And nothing came to spoil it. Now and again, tremulous lightnings would flicker like swords above the purple ruins of the mountains; sometimes little rumblings of thunder came to to the islanders from the river valleys to the east as from the belly of some gorged and slumbering giant, but that was the most of it.

For the rest, albeit the bread and water penance continued, as did the daily reading of the Penitential Psalms, Annes had allowed Eden to invade her couch again. The unpleasantness was over. Has she been having a talk with Mam Indeg and Marged Vaughan? he wondered. Dreamy moments must those have been that they had shared together, if true. A mystery of sybils, aye. For it seemed to him that Annes was even tenderer towards him now than she had been in the days before his adulterous caprice, full of charming coquetry and strange sweetnesses.

Against this, Eva, who had already been upset on two counts—that of her tarnished Venetian plate and her quarrel with Eden—was now in an even blacker mood, by reason of her father's brutal escapade. She blasphemed against her house and spoke of wending her way to the cursing well of St Elian to call down malediction upon Red Iwan's head.

It was, in part, because of this that a concerned Chieftain suggested that the harvest should be held at Rhys Ddu's that year instead of at the Old Hall as formerly.

"She will be missing him, her Rhys, her stay and support. Let us be kind."

"The lady has yet to forgive me, you know," Eden reminded him.

"Aye, there's a great deal of the old Iwan in our Eva, whether she like it or no," Meredith observed. "Still it may soothe her spirits a little, what say you? Anoint her wounded pride with balm."

Their good intentions proved vain as it turned out. Eva continued angry and morose throughout the greater part of the feasting, and cast Eden such hostile looks that they bade fair to dry up the marrow of his bones. It was not long, in fact, before he, in company with the Chieftain and Gerallt stole away from the gloom of the hall and its savage black-browed beauty for a stroll along the hillside to watch the merrymaking.

For that night the men of Mona were drowning the harvest, and they would have reason to remember it well.

It was a beautiful September evening, clear, gay, warm, and fat with ripe autumnal scents. In the cloudless blue skies above the ridges of the mountains beyond the waters the first pale stars were trembling like shrine lamps. Far away, beyond the hall, towards Coeten Arthur and the old burial mounds, seafowl were circling and crying. Oxen drifted lazily through the reeds on the banks of the stream. Men were crouched on their hunkers against the turf banks, passing a meadhorn back and forth, while in the village below a chain of laughing beardless lads and girls with swinging braids and supple bouncing breasts were moving and swaying about the burning heap of furze and heather in front of the wattle huts.

"*Moes un cusan,*" they were singing, "*moes dau gusan, moes tri chusan. . . .*"*

"That's odd," Gerallt said. "There are fires burning on the mountain yonder."

His companions stood and looked towards the east. At first they thought their eyes were playing them tricks for the number of stars brightening in the sky. But no, the red points of light did not move; they stood out like blood drops against the gathering darkness.

"Some herds, it maybe, have set them alight."

"Would there be grazing grounds up there, so high?"

"Well then, the bush could be on fire from the heat."

"Perhaps."

And upon this they gave the matter no more thought, until some little while later. They had returned to the hall. A harper was playing an old ballad, and Eden was lying in the rushes with his head in Annes' lap, when there came a stir in the night. Upon a sign from Meredith, the harper stilled his strings, and all turned their heads, listening. And yes, they could hear shouting now and the clamor of dogs and the sound of hoofbeats thudding over the crust of the earth and surging along the hillside.

"What can it be?" the Chieftain asked.

They hastened out into the courtyard to greet the horsemen. One of them leapt from the saddle before he had drawn rein. In the light from the open doorway his eyes shone as if from an infusion of henbane.

---

*Give me one kiss, give me two kisses, give me three kisses. . . .

"Have you heard? Have you heard?"

"Heard what?"

"Glyndwr has risen, chieftains," he cried. "All of Upper Powys is in revolt."

3
HUNTER'S MOON (1400)

1

It had happened on St Matthew's Day in the morning. In the midst of the fair at the king's town of Ruthin, a band of Welshmen headed by Rhys Gethin and his brother Howel Coetmor had risen upon a sign and fallen upon the startled citizenry. The insurrectionists had swarmed through the town firing the houses, while others had raided the castle, and released all the prisoners. Since then, like a flood that has overflowed its banks, the rising had swelled and spread across Upper Powys and Chirkeland to the walls of Denbigh, Hawarden, Flint, Chirk, Oswestry and Welshpool.

"They are fighting all along the Northern March," the Sheriff of Mona told the Chieftain and Eden when he rode into the Old Hall on the morning after the news. "Watch you do not get dragged into these turmoils."

"O, laughable!" said Meredith

"Wait till the King of England gets to hear of it. There will be hell to pay."

"Caerhun, Cilcein, Trovarth, Trescawen, Penhenllys and Aber of the White Shells—do you know what those were, son of Kenvric?" the Chieftain asked. "They were the mainland estates our faction, the Men of Eden, once held by privilege of our ancestor Ednyved Vychan. They have driven us back into this island and here I stay. Before I cross that water to do battle again—well, do you remember what Bran the Blessed said to his men when they were trying to cross that river in Ireland which had no bridge over it, and could not be forded otherwise?"

"'Bid ben, bid bont.'"

"Just so," said the Chieftain. "He who would be leader, let him be a bridge."

2

"There is a commorthy at Aberffraw tonight," Mererid, the daughter of Father Conan and Mam Indeg, murmured to herself, echoing what she had heard men whispering after mass that morning.

A commorthy, she knew, was now by edict of the Parliament in London decreed an unlawful assembly of the people, punishable by loss of one's head if noble, and hanging if not. Several had taken place in other parts of Wales even before the outbreak of the rebellion, but this was the first to be held on the Isle of Mona.

Mererid was barely fourteen and was more forward than was proper, or so she had often been told. Mam Indeg had spoilt her of course, as she had spoilt all her children.

Other than that the girl was likable enough. She had a clever head and was a good worker. She wore the cut-down dresses of the Chieftain's eldest daughters, had long skinny coltish legs and reddish brown hair, and was besprinkled with freckles about the cheekbones and the bridge of her nose.

It was an October morning and she was in the milkhouse at Penmynydd, taking turns at the churn with Megan and the Chieftain's youngest daughters, Gwladys and Regin, when Mam Indeg came in, all fuss and flutter, holding her younger son Alun by the hand.

"Where is Marged Vaughan? We can come to no result with that poor woman down at the mill and now Long Bet must go home to her family."

"It is bad then?" Megan asked.

"It is going to be a long lying-in, I am afraid."

"Would that Sister Sehostaba were here."

"Aye, indeed," Mam Indeg sighed.

She passed through the doorway into the hall, where she could be heard calling distantly "Marged Vaughan" and in a while the sound of Mam Indeg's throaty lilting voice and the deeper tones of the mistress came in broken snatches from the kitchen and they entered the milkhouse. Marged Vaughan had put on rough clothing and was tying a coarse apron about her waist.

"Where is Father Conan, Indeg?"

"He is over in the turbary."

"With old Guto, aye."

They crossed themselves.

"Megan, do you come with us," the lady then enjoined. "Stay here, my daughters, and finish the churning. Mererid, you are to take your brother and go to the Old Hall. Tell Gerallt to ride to Dragon and fetch Father Idris. And ask Sioned to come here. I do not think you had better ask the lady Annes, she is not strong. And for heaven's sake do not ask that old creature Sibli—it's not that I mind so much, but these silly women around here are frightened of her, she looks so like a little witch-wife."

"Shall I come back with Sioned?"

"That would be bootless, child. Stay there the night."

Mererid went to the stables and led the old brown mare Belene out of her stall to the horseblock where Alun was waiting. They mounted and rode through the hummocks of gorse and broom to the Old Hall. She recited her errand to Gerallt—who set off at once bearing his son Gwyn with him on his saddlebow—and to the women in the hall.

"The child is coming badly, is it?" said Annes.

"Yes," Mererid replied. "They are talking of sending for Sister Sehostaba."

"Good heavens," said Sioned.

"Who is that?" asked Annes.

"A holy nun, lady," Sibli explained. "She used to be reckoned the best midwife on the island. But sweet Mother of Heaven," she said, crossing herself, "I thought her dead and in her grave years ago."

Annes rose.

"Lady, you are not to go," Mererid said quickly. "You are not strong enough."

The mistress looked at her in surprise and then smiled.

"Who told you that?" she said and went off to change her clothes.

"She is stronger than Sister Sehostaba, I'll wager," said Sioned. "So ancient as that one must now be, the miller's big wife could snap her in two like a windle-straw, I am thinking. Have you two eaten yet? There is some flummery in the milkhouse."

It was only a little later that Mererid remembered something. She darted out into the yard, but it was too late. The women had already gone and Sibli with them.

And then there were four people left in the Old Hall: Mererid, Robyn, Alun and Mabon of the Silver Harp. The bard regarded the priest's daughter with a disapproving smile—is she pretty or is she not? She is certainly malapert; I doubt she is biddable. The way she is staring me in the eye. If he had been younger he would have rounded on her sternly, but now he felt too haggled out and weary. He closed his eyes and dozed.

She watched him for some moments, an old man wrapped in a brown robe with a beard to his chest, the little whisper of sleep blowing in his lip-hair and then moved close to Robyn.

"Where is Eden?"

"He left this morning early, I don't know where."

She turned again and stared at the sleeping bard, and then whispered almost without breath: "Shall we go? Robyn, I have a horse."

They looked at one another with wide eyes. Against his ribs Robyn felt the startled beating of his heart.

"And Alun? What of him?"

"Let me come," the boy breathed. "Please, Meri."

His sister peered at him searchingly.

"Are you sure? Will you promise not to breathe a word of this to anyone?"

Alun was ten. About his neck, under his island-spun tunic, he wore an amulet of pebbles with blood spots on them. At Mererid's question he laid a finger against his lips and turned his eyes up to the rooftree.

The royal seat of Aberffraw lay on the south-western side of Mona, on a hill overlooking the sea. Here for centuries the great lords and princes of Gwynedd had held state. Now apart from the encircling stone walls which rose between the huts of fishermen and the sky there was little left of the old palace. Sea fowl nested there and the ancient paths were overgrown with thickets.

The people had begun to come there early that day. By sunset, the headland with its fires and human swarms looked like a large ship beached high among its tidal flats. The twilight was filled with an unceasing roar. Seagulls flew squawking out of their high roosts. Friars were to be seen everywhere. Some were begging money for the rebellion, others were preaching to groups of islanders in front of the church and along the long shelf of shingle.

The children tethered Belene to a tree some distance away and climbed up the slope to the ruins of the palace. A crowd was gathered there, within the broken walls. The dark figures of men moved through the fiery smoke like shadows against a painted curtain. The children pushed their way to the front of the mob, looked around at the faces of their neighbors and waited.

A huge yellow moon was rising above the mountains to the east when a form walked past Mererid, someone in grey robes whom she thought at first was another preaching friar, until she saw his long hair and beard. It was Griffith Llwyd, the most celebrated of Glyndwr's bards.

For a pulpit he had chosen a rock that stood in what was left of the banquet hall of the old palace. Shrouds of sea mist like the white forms of women, smiling and beckoning with their fingers, prowled the bourns of the firelight as the bard mounted his rocky perch. Robyn, Mererid and Alun pressed close to hear him, fell silent and waited.

He said nothing for a space, but glanced around him at the throng, a tall lean man with harsh unfleshed cheekbones and great magnificent black eyes. Then he covered his face as though meditating. Red shadows moved along the bushes and the shattered stones and there was a thick smoke of peat and driftwood. A profound hush reigned. The air grew faint with suspense. Finally and without as yet having uttered a sound, Griffith Llwyd raised his arms so that the sleeves of his robe fell back to reveal the craggy pinnacles of his elbows and in the wailing notes of an incantation began to cry:

> *See you not the drift of the wind and the rain?*
> *See you not the oaks beating together?*
> *See you not the sea scourging the land?*
> *See you not the truth a-gathering?*
> *See you not the sun rushing through heaven?*
> *See you not that the stars have fallen?*
> *Do you not believe in God, fond mortal men?*
> *See you not the end of existence?*
> *Och, my God, why does not the sea come over the land?*
> *Why are we left to linger?*

"Do you remember, men of Mona?" he cried out with passion. "Do you remember those words that were sung here a hundred years ago? Aye, in this very place, in a hall that was hung with branches of evergreen? Let us clothe the bones of memory with the flesh. His bard sang them for Llywelyn, our last leader, treacherously slain by the lackeys of the Black Oppressor. He wept for our murdered pride. He wept that cruel strangers had entered into our rich inheritance. But it was not for this alone that he wept that night. No, he wept for the shining host that had gone before. He wept for Llyr and Coel and Bran the Blessed, for Cunedda of the Red Robes, for Math and Manawydan and Pwyll and Pryderi and for Prince Elphin and the Country Under the Sea. He wept for Hu the Mighty, the golden constable of Constantinople, who led the tribes out of the Land of the Summer and harnessed them to the plough. He wept for the warriors of the Gododdin who rode singing to their death—the old, the strong, the young, the weak. Aye, and he wept for Arthur with the golden crosses on his breast, riding to do battle against the Saxons at Badon Hill. And for Cadwaladr, Caradoc, for Griffith ap Cynan, for Howel the Good, for Rhodri the Great, for the Lord Rhys who took the field against the Normans when he was eighty, for Owain Gwynedd and for Llywelyn Fawr, for those too he wept. He wept for the bards and their songs—for Gwalchmai, Meilyr, Aneirin, Llywarch Hen and Taliesyn. And he wept for the saints and the scholars, for the glories of the schools at Alba Domus, Caerleon, Llanbadarn and the precious libraries at Bangor Under the Wood. And the bright luminaries of our queens, for those too he wept—for fair Elin of the Hosts, for Angharad Golden Hand, for Creiddylad, Enid, Gwladus Ddu and the peerless Gwenhwyvar. For all this and more he wept. Do you remember, Welshmen, do you remember?"

The gathering thundered with a sudden: "We remember! We remember!"

"Is this your own land to live in?"

"It is, it is!"

"Arise then, men of Mona, arise and drive out the robber hordes! Rejoice and lift high your hearts! One has raised his banners among you who is of the blood of the great Llywelyns! Once more the teeth of the sleepless dragon are bared, once more! Rise up, my countrymen, rise up! Sound the assembly through the mountains and valleys of Wales! Let destruction visit the land beyond!"

The bard was transfigured. A thunder-throated prophet out of Holy Writ, so he seemed—weeping and dancing, black eyes ablaze. And as he went on, his voice grew louder and more impassioned; he began to sing and chant, his rich and rhythmic words which spoke to the people of destiny and the blood of imminent battles grew by little and little more obscure. As if they would make the sounds of earth, sky and water a language all his own, his utterances began to pass over the heads of the company thronged in the briar-choked hall, seemed to be caught on running torrents of sound, soaring through the night, far beyond the headland and its fires and its tidal flats.

And in all this it was to Robyn as if he had found something he had often dreamed and longed for but could not express, something astonishing, wondrous and infinite that sent a thrill of mystery and lonely pride through his innermost fibres. The changing voices of the bard came to him mingled with the colors of a primitive past, a very broth of odors and echoes: voices of the wild rains and mists, of the white-maned horses of the trackless deep, of the onslaught of steel and fire—roaring, sobbing, crumbling away, magic voices.

Never had the boy felt like this before—so completely in thrall to one man. His eyes filled with tears, sighs racked his breast, his heart throbbed, he almost felt on point of swooning.

"I am frightened, Meri," Alun murmured to his sister.

The priest's daughter clasped the child to her and looked around in quiet amazement. An old woman, wrinkled as a raisin, was sobbing nearby. Some folk, out of their wits with superstitious fear, had fallen to their knees; some beat their heads against the ground, clawing the dirt and rubbing it on their hair and faces. Others, their cheeks streaming with tears, were crossing themselves and babbling incoherently. Along the walls a thick dark row of men and women made moan, rocking and swaying like a hedge of reeds in a wind. Everyone indeed was as if bewitched, and Mererid was beginning to wonder what if anything would break the spell, when suddenly other voices shook in the air.

"Soldiers!"

In the next moment the hillside was shaken with yells. Men scurried through the bushes, the earth groaned under the tread of feet, the smoke of the fires plumed and tossed in the air, casting fantastic shadows and startling the seabirds from their high roosts. Seizing Alun's hand, Mererid ran beside Robyn out of the ruins and down the slope through the gorse-brakes. Angry thorns plucked at her skirts and scratched her legs. Bellows and curses were inundating the hillside and the pool-starred sands as the children reached the tree where the old mare Belene stood, lazily admiring her reflection in a moonlit puddle.

"Look," Robyn panted. "There's Eden."

He was riding his black stallion not more than a hundred paces away, his mantle snapping and bellying about him in the wind, his big battlesword shining.

What a hero! Mererid thought with scornful anger. Fighting on the side of the Black Oppressor against his own people!

She flashed him one long baleful unheeded glance before giving Belene's flank a kick and riding with Robyn and Alun away.

"Hist, Eden. . . ."

Had he heard that? Someone hissing his name? The master of the Old Hall peered through the yellow smoke, and saw two helmeted heads rising above groundwalls grown over with grass, weed and bramble. Little Garmon was one, a short man as powerful and knotty as a dwarf oak. The other was Asa Coedana, a big, cat-eyed chieftain with long, crooked teeth.

"We have the bard here."

A jerk of the head towards a flight of toppling stone steps leading nowhere.

"God be thanked."

"Very hardly can we turn him in."

"Hardly."

"He would put a curse on us."

"Or worse yet, wish one of his dreams upon you. He's a fine poet, too, from what I hear. It's no small consideration."

"Where can we hide him? Somewhere safe until morning."

"Nowhere is safe tonight, nowhere," Asa Coedana whispered. "They are going to be scouring the island tonight. Eyes everywhere."

Eden reflected, looking down the hillside where soldiers stood questioning people, the flames of firebrands breaking into red and yellow flickers of light as they fell on spear and cuirass.

"The haunted mound."

"Good God!"

"Sweet Jesus! It makes my blood run cold to think of it."

"Some evil doings there at one time. Burnt bones of men."

"In pagan times, Asa. Are you a Christian or are you not? It's a gift. And look, the tide is turning. Soon it will be all around the tumulus. The bard will be as snug and safe inside it as Jonah in the belly of the whale."

"Is that what you call safety?"

"A life is at stake, eh? A precious bit of manmeat."

"Yes, yes."

"Come along then. Who has a lantern?"

"I have," said Little Garmon, sidling along beside Eden to the well of the broken stairway, where the bard was secluded, his cheekbones and black eye-sockets gleaming in the shadows.

"This is Tudor ap Grono's youngest son Eden."

"I wish you a blessing," he said in a curiously soft and mild voice.

"Do you frighten easily?"

"Why do you ask that?"

"Where you will spend the night would cut the nerve of an eagle."

There was a glint of teeth as the bard smiled.

"I am better than an eagle," he said. "I am a being created in the image of the Almighty God."

Eden liked that reply of his. It had a fine manly ring to it, proud, defiant and yet full of wit. Why there may be hope for you, after all, Griffith, he thought.

"Come," he said.

They slipped off down the other side of the hill, moving in the shadows of the boulders until they reached the beach. A flood of cool air met them there, gusting in off the running tide. Walking their horses, they carefully crossed the shelves of sliding shingle towards the sands. A league beyond Aberffraw they turned a bend in the coast and came upon a sight to make the heart shrink. Before their eyes, what might have been taken for a gigantic unswept stables, piled high in the dung, filth, and fetid straw of uncounted years, stretched away before them in the light of the moon. There was a belly-stirring stench. The bard, no stranger to horrors though he was, stopped short in his tracks with a cry: "Bowels of Beal, where are we?" The chieftains explained to him that what he was seeing was what the islanders called *broc y mor*—the scourings of the ocean. "All of it finds its way here, to this one place, for some reason," said Asa Coedana. "Nobody knows why, except it is the devils of the deep."

"Faugh!" the bard breathed, holding his nose, "I could heave up my entrails."

"It frightens folk, do not scorn it," said Eden. "It is your good luck."

For a few minutes more they walked, picking their way among seaslimed rocks and boulders tressed in tussocks of black and stinking weed, and treading the sand of inlets befouled with middens of broken shells and the carrion of crabs, fish and seabirds, and then Eden said:

"There's the mound."

Pale it rose before them, shadows writhing like serpents in the long grass. The rocks stood as though brooding upon their own secrets; even the cold rank rustlings of the breeze seemed full of mystery. They climbed to its summit and there, with the help of the others, Eden lowered himself down into the cave that lay in its depths. Dark nest of the Old People—there was the scrunch of seashells underfoot as he reached the ground, an ancient smell like the beginning of time. The lighted lantern came down after him, then the long, hairy, bony legs of the bard and his grey woolen robes redolent, as Eden's nostrils now told him, of sweat and cloistral mold. He and this pit are made for one another, the young chieftain decided. Arthur's Cave, did not some men call it? Who then would this be but Merlin?

"It is like the womb of the world here," the bard observed.

"Aye, the lair of the Earth Mother, right enough," Eden agreed. "Men will come for you in the morning. The soldiers will be gone by then."

Eden set the lantern down. Half of a fat goatwax candle burned inside it. He could see nothing beyond that small round of light; only the outreaching blackness and that weak flickering glow, and in it Griffith Llwyd's gaunt bearded face hanging like a waxen devil over the flame. That candle is going to go out soon, Eden thought, and then all will be blackness. And the tide will come in, washing all around this tumulus, grisly scene of God knows what bloody sabbats, and this haunted pit will be full of sound. The wild boars of the brine, the two-breasted Leviathan, the calling shepherdess of the waves, the dragons of the salt deep, and the bard can all sing together in symphonious harmony. Goodnight, the youngest of Tudor's brave sons knew he had to get out of there.

"We cannot light a fire for you, I am afraid," Eden told him. "Someone might see the smoke. You will be cold." He unclasped his black mantle lined with miniver, a birthday gift from Annes and handed it to the bard. "Here, take this."

"Give you thanks, son of Tudor. If God see fit to spare me, I will have it returned to you in the morning."

"No," said Eden. "Use it for cover when you leave the island."

"Nonetheless, it is costly, I know. I will hold it for you until next we meet."

"And when will that be, I wonder?"

"Perhaps sooner than you think."

"So may the Lord provide, my friend. Rest well," said Eden, and with the assistance of Asa Coedana and little Garmon he clambered out of the cave and rode homeward.

As he was passing the church-farm at Penmynydd, he saw the swaybacked old mare Belene standing beside the fence of the kitchen garden cropping grass. Is someone from the Chieftain's hall here, Eden wondered? He rapped at the door of the priest's house and walked in.

Alun was sleeping on a bed of rushes in the corner, and Mererid was sitting on a three-legged milking stool beside the fire, with her bare feet on the hearthstone.

"The power of the Cross be with you, Mererid, where is Father Conan?"

"He is over in the turbary."

"And Mam Indeg?"

"She is up at the hall yonder."

"At this hour?"

"Your lady is there, too."

"Annes is there?"

"Yes, everyone is there."

"Except you," he smiled.

She was cracking hazel nuts on the hearth with a pressing iron. A pair of clogs stood nearby, crusted as Eden now saw in the light of the fire with muddy sand. A sudden suspicion flew into his mind, a fugitive memory—had he not seen some children riding a horse earlier on along the sands of Aberffraw? Aghast now and shaken, he glanced at the torn hem of her skirt, likewise soiled and glittering and met her eyes unabashedly directed at his.

"Where have you been?" he asked her sternly.

"Why do you ask?"

"I ask naturally because I expect an answer. Where have you been?"

"Where should I have been, foster brother, but where I am?" she retorted.

The hostility in her glance took him aback. How have I offended her, he wondered? Why is she being so rude and impudent?

"Your hair is getting redder, little sister, and the freckles are multiplying," he said sharply and turned on his heel.

At the hall of Penmynydd the women were sitting in the kitchen, reviving themselves with bowls of warm milk. Mam Indeg was leaning on an arm-end of the big settle, some wisps of her once magnificent flame-gold hair straying about her wide freckled weary face.

She shook her head when she saw Eden enter.

"Ah, joy of my heart," she said, "what a day we have had!"

"The miller's wife has had a worse," said Sioned.

"Where is your mantle, Eden?" Annes asked.

"Look at that!" he exclaimed in disgusted surprise. "It must have been torn off my back in the fray."

Marged Vaughan shook her head frowningly.

"Not that beautiful mantle lined with miniver! Och, what a pity!"

"The fray was a bitter one then?" Annes queried.

"How not?" Eden replied evasively. He sought to change the subject. "What has happened to the miller's wife?"

"She has given birth to her thirteenth child today. A boy."

"Fourteenth," an affrighted Sibli broke in, crossing herself. "Let us not wish such a misfortune upon that poor woman as to say it is her thirteenth child. Sure, that number has been accursed ever since the wicked Judas of Paris sat down to supper with our Lord Jesus and his knights."

Eden and the women stared at her in bewilderment.

"But then," said Sioned, "what you are saying is that last year's misbirth down at the mill must be counted as the thirteenth."

The old woman nodded.

"As I have said, it is a number of ill hap."

Sioned shook her head.

"Sibli. . . ." she began.

"No more of this," the mistress broke in abruptly. "I am weary and must be up betimes to ride over to the turbary to see old Guto's widow. My dear Annes," she said, turning to her sister-in-law, "I wonder if you will send Mererid back here at first light. We shall need her help with the funeral meats."

"Mererid is already here," Eden informed her.

Marged Vaughan looked at him in surprise.

"What a good girl she is!" she smiled then. "She must have known I would have need of her."

3

Some ten days later Rhys Ddu and Gwilym ap Tudor arrived home with their men. They were tired and grim. They said that King Henry and Hotspur were riding in their heels with an army. They were passing through the garrison towns of North Wales, putting to death all the rebels in the prisons.

"Are there any here at Beaumaris?"

"Six that were arrested attending an unlawful assembly of the people at Aberffraw."

"Poor lobs, I'm afraid we shall be assisting at their executions soon."

As Rhys Ddu said, so it happened. It was Martinmas when the sons of Tudor found themselves among those who had been summoned to witness the hangings at Gallows' Point, a spit of land south of Beaumaris on the sea-river. It was a bleak unhappy spot at the best of times, but especially so on that damp cold day. The mountains across the straits were wearing mourning shrouds, and dark white-maned waves chased one another along the strand, sprinkling icy drops of spray on the Chieftains and his brothers.

Meredith ap Tudor was in a bad mood. His crippled leg was giving him trouble as it generally did in such weather. His face was grey and his eyes were dull with anger and pain. Wrapped about and hooded in black wool, he sat in a cradle of rocks, square and terrible, with his chin resting on his hands and the deep frown mark imbedded in the muscles of his brow, staring at the platform where the King and the Chief Justice of North Wales sat. Both were middle-aged men, but whereas Henry of Lancaster was burly and pale with a head that looked as round and hard as a ball of alabaster, Hotspur was lean and florid, with red hair. Near them sat the Sheriff of Mona and Thomas Bold, the new Constable of Beaumaris, looking Meredith thought, as if like himself they would have liked nothing better than to be at home warming their shanks at the hearth.

Soldiers were everywhere, archers and spearmen. And the

townsfolk, too, were out in strength. Goodmen and goodwives. The frequenters of Stew Lane and Addle Alley, boozy-faced old harridans, daughters of joy, tipplers wobbling about on their legs like eggs on staffs. The islanders with their swarthy iron faces moved among them in their robes of red and blue island spun, with their amulets of jet beads and walrus ivory, and their clanking copper ornaments from the old Roman mine at the End of the Ridges. Someone walked past the brothers, a shivering scrag of humanity, with a thin pointed nose, its two taps leaking.

"He has caught a cold already."

"Is it to be wondered at?" the Chieftain fumed. "This is such an indignity. Killing men in the heat of a fight is one thing, but waiting in this evil spot to see some poor wretches hanged—ah, well, God have mercy on them."

"We shall go back to the Old Hall after, why not?" Eden suggested. "Annes will give us some mulled mead."

A glimmer of a smile bent the Chieftain's lip.

"Of a truth, my dear," he said, "those are the sweetest words I have heard uttered all this benighted morning."

There was a sudden surge of bodies, a low roar of—"Here they are!" Eyes full of excitement, eyes full of horror watched the prisoners being escorted by a cordon of men-at-arms to the place of execution where a priest was standing with a cross in his hands. They mounted the steps of the gallows, and then came forward arrayed in their grave-clothes, their heads and faces shaven, their feet bare. Looking more like baleful specters than human beings, the six of them stood motionless as the sentence was read in a voice hard to be heard above the buzz of the crowd.

The islanders were in a stir, calling out in their native tongue.

"They have shaven the hair off their faces. They look like monks."

"It's shameful."

"Aren't they going to give them a pot of beer for their last refreshment?"

"Give the lads a pot of beer, you heartless begors!"

"Do you call yourselves Christians?"

And then there was a quiet falling, the mob stirred uneasily, and for a while there was no sound to be heard but that of the surf. At a sign from the King the nooses were slipped around the necks of the prisoners.

Everyone drew breath. The priest began to chant. But now, suddenly, a wild scream from one of the felons tore through the stillness.

"Down with the tyrant!" he yelled, his eyes glaring out of his haggard face with undisguised loathing. "My curse on that carrion!"

The King had no Welsh, but he must have had no difficulty grasping the man's sense. And yet, apart from what might have been the slightest tightening of the muscles of his face, he seemed unmoved. He made a peremptory gesture and in the next moment the six men were swinging in the air.

Stunned, the people stared at the gallows, with its victims, looming ominously above them. Almost simultaneously, Dirty Dorti, a half-demented woman of the island, flew up to the royal dais, baring her shrunken dugs to the King and shrilling curses. An angry, deep-throated muttering broke out in the crowd. Some of the men, their faces on fire, raised fists like cudgels, others to the rear of the throng fell to hooting and catcalling. Clods of dirt and handfuls of gravel went flying through the air. Shaggy heads, blood-clouded eyes, women screeching, the reek of hatred—the King watched with frozen eyes as a body of soldiers with brandished pikes and knocked bows closed in upon the people and drove them, still glowering and grumbling away.

He turned to the Sheriff of Mona.

"Why do I see no grey friars here?" he asked. "I understand they have a house on this island. Were they not summoned?"

The question put the bowels of Kenvric's son to a churn. He remembered that the Minorites had been Richard the Second's favorite order. Certainly, few had been as assiduous in damning Henry of Lancaster since the death of his predecessor.

"Yes, my Lord King, they were summoned."

"Where is their house?"

"At Llanvaes. Some little way north of here."

The King leaned over to the Chief Justice and said something. Hotspur nodded.

Meanwhile the brothers were at the Old Hall, drinking their mulled mead, while the women bustled about them preparing the Martinmas beef.

"Where does he go now?" Eden mused.

"Back to London, where else?" said the Chieftain. "With us he has reached the End of the Ridges and the waves of the sea, and those not even he can subjugate."

"He has a crowd of business awaiting him there besides," said Rhys Ddu.

"Unfinished business. Yes, a great deal of that."

"What puzzles me," said Gwilym, "is what he has gained by this harshness. Has he hurt Glyndwr at all?"

"Well," said Meredith, "clearly he believes that this show of force will cow the spirits of the rebels, nip the whole mischief in the bud as it were. But it is hard to see what else he could do at present. He has troubles enough at home. They say the hereditary allegiance of his lords is at the breaking point."

"He has the Percies of Northumberland behind him."

"Yes, he has the Percies. But for how much longer? Do not forget that the Percies are allied by marriage to the Mortimers and the Mortimers are kin to the Earl of March, who is, we are told, the legitimate heir to the throne of England. And where do you think that hapless youngster is at the present time? In King Henry's tender keeping. Would you call that a happy situation?"

"Someone is coming," said Gerallt.

One of the Sheriff of Mona's clerks came posting into the courtyard on a panting hackney.

"The most dreadful news, chieftains," he cried. "The King and his soldiers have attacked Llanvaes. The Father Abbot has been hurt, some others. They rode into the Abbey on their horses, have smashed and desecrated the altars, and set fire to the entire house."

No sooner had these words been spoken than everyone was spurred to action. Meredith bellowed orders, men snatched up axes and billhooks, leapt on their horses bareback and whipping them mercilessly put them to a headlong gallop along the garths.

Dusk was coming on when they arrived at Llanvaes and a fierce wind was blowing off the sea. Flooded in a reddish glare and the billowing smoke of the fires, the black spine of the Abbey roofs crackled like a giant boar on a spit. From the walls to the banks of the stream a line of people had formed, passing pails of water from hand to hand, their faces gleaming and ruddy-shadowed. Their arms rose and fell ceaselessly and they seemed to be howling or chanting, although their voices could barely be heard above the wild pealing of the tocsin and the roar of the flames.

The brothers and Gerallt tethered their horses, stripped to their shirts and hurried to help herd out the panic-stricken beasts from the farm buildings. Running through the gardens Eden heard someone call his name. It was the Father Abbot Anianus. He was lying under a tree near the old arbor of the Lady Siwan, surrounded by holy vessels and a pile of gold-embroidered vestments. His face was streaked with blood and soot and he was hugging his processional cross against his breast, but Eden could not make out what he was saying for the noise A young friar with the white and shining face of an avenging angel, shouted:

"The Books! We must get them!"

Some others ran up and they sped away.

They circled the cloisters where men were hacking with axes and firehooks, but it was impossible for them to make their entry there, so they ran back past the farm buildings where Eden's brothers were trying to master the horses that were shying away and rearing over them in terror.

"Where are you off to?" Meredith yelled, but he received no answer as Eden hurried with his companions through the breaches in the walls.

It was no easy task to find their way. Smoking heaps blocked the passageways over which men were staggering like beasts of burden, bearing out chests and other valuables. Choking and coughing they stumbled along. The young friar led the way, nimble as a hare. The rest followed him blindly, their feet pounding along the crumbling lanes, until finally, after having taken a score of false turns and having run their heads into more than one listing beam, they found themselves in the Abbot's parlor.

There, each Epiphany on the anniversary of their father's death, Eden and his brothers had sat after mass for years, drinking bowls of hot goat's milk capped with foam and eating honey wafers with the Abbot. "My blessing on you, hurry!" the young friar cried, on seeing Eden pause. They gathered up armfuls of sheepskin-covered volumes and rolls of parchment, and ran back to the gardens.

From then on it was not clear to Eden what happened. Men kept dashing in and out, carrying away furnishings or rescuing the wounded or battling the fires. There was a terrible delirium. The air above their heads raged, flames darted forth from turf and shingle and flew off into the night like fiery birds. From time to time there came a rumbling crash as toppling walls and pillars fell. Down went the apse, down the reredos. Ednyved Vychan's sculptured tomb was smashed to pieces, while that of the Lady Gwenllian, his wife, remained intact, lacking only her mate. Only the frame of four wooden hovels under the mud wall on the side of the sea, remained untouched. *'De Penitentia Jesu Christi'* read the legend over the door of one of them. Eden saw it in passing, remembered the nights he had spent there once, and a pang of sadness ran through him.

More people kept arriving, streaming across the meadows, a few on horseback, goading their writhing steeds, many more running on foot. By little and little they got the fires under control, but to no end. Puffs of acrid smoke hissed amidst the wet wreckage. The blackened stone walls of church and cloister still stood in places like the charred fragments of a storm-torn forest, but for the most part the Abbey was derelict, destroyed beyond repair.

Eden returned to the gardens, to the lady Siwan's arbor which was now lit with torches. His brothers were there. Meredith turned towards him. His hair was singed and his eyebrows had been scorched away.

"Father Anianus is dead," he said.

Eden stared down at the Abbot. He was lying amid his vestments, his arms still embracing his processional cross. About the body the monks were kneeling, saying over the prayers for the dead, while one of the lay-brothers, his face black with grime was relating to the Prior of Penmon and others how the King and his armed squadrons had arrived.. "They came like a whirlwind," he was saying. "They galloped through the houses, smashing everything in sight. They brought in piles of straw and tar-barrels and fired them. Father Anianus came rushing towards the King with the cross raised before him and they struck him down."

The brothers turned away. What need was there to hear more? A good and gentle man who had done harm to no one had been senselessly slain. Deathly tired, bloody and begrimed and aching with a dull brute anger, the men made their way back home through the darkness.

Gerallt was the first to speak.

"Chieftain," he said. "I wonder if that bridge you spoke about when the harvest was drowned is a-building?"

"What bridge is that?" Rhys Ddu asked.

But neither Gerallt nor Eden was in a mood to tell him. And Meredith, too, was significantly silent.

4
THE CASTLE (1401)

1

It was Maundy Thursday. In the parish church outside the walls of the king's town of Conway the Blessed Sacrament had been reposed in the tabernacle and they were beginning to strip the altars. Meanwhile, at the castle the ancient decayed parishioners were being admitted into the great hall of banquet. Bess Tanner preceded a man she could not remember having seen in previous years. They sat down together on the stone bench next the wall and spoke a while. He wore a hood of budge drawn up over his head and she thought him very charming, although rather slovenly and unclean as old men without women to take care of them are inclined to be—heavens, the dirt that was ingrained in the lines of his face! And yet he had beautiful shapely hands—scarce a wrinkle in them—and his teeth were surprisingly whole and sound for a man of his years. When she remarked upon this, he told her that he had brushed them since childhood with a green hazel twig and salt.

She told him with a smile: "I wish I had known that receipt."

She herself had so few teeth left—God be thanked, she still had her grinders and eyeteeth, but the rest had gone.

"Will they wash our feet before supper?" he asked.

She had to laugh at that.

"Cocks will lay eggs," she said, "before John Massey's lady will wash old folks' feet."

He shook his head.

"At Hereford," he told her, "noblewomen always abide by the custom. I had my feet washed once by the Lady Mary de Bohun, the late wife of our present King. Peace to her ashes, what a saintly woman she was!"

"So you are from Hereford then?" That explained why his face was not familiar to her. "What is your name, if I may be so bold as to ask?"

"Will Chichley. And yours?"

"Bess Tanner. My husband, God rest him, used to be a haberdasher here as was his father before him, but I myself was born and bred up in London."

"My father came from London," said Will.

"And from a good family, too, I'll undertake."

He smiled. "It shows? Through the rags?"

"It's your hands, Will Chichley," she said. "Those are not the hands of a rustic."

He was silent for a space, reflecting, then he went on to explain:

"My father was thrown out of his family for marrying a maid of low estate. You are quite right of course. Mine is a house of some dignity. My father's father Robert Chichley was a merchant of the staple in Cheapside. My kinsman Thomas Chichley was Chamberlain of London during the reign of our late King Richard. One of my cousins Angell Chichley is a Canon at Westminster. And, believe it or not, Mistress Tanner, my great, great uncle Hugh Chichley was the Archbishop of Canterbury during the time of King Edward the Third."

Bess Tanner could find nothing to say.

"But it was my father who had all the luck," he added in a moment.

"How so?"

"He married my mother," Will replied.

Bess smiled.

A wooden clapper was now shaken and the old people rose and began to file past the long table to receive their dole of food and drink. Dressed in a seemly gown of plain dark fustian, the Constable nodded gravely and wished a blessing upon each one of them in turn, but his lady could barely take the trouble to smile. The hussy, thought Bess—that good devout John should never have married her, she was so haughty and uncivil. When Will Chichley came before her she gave a start and stared at him as though he had the leper's sore.

"Pray you, lady," he asked in his gentle tremulous voice, "may I have my pot of ale and my halfpenny cross-loaf of bread?"

She flushed and thrust his portion towards him hastily.

"What ails her?" Bess murmured as they sat down side by side at the board. "The look she gave you!"

He bowed his head

"Alas," he said sadly, "let us pray for her, goodwife. She has not been blessed with the gift of tears."

The old man chewed slowly on his bread and fell to thinking: I must be more careful. She almost burst out laughing in my face. There is far too much at stake.

He was not unfamiliar with this castle. He had been inside it on more than one occasion—once as a liegeman of King Richard's, and then as a prisoner of the Church under the stigma of adultery. At Michaelmas, barely two weeks after the late King had been taken captive by the forces of Henry of Lancaster, he had presented himself before John and Alison Massey.

"You were so kind to me when I was in prison here last year," he told the Constable. "When my own family had abandoned me. I have never forgotten it. Here is a stone my grandfather brought back from Mount Calvary. It is yours."

And he had thought: That delight to the eye next to him and all he can see is a stone. What's life to him? Why, he is dead already, lap him in lead.

Yes, and once he had come here as a market gardener, with herbs and roots for the kitchen. Then there had been the time he had come as a ripper. He had dressed trout, bream and pike here, not to speak of the ocean-swimming cod and mackerel.

"Begone, Howel Vaughan!" she had laughed. "You are stinking of fish."

Through the forests of the Conway two hundred soldiers were moving by stealth and darkness among the trees. They were led by Gwilym ap Tudor and Rhys Ddu and their brother-in-law Einion, the Constable of Dolwyddelan castle. Some way behind them Eden was walking his horse beside two grey friars and Father Sulien, the Abbot of the Abbey of Aberconway at Maenan, his white Cistercian wool covered with a purple mantle.

"The day was," he told Eden, "when Cistercians fled the world and its wickedness to seek solitude wherein to pray, meditate on celestial delights and raise sheep—these are times, my son."

It was darkest night when they reached the wooded hillside behind the town. The white battlements and towers of the castle were like ghostly shapes wrung out of the shadows, and the trees that loomed about them moved with strange whispers in the darkness. The men hobbled their horses and knelt to say their prayers and receive the sacraments. The murmuring of their voices sounded unnervingly loud in the stillness, and Eden found himself looking up warily at the walls, but he saw nothing nor heard a sound other than the heavy breathing of men and horses and now and then the distant barking of a dog. The men wrapped their mantles about them and sat down to wait.

At some later hour there came the tolling of a bell. The monks bowed profoundly three times. "It is beginning," said the Abbot and he made a great sweeping sign of the cross. Eden climbed a nearby tree and others hastened to follow his example. From the lofty branches of a great oak the master of the Old Hall could look out over the dark roofs of the town to the dark waters of the bay, barely discernible now in the cool well of the April night. There was a creaking of pulleys as the portcullis of the castle was raised and a row of lighted candles emerged from the gloom and began to move slowly across the drawbridge. At the same time others began to flicker up along the hilly twisting streets from the harbor. The people, hooded in the blacks and violets of mourning, merged with the darkness, scarcely to be seen. Eden watched them, as at a solemn processional pace they made their way towards the gates of the town and the church beyond.

High up in an embrasure of one of the castle turrets a light appeared and blinked. An owl hooted in the woods and in a moment there came an answering call aloft. "Howel, praise be," Eden thought and clambered down to take leave of his brothers.

"God be with you," he said, as they embraced.

"And with you, too, little brother."

Scarcely breathing, Eden watched the men swarming up the scaling ladders with their grappling hooks. Rhys Ddu and Gwilym were leading. Gripped with anxiety, their younger brother stared after them as they clambered nimbly from one rung to the next as if this was a thing they did every day of their lives. Up and up they went, as sure-footed as cats and almost as soundless but for a chance scraping of a weapon against stone until they surmounted the battlements. There they stopped to help their fellows win the summit of the walls and then with a wave of the hand to the men below they scurried off and dropped out of sight.

"I must return to my flock now," said Father Sulien. "Remember the day. Be merciful."

The company moved quietly through the woodland alongside the town walls. There was the jingle of a stirrup and the groan of a saddle as Einion's sergeant-at-arms mounted his horse and led his men, many bearing firebrands, down the slope to the town gates. A little farther on, a stoneshot away from the church, Eden and Einion came to a halt. The air that was damp and sweet with the dewy mists of spring brought them the distant sound of chanting.

"They are creeping to the Cross," one of the friars whispered.

Dawn was breaking as the smoke of the first fires began to drift upwards from the town walls. This was followed by a mingled babble of voices, of exhilarated 'hurrahs' and screams of 'Help! Murder!' distant at first, but growing by degrees into a long drawn-out howl as the remnants of Conway's inhabitants came limping, hobbling and leaping out of the gates. It was a marvel to Eden that their cries of horror and dismay did not reach the ears of the worshippers. Suddenly he could hear nothing else as folk rushed in a screeching stream along the meadow below the troop.

"Shall we shoot them down?" grinned one of Einion's more bloodthirsty henchmen.

"Whisht, man," the castellan said gruffly. "How would that answer?"

"By the looks of some of those old dotterels," another observed waggishly, "that would be doing the commons of Conway a service."

First into the church was a half-dressed youth with sleep-disheveled locks and witless eyes. Another moment and out ran John Massey. Dazed, pale and horrified, he stared at the town and then yelled: "Profanation! Conway's in flames! Men!"

"Get you back inside that church, John Massey!" Einion bellowed.

In perplexity and alarm the Constable spun round. Shudders of rage convulsed his frame as he raised his eyes to search the thickets where the company was standing. For a few moments he stood thus, as if trying to discover what was happening to him, why the world which had been so orderly and neatly purveyed so brief a while ago should suddenly have come crashing down about his head, then he shook his fist at the trees where the soldiers were hidden.

"Devil fetch you!" he yelled. "What are you? Who are you?"

An arrow three-feet long hummed through the air like a maddened bumble-bee to land quiveringly in the gatepost of the church.

"Inside!" shouted Einion again. "He who sets foot outside those precincts next is a dead man."

The Constable hesitated briefly, then turned on his heel and staggered back into the church.

So passed the best of the affair. Howel Vaughan, Rhys Ddu and Gwilym ap Tudor had seized the castle, the town was fired, and Einion and Eden with their force had the garrison in their power. Worse, however, was yet to come. For Eden this began late that same afternoon when two galleys dropped anchor in a cove a little south of the church, and a company of men-at-arms drawn from the garrisons of Beaumaris and Caernarvon disembarked and marched in warlike order towards Conway led by two kinsmen of his.

"Look," said the castellan. "There's Red Iwan."

"Aye, God help me," said Eden. "And my father-in-law."

Staring down at them as they moved along the sunlit grass that was broidered so prettily with the season's first primroses, he could distinctly make out the flagrant red of the Governor of Caernarvon's beard and the gaunt stoop-shouldered form of the Sheriff of Mona. God's mercy, it's murder, Eden thought, the rest of Einion's men under his sergeant-at-arms having by now rejoined the main force.

The Welsh archers were already bending their bows when John Massey darted out of the church yelling: "Danger! They are in the woods up there." A hail of arrows went rushing through the air. Most of them fell short, but the action was enough to make the enemy ranks break into disorder like streams about a boulder. Then amidst a roar of shouts, the soldiers of Conway came tumbling out of the church.

Einion drew his broadsword.

"Now for it, lads!" he shouted and giving his horse the spur led his men in a gallop down the slope.

During the very first moments of the advance the Sheriff of Mona was struck down by a blow on his helmet. Throwing caution to the winds, Eden flung himself out of the saddle, and catching at his father-in-law's legs dragged him like a sack of flour out of the thick of the fight. He laid him down among the tombstones behind the church. He seemed perfectly at home there. In fact, his son-in-law thought him dead at first, as likely fodder for the earthbred worms as those who lay rotting below. His face had turned a ghastly white, and blood was running into his eyes from a gash in his head. Eden tore a strip of cloth from the Sheriff's surcoat and tried to stanch the flow.

"For the love of Christ," he pleaded, "speak to me!"

The Sheriff's eyes flickered open.

"Eden," he croaked, "what devil's work is this?"

"Fool! Why don't you stay home at your ledgers?" his son-in-law barked at him and returned to the fray.

It went on for another hour. At the end of that time, as if by unvoiced agreement, the attackers retreated to the forest, while their antagonists in their turn attended to their dead and wounded, and herded the terror-stricken townsfolk out of the church. Darkness was coming on when at last their howling voices died away along the path to the ships and Caernarvon. Rejoicing at their success, the tired rebels sat eating their fast bread and joking about the fires. Others were removing the snaffles from the horses and ponies and feeding them oats out of baskets. They greeted Eden cheerfully: "Give God the glory, what a day, eh, son of Tudor!"

Einion was helping a friar straighten and wash the bodies of three men who had been slain before laying them in the cart that was to bear them back to Nantconway. As he moved about Eden noticed that he was dragging one foot behind the other.

"You are limping, Einion," he said. "Have you been hurt?"

"The tithes of old age, my dear. That is something these poor boys will not have to put up with, God rest them."

Throughout the following day and Easter Sunday, groups of armed men came straggling into the encampment. Among the first to arrive were Tango of the Bay of the White Stones and his two younger brothers Rosier and Collwyn, and after them came Asa Coedana and Little Garmon with a company of spears from Mona.

"Well, you naughty knaves, you devils you!" shouted Tango. "What have you been up to, eh? Wresting a town and castle from the overlords! I ask you, is that politeness? Is that how you do homage to your masters? Oia, if you had only seen the faces on our folk when they heard! Four women went into labor in our commote alone."

They brought victuals with them—tansy cakes, wheaten bread, milk cheeses and the first beef Eden had tasted in weeks. It was salty. The last of the Martinmas beef, perhaps, he thought, and he remembered the occasion of its curing-aye, that was when the Abbey of Llanvaes had been sacked.

Early one morning a week later, one of the scouts whom Einion had posted at points overlooking the coastal way that led from the palatinate of Chester and the Welsh Marches to Conway arrived with the news that a punitive force, numbering some five hundred archers and men-at-arms was heading their way.

"Go to, Eden," said Einion. "Pester them a little."

Within the hour a hundred Welshmen were distributed amidst the rocks in the uplands of Rhos. They tethered their horses in a gully and lay down along the boulder-strewn rise that looked down at the estuary of the Conway. The tide was out and the sands, threaded with thin streams and dotted with pools, gleamed like a mackerel in the sunlight. All of them were silent and as Eden lay there with his heart beating against the ground, it came to his mind that it might have been in this very spot that Henry of Lancaster's men had lain in ambush when King Richard had passed this way with the Earl of Northumberland. He was struck by the oddity of this thought. And for a moment a shiver of strangeness went through him, as if in response to some dark design he could sense if but dimly comprehend.

Then Tango, who had his ear pressed against the earth, murmured: "They are coming."

A few moments later they were in sight: a long train of men, horses and carriages winding about the headland. In the van rode Hotspur and Prince Henry, a youth, little more than a boy, riding a white charger sheathed in cloths of blue sarcenet edged with gold. He seemed nervous and excited, whereas Hotspur looked tired and angry, staring with eyes obstinately fixed on the battlements of Conway.

"They are heading for the quicksand," Tango breathed. "It's too good to be true."

The chieftains scrambled into the gully and mounted their horses. Eden rode to the top of the rise and raised his hand as a signal to the bowmen who, so as to give the impression of a bigger force, were stationed throughout the rocks along the path of advance. They drew their bows and let fly a whistling shower of arrows. Four or five footsoldiers dropped in their tracks and there was a confused roar of shouts, orders, and the whinnying of horses as the English scattered across the sands. Wheeling his charger, Hotspur, followed by the Prince, rode after them, yelling commands and waving his sword, in an effort to reform his broken ranks.

"I'm off!" Eden shouted, and bending low over the saddlebow went galloping down the slope.

Stones and clods of earth flew up under the hooves and the air stung his face like spray. All at once he felt such a ferocious glee, such a surge of exhilaration that before he knew it a great exultant cry was torn from his throat, so that he almost ceased to hear the thunder of the men who were riding after him as they headed towards the carriages that were foundering in the pools towards the rear of the enemy train. Tango and his brothers caught up with him, the manes on the outstretched necks of their horses shining and blowing. They bowled over a wagon stacked with fascines and another filled with sacks of meal. Asa Coedana and Little Garmon tumbled a wooden catapult, but hardly had they begun to hack at it with their axes than they saw Hotspur and a band of horsemen bearing down upon them with furious speed. What happened next could not have lasted much more than an eyeblink. The rebels rode out to meet them, drawing them all unwittingly into the quicksand. First down went Hotspur and the foreriders, and as they did so, the other horses shied away in terror, rearing and foaming about the muzzles.

The master of the Old Hall laughed with delight, as full of gladness as a lucky huntsman. Staggering to his feet, Hotspur looked at him, his face muddy and wrathful, then lunged with his sword. Countering the blow with one of his own, Eden raised his foot and gave him a kick that sent him flying back into the water.

"That's for Llanvaes, you sandhog!"

"You scum, you will pay for this!"

"Get you home, sirra!" Eden jeered, and giving his horse the rein fled with his comrades up the hillside. Nor did they stop until they had returned, all safe and sound and laughing to their camp.

2

The Sheriff of Mona was borne back to Beaumaris on one of his galleys. The first thing he remembered with any clarity was waking to see his wife praying at his bedside with her confessor and he thought— my house at Rhosyr. This woman will kill me with coldness.

She had never loved him of course. There had been another - what had been his name? Ah, yes, Eustachius Baud. Holy Mother, what a tantrum she had flown into, the maid Joanna, when she had learned that she was to marry the son of Nicolas Beaupine's partner. They had locked her up in the garret for shouting defiance. Out of the kindness of his heart her betrothed had taken her a bowl of broth on the sly. She had thrown it in his face. Aye, she had been a lively female then, Joanna. She might be so yet, for the matter of that-he had no way of knowing. He had given up trying to force himself upon her fifteen years ago, much about the time, now that he bethought him of it, when Gwervyl, the stewlady and poetess had become his lovewoman.

God be thanked, aye, he had his consolations.

He had bought his house at Rhosyr not long after he had arrived on the island. With its farm it stood at the head of the little marketplace with its well for two buckets and its stone cross dating back to the time of St Cybi the Swarthy, the patron saint of Mona. On the islet across the sands lay the priory of St Dwynwen, the love-saint of Wales, to whose shrine heartsick lovers had beaten a path down through the ages.

The Sheriff was carried there on a litter five days after he had been wounded. On the next morning Annes came from the Old Hall to nurse him. Hers was a lovely presence, gentle and soothing, but the girl she brought with her was troubling—she had reddish hair and seemed to go everywhere at a run.

"Does she never walk slowly? Who is she?"

"Mererid, the daughter of Father Conan. She can read."

"There are not many lasses who can do that. But a priest's daughter—I daresay she could."

"She will read for you if you like. She does so quite well."

"Not today, my dear."

He paused, looking at her searchingly. At last he asked:

"Did you have any inkling that this was transacting?"

She stared at him in surprise and then shook her head with a sad and wordless smile.

"No, of course, how could you have suspected?" the Sheriff said. "It was too cunningly contrived for that."

"Most cunningly."

There was bitterness in her voice. She looked down at her hands on her lap and played with the rings on her fingers.

"It's pity of it," she murmured. "All those poor houseless folk. And on Good Friday."

"What was done at Llanvaes was wicked, too."

"I know that."

She shuddered. The Sheriff saw that her eyes were wet with tears.

"Soldiers are not disposed to kindly acts, Annes mine," he said to her. "It is a cruel world."

"You say these things, father," she observed quietly, "and I do not know why. Are you trying to excuse them?"

He was silent at that. Her words made him wonder. . . .

During those first weeks the Sheriff was almost wholly in the dark as to what was going on. The one piece of information he had received was from the Constable of Beaumaris, who told him that John Massey had reported that the rebels in Conway castle were only provisioned for two to three months.

"The King is going to starve them into submission," Thomas Bold said.

Although the Sheriff suspected that John Massey was exaggerating the straits of the rebels in order to raise his own fallen credit in the eyes of his monarch and Hotspur, he did not hesitate to pass on these tidings to Meredith ap Tudor when the Chieftain in his turn came to visit him.

"You have bitten off more than you can chew, I fear, my friend."

"We'll see, we'll see."

"You are working on a broken wing, old eagle. How are you going to save those chicks of yours, stranded up there in their eyrie on the high crag?"

The Chieftain said nothing. His face was stony, expressionless. But there was a gleam in the deepset blue eyes above the stern and tired cheekbones, a sly and impish gleam which you could not fail to notice. And once you were aware of it, you could see nothing else.

"Why are you looking so?" the Sheriff puzzled.

"Why? How am I looking?"

"Come, tell me what you know that I do not know."

"Hotspur joined battle with Owain Glyndwr in the passes of Cader Idris the other day and has been put to the rout."

"Truly? And where is our Chief Justice now?"

"Wherever he is, that place is not Conway. He has left the young prince to fend for himself there with less than half his force."

The Chieftain was sitting on the window bench that looked out of over the marketplace towards the dunes and the straits. The mountains beyond were lost in mist and grey clouds like mealsacks filled to bursting were hanging over the sea.

"And now," he smiled, "here comes the rain."

Rain, flood, torrent: Eden grimaced inwardly—you would have to be a fish or marshfowl to live under such conditions. Ah, but everything was magnified out of all proportion in this land of fabulists. Maybe this trouble they told him had overtaken his brother-in-law, the castellan, was no great thing at bottom. Would that he could believe it! Would that it were so!

The day he was brought the news had begun with a drizzle. By the time he reached the Abbey at Maenan where they had taken Einion, it had become a downpour, flooding over the cordwood bridges which had been laid over boggy ground and running in streams down the black and wrinkling bark of the forest. The Abbot came out to meet him, carrying a canopy of sackcloth over his head.

"I wish you a blessing, reverend Father. How is the castellan?"

"Ah, it's his leg, my son. He should be at home."

Sure, that leg. Every time Eden had spoken to his brother-in-law about it the older man had passed it off as a joke or had made as if he had not heard. He was scarcely prepared for what he saw. With three of his henchmen seated beside him, Einion was lying on a pallet in the Abbot's guesthouse, and although he had the same old tender jest in his mouth for Eden when he smiled, it was plain that he was a very sick man. Eden looked at his drawn face, his fever-bright eyes, his sweat-matted beard and at his leg that was propped up on a pillow and his heart turned over. The limb was as bloated as dead meat and covered with red, blue and yellow blotches.

"Why did you not tell us of this before?" he asked, trying to conceal his horror.

"You will only laugh."

"By the Lord, my dear Einion," Eden replied, "you must think I live by fooling."

"I fell in a bed of nettles last year," his brother-in-law confessed with shamefaced reluctance. "That's what started it, I suppose."

"And you told no one? Not even Enid?"

"Come now, lad, what do you take me for? Men do not die of a nettle rash, do they?"

"It's true, I've heard of none," Eden admitted. Even so he could not help feeling that Einion was going to prove an exception to the rule, that the old soldier had indeed fought in his last foray.

On the following day he was borne back to Dolwyddelan in a cart bailed over with a leathern cover. Their progress was slow. It took Eden and his troop two days rough travelling along muddy forest trails and through unceasing rain to reach the mountain valley where the castle stood. When they carried Einion into the great hall, Enid went as white as a sheet, but her demeanor was calm. She had her husband put to bed and his diseased limb bathed and packed about with healing poultices. He was fed gruel from a spoon and given a sleepy drink. In a while he felt more comfortable and dozed off.

Yet dropping with weariness as he was, Eden could neither bring himself to eat nor sleep. He sat before the fire in the great hall, brooding over the flames. It was midnight or past and the rain could be heard falling with a pattering as of the tiny feet of a thousand birds along the roofs when Enid came out of the bedchamber and sat down beside her youngest brother.

He sighed. He wanted only to be left in quiet. She wanted to talk, but above that she wanted to scold. Eden could barely bring himself to listen to her—it was such nonsense she was babbling: How it must be that they could not wait to get away from their homes and their wives, he and his comrades; to embrace a life of adventure; capture castles and shed old folk's blood, especially on holy days.

"Do you know," she said, "that Bess Tanner"—whoever that was— "an aged and helpless old woman, who could barely walk, died in that bonfire of yours? Years ago, when I was a girl at Caerhun, we used to buy needles and thread from her husband."

"To die on Good Friday," Eden told her, "is to share the privilege of the Good Thief and win entry into Heaven speedily. It was a blessed death for a crone."

"How you talk!" she said bitterly.

She surpassed him. She went on to cast slurs on his character, his past follies.

"What is this story I've been hearing about you and the lady of Croes Gwion?"

"Mind your own errands."

"Shame on you!"

"Leave me be!"

They quarreled. She went away. He dozed a little. She came back and stood behind him. He could tell she was crying. She put her hand on his shoulder. Without turning, he laid his hand over hers and pressed it.

A week later Eden was at Mathebrud, a hall now transformed—much to the dismay and anger of Davydd, the aged head of the Men of Ithon—into a giant forge for the repair of weaponry, when the Chieftain arrived unexpectedly.

"Hotspur is back in our midst and would parley with us," he told his youngest brother.

"Is he to be trusted?"

"We are to be escorted by the Siri Mawr under a flag of truce."

They moved without delay. The following day found them in Caernarvon, a town which since Segontium and the Romans had been notably liberal to the surrounding natives of its steel. In spite of the presence of the Sheriff of Caernarvonshire and an armed escort, it seemed to Eden for a while that he and his brother would have been better served entering that town in a plague cart, closed and covered with black, a bell ringing in front—so as to clear streets so swiftly filling with their enemies.

"Tidder! Tidder! It's them, the devils!"

Sober citizens were turning into madmen under their eyes. Men made menacing balls of their fists, little children shrilled and spat, screaming women with outstretched clawing hands hung out like gargoyles under the thatched roofs, a wizened toothless crone tottered after them cackling filthy words in the Saxon tongue. And soon stones, cabbage stumps, offal and worse came flying through the damp air, trying to find them.

"Do not forget," Meredith reminded him, "that the townsfolk from Conway are now lodged here."

Eden had not forgotten, but the remembrance did not lighten his heart, nor charm away the bump an old mastiff bone had raised on the side of his head, rather the contrary. No man indeed could have been happier than he when they reached the castle, although lions rampant were in there, sure enough, fit to gorge a tribe of martyrs.

They found Hotspur partaking of a meal with his wardogs in the bleak hall of banquet. For the first few minutes after they had been admitted, he did little but thump the table and curse them, now in Saxon, now in French, telling them that they were hag's abortions and *pissat de crapaulx*, and damning them to the pits of perpetual fire. Meredith was calm; his dark bearded face was as though hewn out of stone, a faint smile hovering over his lips like a trick of the light. His younger brother lowered his eyes and stared at the remains of the meal scattered over the wine-stained board. So this was what put the bowels of a lion into fighting men, those manchets of black bread and dark leathery meat. He looked up and met the gaze of his kinsman Red Iwan, the governor of Caernarvon. He was astounded at the hatred he saw in his eyes.

"It seems to me that you and I have met before," he suddenly heard a voice saying.

Angry eyes were upon him, under fiery brigandish brows. Eyes of a blue so intense and brilliant that they seemed to shoot sparks. But there were dark pouches under them, the cheeks were bony and haggard, and the line of the lips was bitter and cruel.

Eden replied that this was indeed so.

"On the sands before Conway?"

"Yes."

Hotspur smiled grimly.

"Is it possible," he asked, "that we have robbed you so soon of your boast?"

Eden looked at Meredith. The Chieftain put forward his terms: full reparation for the wanton destruction of the Abbey of Llanvaes, free pardon for all the rebels in Conway and no ulterior proceedings to be instituted against them for the offenses they had committed.

Hotspur stared in amazement, then laughed harshly:

"You are mad!" he exclaimed. "Devil if I know where you find the nerve. For such a palpable breach of the peace? No, your kinsmen and their fellows will have to suffer the consequences."

Despite the discouraging note of this utterance, however, his curiosity was fired. He was interested in discovering the motives for the rebels' actions, and the Chieftain was eloquent in their defense. In that gloomy hall, before those iron faces, he retraced the bloodstained course of the past year and spoke in quiet but trenchant words of the distress of the islanders at the attack on the Abbey, the brutal and senseless slaying of the Abbot and the despoliation of his own ancestors' tombs.

Hotspur listened to this with somber intentness, then shrugged his shoulders.

"Well, I am certain," he remarked, "that King Henry had no idea whose sepulchres he was smashing that day. Not," he added, with a wry grimace, "that it would have made any difference to him if he had. But I'll remind you that times are rude and that the King has many grievances of his own to redress. I am told that you are cousins of the rebel leader Owen Glendower, him your people call Glyndwr. Are you allied in this venture, I dare be bold to ask?"

"The action is personal," said Meredith.

"As your father's was in his time, eh? He too was a man of lawless temper, I understand."

The brothers looked at Red Iwan. The governor returned their glance sternly.

"That is a matter of opinion," said Meredith. "He had his troubles with the English Crown, it's true."

"What were they?"

"Taxes were being levied upon us for lands we held by privilege of our ancestor Ednyved Vychan. He was the Chief Counselor of Llywelyn the Great, and Chief Justice of North Wales in his day as you are now in ours. But apart from that, it was a bitter time for our people. The courts were in chaos, our ancient laws and traditions flouted. My father and foster-father, the lord of Bromfield and Ial, rode to London to plead their cause, but to no end. All doors were closed to them."

Hotspur shrugged his shoulders.

"Past is past," he said "These matters are nothing to our present purpose."

He leaned forward and said bluntly:

"What if I tell you that the game's not worth a candle? That the King and his council are fully determined that your rebels in Conway be punished according to their deserts?"

"Then you will leave us with no other choice, Sir Henry," Meredith said calmly and resolutely. "My confederate chieftains and I will raise our country behind Glyndwr."

Hotspur knit his brows in face of this threat, but presently a weary little smile, not without a certain understanding, travelled across his lips.

"Well, we shall see," he said finally. "Come o'Thursday."

And with that he rose, waved his hand at them and strode swiftly out of the hall.

Having thus charmingly and peremptorily retired on his courtesies as a host, there was nothing left for the Welshmen to do but to step out once more into the light of day.

"So what is your thought, Meredith?" asked the Siri Mawr when they had won free of the town walls.

"He lacks cunning," said the Chieftain. "It is plain that he is a man under great stress. I think that bodes well for us."

He took a deep breath of the brightening air and turned his face up to the sky.

"And see, Sir Siri," he said with a smile, "the sun is beginning to break through."

The tenth week of the siege was marked by a curious episode.

On the anniversary of the death of their uncle, Sir Howel ap Grono, the ancient Archdeacon of Mona, it was the usage of the brothers to take turns in bearing a catch of fish as a gift to the priory of the white friars at Bangor. The year Rhys Ddu and Gwilym ap Tudor lay at Conway this duty fell on the shoulders of the Chieftain himself. Creels were loaded on the back of Pengaled, the old grey donkey, Meredith mounted his horse and off he went.

On arrival at the priory he was told that someone wished to see him. He was led into the cloister where he beheld a figure in a black pearl-buttoned soutane leaning against one of the carven stone pillars reading in a missal. On hearing Meredith's step he turned and greeted him. His voice was one of the richest and most seductive the Chieftain had ever heard.

"God prosper you, son of Tudor. I wonder if you remember me."

Meredith stared at him fixedly—that massive dark head, those round, hard, black eyes, those muscular shoulders like a wrestler's—where had he seen them before?

"It was years ago" the stranger admitted directly. "At the house of your uncle Sir Howel ap Grono. Your brother Gwilym and I are old friends."

"Master Griffith Young!" Meredith exclaimed. "Dear my fathers, aye, it has been a long time for sure. You were but a youth then. And now, let's see, what are you? A learned doctor of the Church? One who has graced the schools of Bologna and Paris? What else? Ah yes, if I am not mistaken, your Reverence is also the Archdeacon of Merioneth."

"And Canon of Bangor," the other added with a smile.

In fact, he told the Chieftain, it was in his office of Canon that he was in Bangor at present. He was here at the behest of the Archbishop Arundel to discharge the debts of Lewis Aber, who had been in their midst as bishop so briefly.

"Pope Boniface provided him to the see. But King and Church would not have it."

"I wonder why that would be?"

"Quite simply because he is Welsh. That is unacceptable to our masters. Besides, they had another in mind."

"Who would that be?"

"Richard Young, the Archdeacon of Meath and the Canon of Dublin."

"And he is our Bishop now?"

'He has been Bishop of Bangor for several months."

"But I have never seen him."

"No," said Griffith Young, "none of us have."

That of course made his companion the most powerful ecclesiastical personage present in the flesh in the vicinity, the Chieftain concluded. It was a thought that impressed him even then. Why, you are not doing so badly for yourself at that, Master Griffith, he told himself. But he still could not understand what was wanted of him.

The bells were ringing for terce when at last a clerk, out of puff and red in the face with hurry, came running into the cloister bearing a satchel. "Where have you been, Maldwyn? Counting the waves?" asked the Archdeacon with stinging sweetness. Then he sat down on a bench that ran along the wall and beckoning Meredith to sit down beside him, opened the satchel. Out came several rolls of parchment, neatly tied with purple ribbon, which he handed to his companion for perusal. The Chieftain glanced at one, then at another and his amazement grew. They were copies of all the letters which had passed between Hotspur and the King up to that hour.

"Those two are squabbling," said Griffith Young.

"I had suspected as much."

"But did you suspect *how* much? Did you know that our Chief

Justice has been bearing the entire cost of the siege at Conway? And that now he is threatening to throw up all his commissions? Hotspur himself is on the brink of revolt."

What Griffith Young did not reveal was how these copies had come into his hands and the Chieftain felt it would not have been discreet on his part to have asked him. Some poor clerk angling for a promotion, maybe, or a sergeant-at-arms with a sin to expiate. Like enough, Hotspur's own scribe might have been a hireling of his. Whatever the source, it remained a remarkable achievement and it was with feelings approaching awe that Meredith finally raised his eyes to look at the guileful Archdeacon.

The reverend lord laughed to see his expression.

"Take them with you, son of Tudor," he said. "Read them at your leisure. And be of good heart."

On his return to Penmynydd the Chieftain sent for his youngest brother and showed him the letters.

"It is as you thought, Meredith."

"So it seems."

They were in the small garden next the orchard, the girls' escheat; gentle quadrant in fee to the broidery frame, the distaff and the singing of stanzas. A boss of clear spring water trickling—lavender, thyme, flax and bergamot. The brothers had unrolled the parchments in the grass...'car je ne puisse porter les costages que je face ici sans autre ordenance de vous.' Eden rolled over on his back laughing and watched the white clouds floating high up in the blue sky like lovely flawless isles.

Marged Vaughan came out bearing them mead and a plate of Megan's doucettes.

"What are you two laughing about?"

"The Archdeacon of Merioneth."

"Och, is he so amusing?"

"He is ambitious, Marged," her husband told her. "Beware of such men."

Eden raised his brows smilingly.

"A Doctor of the Church?"

"Come," said the Chieftain. "do you think that we are the only ones who have been given copies of those letters? Our Archdeacon is a man who bears watching, my dears. He is a bishop in the bud."

So far was certain. His timing could not have been better. Owain Glyndwr was about to win a signal victory.

It happened early in July. Some fifteen hundred soldiers drawn from the garrison towns of Wales and the Marches were resting in a mountain glen in the heart of the country. They were awaiting the arrival of another force from Shrewsbury before setting out to engage the rebel leader who was was said to be quartered with his army near the coast.

It was a chilly afternoon, heavy with mist and a brooding stillness. A rain that seemed scarcely to fall clung to the air. The men sat miserably huddled together over their fires. The damp leaked down under their leather jerkins and made their spines shiver. Things loomed up not far away; it was hard to tell whether they were living bodies or shrubs.

Edward Pauncefot, the Constable of Crickhowel, was yawning with weariness when he went off to make water beside what looked at first like a hag with her gnarled arms raised in malediction but turned out to be only a thorn tree. His mailed feet sank up to the ankles in soft wet moss. Suddenly a bird flew up out of the sedge and he saw shapes moving towards him through the dim light. He gave an inward sigh of relief. Here they are at last.

And then he thought—spears! They are all of them spears. They nodded and swayed in the mist like a forest of bullrushes with glittering crests. Amidst them rose the dark bulk of a horseman in a heavy cape and in the van strode a skeletal figure leaning on a staff. The Constable had just time enough to catch a glimpse of a hideous ravaged face before he went running.

"To arms!" he yelled. "It's Glendowrdy!"

His alarm communicated itself to his men. They tumbled over one another in a panic.

"The Fiend is leading them!" someone cried.

In the battle that then ensued among the rain-bent grasses of that glen in the wilds of the Pumlumon range few of the soldiers who had been encamped beside the river Hyddgen that morning were left alive at nightfall.

In far off Mona a week later, in the loft above the feeding walk of the

Old Hall where he was sleeping those summer nights, the young apprentice bard Robyn woke to feel the hanging flaxes trickling over his face like a drowned woman's hair. What could it be that had roused him? He was sick with a chill and at first could not tell whether he was going into a dream or out of it. At last he rose and opened the door leading out into the courtyard. A mournful sea-breeze pulsed in the mesh of his thin shirt and made him shiver. It must have been dead of night. The moon gleamed in and out of the clouds, the straws blowing about the yard shone like silver. Then somewhere nearby there came the tread of men's feet, the jingling of harness. He recognized Gerallt's deep, rather husky voice, Eden's lighter, more youthful chiming. And all at once they were riding across the yard and out through the gates.

Robyn slipped on his tunic and ran down the steps to the feeding walk and into the hall. All the housefolk were up. The aged virgin Sibli was on her knees, running her beads between her fingers and crying up hosannas.

"What has happened?" he asked.

"They are out, Robyn," Sioned said, her face shining.

He stared at her in wonder.

"Yes. Howel Vaughan and our men. They are riding home at this hour. Gerallt and Eden have gone to meet them. We have won, lad, we have won."

"The King has yielded?"

"Yes."

"He will rebuild the Abbey?"*

"Yes."

Annes came towards him and laid her hand on his shoulder. Cool, as to every appearance, she had been to Eden and the whole venture hitherto, her eyes, too, were flooded with tears now and she was smiling.

"Child, you are shivering," she said. "Go back to your bed and sleep. You are still not well and tomorrow will be a long day."

"Do as the lady tells you, my son," said the old housebard, already fretting his brows over the lines of the ode of praise running around inside his head.

Robyn returned to his bed. Whether he slept or not, however, he could never afterwards be certain, but all that night long it seemed to him that he heard laughter and shouting and the sound of horsehoofs throbbing along the rides.

* See Note 4

5
DEPARTURES (1401 -1402)

That September Mererid went to live at the Old Hall. Annes had asked
Father Conan and Mam Indeg whether she might come. Although known
then to but a few, the lady was again pregnant. After a series of painful
miscarriages she shrank from inviting another through overwork. Hence
the priest's daughter arrived at the Old Hall as an extra hand.

"Well met," the young apprentice bard Robyn thought with delight,
"Mererid is here."

At fifteen she was blossoming almost imperceptibly into a very
attractive girl. And yet she was completely without airs. Everything she
did, whether it was spinning or weaving or gathering in the kine or
reading some edifying tale out of the Lives of the Saints to the wives and
maids in the weaving room, she invested with an innate and artless grace.
Her ways had about them all the purity of a bird singing or a freshet
running and Annes loved her well.

And Mererid worshipped Annes. She had little but scorn for Eden.
Until she came to live under his roof she had never realized what an idler
he was. It was Gerallt who did all the work. If there were not fun and
games to draw him forth the lord and master seemed content to loll about
the hall playing chess with old Mabon or dozing beside him.   And
everyone had to be so quiet then—as on Easter morn, she thought, that
holy time when folk went about on tiptoe for fear that they would disturb
the earth.

"In the name of charity, hisht, girl!" old Sibli would scold.
"Running and clattering around so! Don't you see that the master is
resting?"

Besides, he was faithless to his wife. That empty-headed wanton,
the lady of Croes Gwion, had not been his first light o'love, Mererid
knew, nor was she likely to be his last. As it happened, she herself had
received more direct evidence of his infidelities.

It had taken place during her first week at the Old Hall. It was late
in the afternoon and she was tired. Near the houses there was a heathery
hummock with a stone roundel cut into the side of it as a shelter for herds
watching over the cattle and goats. There she sat down and looked at the
seagulls dipping and circling overhead. She did not see him until he was

only a few paces away.

"What are you doing there, Mererid?"

"I am watching seagulls," she said.

"Watching seagulls?" he marveled, sitting down beside her. "Come, little sister, can you find nothing better to do?"

"I have been up since daybreak," she told him coldly. "I have baked bread, I have milked cows, I have churned butter, I have helped sew shrouds for poor dead folk and I have been to Penmynydd and back on an errand for your lady."

He smiled.

"You are going to make someone a notable wife."

She overpassed that as a silliness unworthy of remark.

"How old are you now, Mererid? Fourteen, I'll undertake."

"Fifteen," she said curtly.

He gave a surprised whistle.

"Fifteen? High time to find you a husband then. I must have a talk with Gerallt about it. Let's see now. Asa Coedana's son Cadwaladr is a likely lad. The pity of it is, I don't think the family can afford a maiden fee. Not after all those weddings. Wait now, there is always Bras of Penbol. A widower on the scout. It's true he is old and has no teeth, but he is of good blood. And rich!—he would take you with no dowry, I'm sure."

She sighed. She wearied of his puerile prattle. She wished he would go away and leave her at peace.

"And then, of course, there is Long Bet's son, Aron the Necromancer. . . ."

She turned and looked at him with a direct and fierce gaze.

"The man I marry," she told him scornfully, "has not been born yet."

Eden stared at her in astonishment. And then suddenly, he threw her on her back and began showering kisses on her face—her brow, her cheeks, her lips, her throat. She thrust him aside vehemently and sprang to her feet. "You!" she panted and set off between walking and running towards the hall, her cheeks stung red as raspberries by the hoots of laughter that pursued her.

"Walk with pretty mincing gait, longlegs. We shall only be able to find you farmers prancing along like that."

She rushed into the milkhouse and pressed her burning cheeks against the cool stone slab where the pans were kept. Aghast at what had happened, she stayed there, she did not know how long, trying to gather her wits.

Och, the shame of it! How could she go in there and face them?

But when at last she did so, Eden was sitting beside Annes at the board as though nothing untoward had taken place. He seemed unaware of Mererid's presence. He and his wife were chatting pleasantly together as they ate. Once he bent forward and quickly kissed her on the brow. And she laid her fingers softly against his cheek and stroked it.

2

Throughout this time the troubles were growing in the land. Since the events of the summer the revolt, like a raging gorse fire, had spread far and wide across the hundreds of South Wales. By the end of August the men of Towy and a multitude from those parts had come to the side of Owain Glyndwr. Then the King struck. Early in October he assembled an army at Worcester and crossed the Marches into South Wales. Blood and fire marked his passage. The straws of marketplaces ran red with blood and the shadows of the swinging dead darkened the scaffold's wooden square. A thousand children were taken hostage and villages put to the torch. At Strata Florida the Cistercian monks, as known supporters of the rebellion, were scattered before the searing breath of the King's fury like so much chaff at the wind of a grindstone, while his soldiery cried havoc, sacked the Abbey, robbed it of its valuables down to the sacring bell, looted the tombs and stabled their horses at the high altar.

It was at this time that Einion, the Constable of Dolwyddelan, died. He had been a squire of the King's father, John of Gaunt. In fact, it was while he had been in Wales feeing men to the old Duke's sword, that he had met Enid and fallen in love with her.

The widow and her brothers spoke of this as they reminisced in the hall of the castle after the Constable's burial. They recalled Einion in many ways. Enid listened to them with a smile, then a sob would unexpectedly rise in her throat and the tears would flow down her cheeks without check.

"Come away," Marged Vaughan told her, "if it pains you."

She shook her head: "No, I want to hear."

Meredith said, "He was an indulgent husband. Am I right in

believing that it was by his license that you were the first woman in North Wales to ride a horse side-saddle?"

Enid nodded. "The old people were so shocked. Tudor's daughter is riding for a fall, they said. It was Anne of Bohemia, King Richard's first wife, who brought the fashion into the islands, I understand."

"So you were among the foreriders in every sense of the word," the Chieftain quipped.

It was a glorious evening. Above the towering darkness of forest, crag and mountain, the sky was rent with clouds like crimson banners. A scented breeze whispered across the water meadows and stirred in the straw where Eden sat peering into the red nest of embers flaming on the stone.

And his mind was blown about by fancies. It was so strange to be here without the castellan. For as far back as he could remember Einion had been here. To the boy he had once been he had been the very soul of the castle—head, shield and defender of a magical world. What a remarkable man! Was there anything he could not do, Eden used to wonder as a child? No, that miscellaneous fellow was always at your service. Apart from the fact that he was a celebrated warrior, thus inspiring in his young brother-in-law's heart stirrings of the most heroic order, he could play the harp, crowth, cithern, psaltery, was a chief of song in both of the old traditional forms, was a fair smith, something of a chirurgeon, could marvelously mimic the calls of the birds, and if it was your wish to have some wild meat for supper—tirra-lirra, he was off, tirra-lirra he was back, with a brace of pheasants, a bag of rabbits, or a lusty buck.

God rest him, and now that he was gone, it was as if the other spirits of the place, so long overborne by that warm and boisterous presence, were beginning to emerge from their coverts. Eden remembered that of old this had been one of the castles of Llywelyn the Great. Tangwystl, his concubine, the Peace Hostage, had lived out her days here. Her couch had been covered with skins of bears hunted down in the high gorges. She had heard the wolf-packs howling in the forests yonder. She had heard the wild geese flying south over the Pass of the Arrows.

"Tell me, Enid," Rhys Ddu asked, "when did Einion receive his last yearly stipend from the House of Lancaster?"

"A month before you took Conway castle," she replied.

The brothers laughed.

They were making ready to leave with their families on the next day when they were advised by the sergeant-at-arms of the castle not to return to the island by way of Caernarvon.

"The town is under siege since two nights ago," he said, "and all the country round about is up and rising. Glyndwr's warboys are there, with some Frenchmen. A shipload of them under the blazon of luces of the sea."

"Jean d'Espagne!" Rhys Ddu exclaimed with delight. "Ah, if only. . . ."

"Rhys!" the Chieftain broke in abruptly. "Remember you are under oath to the King of England not to bear arms for a year."

"Why a year?" Enid asked.

"Plainly, he expects the rebellion to be crushed by then."

"But it is spreading."

"Plainly."

They went home by way of Mathebrud. Howel Vaughan was master there now, the old chieftain having died in the course of the summer.

"What need have I of trotting round shrines to worship holy relics?" he had asked once. "I have my father."

And now it was he who was the head of the Men of Ithon. He was as full his skin as a pig sausage.

The company stayed under his roof for a night and a day. The women went to visit Father Mathau and his pupils at the nearby village of Llanrwst, and to admire the loomwork of Mabli Silverhand, a celebrated weaver of the district. The men roamed the woods with their longbows for half a day, and then sat down in a sunlit glade to drink ale from a tub which had been brought in their heels in a handcart.

"What happened to Alison Massey, Howel?" Eden asked when they were alone together.

"I don't know. We parted most lovingly near midnight of Maundy Thursday and naturally I saw nothing of her after that. She has gone back to Shrewsbury with old John, I'll wager Well, her dream was to escape that castle, so you could say that I was her liberator."

"You are a dog, Howel," said Eden.

"It's a dog's world, my heart," said he.

The siege of Caernarvon went on until winter. It did not succeed, for the fortifications were almost impregnable and the garrison strong and well-purveyed. Nevertheless, it was small blame to the townsfolk if the presence of such a hostile force outside their walls should have terrified them. Under a flag of truce they scurried about like mice in a burning barn, fitting out barks and baggage trains to bear their families and goods to the safe haven of kinsmen beyond the Welsh Marches. In the prevailing panic other garrison towns hastened to follow suit. Nor, if it was only by one notable example, did Beaumaris prove itself an exception.

One day, late in October a message came to the Old Hall summoning Annes to Beaumaris. Joanna Beaupine was departing for the palatinate of Chester, to visit her recently widowed sister Philippa, and she wished to see her daughter before she left.

It was cold and windy near the sea-river that day. The empty marketplace that fronted on the castle moat looked as big as a field. A bark rocked at anchor at the quay near the merchant's warehouse waiting to bear Joanna away to kith and kin. Upon the brine-whitened semblance of St Christopher over the stout oaken doors with their studs of steel, a disheveled seagull sat.

While Annes crossed the mew and mounted a stairway leading to the kitchen, Eden called upon his father-in-law. Clad in a robe of violet velvet trimmed with fur, he was busy over his account books. The raw-looking scar on his forehead made Eden's old one ache. He sat down over against him and spoke a while. Once or twice, the brisk sea-breeze that rattled at the window shutters brought them, gruff and hoarse from beyond the headland, the distant cough and retch of battle.

"They will never take that castle," said the merchant-sheriff.

"But the town? What of that? The burghers are being scared away."

"Like birds of passage, aye. Fleeing before the storms."

"So you think there will be storms, in-law?"

"As like as not," he said. "Did you know that we have some Frenchmen on the island now?"

"Jean d'Espagne?"

"No, he is outside Caernarvon. This is another crew. Renaut and Patrouillart de la Trie."

"Oia, where are they all coming from?"

"Duke Louis of Orleans," he said. Then he asked, "Did you ever meet Llywelyn of Caeo?"

Eden reflected.

"Yes," he said, "years ago when I was riding through the land shooting matches and masteries with my friends, the sons of Jenkin. We stayed at his hall one night. Why do you ask?"

"He has been beheaded before the market cross at Llandovery. He told the King he would show him and his army where Owain Glyndwr was encamped, and he led them all into Tregaron bog."

Eden was amazed. In his mind's eye there formed the image of a thin quiet sharp-chinned little man. He remembered his shy absent smile and his artless twinkling eyes.

"So your wife is leaving you for a season?" he observed.

"It is just as well. She has never been happy here. Go pay her your devoirs, lad."

Eden left through the inner door of the warehouse. A cold dank stone passage and a flight of stairs led him duly to an apartment familiar to him of old. Dressed with rich suits of tapestry worked in silks and or, and fragrant with spices, it faced on the straits of Menai and the forested mountains of Arvon. Annes was sitting alongside her mother at the window. Joanna was wearing a great hat with wide upsweeping wings, which made Eden wonder for a moment whether she purposed to attempt the velocity of flight. In his struggle not to laugh, he succeeded only in pulling a disagreeable face.

His mother-in-law was gracious enough to overlook it.

"Dieu vous doint bon jour, mon filz," she smiled, offering him two fingers to kiss.

So that is the way of it, Eden thought. French today. I am not being invited to partake in this tender interview, that is obvious. So be it.

He sat a little apart, watching the two of them chat. In justice to Joanna, he saw that it was from her that Annes had inherited her good looks, although the mother was of a coarser creation than her daughter by far. The frail nunlike quality that was his wife's peculiar charm made the merchant's lady look like a courtesan. In her eyes, in fact, Eden had often thought he could detect gleams of what seemed to him a frozen lewdness. For sure he had always fought shy of being left alone in a room with her. He wondered whether it was true what Gwervyl Mechain, the tavernness at the ferries, had once told him—that she and the merchant had not slept together for fifteen years.

Ach, but that was laughable. Gwervyl was the Sheriff's lovewoman.

She would be the first to invent such a fable.

And yet, the Chieftain had believed it when he had told him.

"Were I Joanna I don't think I would want to sleep with him, either, so bony and yellow of skin as he is."

"But in descent from St Brychan," Eden reminded him. "The blood tells."

It was perhaps to that saintly ancestor that Annes owed that lovely pure inviolate air that had so enchanted him from a boy. She had been Mistress Dauncey in that time. Then she had been Lady Dauncey briefly—her husband Hugh having been knighted on the battlefield moments before being given the sacraments in extremis. It was a pity she was so often sad. He wondered if her former husband had been cruel to her. She'd had a child by him, a boy. When she had become mistress of the Old Hall he had been taken from her and bred up among his father's people beyond the Marches. Perhaps it was this that had wounded her. The women thought so. Maybe they were right. She would never tell, of course, unless it was to Father Conan, no, never.

But now Joanna was embracing Annes. Sobs rent the air. The moment of parting had arrived.

"Take care of my daughter," she wept, pecking him on the cheek.

"I always do, lady, " he said.

"Please God," she said, "that this time she brings forth a living child."

"Please God," he echoed, once he had recovered breath.

It was not until they had won free of the walls of Beaumaris that he raised the matter with his wife.

"Why did you not tell me of this before?"

"You worry, my dear," she said. "And then," she added with a small, bent smile, "perhaps I was afraid to tempt Providence."

"What does that mean?" Eden frowned. She makes it sound as if I am under a fate.

"You see," she observed, giving him a sidelong glance. "I have told you and already you are fretting."

"No, it's not that," he said. "I have now begun to understand why Mererid is at the Old Hall these days."

And he thought of the priest's daughter. Almost without being aware of it he began to smile.

3

At the beginning of Advent Mabon of the Silver Harp left the Old Hall. He was growing progressively more tired and feeble and wished to spend his last days amidst the solitude of the graves on Ynys Enlli, the isle of the saints.

"Ah, this growing old," he told his apprentice Robyn, "what a weariness it is between the suns. I'm creaking, lad, a pack of aches and pains. It's like an almshouse, this mean body, every day a new tenant. Come you, not all the enginry of earth will be able to budge it from its bed before long. One day you will know what I am talking about. "If," he added, "you have the misfortune to live so long."

For nights moreover he had heard the old brown owl screeching among the dwarf oaks this side of the burial mounds. In times gone by such signs had meant little to him. He had never thought of himself as a superstitious man. But now, all at once, those cries in the night engendered in him a mood not unlike that called up in the human breast at the memory of a woe that has happened so far back in childhood that it seems less to be remembered than felt, deep down inside oneself, a dark dream moldering at the roots of the sense. He found himself shuddering.

"I am afraid you are going to see terrible days, my boy," he told Robyn. "Treasure these moments of your youth. Do not wait on wonders."

Bards were supposed to be born with prophetic powers, but Mabon had often wondered if those powers did not arise from a long accumulation of memories. The image of the past is upon the future, he told himself, and can never be effaced. And in the grey of time what is anything but a remembering?

Everyone at the Old Hall was upset when they heard of his intent.

"Sure, you do not mean it, Mabon," said Eden in consternation. "What will we do without our old housebard?"

"The Lord Jesus Christ direct all to his glory, you will survive, Tudor's son," he smiled. "I am in the manner of mortals a most expendable creature. There will be other bards."

"But none like you, Mabon. I beg you stay."

"Yes, old friend," said Annes. "This is your home."

"It has been my home and a most kind and beloved one has it been to me. God knows, all my life and dreams and songs I leave here with you, my little ones. But I have my way to go and you have yours and where I go the journey's short."

And so one morning, at earliest light, the bard put on him a coarse woolen robe and the Joseph's shoes which he had worn when on pilgrimage to the shrine of St James at Compostella in Tudor's time, took up his pilgrim's staff, laid his gout-knotted fingers for a moment upon the frame of his harp—and ah, what a wealth of feeling lay in that wordless caress!—cast one all-embracing look about the hall and with only his apprentice Robyn for company, departed.

He had scarcely passed through the gates when he heard someone calling after him.

"Wait, Mabon!"

He stopped and turned. It was Annes. He peered at her closely as she came up to him in the dim light. Over the bones of her face the skin was drawn so tightly that it glistened with the pale translucence of a pearl. But her eyes looked huge—sunken and glimmering in funereal sockets.

"Death is touching you," he thought. "It will not be long until we meet again, you and I."

"Here," she said. "I had almost forgot. I had packed you this wallet of food against the journey." She kissed him. "God be with you, Mabon."

"God be with you, too, dear lady."

Robyn went with him as far as the ferries. But the old man would have him go no farther.

"Remember all those things I have taught you and told you in the years we have been together," he enjoined him. "Serve your house well. It is a house upon which a destiny is sworn."

The boy stood on the bank of the sea-river watching the ferryboat until it reached the other shore. The old bard stood there briefly, looking back at him. And then he raised his hand in what would ever seem to Robyn the most moving of human gestures—that of farewell. The dark poignant line of that uplifted arm and in the next moment Mabon of the Silver Harp was gone, lost to sight under the hood of trees.

For long Robyn stood there, seeing in his mind's eye the way the old bard would go, and then he turned and took his way back. When he arrived at the hall he learned that Annes had collapsed and been put to bed. It was a perfectly natural thing to happen to a woman in her condition, old Sibli assured him, cackling and winking her eye. But Sioned, he marked, was unsmiling and silent and her eyes were grave.

Annes stayed in bed for much of the time through the rest of the month. Hence she could not join her husband in the Christmastide round of festivity at the island halls.

"How many feast days have you cheated me of your company," Eden grumbled humorously, "taking to your bed in this way?"

"Aye, blame her do!" Sioned exclaimed between laughing and scolding. "Men! Jesus Maria!"

By January Annes declared that she felt much better. She moved about the hall and went about many of her daily chores as of old. To venture outside, however, was not to be thought of. The weather was freezingly cold. Then as February began it took an unexpected and alarming turn. An unseasonable thaw accompanied by tempests of wind and rain swept the country. For fourteen days it did nothing but rain. You could hear it ceaselessly, whispering among the naked trees and the deserted grasslands, pattering on roofs and window-ledges, while in the byre and stables, water trickled down the walls and gathered in puddles in the grooves and hollows of the clay floors. It seemed as if it would never stop.

It was at this time that the loss of Mabon was felt most deeply. He had been the best of company on wet and stormy days—his store of tales had been rich and extensive, his music enchanting. Robyn, the novice, was as yet a poor substitute and Sibli's old wives' fables ended by being tedious. One night Mererid brought out the *Barcud Mawr* (the Great Kite), that weighty household chronicle that waxed fat on weddings, births and troth-plightings, and they had some fun with that for a while.

"See what a trumpery gaud Sabel of Penpadrig gave Cadi for her wedding on Rogation Day in 1362. A gilt neck-chain."

"Perhaps a gilt neck-chain was worth more in 1362."

"No, for someone has written down beside it: 'It was her thought we would take it for gold, no doubt, but we are not all void of sense and understanding. Gilt: a groat.'"

"Those folk at Penpadrig were ever stingy," Sibli observed.

"Not all of them surely," said Annes.

"All. They would not part with their spit, lady, so miserly as they are. I can remember the lady Margaret, Sir Tudor's wife, getting very angry at that house once. Something to do with a christening gift that was. Some old breech-clouts, I think."

"I'll look for it," said Mererid.

"Don't look for it, little sister," said Eden.

Sioned said: "What's that cock crowing about?"

"The cock's crowing?"

"Listen. It has gone so quiet."

"The rain has stopped."

"Praise be!"

"Are those hens I can hear fussing out there?" Sibli fretted. "Sure they can't be out of the coop." She turned to Mererid. "Did you not shut them in, lass?"

"Yes, I did, Sibli, I'm sure of it. Let me go and see."

"Stay where you are!" the old woman said crossly. "This is what comes of teaching maids how to read. I will see to it myself."

She went out mumping, and maundering.

"It's a wonder that Sibli would go out with that cock crowing," said Sioned.

"Is that an ill omen, too?" Annes asked.

"At this hour of night? O yes."

In the next moment Sibli came tottering into the hall from the yard. The aged maiden was trembling all over like a bird caught in a fowler's net. She was wheezing so that she could not speak.

"Sibli!" Annes cried. "O, catch her one of you!"

She fell into Eden's arms, her thin little body racked with sighs and hiccups of fright.

Gerallt ran out, then as quickly ran back.

"You must come and see this, it is astounding."

"No, no!" the old woman gasped, clutching at Eden's arms desperately. "Do not let the lady see it, I beg you. For the baby's sake, no, no!"

"Stop it now, Sibli," said Annes. "What nonsense!"

"A dragon thing out there, o, frightful."

Eden set her down carefully in Mabon's old chair of bardship and with the rest rushed out to the courtyard, then out to the slope beyond the walls and turned his face up to the sky.

And there it was! And what it was that they saw, as they stood together on that hillside, staring up into the heavens that February night, was so incredible, so unlike anything which any of them had seen in his life before, that at first it might not have been too hard to convince them that it was indeed a dragon that was dazzling their eyes up there—that white star blazing in the north-western sky, trailing its plume of bright smokeless flame.

"It must be a stella cometa," said Eden, as they crossed themselves.

"Yes," said Gerallt. "That is what it is for sure."

And the night air was chill and damp from the rain. The smells of wind and wet and turf were upon it and Robyn's backbone shivered. Black rolling clouds drifted westward across the sky. The boy blinked his eyes and stared. But the great star remained where it was, moveless, wondrous, awful; and the night was filled with a pale glow like the dawn.

"It's beautiful," said Annes.

"Listen," said Gerallt.

A ringing far away.

"It is beginning."

And by little and little, from parish to parish, from commote to commote, from near and far across the island and as, muffled or shaken out into broken chimes, they were borne to the hall on the wind, there was a grim interchange of bells—a somber tenebrific tolling. Folk were going to prayers.

So it went on until the end of the month and also through most of the next. The great star held the island in its powerful sway. The moiety of the time that was not dedicated to night seemed dull in comparison. There were gatherings of the people everywhere: in church and dingle, in clod hut and timbered hall. The bards explained to the islanders that what they were seeing was the third great star of history: the first being the Star of Bethlehem, harbinger of man's salvation; the second, the great comet which portended the might of Uther Pendragon, and through him of Arthur; and this, betokening the liberation of the Welsh from the yoke of the Black Oppressor.

"There is longing for him, the Prophesied One," it was sung. *"There is hope for our race. His name comes down from the mountains as a two-edged sword and his descent from high blood."*

And in its mysterious wildering light an inarticulate and helpless dread was born in the hearts of the islanders. Crazy stargazers filled the churches, rolling and screaming, foaming at the mouth and flinging themselves on the altars. The monks and priests were out at all hours with pyx, holy water and the blessed bread. Tales of fearful character and dubious value were given currency. It was told that the graves were walking at Aber Gwenoli and the Hill of the Old People. The long dead were shouldering up out of the black and soggy wastes of Cymminod and Cors-y-Bol. Demons with bloodbright eyes were trafficking for human souls at the End of the Ridges. A pilgrim seen trudging along the road from the ferries to the shrine of St Cybi on the Holy Head did not arrive there, and the rumor was that he had been murdered by celebrants of an obscene mass among the stones on the haunted mound. The Sheriff and his men went there looking, but found only the charred remains of a fire and some smoke-blackened sheep bones.

"The Devil's own self must be growing weary," he complained to his son-in-law.

In a world where crows cawed at midnight and cocks were heard crowing to the limits of earshot, who paid heed to outlaws and rebels? They came and went at will. So on Shrove Tuesday Eden announced to his hall: "I am off to Rhosyr to burn the straw man," and went instead with his brother Rhys Ddu to the hall of Myvyrian, to meet Owain Glyndwr's chief war-captains. They were ugly men, each in his own fashion—Rhys Gethin dark and ferocious, Howel Coetmor, smiling and owl-like.

"Do you know," Rhys Gethin observed, "that when we look at the comet in the Glens of Dee it seems to shine directly over this island?"

"And how do men in the Glens of Dee interpret that?" asked Emrys, the lord of Myvyrian.

"The Prophet of Ffinnant foresees that the times are now going to bring forward men as much like our ancient leaders as are to be found in the houses of this island."

"Ah, but in which houses?"

There was a sudden burst of movement in the yard outside. The door to the hall was flung open and Gerallt came rushing in. His eyes were wild and he looked weary beyond all telling.

"Eden," he cried, "come quickly. Annes is dying."

During the afternoon she had been seized by violent pains. Word had been sent at once to Father Conan, the Sheriff her father, and the halls of the brothers. Gerallt wore out a horse riding at breakneck speed to Rhosyr to get Eden, but he was not to be seen among the merrymakers who were burning the straw man. He was nowhere to be found. Beside himself with anguish he borrowed a horse from the Sheriff's farm there, and rode back to the Old Hall.

By that time Annes had been delivered prematurely of a child. The baby, a boy, was stillborn, but as it chanced nobody had a thought or an emotion to spare for him, since it was immediately apparent that Annes was desperately ill. Although in high fever she was not delirious, but there had been a considerable loss of blood and she was very weak.

"I cannot find Eden," Gerallt told the Chieftain.

Meredith frowned.

"Wherever he is, he must be with Rhys Ddu. For that one is not here, either."

At that Eva beckoned Gerallt aside.

"Go to Myvyrian," she told him.

Marged, who was standing nearby, looked at her but said nothing.

In the bedchamber Father Conan, haggard himself from sleepless nights and endless worry about the half-demented people who had been plaguing his threshold begging advice and succor, anointed Annes with the holy oil and gave her the viaticum. He began to recite the prayers for the dying.

"Where is Eden?" she asked.

"He will come soon."

Mererid and Robyn sat on a bench against the wall, so stunned with grief that they could have been carved in stone. Kneeling beside the bed, the Sheriff saw his daughter sinking swiftly towards death. Even as he watched her face was changing—her cheeks were grown whiter than the sands of the love-saint's isle, the nose stood out sharply, the lips were drawn back over the glitter of teeth. What life was left in her must all have been in her eyes. Tenderly they gazed up at her father out of their huge, dark, glimmering pits like the wild pansies that tremble out of pools in woods. Her thin fingers rested on his, lightly, caressingly.

"Eden. . . ."

"He will be here soon."

"Tell him I have loved him dearly."

She closed her eyes. Presently her hands began to flutter over the coverlid like little birds.

"She is feeling for the earth," Mam Indeg murmured with awe and crossed herself.

She had been dead an hour by the time Eden arrived.

At first his behavior was that of a madman. He flung himself upon the body of his wife, sobbed uncontrollably and had to be laid fast lest he do harm to himself. With mingled feelings of horror, pity and sorrow, Mererid escaped from the deathchamber into the hall.

Marged Vaughan was confronting Eva there.

"You knew Eden was with Rhys Ddu at Myvyrian when you arrived here," she hissed. "You knew we had sent Gerallt to Rhosyr on a fool's errand. Why did you not say so?"

"And the Sheriff of Mona at my side?"

Marged was so staggered that at first she could not speak.

"What are you saying? Her own father?"

"Glyndwr's war-captains were there. Rhys Gethin and Howel Coetmor. The ban of outlawry is upon them. The Sheriiff has been watching Myvyrian for months. It is a hotbed of sedition. He would have suspected something."

"You foolish wicked woman!"

"Don't talk to me as if I am one of your maids, Marged," Eva flared up, "I'm not used to it."

"I never talk to my maids so. But you are a woman of rank. You ought to know better."

"Well, what of it?" Eva retorted, casting around in her head for something cruel and biting to say. "He never loved her at heart. It was always that other."

"I will speak no more with you," Marged snapped and turned away with an angry writhing of her skirts.

Both women were white to the lips with fury, Mererid saw. All at once she began to weep helplessly. She sank down to the floor against the silentiary's post and buried her head in her arms.

The catafalque, hung with heavy brocaded cloths, had been raised upon the dais boards at the upper end of the hall. The body however had yet to be moved from the bedchamber.

"Leave us here awhile," Eden had said.

So there they were, just himself and Annes. No, not Annes, that was wrong of course. Say rather the husk of a woman he had loved. Appareled in garments of gold and crimson, the body lay upon the bed, as stiff and lifeless as an effigy cut out of a shaft of alabaster. The hands were arranged on the breast in the pious attitude of praying. The yellow light of the wax candles which burned round about gleamed in the gold rings which adorned the chaste fingers; it flickered over the ravaged cheeks and played with the lamentable smile which death had graven on the pale lips.

How long he stayed there or what thoughts crossed his mind, Eden could not afterwards recollect. He knelt without moving at the side of the bed for such a length of time that his whole body ached. There was an uncanny stillness in the room. Every now and again the sounds of women keening would come to his ears like the wind rising and falling in trees, and somewhere outside he could hear the dripping of raindrops into a hogshead or a drinking trough. But these things seemed oddly unreal and far away to him in those moments, as if they came to him from a far distance, as it were from the bounds of the earth.

At last he rose. He bent over the bed, searching his dead wife's face with haggard eyes.

"Annes," he murmured.

He pressed his lips to her brow. A chill not of this earth enfolded him and went shuddering through his veins.

"Annes," he kept on saying. "Annes."

Perhaps in the depths of his hurt and bewildered heart, there still trickled a bright blood-drop of hope. That maybe it was all delusion, a bad dream, that in another moment she would open her eyes and say with a smile: "Yes, my Eden."

Alas, she would answer him no more—never more in this world.

He returned to the hall. There was no light there that night save that of the fire that glowed and roared in the heart of the shadowed rock. It made bright like autumn leaves the russets, browns and greens of gowns and island-spun tunics. It shone full on the heads of the folk who knelt at the hearth praying. But where their feet were rested it began to fade, wasting its strength amidst rush and straw and running out between the mourners and the dais where the catafalque loomed, into sighing pools of darkness, so that what lay beyond could be seen only for the wink and flash of weapons along the massy oaken crucks that bore the walls upward to the length of the hall.

Father Conan saw him first, then Meredith. Both rose, priest and Chieftain, and came towards him.

"Peace to the dead," said Eden. "We'll bear her in now."

At the Old Hall on the night of the burial there was a somber feast. Eden sat alone in the high seat partaking of funeral meats that were without savor for him, and watching the faces of the mourners about him with indifferent curiosity. Marged and Eva were at daggers' drawn about something, he noticed. Och, they had to quarrel at such a time!

I shall have to leave, he thought. What other resort is there? Like our old housebard I have quite reached bottom here. God's my life, what a season of partings this one has been!

Afterwards he went out on the hill beyond the walls. The fires of the comet were beginning to wane by then. Enough burned in the night's black, for all that, to illumine the ugly cloud-shapes, like goblin shreds and hags' clouts, that went scurrying across the face of the sky. A wind was blowing out of the sea, bending in the sedge and the high grasses. It was wild and bitter, but the first gay eddies of spring came dancing in its wake and there was a smell of new-turned earth.

Eden stood in the shelter of the gates and leaned his head back against the wall. He felt weak, lightheaded and deathly tired. It was as if the torment of the last days had drained him empty of emotion as you would drench a horse or steer.

And when in a little he put his hand up to his face to brush away what he took to be some tickling cobweb which had fluttered loose from the old and mossy joinings of the stone, he was almost surprised to find that his cheeks were wet with tears.

A Destiny is Sworn

Book Two

The Stone Cauldron

6
THE CAPTIVES (1402)

Horns sounded deep in the forest—the baying of hounds.

Scabbed with dried mud and covered with patches of bristling brown hair, with black markings on his dangerous yellow tusks, the great boar stood listening. He was lost. The thicket in which he found himself was unfamiliar to him. With a lowering glance of his small red eyes, he looked around and sniffed at the wind with his brown-mottled grey snout.

It was early in the morning of a spring day. Misty trails of sunlight ran wavering and trembling through the gloom. Among the age-old branches of an oak a large dark bird flapped its wings clumsily and flew upwards. Squirrels skittered among the rotting logs squeaking alarm; a lynx with tufted ears and blazing eyes cautiously peered through great webs of bleached twigs.

But now the hounds were giving tongue nearer at hand. And then there came other noises, ever more sinister—the cracking of a dead branch close by, whisperings, the furtive tread of some heavy creature bent upon passing unseen. Catching the hostile scent, the boar swung round and ran forward a few paces, confused, his blood throbbing with fear and rage.

The air was growing lighter, the moss on the trees glowed with an emerald brilliance, spiderwebs glistened in the wet grass.

"By God, you did not lie, Hamo. What a brute!"

A man on a glossy sorrel drew rein on the brow of a hill looking down into the thicket. He was a commanding figure, tall and broad-shouldered, stately in the saddle. His large florid face was clean-shaven but for a small forked beard, and when alight with pleasure as it now was, could not have seemed more affable or kindly.

"Go to! Get him!"

Urged on by the two mounted whippers-in, Hamo and Janyn Breton, a dark chain of hounds burst out of the trees. At a lumbering run the great boar made for a nearby glade. The grass there was thick, lush and trampled, and the smell was rank—a friendly reassuring smell that made the boar hesitate for a moment before hastening on to the further side of the glade. A little way beyond it, among the trees at the head of a gully, he found his path blocked by piled up rocks and logs. Baffled, he turned about and ran back into the glade. The hounds encircled him on three sides. A black bitch leapt on him and he tossed her off with his tusks. Then he charged. The next thing that Hamo knew, something had hit him like a thunderstone and he was on his back on the other side of the clearing. His pony was lying nearby in a pile of broken twigs, kicking his hoofs in the air. His belly had been ripped open and the entrails were hanging out in a horrible mess of steaming and bloodily oozing flesh. Then the boar was coming at Hamo again. The whipper-in leapt to his feet, holding out a branch before him in order to ward the boar's powerful swipes. There was the crunching sound of breaking wood; Hamo could see the white glinting of the driving tusks, feel his heavy weight bearing down on him, the hot fetor of his breath.

"Go to! Get him!"

There was a black coil and whistle of wolfgut as Janyn Breton plied his whip over the backs of the pack. The hounds closed in on the boar again, springing on top of him in a writhing mass, dragging him down and tearing at his flesh with their teeth.

"He's mine!" the big huntsman shouted. "Let me take him!"

In the grip of an excitement more intoxicating than the vapors of spring, he leapt off his horse and plunged his knife in the boar's throat up to the hilt.

"God in Heaven, get them off!" he exclaimed furiously, kicking out at the hounds that were still snapping at the carcass.

"Father"—it was a younger man who spoke—"they are all about us."

At the same time, another of the hunting party cried out: "It's a trap!"

Very pale now, blood-stained and gasping, the big huntsman rose to his feet. He saw at once that to flee or fight were both out of the question. There must have been close to a hundred men about them in the glade, Hamo and Janyn Breton in their midst. So it was they who had betrayed him, those two. White with rage, he spat on the ground. God damn the whoresons! He would not forget!

"Good morrow, Lord Grey."

It was Glendowrdy, of course! Chief of all the outlaws in this benighted land. And beside him, mounted on a fine chestnut—stolen as like as not— behold that other work of Satan, the sometime Keeper and Master Forester of Chirkeland, with his hard stare, his rascally grin.

Lord Grey drew himself up stiffly.

"So we meet once more, my lord Glendower," he said with a sour smile.

"And not under the happiest of circumstances, alas," his captor observed. "But I am glad you enjoyed hunting the boar we provided for you. He was something of a legend in the lordship of the Knights Hospitallers. The men who live there used to call him *The Hewer*. I think he served us well."

Bound and hoisted on their horses, Lord Grey and his companions were now led for half a day's journey over forest roads. Once in the open, they were made to dismount. In chains and bound to carts, their faces turned ignominiously to the tails of horses, they were drawn through the Vale of Clwyd. It was a countryside that lent itself to the same mood of deception that marked the day. The pleasantly wooded green hills in which the Vale was cradled hardly suggested the greater ones that lay behind—the bleak silences of uplands where strange winds moved and eagles cut the sky with an even sweep of wing.

In the heart of this world lay the ancient fortress of Caer Gai.

Nothing could have been more natural than that this site should have seized upon Owain Glyndwr's imagination. Here it was that Cynir had ruled and that his son Cai Hir* and his foster son Arthur—those two fabulous fools of destiny—had spent their boyhood. A league away, lost to the view in a purple cup of the hills, stood Carndochan of the cockle-shells, with its enchanted harp and Merlin gold. On the farther side of the nearby lake, amidst its hazel woods, there lay crumbling away to time the grey tower of Llywarch Hen, the ancient poet-king who had survived the loss of his kingdom and his twenty-two sons, to sing of death and exile in the brooding shadow of the Aran. Aye, and this too had been the domain of Grono the Radiant, who had stolen the love of Blodeuwedd, the flower bride—grey Meirchion's daughter, she that was quick and bright as the moon.

Owain Glyndwr had moved his household here in the autumn of 1401. Then, as his lady, Margaret Hanmer observed, he seldom stayed there. He was either arriving or departing. That unsightly creature, the Propher of Ffinnant, would look in his crystal or sit up among the chimney-pots listening to the music of the heavenly spheres, and if the

---

* Cai Hir (Long Cai)—the Sir Kay of Arthurian legend.

omens were favorable—fare you well! Glyndwr would put on his cuirass and black purple mantle, his helmet plumed with the feather of an Egyptian heron,* take up his sword and battle-axe, and ride off with his horde of barelegged spearmen, the dear knew where.

Hence for the greater part of the time it was the Lady who was the ruling presence at Caer Gai. "Nothing is good enough that can be excelled," she liked to say, and folk were often given to believe that she was bent on making the byword flesh. Every morning dawned on the stronghold as if at a gallop, with the running clogs of serving maids and scullions. Mass first—the Lady was much given to good observances and plied her devotions loyally. Then she set out to inspect her domain— a full-bosomed matron with an air of calm and dignified assurance, smiling a grave, mild, urbane smile, a fold of her heavy trailing skirts caught up over her arm, floating along as stately as a galleass through the chambers, the winehouse, the bakehouse and the kitchen.

Nothing escaped her fastidious eye, certainly not the encampment at the lake—that host of hungry bellies and birds of passage. Every day came more, some with goats and pigs, some with but the clothing on their backs. God knows it was a concernment to her. Clod huts, goatskin tents and cabins of wattle and daub went up overnight. She went about them from time to time, looked at the babies, inspected the gruel and stew being cooked in the pots, asked the children "Where was our Lord Jesus born?" and studied the maids to see if they were chastely dressed.

"Why are you doing that?" she asked one man who was searing fungus to the doorpost of his hovel.

"To keep away the Evil Eye, my lady," he replied.

"If that is your mind and purpose, tell your wench to cover up her bosom," she told him.

One April evening she was sitting at the heart of her redoubt of women in the hall of the castle. The great lady's needle darted and flashed under her eyes as though it had nothing to do with herself, nor with the wilful independent motions of her mind, which was thinking now of her husband who surely should be here by this time, and now of moments of her childhood at Hanmer, and then of tomorrow's supper— this salmon in the waters here, she had heard it said that it was the only fish that the lake-fairies would eat, the generality of their diet consisting of milk mixed into messes with saffron. Paganish nonsense of course;

---

* A flamingo feather, it has been surmised.

still, was the salmon fit for human consumption?

An unwonted silence among the women made her look up. Three newcomers were being conducted towards her by her youngest son Maredudd, a smiling fresh-faced youth with nutbrown hair. The Lady recognized one of them as Howel Vaughan of Nantconway, a rogue and skirt chaser of whom she disapproved highly, in spite of his reputation as a bold and fearless warrior. The other man was tall and dark, and one of his eyes turned outward a little. A swarthy lad stood beside him, perhaps his son.

Howel Vaughan bowed low, sweeping the rushes with his plumed cap.

"Altesse!"

A flurry of amusement stirred in the feminine ranks. The Lady bestowed on them a brief silencing stare.

"God rest you merry, chieftain, you do me far too much honor," she nodded with an amused gleam in her eye, and turned to his companions. When they were presented to her she raised her eyebrows in delighted astonishment.

"Say you so?" she exclaimed. "Tudor ap Grono's son Ednyved? I can scarce believe it. How long ago has it been? I am hard put to remember how all the unpleasantness began."

"It began fifty years ago, my lady" said Eden. "With a wedding."

"Aye, that wedding!" she said. "How run the wheels of time to be sure! Well, God be praised that I have lived to see this day and God's welcome be to you and yours to Caer Gai."

The three were assigned a well-appointed turret room which looked over the rolling grassland towards the lake and the mountains beyond. Not long after their arrival a bundle was presented to Eden by a flunkey. It was the black mantle lined with miniver which he had loaned to Griffith Llwyd, the bard of the haunted mound, more than a year and a half ago. He pressed it against his face and closed his eyes. It had been Annes' gift to him. He almost thought he could smell the wild tansy she used to put in the chest where she had kept his clothes. His heart was wrung and made him think of days that no longer were and of the beloved dead gone beyond recall.

Owain Glyndwr returned two days later. It was near sunset when the rebel leader's son Maredudd ran into the hall of the castle, eyes and teeth shining.

"They are coming!"

Robyn ran up to the roof of the keep at the heels of his foster father and Howel Vaughan. Even before they saw the homecoming warband, they could hear the hoarse cry of the horns, far off over the wild outcroppings of crag and the rolling hills. Robyn could feel the triumph of those horns reaching over the countryside and an intense tremor of excitement passed through him. He had all but forgotten, it seemed to him, that such things still had power to stir his blood.

And the incessant bubbling life, as in a cauldron of the camp, fairly boiled over as people in their hundreds swarmed out of their tents and cabins or left their chores to greet the chieftains and soldiery as they came walking and riding over the brow of a hill to the north of the lake— a lightly armed force, winking in and out of the rocks and trees, and spreading out along the grassy paths like moving scales of silver.

"It looks as if they are bringing back a great deal of plunder with them," Eden observed. "Look at those wagons and sumpter horses."

"Aye," said Howel, "and will you look at what else they are bringing us! If my eyes do not mistake me that is the Chief Marcher Lord himself."

"Grey of Ruthin? Away!"

"Look for yourself!"

There was a general rush down into the courtyard as the gates yawned open. And it was he, right enough, that Robyn and the other two now saw coming towards them in a dung cart—Lord Reginald de Grey of Ruthin with a handful of companions. And in what a state! In chains, their clothing filthy and torn, their haggard faces encrusted with dirt. Folk thronged about them, their faces full of exultation and hatred. An escort of spearmen cleared a path for the hostages through the jeering mob. At their head, Owain Glyndwr having been detained some little way back by the greetings of the crowd, rode the leader's eldest son Gruffydd, his deeply tanned face framed in a curly black beard, his nose broken under a white scar.

He dismounted and embraced his mother, who was looking at the prisoners with horror and a sort of stern pity.

"Must they be chained?" she asked.

Her son walked over to the guards.

"Unchain them," he said.

It was done And then, summoning up the last of his powers, one of the prisoners spat in his face. What happened next was over in an instant. Eyes ablaze, Gruffydd swung back his sword. There was a terrible whistle of steel through the air and the man's head was struck off at a blow. The blood jetted up from the severed neck in a fountain. Howel Vaughan, his tunic splattered with gore, sprang back.

"Christ Jesus!" he cried out, astounded almost to laughter.

Pandemonium followed. Howel's shout in concert with the screams of others infected the mob. Not understanding exactly what had happened, some to the rear of the crowd were heard to yell: "Kill the devils! Look what they have done to us, the brutes! Look how many orphans they have made! They don't deserve to live!" Mindlessly then they fell to brawling, striking out with their fists at random, and charging about like drunkards. While the soldiers busied themselves restoring order and clearing the court, Howel and Eden helped escort the women, many of them stunned and helpless with horror, back into the hall.

"King of Mercy, I do wish they would spare us these horrible sights," fumed the Lady, who apart from her anger, was her usual superbly competent self.

Moments later Owain Glyndwr entered the courtyard. He stared gloomily at the headless body sprawled out amidst its red refuse in the straw.

"Clear away that offal!" he said.

He turned to Rhys Gethin.

"Who is at Dolbadarn castle?"

"The Siri Mawr."

"Take Grey and company there. Their lives are not worth a day's purchase hereabouts."

Inside the castle he was greeted by his brother-in-law, John Hanmer, a dark smooth-faced barrister-at-law with a clear unwinking gaze. They went together to Glyndwr's retiring room where the Welsh leader washed and changed into a soft brown woolen robe tied at the waist with a belt of white fleecy cordwain. "Your sister's hand has been busy here since I left," he said with a smile. A lichen-red rug lay upon the blue flagstones, bright cushions of bliant and sendal were upon the window seat, and the white walls were adorned by a crucifix, a picture of St Garmon, chief saint of Powys, and a black Crusader's shield, polished to a brightness, wherein Glyndwr's great leonine head glimmered like a small moon of the fairies.

"I do not remember having seen this shield before," he remarked.

"It comes from Hanmer," the barrister said. "I'm told it belonged to a Norman forebear of mine who fought in the Third Crusade."

"He must not have fought too hard. There's not a mark upon it. Are you sure it did not belong to one of your Welsh forebears, John?"

"You mean," the other smiled, "one of those who did not keep his covenant of faith?"

"*Horribile dictu,* yes. Of course, Archbishop Baldwin should have known better than to swear the Welsh on the Book of the Gospels. If it is not a portable bell or a miraculous staff or a sainted bone no man can be held to an oath in this land."

"Not even a king?"

"Why he more than another? The Lord Rhys, the king of Dyved, was prevailed upon to forgo crusade for no greater thing than the tears of his wife. And then there was that broth bowl, Prince Owain Cyveiliog, the singer of *The Hirlas Horn,* he too was forsworn."

"*'Fill the horn with foaming liquor. Fill it up my boy, be quicker,'*" John intoned gaily.

"*'Hence away despair and sorrow! Time enough to sigh tomorrow,'*" Glyndwr caroled in his turn. "That reminds me, my pulse, I have a thirst. Let's away."

They returned to the hall, thronged now with a festive crowd. As they entered, John Hanmer plucked Glyndwr's sleeve: "Do you see this chieftain coming towards us?"

"Him in wildwood green? That is the head of the Men of Ithon."

"No, his companion."

"Should I know him?" said Glyndwr, staring.

"Your mothers were sisters."

"Ah, yes. *'Fill cupbearer, as thou wouldst live, the horn held in honor at the banquet, the long blue horn, high in renown, ringed with rich silver, and bring first to Tudor, eagle of battle, the first draught of ruddy wine!'*" he murmured as the two men came up. "Have welcome, Howel Vaughan."

"May God prosper you, supreme chief of kindred."

Glyndwr turned towards Eden.

"My heart grows tender towards thee. I know thou art of my

blood,'" he said, with a fine bardic ring and relish to the words.

"He is Ednyved, the son of Tudor of Mona," said Howel.

"I know well who he is," said Glyndwr, opening his arms wide. He embraced the younger man's lean shoulders and kissed him. "The years, eh, kinsman?" he exclaimed. "The years, the years, such years!"

That night Glyndwr rode out through the encampment. The smells of turf fires wrapped him about in the wild scents of thorn and whin.

"Pendragon," someone called out, "what will you do with that tyrant Grey? Will you have him put to death?"

"Dear my fathers, no," he replied. "But I am asking such a ransom for that dog of darkness that all his estates here and in Ireland will have to be mortgaged to meet it."

"Lord," another cried in amazement, "you will be as rich as kings in old Babylon."

Glyndwr laughed. "And richer than the dreams of kings in old Babylon shall you be, my children," he proclaimed jovially. "For this will be your own land to live in and you will be free."

Less than a month later Eden, Howel and Robyn were on the march southward with the host. Three days after their departure from Caer Gai they crossed the estuary of the Dovey and entered the province of Glyndwr's old comrade Black Rhys, lord of a hundred vills, the dragon* of Penweddig, the backbone of Ceredigion.

The great clearing as of a river plain in the heart of the vast and shadowy forest was humming like a beehive in the gathering dusk. Fires burned in the clay and wattle huts, painting the faces of men, women and children in the colors of flame and shadow. Sensing the excitement, other people had trickled in along the forest paths from their neighboring homesteads. Even the red-bellied sows were stirring and grunting in their pigbeds.

"What's to do?"

"Big things, lads. For sure, for sure. Look there, Slow Sinnoch is out on the hill."

All raised their eyes as one to stare at the great hall. It could have been the stronghold of a giant—those big, black houses sprawled out at

*dragon—leader. pendragon—chief leader. The Welsh name for the monster of myth is draig.

haphazard over a mound which rose as high as the treetops to catch the crows and their droppings. Around it ran an insurmountable wall of stout timbers, each one a hewn tree of the forest. There were a thousand iron studs in the big gates, and the spikes at the top were hung with the whitening skulls of wild cats, tenbranched stags, and great tusked boars.

Torches kept running in and out of the houses—from afar they looked like shaggy dwarfs afire. And in their light, from time to time, could be seen the figure of Slow Sinnoch, immovably standing, his smoke-white hair fluttering about his shoulders, his face of an ancient tortoise turned northward, far over the forest tops, to where the great constellations of the Wain and the Herdsman were wheeling in the heavens.

"Why is he looking to the north?"

"It must be from that way he is coming."

"Who?"

"Who else?"

And a sudden impetuous whispering ran in the night like the feral rush of eagles:

"Glyndwr! Glyndwr! Glyndwr!"

Inside the huge hall, with its two fires burning at top and bottom, the four sons of Black Rhys and the Lady Madlan sat ranged along the wall in their bloodbright ceremonial tunics and stout leather belts, as still and sober and round in the face as a row of ruddy milk-cheeses. On the other side of the hall sat the three daughters: Glenys, Gwyneth, and Elliw, in their heather-colored gowns; their new-washed and curried hair shooting little lightnings in the firelight. Once, Elliw, the youngest of the three nudged her eldest sister furtively and following the other's glance, Gwyneth caught the wolfish white gleam of eyes and teeth of a man lurking in the shadows of the central pillar of the hall. It was Robyn Holland, her father's captain of the guard. As she looked at him he moved his lips in a kiss. She dropped her eyes, smiling.

Legs astride, arms akimbo, the lord was standing in a muse near Robyn Holland, staring downward at his feet as though he were overseeing the yearly cleansing and scouring of the town ditch. Every now and again he glanced up at his wife, puffing and fussing about the tables, her errant hair escaping from her headlinen in fluffy wisps, sweat gleaming on her blood-suffused face. The Lady Madlan was great with child again. O, why must they be so late? She sprinkled her cheek with the scented water in the finger bowls.

"Sit down, lady," Black Rhys shouted at last. "Have you not serving women to help? It is making me nervous only to look at you."

She leaned forward on her elbows on the high table to ease the cramps that were clawing at her thighs and groin.

"Where are they?" she asked him despairingly.

"How am I to know where they are? They are on their way, is that not enough?"

"How many do you think will be coming?"

"If I have told you once I have told you a hundred times—a few thousand, perhaps five or six. By the week's end we might well have ten thousand here at least. What care?" He saw that she was on the point of tears. He loved her dearly. He sought to cheer her.

"Remember our wedding, my Madlan? How many of your kinsmen came with you then out of Gwidigada and Toadtown and the east, eh? I never knew you had so many relatives. Thanks to my purse for this, said I, when I saw that multitude. All the population of Gwentland sure and half of Glamorgan. . . .What is it, Robyn?"

"Slow Sinnoch is coming in."

"Did he ever go out?"

"Lord," Slow Sinnoch announced in grave and measured tones, "they are here."

There were wild whoops on the hill outside.

"Sweet Jesus help us!" the Lady Madlan gasped, and sat down.

"Get up, wife!" Black Rhys exclaimed, suddenly beside himself with excitement. "Is this the time to be sitting?"

There sounded the terrific blows of the gate-hammers. Black Rhys went leaping down over the mound.

"Who goes there? Declare your right and chaunt of entry."

"La double mort, c'est a dire, la mort corporelle et la damnation infinie."

"In the name of Heaven admit him!"

Owain Glyndwr rode in and dismounted. The two men embraced.

"God rest you merry, Rhys, my old comrade. Is all well with you? How is your good lady?"

"By the Blessing of the Mothers, most fruitful. She is breeding again."

"What is that?"

Glyndwr came to a halt. His face was set in stern lines, his eye had a fierce censorious gleam.

"That was ill done in you, Rhys," he said. "I was hoping to sleep with her tonight."

"Be of good cheer," his host assured him. "She may well drop that child before you leave and then she is yours."

As they entered the hall the Lady Madlan, followed by her three daughters and her four sons, walked towards her husband and their guest like a ship trying to make head against a wind.

"My lord Owain . . . an honor," she breathed hoarsely and before he could stop her she had sunk to the ground in a profound curtsey.

"O no, dear lady, I beg you, don't do that!" Owain Glyndwr called out in sudden alarm.

Gently raising her to her feet, he kissed her warmly on both cheeks and duly conducted her, still gasping and red of face to the dais where he gallantly deposited her beside him in the high seat with cushions at her back and under her bottom.

"And do you come hither now, too, Rhys, my dear," he told his host genially, "and sit beside me on my other hand. We shall break lagana together tonight and share our messes from the same platter. We three like the Trinity, eh?"

The Abbot of Strata Florida recited a long grace at the table's end. And with that the feasting began.

For five days it went on and throughout this time other contingents joined Glyndwr's force. The Siri Mawr came from Dolbadarn castle in the north and Henry Don of Kidwelly from the southern coast. Men came from all over Ceredigion and its bourns. They walked in along the forest path that went winding for miles through the thickets to the Abbey of Strata Florida and its broken tombs. And from the Land of Pryderi, the Red Bank on the Teivy and the Glen of the Cuch in Emlyn, from Caeo and the Valley of the Cothi, from the Vale of Aeron with its flowery meadows and its acorn-floored woods, from the miraculous mount of St David, and from the ancient high grey beacon carn of Crug Mawr, they came streaming in with their longbows and their spears as tall as larch saplings.

More and more of them coming; they were massing throughout the pastures and the woods beyond. Wild faces, shining eyes—the air seethed with excitement, the babble of voices, shouts, laughter. The village was rocked in sound; there was no escaping it, the throb of that full blooded life.

Then on the night of the fifth day, the after supper noises in the hall of Black Rhys were stilled to hear Owain Glyndwr say:

"Perhaps you are wondering why I am here and what is my mind."

Seated on the chair of honor, which was large, black, oaken, and carved about with heraldic beasts, wearing a long damask gown of green color with a green belt harnessed with silver, he was graciously, affably at his ease. Earlier that evening he had presented a silken purse fat with coins to the lord of the manor's housebard for a spirited rendering of *The Warchant of Uther Pendragon*, and before that he had delivered himself of some timely homilies to a choir of little children from the neighborhood who had sung him anthems. But never was such an attentive silence in all that great smoky hall until that moment.

"We are going to call upon Sir Edmund Mortimer," he told the chieftains.

He smiled at their expressions of blank amazement.

"What is it, my friends? Are you afraid?"

"Afraid?" Black Rhys laughed. "You are our captain and our good luck. Why should we be afraid?"

"But why now, my lord Owain?" asked Henry Don of Kidwelly. "And why Mortimer?"

"Call it a happy conjunction of the stars, if you will."

Presently, however, he became more explicit. As he reminded the chieftains it was no secret that for a long while Sir Edmund Mortimer had been much put about because King Henry was still keeping his nephew and namesake, Edmund Mortimer, the Earl of March in custody when the boy was the rightful heir to the throne of England. Without disclosing his sources of information, Glyndwr explained that he had now been given good reason to believe that relations between the House of Mortimer and its sovereign had so far deteriorated that they had reached the breaking point. The time was thus ripe to invade the large Welsh estates of Sir Edmund and wrest them from him.

There was quiet for some moments.

"And what then?" someone asked.

"Well, and what do you suppose is going to happen then?" Owain Glyndwr replied with assurance. "Do you think this King will lift a finger to help a man he hates and dreads? Will he make war on us for

Mortimer's sake?"

"No," came the reply.

"Very well then," said Glyndwr. "Let us go forth and bring back those stolen fields of Powys to our people."

So it was that on St Alban's Day a week later, amidst a chorus of warshouts and the blowing of a wild music on horns, Eden found himself riding with his comrades down a hill many leagues away from Ceredigion and the fastness of Black Rhys to meet an advancing line of horsemen led by Sir Edmund Mortimer. It was his first battle and, as it proved, it was almost his last. In the first tumultuous minutes of the conflict his horse put his hoof in a rabbit hole and he was pitched from the saddle. It was as if rough hands had plucked him up, tossed him in the air, and hurled him to the ground all in an instant. The world reeled about him, the bloody ball of the rising sun disgorged a battalion of writhing red devils into the sky over the hills, the green mantles of the forest shook and swayed. Stunned and bruised, he staggered to his feet, only to see a knight bearing down on him with furious force, sword raised. Curse of my stars, he thought, it is my death. His shaky limbs would not obey him; they had turned into bread. The blue light of the blade was falling on him, even as in that very breath and tick of time another horse surged up out of nowhere and the knight went tumbling, felled by a blow so powerful that it took half his head away.

Eden stumbled back against the rough breast of an oak. And then stared and stared for what seemed an unending moment into the face of his deliverer.

"Howel Vaughan. . . ."

"Are you having fun, son of Tudor?"

Another came hasting up, leading Eden's horse by the rein. It was his fellow islander, Caradoc of Penhesgin, a man with whom he had not been on the best of terms during the past year.

"How is it that devils like you have all the luck, Eden?" he asked, running his eyes over him with a bitter smile.

Those were the last words Caradoc was fated to utter. Scarcely had they left his lips than an arrow found its mark between his shoulder blades, and Gwennan of Croes Gwion had lost the gallant who for years had given her comfort in a loveless marriage.

All this took place, as Eden later surmised, within the space of the first hour. The battle went on for half the day. Small wonder then that so much of it would remain confused in his memory. Amidst the bloody and inescapable fragments of the carnage, however, there was another incident he would never forget. With some of his comrades he had fallen back about a bowshot from the main body along the slope of a hill. There was some hard cutting going on when Rhys Gethin and Howel Coetmor, Glyndwr's chief captains, burst out of a nearby thicket and their enemies began to scatter. Rhys Gethin was a sight to behold. He was splattered with brains and gore, an eyebrow was down over one eye streaming blood, and he was spitting out bits of tooth. But his other eye as he reined in and looked past his companions was shining with wonder and delight.

"Good God!" he shouted, showing the bloody roof of his mouth as he laughed. "I cannot believe it."

And then the rest turned and saw: Mortimer's Welsh had turned against him.

Like the riptide swirling in the rough inlets of Mona, that is how the field looked to Eden, as with wildly leaping heart, he watched wave after wave of Welsh footsoldiers in the service of Mortimer, break, recoil, and sweep back through their own ranks. From the slope where he and the others were standing they could see them running like hares at the tails of the enemy cavalry, hacking at the bellies of the horses, or, knives in teeth, leaping up behind the riders and dragging them down. Glyndwr's flamboyant heron feather, too, could be easily distinguished; one could even make out the golden lion of Powys on his shield, as he raced around exhorting the men of Wales to follow him. And hither and thither over the heads of the seething crowd darted the red dragon banner of Cadwaladr, its tongue of flame licking and smacking the air.

From that moment the outcome of the battle was in no doubt. By mid-afternoon when the struggle was finally ceded, the valley and hillsides were strewn by the thousand with the bodies of the dead and wounded, and of all the border chivalry that had ridden out against Glyndwr, the only survivors were Sir Edmund Mortimer and his friend Thomas Clanvow.

Those two nobles were taken to Pilleth, a diked-about little settlement of clod huts nearby, where the victors had left their stores and baggages. A red and white striped tent over which the standard of the golden lion of Powys fluttered had been set up in the plain field, and preparations were already underway for a feast to crown the triumph.

"Stewed goat's meat will be the best of it, I am afraid," Glyndwr told his prisoners in humorous apology. "We hope to approve ourselves better cooks when we get you home."

A miserable smile slipped over the exhausted face of Sir Edmund as he gazed with dull eyes at his host. A man of thirty with fine-boned features and long-lashed eyes like a girl's, he was not hungry. Owain Glyndwr was cheerful with him to no end. His comrade Thomas Clanvow was in even worse case, sitting dead-eyed as a cadaver over his untouched platter. The candles that burned along the board smoked without giving much light, and the tent was filled with weird shadows; the embers in the brazier muttered and glowed and wisps of acrid smoke stung the eyes.

For this reason Eden was glad, because of the scant room within, to eat outside. Howel Vaughan kept him company. They sat crosslegged like cobblers on the ground, chewing their meat and sharing a two-eared dish filled to the brim with bread and beer.

The evening shadows deepened, and dark feathery clouds hung in the sky. In the tent behind them Griffith Llwyd, the bard of the haunted mound, was playing the harp with his usual effortless mastery. There was dancing and singing along the narrow, thatched, flame-bright lanes of Pilleth, and scores of torches flickered along the meadows and black wooded slopes beyond.

"Can they still be gathering up the wounded yonder?" Eden said.

A deathlike chill pinched the nape of his neck.

"I wonder where Robyn is."

It was an arrow that had struck the boy while he was running on an errand for one of the monks. It had severed a large tendon in his right leg. He had fallen down at the edge of a small glade where several corpses had been tumbled out of the way. When he tried to get up, he found to his horror that he could not. Blood was flowing down his leg. Overcome with pain and trembling helplessly, he fell flat on his back, and the world went whirling and flying about him.

Hours must have gone by—he was scarcely aware of their passage. So long as he did not move, the pain was not too bad, but he felt light-headed and very weak. They had built a big bonfire about a quarter of a mile away from where he was lying, and all sorts of high jinks were going on there, much as on one of the festive ghost nights. A fiddler was striking up a merry tune, shadows were swaying, and the lighted circle was thronged with wine-red forms like hobgoblins, waving their arms and screeching. Once Robyn thought he saw the Prophet flitting about, black and batlike in the reddish glare; and another time, in a sudden blazing up of the flame, the form of a woman emerged, her hair whirling loose about her shoulders, her strong lithe body writhing like a serpent's, dancing to the accompaniment of shouts and clapping hands.

Perhaps what he saw was not real, perhaps it was no more than a dream that would break at waking, and fade away into the light and hubbub of the coming day. But no—he stirred; he felt the pain in his leg, his head swam, his heart throbbed.

It was growing darker and darker. Things moved about him in the gloom; there were strange and sinister shiftings of shadow. A thin high scream came from afar—it was like one of those strange lonely cries one hears sometimes at dead of night. What is happening out there, Robyn wondered?

Fright gripped his stomach and wild thoughts troubled his brain. Old Sibli came before him—she of all people—whispering to him of Death: "He is thin and long, lad, with arms to his knees and pale hands with hooks on the fingernails and head a-drop. He comes in quiet as if walking on feathers, but he strikes as with a leaden fist."

An icy breath fluttered in his cheeks as he began to say his pater— every saint he could think of, he prayed to him. A horned and speckled moon peered down on him through a ragged hole in the clouds like the eye of a spectre. The faces of the dead men near him gleamed with a bluish light. The skull of one of them had been split in two, another's mouth was gaping open, wrenched in a frozen grimace; yet another lay with his teeth bared in his upturned face as though smiling. Robyn turned his eyes away. The streaming flame of a torch was coming towards him—there was the sound of footfalls. Someone gave a whistle, gay and frightful.

Grating his teeth with the pain, he pushed himself through the grass and rolled behind a bush. He felt hot and yet he could not stop trembling. He dug his fingers into the turf and watched a figure approach and stop not ten paces away from where he lay. It was a woman. He could see her well in the light of the torch she was holding. She seemed to be staring right at him through the interlacings of the twigs and leaves. Never he thought would he forget that face. Big nostrilled, with broad high cheekbones, a wheat-gold skin and brilliant black eyes, it was an ugly face—the face of a she-demon-and yet in its own way it was strangely beautiful.

"Saranhon, Saranhon," a voice called. "This way."

There were other torches—others were running, laughing—women holding murderous skean knives, more than a foot long. The she-demon sped after them. Their cries grew fainter and fainter,

Sometime later he saw the white glimmer of a cassock not far away, the yellow flicker of a lanthorn. He cried out. A Cistercian bent over him, eyes gleaming moistly.

"Here, Brother Marco, I think I have found him," he exclaimed, "the lad they are looking for. Robyn of Mona, are you?"

The boy gave a shuddering sob.

"There, there," said the monk, "all is well now."

Two men came hurrying up with a litter. They laid Robyn upon it and bore him away to a barn which stood a mile away at the edge of a heath. Groaning men lay all about, while the Abbot of Strata Florida and other monks tended to their hurts by torchlight.

They gave Robyn a sleepy drink—poppy or mandragora.

"Father Abbot," he heard someone say, "our people are drinking too much. They are turning into devils."

"It is not unknown to me."

"It is a very Dance of Machabray that is going on out there. . . ."

"*Procedamus in nomine Domini. . . .*"

Their voices began to fade away.

When he next awoke, a pallid misty light was stealing in through the gaps in the thatch, and Eden was sitting beside him in the hay, chewing on a grass-stalk. A surge of gladness filled the boy's heart to see that beloved and familiar face, bruised and scraped raw in places, yet tenderly smiling.

"Robyn, my brave little fosterling," Eden said. "You are alive. Thank God!"

Trembling with the effort, the boy tried to rise, but could not. The pain made him gasp. Sweat prickled in the pits of his arms and hands. He was frightened.

He heard himself ask in a shaking voice:

"Will I be a cripple now? Will I ever walk again?"

"The Lord's will be done, my son," said a monk in passing.

"Begone, shaveling!" Eden barked after him angrily. "The Lord's will, my foot! Pay no heed to him, Robyn. That is how such crabs justify their existence, by scaring folk. Of course, you will walk again. And if you are lame, what of it? So is your Chieftain lame, remember. And where is there another the like of that one?"

Later that morning the wounded boy was taken back to Caer Gai.

7
CAER GAI (1402 - 1403)

1

Robyn had small memory of the way, only that now and again when he was not dozing or hurting, he was dimly aware of voices singing or laughing nearby, and of the sounds of wheels knocking along the stones of the road, and of the scents of newmown hay and wild mint drying in the sun.

Once at the castle he was borne to that same chamber which he had formerly shared with Eden and Howel Vaughan. Now his companion was Maredudd, the Lord Owain's youngest son. A gentle good-natured youth, he had Robyn's bed carried over to the window, so that he might look out upon the meadowland and mountains and watch the coming and goings about the fortress. It was kindly done in him no doubt, but Robyn was scarcely in a condition to profit by it. At first the world was nothing to the sick boy but an aching limb of flesh. His injured leg throbbed constantly—never, he thought, was there such hurting.

Each day an old woman came to bathe him, dress his wound and rub his body with sweet oils. Had he not been so ill she might well have frightened him, so ugly as she was. Whiskers were on her like the fluff on a thistle. But her hands were deft and healing and her voice was kind.

"A pity she is not young and biddable, is it not, Robyn?" joked Mared.

Then gradually he began to get better, and although at the outset he came close to tumbling on his face, he even tried to rise and move about the room, hobbling about as best he could on one leg to begin with, as subsequently with the help of others and with crutches. Days became weeks. By August he was allowed to take the sun with the maids of Caer Gai on the meadows between the castle and the lake.

Those were hot still days. The faintest of haze veils, like the hoar frost that clings to the manes of horses on winter mornings, hovered over the hills and distant crags. Ducks and other waterfowl paddled and fussed in the bullrushes and reedbeds along the shores of the lake. Grasshoppers and gnats filled the noontide still with their churring music. And nearby could be heard the faint tinkling of goatbells, and the cooing of wood pigeons, and now and again the voices of soldiers as they called to one another from the platforms.

The girls wore bright headcloths and aprons. They sewed handkerchiefs, played ball and knucklebones and giggled a great deal. Robyn did not much care for their chat, which struck him as mindless and silly. He missed Mererid.

Of only two did he make an exception. One of these was Elin of Brynhodla. Brown-haired, with big laughing brown eyes, she had apple-red cheeks and a gay and confiding heart. The other was Owain Glyndwr's daughter Catrin, a girl of sixteen with straight silky barley-light hair. Her face was rather sad and pensive in repose, but it lighted up when she smiled like a woodland pool touched by the sun.

One afternoon Elin of Brynhodla said to Robyn:

"Let us ask one of the fishermen to take us out on the lake."

The boy saw no reason not to—the air was warm, heavy and still, and the water was placid. Besides, he was curious to see if in truth a town did lie in its depths, as it was so often rumored.

They had barely reached the heart of the water, however, when their boatman cried: "Look at that!" Following his gaze, they saw a cock of moorland hay which had been left out high on the mountainside being sucked up and whisked away, far, far off across the crags.

"A storm is brewing," the boatman said. "We had best turn back."

He was not mistaken. Within moments a bleak gray haze began to spread across the sky and the water, stirred by the rising wind, lapped noisily against the sides of the boat. Thunder was growling in the mountains and the underbrush was alive with waterfowl. Ducks were quacking, wild geese crying, and as the boat grounded amid the shallows, a heron rose with flapping wings out of the wind-threshed reeds, its long thin legs trailing behind it.

An hour later the courtyard of the castle was a moat of yellow mud, and the lake and mountains were lost in rain. The weather remained bad after that for weeks on end—raw savage days, ragged wailing skies, trees thrashing and making roar. Sometimes as Robyn lay awake in his bed at night listening, it seemed to him that the castle with its human cargo must be whirling away from earth, into the black and howling immensity of chaos.

And in the midst of this, like a flock of storm birds, Owain Glyndwr's brother-in-law Robert Puleston, rode in from the Mortimer estates in Powys with a band of horsemen.

"What weather, eh?" he said to the Lady Margaret and his wife Lowri, Glyndwr's sister. "Do you know that the common folk hold our leader responsible for it?"

The Lady gave a laugh in which was little gaiety.

"And do they bless him for it?"

"Dear Margaret, did you not hear what happened to the King of England then? Invading our land? His camp was washed away in the tempest—goods, mules and soldiers. Henry's tent fell on him while he slept. It might have proved his death-sentence, if he had not been wearing his armor."

"Going to bed in his armor?" Lowri Puleston exclaimed. "Who would be King of England truly?"

In Robert Puleston's party was Owain Glyndwr's secretary, Master Howel Deget.

Robyn had first seen him in April, when he had arrived at Caer Gai with his foster father and Howel Vaughan. The story was that the young scholar had been expelled from Oxford with his fellow Welsh students in the year of the rising. What had seemed undoubted to Robyn at the time was that the women had been much taken up with him, with the mellow sweetness of his voice, his handsome presence and his learning. He beguiled the ladies with the rudiments of dialectic—if a shield is white on one side and black on the other, what color is it?—and the structure of a syllogism. Or he would discourse them on historical themes—the fall of Troy, Charlemagne and his paladins, and goddesses of antiquity.

"That is unfair," Howel Vaughan objected in tones of humorous exasperation. "He is teaching the lasses things I don't know myself."

Now the young scholar could have been another man. He kept aloof from the women. His bearing was altogether colder and sterner.

At the same time a change came over Glyndwr's daughter Catrin. She moved about as though in a daze. She seemed helpless, incompetent, and always on the point of breaking into tears. Sometimes when Robyn spoke to her she looked through him as though he did not exist. Have I offended her in some way, he wondered?

So matters stood when Michaelmas arrived. Preparations were under way for the feast when suddenly Lowri Puleston was brought to bed with child. At once the castle was set by its ears. In the midst of the noise and confusion Elin of Brynhodla sidled up to Robyn in the great hall.

"Will you do me a favor?" she asked.

"What is it?"

"Will you tell Master Howel Deget that Catrin wishes to see him?" she breathed. "Tell him it is a matter of life and death."

Robyn stared at her in surprise and alarm.

"What do you mean?"

"O, mean, mean!" Elin exclaimed, stamping her foot with impatience. "Why must you ask such questions? Did they never teach you anything in Mona? Please, Robyn."

Reluctantly he agreed to do so and sought out Master Howel. He met him coming from the chapel. The young scholar was walking close to the wall in the manner of the monks, with his hands tucked up inside the wide sleeves of his black gown, and he was staring down at the ground so fixedly that when he first looked up to see who was addressing him, it was as if the wave-like patterns of the ancient flagstones were still drifting before his eyes. Upon hearing Robyn's message, he flushed.

"No," he said bluntly. "It is not possible."

"It is a matter of life and death, Master Howel," Robyn told him.

The other raised his brows.

"So bad as that even?" he said, and a faint smile flickered over his lips. "Who said so?"

"Elin of Brynhodla."

"Did she ? And what would a highborn maid of her few and innocent years know about matters of life and death?" he asked bitterly.

"Catrin is not herself these days," Robyn told him. "There is some sad weight upon her spirit."

The somber young scholar sighed: "God bless you, lad, I know that," he admitted then. "I too am not myself these days. Forgive me my sharp words. Of course I shall see the maid Catrin, if that is her wish. But where? The hall is crowded and the weather unfit. The stables, perhaps."

"The horseboys and the oxendriver have their beds in there," said Robyn.

"I shall have to arrange for them to leave their quarters for the nonce then. Mary and Joseph, what a coil!" He shook his head and gave a wry laugh. "You and that wise little woman, Elin of Brynhodla, had best attend us," he told the boy at that. "We may need your witness."

"When shall we meet?"

"After Vespers."

Robyn returned with the message to Elin of Brynhodla, who awaited him in the hall. The men who were seated with Robert Puleston around the aletub had fallen quiet now, the boy noticed, and in the fire-dagged shadows sweet with wisps of incense, the heads of housefolk, whispering their litanies and paternosters, rose and fell.

"What has happened?" Robyn asked in alarm. "Is the lady dead?"

"Good heavens, no! But it it is a difficult labor. It may well go on all night. Let us hope so."

"Why do you say that?" Robyn asked her, thinking at once and with fright of Annes.

"It will keep folk busy, of course. They will have no thought of us."

At the appointed hour the two girls and Robyn crept away to the stables. They sat down at the head of the feeding walk among drifts of straw and bracken, and watched the rain pattering in the black pools beyond the open doorway. Chickens were roosting on the beams overhead, and the gloom, which was dimly lit by a single lantern, was full of their fussings, and the heavy breath of horses and cattle.

They had been waiting no more than a few moments when the tall figure of Master Howel, mantled in black, appeared in the doorway and called Catrin's name. She ran towards him weeping and flung herself into his arms. He held her close, comforting her, then drew her down beside him in the straw. Robyn could not make out what was said, but from the tone of their voices it seemed to him that the man was reasoning and the girl was pleading. Robyn was mystified.

"I did not know that they were such dear friends," he whispered to Elin.

"Did you not?"

"How should I?"

"When Master Howel was driven out of Oxford—he led the riots of the Welsh students there, you know—Owain Glyndwr gave him shelter. The Pendragon took him to his heart like one of the family. He was Catrin's teacher. O, but it's the old story," she murmured. "They are in love, can't you see, boy? And it cannot be, that is the pity of it."

Robyn turned his attention back to the two lovers, who were sitting over against one another now, their heads almost touching, holding hands. The curve of the young man's head and the coil of his shoulders were as eloquent as a prayer. Without fully understanding what was going on, Robyn felt a sadness beyond words.

Afterwards, indeed, he was never to regret the part he played in that clandestine meeting, although the consequences to himself were unpleasant enough. A boy baby was born in the castle in the course of the night, and although to Robyn's mind it looked a thing fit but to dance on the head of a thistle, father and mother seemed to be well pleased. Jollity prevailed everywhere. And yet, at the morrow mass the Lady Margaret's face was like a thundercloud.

"Be so good as to attend me in my closet, both of you," she told Robyn and Elin as they were leaving the chapel.

The two stopped in their tracks and looked after the Lady in horror as she walked with a quick and angry step down the passageway. There was the sound of a door slamming . The silence rang out around them. To the two miscreants it was like a dungeon door closing on the last night of the doomed.

"She knows," Elin breathed at last. "Who could have told her?"

"The steward had it from one of the horseboys, perhaps. What does it matter? She knows."

And the Lady scored them off thoroughly without question. Robyn could not remember when he had been the object of such a tirade. What neither he nor Elin of Brynhodla knew then, what few in the fortress knew for the matter of that, was that Robert Puleston had come to Caer Gai to fetch Catrin to her father in Powysland. It was designed to marry her to Sir Edmund Mortimer before the year was out.

The Lady was oppressed by gloomy feelings. Pieces in a game, that is all we are, she thought, as she fell silent at last and stared at the two before her, the weeping girl and the poor crippled lad with his dark morose snub-nosed face. What am I about venting my bad humor on this pair of children? Howel Deget, now he is turned of twenty, he is privy to Glyndwr's counsels—sure, he should have had more sense and discretion.

She asked the two delinquents more gently: "Answer me truthfully, were you present throughout the entire interview?"

"Yes, my lady," Elin sniffed, "and if I may venture to say so the behavior of your daughter and Master Howel could have been that of a monk and a nun passing the time of day."

"And I venture to question that, child," said the Lady with a sad and spectral smile "I rely on you not to let a word of this pass beyond these walls."

That night there was a banquet in the castle. The hall was seething with people like herrings in a creel. Robyn sat down with his platter among the children in the rushes at the lower gable end. He could see Master Howel Deget nowhere, but Catrin was seated beside her uncle Robert Puleston on the dais beneath the banners. How far away she seemed all of a sudden, Robyn thought, and oddly unreal somehow—a manon painted in a church window.

While he picked away at his food, a small girl child sat down beside him and watched him eat, following the movements of his spoon with solemn curious eyes. Robyn moved his ears up and down at that and her face broke into a smile, a merry thing to see.

"What is your name?" she asked.

"I am Robyn of Mona."

"Do you have a grandfather?" she wanted to know then.

"He is in Heaven," he replied, "among the saints."

"I have a grandfather," she went on. "He is Brochwel of the Spears. He is very old."

She looked before her dreamily, softly singing as she sat there some phrases of an indefinite lay known only to herself, and rocking back and forth on her heels. "I am not going to grow old," she said. "I shall grow up but I shall never grow old." And then she showed Robyn the faded remains of some little wood-anemones that she kept in her purse. "They grow like stars in the forest," she informed him gravely, "and there are little rows of silver birch there too. If you go there at night, Robyn of Mona, they look like white ladies. Fairies come there too in the moonlight. My nurse has seen them. But you must be careful. Do not go near them or they will bear you away. . . ."

Robyn listened to her with a smile. He eased himself down in the rushes with his arm as a pillow. The pretty lilt of her nonsense flowed about him and slowly warmed him out of his sadness.

Towards the beginning of November the weather cleared and all the great folk at the castle moved southward—a gay procession of horsemen, whirlicotes, painted wains and sumpter mules. The end of it? A wedding and a most splendid one, as Robyn heard it told. In a word, before the month was out the daughter of Owain Glyndwr became Lady Mortimer.

Aye, the young Catrin with her dark sad eyes, her wistful smile and her gentle presence—the boy could scarcely bring himself to believe it when he first heard.

As for Caer Gai the whole atmosphere changed there once the merry crowd had gone. Suddenly it was as if the shadow of a devout and scholarly thought lay over the stronghold. The Abbot of Valle Crucis arrived with treasures for safe-keeping and the monks entered into possession. Their grave voices were to be heard sounding along the chill passages by day and night, moaning, praising, and imploring. Mingled with the sighing and sobbing of the wind, this chanting of theirs, albeit beautiful, had a melancholy effect on the spirit of young Robyn of Mona. He was woefully homesick and had only to close his eyes, it seemed, for there to float before him the figures of those among whom he had been bred up: of the cornhills, the yellow sands, the rushy bogs, the ploughlands shagged and shining with seaweed, and the big blowing skies of his island.

And there was Mererid, always Mererid—Mererid singing, Mererid laughing, Mererid angry, Mererid dreaming; Mererid hanging up flaxes to dry in the kitchen garden, Mererid reading sermons at the lectern, Mererid's fingers inquiring into the heart of the fleece. And the vivid, breathtaking comings and goings of her—swift and lightsome, kirtle whipping, feet sparkling, ribbons dancing, as though a being yoked to the wind.

Ah, if only he could go home! But how? Every desire has wings, the byword has it. All very well to say. So far at any rate as Robyn was concerned, matters were hardly that simple. Meanwhile, the Abbot of Valle Crucis had lost no time in discovering that the boy was a skilled penman.

"I had no idea that you could write so well, my son," he exclaimed with delight. "You can be of assistance to us."

The boy was promptly installed in the chamber that now served as book-hall, at a writing desk upon which were set inkhorn and quill. There he was to be found most days after that in company with one or two monks, copying old manuscripts which had been damaged by rain, rot or fire in the course of the rebellion.

He was there one afternoon near the Feast of Christmas when the Abbot entered and asked him: "Are you the grandson of Jenkin, the ancient lord of Welsh Maelor?"

"Yes, Father Abbot."

"Come with me."

In the hall, before a huge fire of brush and logs a man was standing over the gutted carcass of a deer—a short, sinewy figure with a barrel chest and powerfully built shoulders. Robyn noticed that although his green garments were soiled and patched, his belt and dagger were richly ornamented in silver. There was the look of a proper rogue about him. His lean weather-beaten face was covered with a straw-brown bristle of beard . His green eyes were merry and cruel.

"Is this the lad, Holy Abbot?" the man asked, studying Robyn with an intense probing gaze. "Well, by God's tooth!"

"Mind your speech."

"Craving pardon, Holy Abbot. By Beelzebub's tooth! Ha, ha!" he cried, slapping his thighs and laughing. "Do you know who I am, lad? I am your Uncle Davy."

Robyn was thunderstruck.

"The outlaw?"

"O, as to that, who is not an outlaw in Wales these days? Even our supreme chief of kindred, that bullbright thunderer Owain Glyndwr is an outlaw to hear our enemies tell it. I like to think of myself rather as a dispossessed lord."

"But I thought you were in Ireland."

"Think on. Here I am."

He spent the rest of the afternoon at Caer Gai. The uncle let the nephew talk as much as he liked, and when Robyn told him of his wounding on the hill of battle near Pilleth, he looked suitably impressed.

"So young and already a hero," he marveled.

He himself lived with his company in the lordship of the Knights Hospitallers. He had his lair in a cave in the Grey Rock Woods.

Robyn did not see his uncle again until the Shrovetide next following. It was on the same day that the Siri Mawr rode in from the castle at Dolbadarn, in the heart of the wilderness of the eagles, with the news that after protracted negotiations between the envoys of Owain Glyndwr and those of the King of England and his Council, Lord Grey had at last been set free.

"Ten thousand marks,* lads!" the Siri Mawr exclaimed.

"Give God the glory," the Abbot laughed, clapping his hands. "That

*A mark at this time was equivalent to two-thirds of a pound sterling.

will help pay for the wedding."

A few hours later David ap Jenkin arrived with some of his men. The devil's own they looked, Robyn thought, regular gallows' birds with shaggy faces and red glittering eyes. The Siri Mawr eyed their chief narrowly.

"By my soul, if it is not Outlaw Jenkin," he exclaimed at last. "It must be near ten years since the hue and cry was out after you throughout these hundreds."

"Aye, and now it is like to be out after the Great Sheriff himself. So you have lost your prize prisoner."

"And his boon comrades, Sir Richard Thelwall for one. Does that name ring a bell?"

The outlaw laughed. Afterwards he told his nephew why.

"Sir Richard's brother Thomas married a woman of the Trevors. Their son was Simon Thelwall."

"The man you killed?"

"Your father and I."

Uncle and nephew were up late that night, taking their ease at the hearth in the great hall of Caer Gai. Only one other was awake in their vicinity, and that was the outlaw's minstrel Odo, a ghost of a man in filthy sheepskins, with red-lidded eyes and a sparsely bearded white face. Outlaw Jenkin was full of reminiscences of the old days, and as he sat there at the hearthrock, leaning forward with his hands spread outwards on his knees, musing into the fire, it was easy to see him summoning up images of those people and events he was talking about—the old life in Welsh Maelor, the highblooded youths riding forth in the young of the day in all the laughing scorn of their prime, noonday wine and harpsong, running with spears at fairs, ambuscades in glen and forest—the hall of the Trevors.

"What was she like?" Robyn asked. "Angharad Trevor?"

"I did not care for her," his uncle replied. "She would not let me kiss her in a skipping game. Any she who can put such an affront on a fellow is not worth a pissabed to my mind. I warned Eden about her, but he would not listen. He was in love. Or thought he was. And to be fair, she seemed to love him too. In the beginning."

"It is a cold love that is blown out by the first gust of wind," said the minstrel in a surprisingly sweet and lilting voice.

"Aye, Odo," the outlaw agreed. "Love lay dead and cold in that hall for sure when we went there the next time. There was not a she-creature in sight, not even that old hag, Auntie Corwen. Hairy, rank old men everywhere—the chieftain, the governor of Dinas Bran castle, and *retro Sathanas*, the Bishop! Sons, foster-sons, collaterals, mastiffs. And that hag's abortion Simon. By the Lord, but we had a merry brawl there that night. A scutcheon I threw missed the Bishop by inches."

"You stole Simon Thelwall's horse, too, I heard."

"Why not? It was too fine for the likes of him. The braying jackass! He should never have pursued us. What folly! Eden was knocked senseless in that pretty encounter, you must have heard of it. Aye, his skull was laid open. No great a thing in truth—the wound did not penetrate the brain. Ho, ho, but the Chieftain made a right hullabaloo about it, mind you. A blood fine was levied on the heads of the Trevors with the understanding that Tudor's sons not seek revenge. Of course, Rhys Ddu was out of the country then. So he could not swear."

Robyn stared at the outlaw dumbly.

"Remember, there was also the *sarhad*,* nephew."

"The *sarhad*?"

"The slander. It was what started the whole brawl. Simon Thelwall called Rhys Ddu's wife a wanton. An incestuous slut. You can see it now, can you not, Robyn? That barren noddle was too noisy to live. Ah, Eva, now there's a woman for you. That haughty bitch Angharad is a drab beside her, eh, Odo?"

"O, pulchritudinous epiphany!" the minstrel chanted. "O, divinity."

"Are you saying that you were in Rhys Ddu's fee then, uncle?" Robyn ventured.

"I am saying no more than this. I have been in fee to dragons."

He paused and sent Robyn a sly, green-glinting look.

"Who do you think trapped the Hewer, the great boar that trapped Lord Grey?"

Robyn sat wide-eyed, tossed between wonder and horror. And his uncle's bristling straw-brown beard was split in two by a roguish grin.

2

During that spring Prince Henry, whose headquarters were now at Chester, led an army across the border into North Wales. In the course

---

*sarhad: insult, also the fine for the insult.

of this raid villages were put to the torch, the Abbey of Valle Crucis sacked, Glyndwr's halls at Sycharth and the Glens of Dee burned to the ground, and all who were found in residence there slain, including that doughty warrior and prince of horsethieves, the former Keeper and Master Forester of Chirkeland.

Two women grieved: the Keeper's widow, Angharad Trevor, in a hall that was strewn with flowers of rosemary and rue, and Owain Glyndwr's wife at the ancestral seat of the Mortimers at Maelienydd, in a Welsh valley bearded with silver streams. The Lady Margaret had lost her heart's home—God knows so much of her life had gone into those two great halls—and at first she was inconsolably bitter.

"And where are we going to live now?" she asked her husband with some asperity.

Glyndwr gazed upon her with calm forbearance.

"Can this truly be my Margaret?" he mused. "Blood, flesh and bone of that wise and sagacious nobleman, the lord justice Hanmer of Hanmer? And is this the same lady who was ever reminding her tender charges of the frail fabric of earthly splendor? *Sic transit gloria mundi*, aye, my little ones, 'tis the way of the world, indeed. Come, my dear," he added reassuringly, "don't you know that like the hares and foxes we have a hundred earths? We have bedchambers all over this land."

What am I supposed to make of that, Margaret Hanmer wondered? Does he imagine a home amidst rocks and scrub would delight me? Men! What do they expect of us? That we be content to bake, stitch, rock the cradle and sing stanzas on the harp, while they draw these rings of everlasting pain and worry about our lives?

Already she felt an estrangement from him. If she had been told that, as in the old folk tale, the King of the Underworld had changed places with his twin in looks, her own husband, she would not have found it too hard to believe, so much more remote and well-nigh mysterious this man seemed than the one she had known formerly. He moved with a weightier stride, his voice rang a deeper, more resonant bell.

"And where is your father off to now?" she asked her youngest son Maredudd.

"There are some people out there."

"When are there not, my dear?"

Eden who was standing nearby with Howel Vaughan could not forbear smiling.

"Good luck to her," he said, "she's a noble old goose."

He meant her no disrespect in saying so. Sure, there was nothing wrong in a woman resembling a goose, particularly if the fowl was a proud and noble brood-mother as the Lady so manifestly was.

"Living with Himself can't be all honey and oil, I'll grant you," Howel Vaughan observed.

On Glyndwr's side, Eden often had the feeling that his light-hearted manner of scoring off his lady reflected his despair at ever producing an effect upon her by taking a more serious and logical line. Certain it was that he made a greater impression on the people than on his wife.

It was getting on towards nightfall then. The sun had gone down, leaving a drift of red streaks in the sky to the west. A crowd was thronged about the gates. Rumors of the English raid on Sycharth and the Valley of the Cross had sown alarm and doubt in men's minds. Glyndwr moved among them with assurance, patting the heads of the children and jesting with this one and that in passing. Once, looking about him at hazard, his eye fell on a thin, silent youth, in a coarse flannel tunic, with big, shining, earnest eyes. He asked him his name and where he came from, but the boy was so tongue-tied, he could do nothing but stand and stare. At this one of his companions spoke up:

"He is Deio, the son of Jockyn the sievemaker, Lord, and his home is Carmarthen."

"Ah, so that's it. I understand now," Glyndwr said with a mischievous lift of his brows. "Carmarthen to be sure. Merlin's township. If I am not mistaken, you had a royal visit there last year, did you not? The so-called King of England was there—in a dreadful mood, it seems. He passed a law, I'm told, prohibiting the Welsh of Carmarthen from speaking Welsh, for some reason or other. He could not stand the competition belike. Such a noisy, gobble-jawed, bloody-headed fellow as he is, eh? A regular King Furioso."

His listeners grinned delightedly.

"But it seems that you are laboring under the delusion that this cruel law is still in force, lad," Glyndwr continued humorously. "You have not heard the latest tidings, it seems. King Furioso has had a change of heart. Aye, he has now in the infinitude of his mercy and grace, been pleased to let the word go out: 'Very well. Swear that you will behave yourselves, no more naughty pranks, cap to the sheriff, make low legs to the constable, lick our spittle, and we shall allow you to speak your crooked

Greek and not crop your tongues for trespassing upon the air we breathe.' So you see, Deio, you have the royal permission to speak to Glendowrdy in your native language."

"The power of Holy Cross be with you, Lord," the youth said shyly and simply.

"Good, Deio," said Glyndwr. "May you be happy."

The Welsh leader moved on towards a boulder on a rise of ground. There he stood for a few moments in silence and swept his eyes over the crowd that bristled like a thicket along the meadowland before him. The red flames of torches shone upon glittering eyes and teeth and spearheads, and there was a whisper of tense, hushed and expectant voices.

And then he spoke. In a big and ringing voice he began by telling the people that like them his heart grieved for the Keeper and those who had been slain. He was sad that his own halls had been burned and that the great abbey in the Valley of the Cross had been sacked. But he mocked those who at that hour were triumphing.

"What are they saying, think you? 'See how we have broken the back of the wicked Glendowrdy. We have killed his cubs and destroyed his lair. Where will that mangy old lion go now?'"

He snapped his fingers in the air and the crowd roared.

"Away," he scoffed, "this is ever the way with men of warlike temper, you know. They murder the tiniest whisper of doubt within their hearts with the imagination that the only source of power lies in force of arms and strong walls. How wrong they are! Consider the fate of the City of the Legions. Here was once the greatest city in Britain. The Romans built it. Arthur ruled there. Ambrosius, St Garmon, the famous doctor Morgan Tud and many other wise and learned men dwelt within its walls. The martyrs Julius and Aaron were buried therein. Here it was that the Archbishop Dubricius ceded his honors to St David, our patron saint, all praise be to his name! Its temples, schools, theaters and palaces were among the wonders of our Isles. And if Caerleon was great, the cities of Babylon and Caerdroia, so it is told us, were even greater. But where now is the mighty City of the Legions and where is Troytown and where is magnificent Babylon? They are dust and rubble, my countrymen. For, of course, it is folly to believe that strength has its issue only in piles of sticks, stones and mortar. No, the true strength is here," he said, touching his breast, mouth and forehead in turn, "and here and here. It is in the hands of the potter at his wheel, the ploughman at the plough, the physician on his errands, the harper at the harp. It is in the eye of the painter of images, in the mouth of the poet, in the feet of the pilgrim, in the resolve of the hero, in the loyalty of the patriot, in the faith of the true believer, in the heart of the mother, in the mind of the scholar. What I talk about has nothing to do with death. It does not stand still like castles and monuments. It does not grow old and rot and turn to dust. It is a living immortal spirit, restless and migratory as are the winds—ever questing, ever magical, ever young. Wherever we wander and draw breath we bear it with us—aye, carry within us our fortress, our manor, our township, our home. Indestructible, imperishable—here, indeed, my children, is the strong place!"

"You tell them, Lord!" an old man to the fore shouted. "Tell them!"

"Our cause is of Heaven and must prevail, do you believe me?"

"We believe you!" came the cry.

"If we hold together, they cannot withstand us. The castles will fall to us one by one, for what are they but stones and mortar? And what are we, my children, what are we? We are a moving destiny under these stars."

The people stood as though benumbed. The silence was deep. And then, as though a mysterious vibrant wave were passing through the air about them, a gasp, a whispering, rose as from one great throat, crying one name over and over again, and it was as if the seas had murmured it, and the winds had picked it up, and the trees of the forest were echoing it, and the waters of the mountains were singing it, and the strings of a thousand sleeping harps had borne it back upon the thrill and ecstasy of their awakening.

"Glyndwr!—Glyndwr!—Glyndwr!"

Suddenly, astoundingly, there was nothing else to be heard but that name.

Eden looked across at him where he stood, before the boulder on the rise of ground, a motionless figure, ringed by torches, quietly standing with his arms outstretched before him. He looked transfigured. And why this should be Eden could not tell, but as he watched the Pendragon standing thus, a dark unmoving figure between earth and sky, it was to him at that moment, as if like an eagle, their leader searched the land as one whose rightful place lay above it, above the smoke of the fires, that black seething meadowland, the excited cheering crowd, and the common measure of the hour.

His heart was marvelously uplifted. It beat joyously for minutes on end, only to sink back sighing at last, like a weary bird into the refuge of its own feathers.

Ah, thought Eden, these are words and they are so fine, but what lies beyond this night? I am clay. From the first to last of the sun I am of this earth. Brute force can bruise me. It can crush my little life and grind my bones into meal for the blood crows and wild dogs. O, stay away from me a while longer, brute force. Give me grace to breathe out in joy for some few years more—I am Eden and this is the world and I am in it and I am alive.

With ten thousand insurgent spears and longbows at their backs, the course of events bore Glyndwr and his captains irresistibly through the last of the springtide and into the summer. By July the towns of Newcastle Emlyn and Carmarthen had fallen and the great fortress of Dryslwyn near the river Towy was yielded up without a fight by its Welsh constable, who fell on his knees and kissed Glyndwr's swordhilt directly. A force of men from France and Brittany in support of Glyndwr had laid siege to the town and castle of Kidwelly, and farther north, the garrisons of Harlech, Aberystwyth and Caernarvon were in desperate plight.

Such were some of the happenings, which as told and retold and embellished around fires in chieftain's hall and crofter's hut, led in that same month to the popular recognition of Owain Glyndwr's title as Prince of Wales. This happy event was duly celebrated in the Vale of the Towy with a festival. The towers and ramparts of the castle which dominated the surrounding countryside were bright with a whirling rout of flags and pennons. Chieftains rode in from far and wide with their kinsmen and warbands to do homage, to feast on wild boar, venison and potbaked oxen, and to join in or watch an unforgettable game involving a large beechen ball boiled in tallow to make it slippery.

At the stroke of noon, when the game began, there must have been a thousand participants arrayed on either side of a river meadow, most on foot, but many horsed and bearing long clubs. By sunset, Eden would have gone bail that he had not seen such an amount of rainbow-hued flesh and so many ungently trimmed long-locked heroes in his life. Where folk were not laughing they were groaning, and everywhere women and physicians were busy bandaging joints, and anointing bruises with butter, betony and white wine.

That evening the water-meadows were bathed in a fiery mist through which throngs of revelers moved, singing and dancing. Among them emerged a striking figure, tall, sallow, hooknosed and extraordinarily thin, in a pigwife's bonnet and a shabby black gown turned green with age that reached down to his heels. When Glyndwr learned of his arrival he had him ushered into the castle hall.

"Chieftains," he announced to his company, "may I present to you Hopcyn ap Tomas, the Wizard of Gower Above the Wood. This remarkable man claims to have read the Stones of Gwithon Ganhebon upon which are set down all the arts and sciences in the world."

"Who would read them?" shouted Black Rhys of Ceredigion, one of his eyes half-closed in sooty blackness, the other blinking bloodshot through the tears, "Only show me where they are and I will give you a plate of gold as large as your face."

Into the fire that blazed on the long hearth the wizard threw a powder that filled the great hall of the castle with a greenish light and a penetrating odor. Grotesque shadows leapt up the walls and tongues of flame licked the hearthrock, illuminating the bones and deepening the pits in the wizard's cadaverous face as he sat down with his legs crossed and stared into the heart of the burning logs. After he had sat thus for several moments he began to rock back and forth and chant:

"Hist! Hist!" he cried in a voice hoarse with the smoke of fire and reverie. "Listen, listen, do you hear? Hwa, hwa, gis, gis, the great hunt for souls is on. The Dark King is galloping out there on the back of his blackberry-black steed Du March Moro, and his bugler is bugling to split the wind, and his black lead hound Dormarth is baying to freeze the blood at the head of the pack. Such wild sport, such revelry out there! Eastward, eastward, they are riding! Witches cackling and cats screeching and broomsticks travelling and clouds flying and the bones dancing. And there is woe in the twice-six houses of the stars. The helmet of Mars is casting a shadow. The moon is raining blood. I foresee a terrible carnage."

"Ochan," someone wailed, "not another game with the beechen ball."

A gale of mirth swept through the hall. Only Glyndwr sat as before, brows knit, a faint smile playing over his lips like the shadow of a riddling thought. The Wizard of Gower Above the Wood raised his head and cast the company a glance that was at once cold, contemptuous and sad.

"Can you see the He-Goat of the Castle of Venus?" someone demanded.

"I can see him," said Tango's brother Rosier, fixing a hard, unwinking gaze on Howel Vaughan.

"Help!" sobbed Black Rhys. "The knaves have cursed my eyes with blindness."

"I crave pardon for these tipplers, Hopcyn ap Tomas," said Glyndwr, shaking his head in amiable and courteous disapproval. "You and I know that one day their merriest frolic will fill the hearts of men with but the most pitiful solemnity. Proceed."

"The black banners of Death are riding towards our Marches at this hour, my Prince," the Wizard told him. "Hold aloof!"

"Be of good heart," Glyndwr replied. "Death will hunt us out in his own good season. Who would hasten towards such a dark encounter?"

Less than a week later the Welsh crossed the river Towy and rode towards the castle of Dynevor. Early that morning, under cover of darkness, the constable Jenkin Havard and his men had sneaked out and away to the township of Brecon, leaving the castle to the wheeling bats, the hooting owls and Glyndwr. The silver round of the moon was bright in the sky and the valley a dreamy lakeland as the men crossed the tilting meadow towards the hillside where the castle stood—Dynevor, the old seat of the Kings of Dyved.

Here it was that Gwenllian, the daughter of the great Lord Rhys had been born and bred up. When she had been sixteen the princess had sat in this meadow, watching men from all over Wales try their skill and strength in the Whitsuntide games. Among them had been a young captain of troops from the North. On his shield he had borne the device of three lopped-off Englishmen's heads, in token of the three knights he had slain in battle against Earl Ranulf of Chester.

Two hundred years ago that pair whom their descendant had known only from the stone effigies carved on their tombs at the Abbey of Llanvaes on the Isle of Mona had walked these paths, laughed and loved in these woods. Their eyes had looked upon these towers, that river, those hills. And yet Eden would have gone on his oath that their eyes had never seen what his eyes saw there that night.

All at once everything about the company began to darken as if clouds were gathering. From the castle slope that was high in fern and foxgloves, Eden looked back across the hushed meadow that was graven with a black unmoving frieze of figures. Above the Black Mountains the moon showed a dusky red, as though a sooty veil of smoke hung over the fiery ball of the setting sun. Men murmured in awe and fear and crossed themselves. It grew darker and darker as they continued on their way up the hillside towards the castle. At last there was no more to be seen of the moon than a dim disk which glimmered in the heavens with a light as faint and uncertain as that of the false dawn.

"The earth is casting a shadow," Glyndwr said.

An earth grown swollen, perhaps, from drinking the blood of her slain sons.

The Battle of Shrewsbury* had happened. It had happened that very day and they did not know it. Never must King Henry have moved with such dispatch as he did then to crush his rebel barons and the pride of the Percies. By evening the fields outside the town were a huge slaughterhouse of dead and spoiling human meat. In this horrific shambles fell John Massey, the sometime Constable of Conway. And that night under the blood-dimmed moon, the hastily buried corpse of Hotspur was dug up and brought to the red sandstone castle of Roger de Montgomery on its bluff. There the King sat at the bedside of the wounded Prince, his son and heir, whose cheek had been rent by a rebel arrow. Terrible in his fury, the royal father ordered the body of Hotspur to be cut into quarters and hung on posts in the chief towns of the Welsh Marches, there to stand in token and warning until the crows had picked them clean.

A few days later with the Welsh force at Pengelly castle, Sir Edmund Mortimer rode in with his wife to visit Owain Glyndwr. He was a melancholy man, Eden thought—more the courtier than the warrior, with a fine-boned face, long beringed hands, and a graceful, almost feminine manner. Catrin, the young girl they had given him for wife, appeared to charm him—he held on to her hand as though afraid she would fly away—but Eden saw that already she seemed almost as sad as he.

*The Battle of Shrewsbury—See Note 5

Sir Edmund was grief-stricken over his brother-in-law's death. The two had been close friends. In fact it had been the King's reluctance to pay Mortimer's ransom that had finally driven not only Sir Edmund to embrace Glyndwr's cause, but had also precipitated the terrible scene in which Henry of Lancaster had struck Hotspur in the face and called him 'Traitor', thus driving him at last into open rebellion.

Poor irascible knight, thought Eden, it was not for courage and resolution that he had lost.

He remembered the last time he had seen him. It had been early in the spring, at Dinas Bran castle, hooked high and watchful as an eagle to its eyrie between the cloud bastions and the gorges of the Dee. It had been vespers and the far-off sound of bells had drifted up to them from the Valley of the Cross. They had walked up and down the platforms for the better part of an hour, talking of bygone days and worthies and of Owain Glyndwr. Hotspur was baffled by him.

"He is a man of many ways of being," Eden said.

"Many ways, aye," the other said, smiling joylessly.

He went on to say: "That is what I liked about your brother, the Chieftain. A stubborn-headed, argumentative man, for sure, but at least I knew where I stood with him. By the way, let me warn you about your cousin, the Governor of Caernarvon. He hates you and he is a fool. Such men are dangerous. He will do you great harm if he can."

"Yes, I know," Eden said. "And the hatred has risen from such a trifling issue, that is what is so absurd. The matter of a fostering."

"Only that?"

The knight paused, his eyes narrowed with reminiscence.

"Was there not also some trouble to do with a daughter?"

Eden stared at him.

Eva, he thought suddenly. As always. As in the beginning.

Towards the end of August Eden returned to Caer Gai. One morning Robyn awoke and hobbled into the hall and his foster father was there. Laughingly, Eden stood to greet him.

"Robyn!"

He embraced the boy, rumpled his hair affectionately and holding him away at arm's length, appraised him with an approving grin.

"How is it with you, bogbean?"

"As you see, I can get around now."

"Praise be."

Later when Robyn told his foster father about his encounter with his uncle, the outlaw, Eden was marvelously diverted.

"So the old Davy is back then? Well, well, what a surprise! I thought we'd never riddle him home from his Irish roost. Upon my soul, life's strange. How did he look? The last time I saw him he was fleeing the country in guise of an old pilgrim woman with a blackthorn stick. Goodnight, I'll wager the cock-and-bull stories came thick, eh, Robyn? Enough to choke the tongue of an honest man."

"He had only one story for the telling," Robyn said, "but that one kept him going well on into the night."

"Yes," Eden smiled, "I think I know that story."

On the following day they returned home to Mona. The corn harvest was under way on the island when they arrived. Fifteen stalwarts were at the scythe in the home meadow at the Old Hall. They were wearing ferns on their heads to shield them from the sun, rags were about their ankles to protect them from the thorns and thistles, and their jolly jeering faces were running with sweat.

"Well, look who it is," Gerallt grinned.

"Greetings, son of Tudor. Home, eh, to lend a hand with the harvest?" another shouted amid such laughter as one might figure.

Entering the hall Eden felt a strangeness creeping over his face upon first looking around. A sudden spasm of grief seized his throat and his eyes filled with tears. Annes. When his eyes had cleared enough to look around again he asked the very question Robyn had wanted to ask.

"Where is Mererid?"

"She is at Dyngannan," said Sioned.

"Mercy on us, why?"

"Old Elianor has had a paralytic stroke, so Mererid has gone over to help with the household and read to her."

"I always told the priest-father," said Eden, "that he ought never, never to have taught that girl how to read."

8
ROUGE DRAGON (1403 - 1404)

Elianor, the lady of Dyngannan, was not a bad woman at heart. Once she had even been gentle and shy, but marriage to a hateful old man had hardened her considerably. After burying him, she had grown greedy and despotic. She squeezed her tenants and debtors—for she loaned out money for securities—and bullied her servants and dependents. But under her rule the manor had prospered as it had not done in time of mind.

In November in the year 1402 from the incarnation of our Lord she was in the pig yard, supervising the annual slaughter of the swine, when she was struck down as if by a terrible blow. She lost her powers of speech; her tongue lay like a slice of bread in her mouth, the whites of her eyes turned red, her ears roared, and her throat rattled. Two bowls of black blood were drawn from her veins that night by Long Bet of Bodrida. Those she had not seen for years—her three married daughters and her younger son, the ne'er-do-well—turned up at her bedside to wail and pray, but she cheated them of their hopes by getting better. Soon she was so far recovered, indeed, that she caused her bed to be brought out of her sleeping chamber into the hall, the better to oversee the serving folk who would otherwise be certain to idle. Her daughter-in-law, Em of Tregele, was a helpless creature. She knew nothing about running a household. All they had taught the lass at Tregele, it appeared, was how to sing and dance and embroider stitch. When the old woman urged her to learn how to read and write as she had done, in order to keep the account books of the estate, she balked. She was afraid to tax her wits, no doubt, and such as they were, perhaps she was justified in her fear. As for Elianor's older son Andras, he was Keeper of the Mona ferries and was thus often away, especially of late when so many odd and outlandish folk were coming and going about the island.

One day she bethought her of Father Conan's daughter. The mother, from what she had heard, was an absolute fool, but the father was reputed to be a good and learned man. At her summons the priest brought Mererid to Dyngannan. Elianor was shown a sample of her handwriting and heard her read—she did so easily and her voice was pleasing. She had reddish hair and sunburned skin like a rustic, but she seemed shy and respectful. A bargain was struck: Mererid would stay with her until she was on her feet again; she in return would leave legacies to the church at Penmynydd and the poor of the parish. Since Elianor intended living forever, she naturally considered that she had come out of the business cheaply.

"Enough!" she growled irritably one September evening as Mererid was reading to her. "I am sick and tired of listening to the tale of St Paul's travels in Hell. I have troubles enough of my own without hearing about the sufferings of the damned."

Propped up among pillows, the old woman with her beaked and mottled face lay like a vulture in decay, a black patch over one eye, her mouth twisted halfway up her cheek in a terrible grimace. She screwed her head about to look at her hall with its hollybright tapestries and limewashed walls and wondered why she must always find something amiss—one of the shields hanging askew or the fuzz of a cobweb in a joining of the stones.

"What is boiling in the great pot?"

"Water."

"For what?"

"For when it is needed."

"Is there need for it now?"

"No, my lady."

"Then raise ithe pot from the third ring of the chain to the tenth and turn the tilter away from the fire—no, not to the left side," she snapped testily, "to the right. Has no one told you that the left side is one of ill hap?"

Closing her eyes, she leaned back and thought of her native hall of Nannau, far away across the sea, in the heart of the mountains. She saw herself—a young maid, the life quick and rich in her, sitting breast high in grass thick with daisies. From under the palm of her hand she was watching her father, the lord of Nannau riding towards her on a white stallion—a majestic, gold-rimmed figure against the blaze of sunlight. There were the true men-there!—these islanders were barbarians in comparison. A sudden uninvited memory of her husband and the brutal misery of her wedding night arose in her mind to torment her. She opened her eye with a shudder.

"When I was a girl at Nannau we had a book about King Arthur," she said. "I want to be entertained. Is there no jollier reading on this island than these dull books?"

"Our Sheriff has the 'Fables of Aesop'."

"What are those? Who is Aesop? Is he Welsh?"

"He is a storyteller out of antiquity. Father says he was Greek. Or perhaps an ancient Roman."

"Roman, you mean. There is no need to say 'ancient Roman'," the old woman scoffed. "All Romans are ancient."

One of the forebears of the house of Nannau had been a leader in the revolt of the Brythons from Nero in which seventy thousand Romans had been slain, so Elianor felt she knew whereof she spoke.

"How do you know the Sheriff has that book?"

"His daughter Annes was my foster-brother's wife. I read out of it once to the spinners at the Old Hall. It is about animals."

"Animals? How curious! Animals. That would be a change."

"I think the book may still be yonder."

"You could go there and fetch it."

"As you will."

There was a nervous shuffling of feet at the door as Em shepherded in her small son and daughter, Iori and Betris. "Kiss Nani goodnight," she urged them in a trembling whisper. The children's hearts beat painfully, Nani looked so like a witch. Her one round yellow eye shone out at them terribly and the shadows gave her mouth an even more ludicrously evil twist.

"Well, come along, come along!" she croaked crossly.

The boy's lips quivered and he fell back a few paces, while his little sister pressed her quailing body against her mother's side. Em bent over her, coaxing, not shifting her own uneasily smiling gaze from Elianor's face.

"Silly, Nani is not going to eat you, are you, Nani?"

Why do they not forgo this ritual? thought Mererid with pity and impatience. She rose and taking the children by the hand drew them forward to the bedside. "See," she smiled as though to dare them, and boldly pressed her lips to the old woman's withered claw. Then they too hastened to kiss the heavily-veined and speckled hand; their grandmother growled her blessing and they left the hall almost at a run.

"My children are your slaves already," Em told Mererid when they had gained the refuge of the kitchen.

"The dear knows there is little fun for them here."

"No," Em agreed. "Dyngannan has never been a happy place. Your foster-brother is home, I hear."

Mererid glanced at her quickly.

"Eden? Has he brought Robyn with him, I wonder?"

"That I do not know. Andras says the talk is that the son of Tudor has come back to help with the harvest, they are so short of hands at the Old Hall these days."

Mererid let her laughter peal around the room.

"They are jesting sure. Lazier man than that has never walked this earth."

Em smiled.

"And yet I think you do not dislike him."

"O. lal di lal!" the priest's daughter said.

For Em the arrival of Mererid was like a liberation. Since she had left Tregele as a bride she had almost forgotten what it was to laugh and chatter freely. The priest's daughter was easy to get along with and in her company she could rid herself of feelings long pent. She dreaded the thought of the day when Mererid must leave. Yet, gloomy and taciturn as he was, Em loved her husband well. It was his mother who had made him so, she told her new friend. "He is the best of men, if you but knew."

Mererid wondered. She was thinking of a night when she sat alone, spinning before the fire in the kitchen. She felt rather than saw him first. She turned and there he was, building a darkness about himself where he stood.

"Your hair looks as red as the flame," he said, "and your eyes as black as night."

"Well, I assure you," she said, once she had collected her wits, "that my hair is far more brown than red, and my eyes are blue."

Hawknosed and swarthy in a bush of hair, he stood there staring at her unsmilingly for a few moments further. Then he left. The air itself seemed to breathe out a sigh.

It was strange that in spite of Mererid's apparent scorn for Eden, she should have dressed with such care on the day she set out for the Old Hall. She washed her hair, put on a silken shift, her green dress and mantle, the silver ornamented girdle she had received as a gift from Annes, and her best shoes with the silver buckles. Her step was light and quick as she crossed the yard to the horseblock where Em's palfrey had been saddled for her. And to get away from Dyngannan for a while! The ride homeward was a joy. The air was full of autumn, of nuts, bright leaves, berries, salt wind, screaming gulls, and the island lay seaward and shining from the End of the Ridges to the Menai shore.

Strings of geese scattered before her like drifts of snow as she rode into the Old Hall. Gerallt appraised her with a broad grin as he helped her dismount.

"All in green like the Queen of Fairyland," he declared. "Life at Dyngannan is using you kindly, it's clear, my sister."

"I'm glad that you think so," said Mererid, her lips taking on a wry curl at the corners.

She walked beside him into the hall. Robyn, leaning on a crutch, hobbled towards her with a moist-eyed smile. She was moved to tears.

"God be praised, dear Robyn, it's good to see you home and alive."

She embraced his thin shoulders and then caught her breath at Eden's voice.

"They tell me Mererid is here. Where is she?"

He took her in his arms and kissed her. Looking with a laughing gaze at her flaming cheeks, he said: "It's a long time since I have seen a girl blush."

"It's plain to see what sort of company you have been keeping then," she retorted.

"Still the same sweet biddable tongue, too. A woodland violet," he smiled.

"She has come here for a book—one we borrowed from the Sheriff. It has been returned to him, as it happens," said Gerallt. "Are you going to Beaumaris soon? Perhaps you would get it for her."

His foster-brother, who had yet to pay his devoirs to his father-in-law, the Sheriff, willingly agreed. On the next morning he rode to Beaumaris to visit him.

Eden gave a low whistle of surprise when he saw the Isle of Mona's garrison town again. The greater part of the commonalty had taken their departure and gone into England with their wives and children. Sunk in the shadow of its towering castle and ramparts, Beaumaris was like a town of the dead. The smell of rot was everywhere. The gaping thatch of the cottages, and the broken doors looked both forlorn and forbidding. Harrows rusted in lots; thistles and nettles were thick in the kitchen gardens. Herring gulls gleamed like sea-froth on mixen and dungheap. A bundle of rags lay snoring in a drunken stupor in the porch of the Chapel of our Lady. Behind a half-opened window a woman stood combing the haystalks out of her sleep-tousled hair and silently watched the lone horseman pass. Apart from these two and the sentries on the walls Eden saw no other living soul as he moved along the narrow twisting streets.

He found his father-in-law holding his hands to a fire of burning logs in the great hall of the castle, a bent branch dressed in hangings of velvet and fur. Crosslegged in the straw nearby sat the old sergeant-at-arms Dickon Lescrop, blissfully sucking up peasoup into his sunken mouth. Five other soldiers were dozing in a huddle against the wall. Eden could see the Constable nowhere.

"Where is Thomas Bold?" he asked the Sheriff, after he had embraced him.

"He is gone into England to get reinforcements."

"Why?" Eden smiled. "Are you expecting an assault?"

"Ask your kinsmen."

"I know what they would say. Give up the keys of the town and the castle. You are in a hopeless position and you know it. You have forty soldiers defending an empty town against an island swarming with rebels. Surrender."

The Sheriff gave a grim laugh.

"Would that it were so simple," he said, and then he went on to tell Eden that one of his vessels, homeward bound from Italy with a full cargo, had been unaccountably arrested and detained at Bristol since the octaves of St John's Day. The son of Kenvric had lost no time in supplicating the King and the bailiffs of the port, but to no avail.

"It is his way of telling me that he can ruin my trade, I suppose. Unless I play his game."

"But what a game it is! You are caught between the Devil and his tail, in-law."

"Aye, son, I know I am."

A little later they left the castle together and made their way back to the Sheriff's house. They walked silently, full of memories, stirring up ghosts at every step along the dead quays. The merchant's apartments were dusty and smelt of mold, for the owner no longer slept there; but he brought out some old wine from his store, and the two men sat a while drinking and staring broodingly at the dirty grey light falling through the brine-fogged windows upon the unswept tiles. Each, in his own way and without speaking of it to the other, thought of Annes.

"Did you know," the Sheriff remarked at last, "that I have been advised that your mother-in-law is seeking a separation from me?"

"Joanna? On what grounds?"

"On the grounds of having detected me in adultery three times."

That was plausible enough, Eden thought. But when the Sheriff went on to say that his wife might even have been considering remarriage, he found that far more diffcult to believe. Seeing his son-in-law stare at him as though through a mist, the Sheriff demanded of him, why not? Joanna Beaupine was still a likely female, was she not? Handsome and affluent?

"Holy Church will not permit it," Eden argued.

"But you'll have heard the talk that is going around for sure. That Wales may soon go over to Avignon? Whence it must arise that Rome anathematize and excommunicate us all. And Joanna will be free to choose another mate."

"Would that trouble you?" Eden asked, falling in with the in-law's jesting mood. "If so, remember, son of Kenvric, that according to the old Welsh law you have only to pursue and overtake her before she plants her two feet on the bed of her new husband and she is yours."

"Och, my heart, you overestimate my agility, I assure you. I am gone so to seed these days I fear the seagulls would pick me up before I reached the other side of Aber Menai."

He broke into laughter at that. And because his son-in-law was glad to hear of anything befalling him, be it ever so small, which might be counted as a gain, he joined him in mirth, and they laughed along together in this manner for a space, as brisk and jolly as beer in a vat.

Then, having been given the book he begged for, Eden rode away with it gladly to Dyngannan. There he had hoped to see Mererid and have a talking time with her, but to his dismay she was off on an errand somewhere, so he handed the book instead to Em of Tregele. He stared at her in surprise. It was not so many years ago that he had seen her dancing for garlands at one of the festivals, a proper bonny little woman, as bright and pretty as a bees' honeycomb. She had grown thin since then; her face was pale and she had a furtive, fearful look. They are killing her here the begors, he thought, and he wondered about Mererid—by the Lord, no, they would not overbear that lass so easily.

And then his thoughts turned back again to his father-in-law. Eden was often to tremble for the man's life in the weeks that followed.

"Can you not reason with him?" he asked the Chieftain.

"What good would that do, think you?" Meredith replied. "Trade is blood and bone of the Sheriff's being. It's hard for him to give up the habits of a lifetime."

"It's mad not to."

"Well, these are mad days," said the Chieftain.

Mona, as it fortuned, was merry in its madness. In later years, when the islanders looked back upon that period, they spoke of it as a golden time. Never were such splendid days as those—even the stars seemed larger and brighter somehow. A wild, sweet, intoxicating sense of freedom ran across the island from the gale-bitten cliffs of the Holy Head to the saltings of the sea-river. The natives roamed at will in the royal dower lands, hunting the hart and the hind. Bands of French auxiliaries were everywhere. At Christmas six ships flaunting the royal oriflamme of St Denis sailed into Porth Cadwaladr carrying a cargo of wine and spices as a gift from Duke Louis of Orleans to the island chieftains who were harboring his men. Scots vessels dropped anchor in the Bay of Dulas, bringing strong water and arms from King Robert of Scotland. Fires were lighted on the hills, steers and pigs were roasted under the stars, and there was a happy music in the villages and along the grasslands.

And still the Sheriff of Mona, that pale gaunt horseman in his long black mantle, rode out across the island, collecting dues for the King of England, and with that comical band of troops trotting in the heels of him—grizzled, shrunk-shanked and shrivel-buttocked.

The wonder of it, of course, was that he went unharmed so long. Perhaps people remembered how fairly he had dealt with them in the past. Or then again, perhaps it pleased Rhys Ddu to be indulgent.

"You know," he told Eden laughingly once, "seen from afar one is hard put to decide which one of the two is the lively reliquary of the Holy Ghost, your father-in-law or his big spear."

And then Rhys Ddu stopped laughing. Eden remembered the day. It was a damp misty afternoon and he was stretching his legs at Penmynydd when Gerallt arrived, breath in fist, with the news that Rhys Ddu and Jean d'Espagne had attacked the Sheriff's force at Llanddona and had seized Beaumaris and the castle.

"Oia, those poor ancient jesters," said Eden.

"How of the Sheriff?" asked the Chieftain.

"They have taken him captive. He has been hurt. A spear thrust in his side."

"God help us, where have they taken him?"

"To Rhys Ddu's."

There they rode. The hall was bristling with spears as though for a siege when they arrived. Some forty to fifty men were crowded into the courtyard alone, laughing, chattering and shouting jests at one another across the fires. Seeing the newcomers they fell silent for a moment while the Chieftain, his robe and beard powdered white from the rime from the mist that was billowing damply over the rides, walked into the hall in front of Eden and Gerallt.

"Where do you have the Sheriff hid?"

"Who is hiding him, faith?" Rhys Ddu laughed. "He is in the bedchamber yonder."

They found the wounded man lying in a bed hung about with blue curtains embroidered with mermaidens and other curious creatures of the deep worked in gold thread. A young priest was saying over his prayers on one side of him, and on the other sat Eva, holding his hand and soothing his brow with motherly kindness, but there was a gay triumphing in the smile she sent her brothers-in-law and her dark eyes gleamed archly. The Sheriff lay with his eyes closed, his bruised and pallid face glistening with salves, breathing hoarsely like a worn-out bellows.

"How is he?"

"He could be worse," said Eva. "We have let blood."

"Ach," said the Chieftain, "was that necessary?"

At the sound of their voices the Sheriff opened his eyes and stared at them uncomprehendingly, as one shaken out of a deep slumber. His glance, filmy and somber, came to rest on his son-in-law. A faint, miserable smile touched his lips.

"What a stew, eh?" he croaked weakly. "They have slain old Dickon Lescrop, did you hear? Ned Blonkett and Jake de la Diche, too. They were here in the time of your former Sheriff, what was his name?"

"Baldwin Radington," the Chieftain replied. "How is it with you, son of Kenvric?"

"Ah, they have done for me this time."

"Come, you are a battleground for scars, my friend. You will surmount this one like the rest."

Pity clutched at Eden's heart. Och, life was such a bawd! What his father-in-law had so long feared had at last come to pass. He was a ruined man. Ships, high office, trade, good health had all been wrested from him at a cast. Only the house at Rhosyr was left.

Gwervyl Mechain, the tavernness and his lovewoman for many a year, awaited the Sheriff there. When he had brought her with him out of the distant Valley of the Cain, a purchase from her grandfather, the local wizard, she had been very pretty and winsome. But with the years she had grown stout and jolly from drinking her own beer and laughing at her own verses, most of them so ribald that only a man in his cups would dare to repeat them—that is to say, of course, if he could.

It was good luck for the Sheriff that he had her, his son-in-law thought. She was the soul of kindness.

Eden next saw his father-in-law two weeks later. It was Candlemas, and the weather although cool was sunny. Bundled up in furs, with a woolen cap on his head, the sick man lay in his window bed in the hall, looking out over the small marketplace with its stone cross and its well for two buckets. A huge, tusked hog fattened for bacon had been slaughtered there that morning. Spears of frosty sunlight glittered brightly in the blood-stained straw, and out across the straits a fresh breeze was ruffling the waters of the Menai to silver. Now and again it brought them, gruff and hoarse from beyond the headland, the distant cough and retch of battle. Two French ships captained by Jean d'Espagne had lately been brought to bear against the fortifications. Rhys Ddu's vessels, the 'Prydwen' and 'Seren y Mor' had been laying on before that, along with Asa Coedana's carrack and 'Morwyn Maenan', the ship of the monks of Aberconway. "Talk about fishers of men indeed," grunted the son of Kenvric, and he asked Eden how the siege was progressing.

"The town is devastated," said his son-in-law. "A heap of cinders. It will fall."

"Unless King Henry raises the siege."

"How can he do that? He has his hands full."

"Let us hope so."

Meanwhile, over the ramparts of Beaumaris the red dragon banner cracked and bellied in the wind rising out of the sea and the natives ran whooping and brawling through the streets, noisy enough to be heard at times through the hammering of forges in the castle. It was an arsenal in there—full of the fume of war, of sweat, harness, carbon and smoke. The very stones simmered and rang with military bustle and enterprise. Beaumaris was the center of activities along the Menai water. As such, the warriors and sailors came there to take their ease, repair boats and weapons and wash away the stains of battle.

Day and night the hall of banquet flamed with welcoming fires. The ruling presence was Rhys Ddu. And Eva, decked out in a magnificent new gown of foxglove red, slashed to reveal a silken shift as golden as the broom, with gold at her throat and girdle, queened it finely.

Meredith ap Tudor never went there, Gwilym ap Tudor rarely, Eden frequently.

It was a cold night, pitchy black and wild with wind, and the crescent of dilapidated wooden houses fronting on the moat and the seawall was creaking and groaning like the cordage of a ghost ship blown about at its moorings, when a solitary rider came knocking at the gates. A young man with a monkish mat of hair, wearing the habit of a Dominican friar under his heavy sheepskin mantle, was admitted into the hall. Eva stared at him hard. Something about him seemed familiar to her—the cut of his head, the broad wide-nostrilled nose, the morose beetle-black eyes. And then she knew. It was her half-brother Gwern, a bastard son of Red Iwan's. She leaned over and whispered to her husband. Rhys Ddu nodded and smiled.

"Greetings, kinsman," he said. "I crave pardon that we did not recognize you at once, but it has been such a long time since we last met, has it not? Why, you were little more than a brat then, and now look at you. A friar even. Well, what is it, Brother Gwern?" he chaffed. "Have you come to execute the judgements of Heaven upon us?"

"No, Rhys Ddu, I have come to tell you that Red Iwan your father-in-law is dead, may God rest his soul."

There was a silence before Rhys Ddu spoke again.

"How did this happen?"

"He was killed fighting on the walls of Caernarvon a few days ago."

The friar explained that his stepmother, Pia, had summoned him to her side as soon as she had heard the news. Red Iwan's hall had been burned to the ground by the forces of Owain Glyndwr some while ago, so she now lived in her old home at Nanmor with her youngest children.

"She asks permission to have the body brought out for burial."

Rhys Ddu nodded.

"Be it so. I have no quarrel with the dead. I am however much interested in the living. Where are my wife's dear brothers, Madoc and Huw, keeping themselves these days?"

The Dominican paused.

"They are like the curlews, Rhys Ddu," he said then. "No man knows where they nest?"

"Curlews do you call them?" Rhys Ddu laughed. "Cuckoos rather. For I think I know enough about their ways to tell you that they make their homes in the nests of others. But which others?"

Brother Gwern did not reply. He looked at Eva. She had yet to utter a word. As regards emotion she was a woman of marble, cold and beautiful. Her he loved more than any living soul, he thought, and she cannot spare him as much as one tear.

2

During the early months of the year the castles of Harlech, Criccieth and Aberystwyth fell. Owain Glyndwr's power was now supreme over most of the country. On the calends of May four men from every commot* in Wales under the Prince's sway were summoned to attend his coronation and first Parliament in the township of Machynlleth in mid-Wales.

The throng of chieftains, ladies, priests, bards, minstrels and soldiers was so great that not enough room could be found for them. Tents and pavilions blossomed overnight in the meadowland. Eden and Howel Vaughan were hailed by Black Rhys, who was spreading his broad buttocks about the huge splayed roots of a giant oak, with Henry Don of Kidwelly sitting on one side of him and an alepot on the other.

"Did you hear how my captain, Robyn Holland, took Harlech, chieftains? He beat John Henmore in a skirmish at the gatehouse and bore him captive away. So the English sent another constable there,

---

*commot (from W. cwmwd): In Wales a territorial and administrative division, usually subordinate to a cantref (a hundred or canton.)

William Hunt by name. The pestilence there, boys. Everybody dying. So Will rides out under a flag of truce and devil fetch me if Robyn does not take him captive, too. 'This is an outrage,' says Will, 'it is in violation of the rules of war.' 'What rules?' says Robyn. 'I did not know there were any.'"

The coronation was very fine, Eden thought: all those bells of jubilation—so many it was a wonder they did not sour the drink, as Howel Vaughan remarked—and the choruses of friars and clerics singing canticles. The path of the procession was luminous with flowers. Eight captains of troops bore aloft on their shoulders the image of St Dervel, the warrior saint, attired in a burnished coat of mail, glaring out black-browed and fierce from under the glittering beaver of his helmet—beaked shield on arm, spear in fist, lips and cheeks painted with an incarnadine brush. A horseman rode a few paces behind, bearing upright before him the sacred sword of St Eliseg. Owain Glyndwr followed on foot, a big imposing figure in red-purple robes adorned with gold. His stern fork-bearded face was wreathed in genial patriarchal smiles. And you could see the people warming, melting to him as he came on, the way they will to the old hearthrock after a cold season among strangers. Tears came to the eyes and smiles to the lips. Everywhere fingers were stretched out towards him. Fathers held up their children the better to see; others fell on their knees with their hands raised as though in prayer; toothless crones, their faces bitten by toil and suffering, darted out to pluck at his sleeve or the hem of his robe.

The procession moved at a slow hieratic pace to the heart of the great meadow. There, under a baldachin of leek-green silk embroidered with the four golden lions of Gwynedd, a dais had been set up bearing a throne of heavy, polished, sculptured oak. Glyndwr had so ordered it, in order that as many people as possible could witness the coronation. Gradually the stands which had been raised nearby for the convenience of the ladies and dignitaries were filled. And the formal ceremony of the coronation began.

A hush fell over the multitude. For a while there was nothing to be heard but the incantations of priests and a faint susurration of voices through the host like the humming of bees in distant hives. Small stirrings of wind wafted smells of incense to Eden's face. Occasional mumblings of Latin went drifting by: . . . *ubi honor est . . . felix qui in domino . . . anno humanae salutis . . . amen.*

And then:

"Owain, Prince of Powys, Owain, Prince of Gwynedd, Owain, Prince of Dyved, Owain, Prince of Gwent"—so boomed out the magnificent voice of the newly appointed Chancellor of Wales, Griffith Young, the Archdeacon of Merioneth, aye, and Bishop *in prospectu* - "Owain Prince of Wales."

"Alleluia!" chorused the priestly train.

"Alleuia!" shouted the crowd.

Dancing there was that eve in the meadowland by torchlight— roundel and rigadoon. And on the next day the Prince presided over the diversity of games which had been arranged for the occasion, in which there was a jolly and triumphant jousting on horseback and on foot. Whereon he conducted his foreign guests to his pavilion for a banquet.

The day was drawing to a close by then, yet several gentlefolk still lingered on in the stands, as if at a loss to know what to do with themselves. Eden marked Lowri Puleston among them, as well as the Lady Madlan, Black Rhys's wife, and some antiquated dames, wimpled like nuns. And then his attentions were seized by one who sat a little apart from her she-comrades—a woman dressed in a simple blue-grey gown with white facings. Supporting her chin with her hand, she was staring off past the heads of the merrymakers with an air of boredom and disdain. Who was she, he wondered? And why had there come this trembling to his heart?

Eden drew closer, until he was only a few yards away from where she sat, as indifferent to his presence as the evening star which was beginning to glimmer behind her in the western sky. Indeed she had about her much of that same cool, remote, tranced quality. And all at once he knew who she was.

"Angharad," he said. "Angharad Trevor."

She gave a start and looked down at the man looking up at her. Against the black of his tunic with its wide orphrey of gold thread at the neck, his face seemed almost pale. His dark-rimmed black eyes glimmered at her in a daze and his lids trembled.

Or, perhaps, after all, it was her own lids that were trembling. She no longer saw as well as of old.

"Who are you, sir?" she asked, peering at him as if through the eye of a needle she was threading.

"Angharad, Angharad, don't you know me, Angharad Golden

Hand?"

"Heart alive, can it be?" she breathed.

She brought her face close to his, searching his features with a ruthless gaze, and in a little her eyes widened, brown and clear as sunlit pools in a mountain bog, with something of frost sparkling in them and something of flame, and she exclaimed delightedly.

"Ednyved! In Holy Mary's name, you must please forgive me the incivility, but it is my eyes. They serve me so ill nowadays. In fact, my friend, I am as bad as a flittermouse."

They laughed then. And they lost count of the minutes talking there. It was almost as if some vagrant zephyr out of that vanished summer they had shared together long ago had suddenly whisked past them, setting them apart from other air.

It was Mam Indeg who had put the whole glamour in Eden's head to begin with. Even now, it seemed to him, he had only to close his eyes and there would float through his fancy pictures of flowering meadows, and impeccable maidens spinning in dream towers, and youths setting forth in the young of the day to fight ogres and fabulous beasts, all as they had been created for him by his foster mother about the coiling smoke of childhood fires. And Angharad had stepped into that magical world so easily and naturally when he had first met her that thenceforth, it seemed, he had never been able to think of the one without the other.

"Your husband was a gallant chieftain," he said to her. "The Keeper's name will be on the lips of boys yet unborn. The great horsethief who raided the studs of the wicked Lord Grey."

She raised her brows.

"Is it a horsethief you are calling him?"

"There is no shame in it," Eden replied. "You know how mothers used to counsel their departing sons in the old time of the princes: 'If you see a fair jewel, take it and give it to another and you shall have fame thereby. If you see a fair lady make love to her, even though she desire you not. A better man and a nobler it will make you.' I had a couple of friends once who were horsethieves."

"I know you did," she said drily. "The sons of Jenkin of Welsh Maelor. But I wonder that you call them friends. They stole my cousin Simon Thelwall's bright brown bay with the two white hind feet. They did not like me, I believe."

"One of them did not like you. You did not let him kiss you in a skipping game."

"I did not like him either. I never gave my kisses idly. God has not given me such a heart, although I suppose you must have thought so at one time."

"Lady," he said, "I loved you so."

Her expression softened.

"I loved you, too."

"Did you? And yet you ran away."

"Ran away? When?"

"When I came back to your father's hall that second time."

"Running away?" She gave a bitter little laugh. "Is that what you call it? Do you think I had any say in the matter? A mere slip of a girl? Have you never marked it, my friend?—men govern this world. Can you imagine me going in the teeth of my uncle the Bishop, let alone my father and kinsmen? God knows the tears I shed. And then when they beat you so cruelly. . . ."

He was touched.

"Angharad," he said, "I did not know. I thought for sure that you had forgotten me."

"Forgotten?" She gazed upon him wistfully.

"Don't you know, my friend," she said then, "that a woman never forgets the first love of her heart?"

And leaning towards him, she put her hand to his face and stroked his cheek with her fingertips—dear God, so softly, so caressingly.

His head swam. And deep down in the rank, dark, warm lair of his loins the beast stirred, yawned, uncurled his mischievous tail, and lazily stretched his voluptuous limbs.

"Ah, my Eden," Angharad sighed.

Afterwards, in recalling this tender exchange, he could never be sure where it took place, whether in her tent with the train-oil lamp and bowl of primroses at the edge of the festive encampment, or at Garth Ivor, the nearby hall of Siân Heiling, a kinswoman of hers, where he spent the next week. The mistress and her family had gone to a funeral in Towyn, leaving behind them only Lucy Telynor, an extremely old and feeble harper and two handmaidens coeval with himself. All three were hard of hearing, giving Siân Heiling's niece and her friend full license to reminisce.

"What happened to that old aunt of yours who used to lie there beside us to see that the mischief did not go too far?"

"Auntie Corwen? She is no longer with us, Eden."

"God sanctify her dust."

She sent him a sly and mischievous smile.

"Are you happy?"

"Purge me with hyssop, aye," he said, coaxing out of her then one of the most marvelous laughs he had ever heard,—so joyous and lovely it was.

"You are the best thing that has happened to me during this festival truly," she said. "You are better than all the trumpets and crowns and Te Deums."

"I too feel that way," he said, and did not lie.

The years had adorned her like the trees of autumn, with princely banners.

The hall stood on a wooded hillside overlooking the Dovey estuary. For the first five days they saw little of it. Fogs rolled in off the sea with the dawn and across the sands the woods looked like troops of ghosts combing the air with white fingers. On the sixth day, bundled up in their hooded mantles, they rode out eastward to find the sun. Soon they were caught in a downpour. They took shelter in a fisherman's hut, the door torn off by the gales. Coracles lay upended like wet black turtles along the glittering windrows.

"To think," Eden observed "that our ancestors came here from the Land of the Summer."

"Where is that, pray?"

"Well, the old ones called Hu the Mighty, the golden constable of Constantinople, so I judge it must have been in that region somewhere," he mused. "There all the days are sunshine, of course, and the birds hang like jewels in the trees."

"Why would men leave such a Paradise?"

"Why do men ever leave Paradise?"

"They are driven out by the covetous."

"Or by the hand of God. Perhaps," he speculated, "another lady dares pluck an apple from the tithe tree."

"Another Eva?"

They looked at one another and burst out laughing.

"How does your sister-in-law fare these days?"

"Like Eva," he said. "The Mother of us all."

"It is clearing," she said. "By my soul, look at all these seafowl, only look at them!"

White they were drifting and falling through the sparkling rainmist, like a myriad flecks of foam, lilies of ocean.

He fell silent, watching them, strangely stirred. She looked at him and after a while said:

"Far travel the thoughts in early summer. What are you thinking of, my friend?"

"So little a thing," he replied. "I was thinking of a girl watching seagulls."

On the following morning he left the district. In parting he gave her some skins of ermine and a gold ring. He held her face between his hands and gazed for one last infinite moment into those eyes towards which dreams and river valleys had once flowed as simply and magically as the phrases of an old song. Then he rode off into the young of the day without looking back. Their paths never crossed again.

9
HARLECH (1404 - 1405)

1

The castle stood on a craggy height washed around on three sides by the sea.* Seen from afar, across the grassy plain that rolled away eastward to the mountains, its lonely towers looked both majestic and forbidding, like the wings of a dark angel prowling the bourns of Heaven. In the way of his fabled forerunner, Bran the Blessed, when he had been crowned King of Britain and exalted with the honors of London, it was here that Owain Glyndwr, the Prince of Wales, now established his residence.

One night, towards the end of August in that year, three ships anchored at the mole at the base of the crag. They were accompanying Griffith Young, the Chancellor of Wales, and John Hanmer, the Prince's brother-in-law, back from France where they had recently concluded a treaty with Charles VI, King of the French. Funereally violet clouds were gathering over Sarn Badrig and St Tudwal's Isles and a wet wind was winnowing the sand as they disembarked and rode up the side of the hill to the castle. Owain Glyndwr awaited them in the courtyard. As he greeted them a thunder growled in the heavens. Could that have been by arrangement, John Hanmer wondered waggishly? Raising his face to the cool seaweedy gusts of the soft falling rain, he saw a fluttering standard caught in the sudden flare of a torch from Branwen's Tower: the red dragon banner of Cadwaladr. It burned with a fierce, lonely anger into the night for a moment, hissed, writhed, and fell back into darkness.

Exhaling an air of ease, aplomb and well being, Glyndwr conducted his legates and guests into the great hall, whose timbers removed of old from one of Llywelyn the Great's palaces, were worn by age to a silken lustre. There, after they had rested and eased their garments, the French envoys presented him with the gifts of their monarch: a golden casque, cuirass and sword. He fell down upon one knee directly and kissed the sword-hilt. It was an arresting sight. Everything, all that was common to Glyndwr, the great pride and assurance of the man, his fearless magnanimous bearing, his occasional air of being in touch with the Otherworld, the way he had of freezing you with a glance, of charming

*As the castle crag once was.

the eyes out of you with a smile, and of being miles away from you in thought while appearing to be giving you his undivided attention, seemed to vanish for a moment in that one simple and moving gesture. There was a profound hush. Then he rose, he smiled, he talked, and as if by the touch of an enchanter's wand, the ordinary activities of the castle were resumed.

For all its royal appointments it was the same common hall and marketplace at Harlech, John Hanmer observed with pleasure, as it had once been at Sycharth and after that at Caer Gai. You could not take it in all at once, there was so much going on.

At a table covered with parchments and correspondence, the Prince's secretary, Master Howel Deget, was dictating to two clerks who were scribbling away, their faces set in lines of Lenten sobriety, as if engaged in transcribing the Decalogue. An isle of women presided over by the Lady Margaret and her daughter, Lady Mortimer, blossomed in their blues, greens and crimsons about a loom in the heart of the main floor, stitching away, gossiping, laughing or warmly disputing some interesting fact of life about a cradle from which a feeble human music stole. Soldiers sat crosslegged in the straw, mending their gear and throwing dice. Upon the benches ranged along the walls friars were telling their beads, and minstrels were tuning harps and pibcorns and putting strings to fiddles. At the farthest end of the hall children were playing hoodman blind while scullions and maids kept running back and forth from buttery and kitchen with comfits and sweetmeats.

John paid his devoirs to his sister and the ladies. Then, while the Chancellor introduced the French envoys to Sir Edmund Mortimer, he joined his brother-in-law at the high table under the blazon, which as successor to the Llywelyns he had now adopted: the four lions rampant of Gwynedd. He is growing his hair, thought John. Such a leonine amplitude to lend coverts to the telltale wink or grimace.

"How did you find King Charles, John?"

"In health. That is to say, whatever passes in his royal majesty for health. He looked beaten out to me, a sad childlike man and as pale as mushrooms, if I may say so."

"Or a ladle that has been left in the porridge, say on."

"We were told to speak to him softly, not to excite him. They are afraid to blow trumpets in his presence lest the noise distract him into a delirium. I think he laughed no more than once while we were there.

The Duke of Orleans told us that in letters to the French court Henry of Lancaster styles himself as 'Henri d'Angleterre, roy de France'."

"Ha! So they are left in no doubt as to his ultimate intentions. That will help us."

"And he addresses the French King as 'Serenissime, illustrissime, tres-preudhomme *Prince* Charles'."

"Sweet his tooth as sugar candy. And that amused the King?"

"Highly," said John, and he called up in his mind's eye an image of the French monarch in his big red chaperon with the velvet caruncles hanging as he presented to his Queen a peaked and bloodless face puckered up with stitches of wild elfin mirth. "Prince Charles," piped he, clapping his hands as at some delightful jest.

"And how of his brother the Duke?" Glyndwr asked.

"He smiled."

"Yes, I think I can see that smile. Our Chancellor says Duke Louis is not well liked by the people of Paris."

"They believe he plays on his royal brother's infirmities to further his own ends," said John, and he recalled for Glyndwr the notorious ball of years past when the Duke of Orleans had scampered about with a lighted torch among revelers disguised as savages in suits of grass and tow. Four knights had died in the conflagration which had ensued, thereby winning for that incendiary frolic the name of *'Le Bal des Ardents'*.

"The King fell into a fearful frenzy directly. They had to hide him away in the Chateau de Creil for months."

Glyndwr pondered a moment, stroking his beard. He glanced, half-absently, at the French envoys, who were now seated among the ladies.

"So it is Burgundian Jack who is their lad then-the citizenry?"

"Not only theirs. The University of Paris rings out in the Duke of Burgundy's support."

"Jean Sans Peur. Is he so fearless, think you? He is a crafty and hard-headed man for sure. His cousin of Orleans is by far the better of the two to my mind. The pity of it is, of course, that Duke Louis has stayed wild and foolhardy so long. He begins to be wise now. Let us hope it is not too late."

"The French Chancellor gave us to know that word of our presence had been sent from the Burgundian headquarters at the Hotel d'Artois to Bruges."

"And of the expeditionary force we have been promised, naturally," Glyndwr observed. "And since Burgundy and Henry of Lancaster are hand in glove, it is to be assumed that England knows now, too. What a world we live in, eh? Ears cocked everywhere to meet every whisper of the wind."

"Messire Arnaud de Corbie calls it *un jeu de chat et souris*. What happens next I wonder?"

"Let your fancy play revel, John. For my part I would like to hear of your visit to the lecture halls of the University. Let us begin with the celestial deliberatives of the learned master Jean Gerson."

Towards the end of that month sixty French ships put out of Brest bound for Wales, only to be turned away by the news that an English fleet was crowding sail towards the Normandy coast. Rhys Ddu and Jean d'Espagne, who had been appointed to guide the French ships, returned to Wales in September with the story of rude parleys off Harfleur and Mont-Saint-Michel-in-Peril-of the-Sea, and of a ferocious brawl at Calais, and on top of this a storm blowing up: waves high as cliffs, rain, fog, winds howling shoreward like devouring harpies, with ships foundering and running aground to grapple with rocks and catapults, and others being towed to harbors up the river Seine for repairs. It was almost a year before they were heard of next.

Meanwhile the Welsh rebels suffered one of their worst setbacks. The beginning of it was when it was learned that the men of Glamorgan and Gwent were in serious difficulties in the Valley of the Monnow along the Marches of South Wales. They had been besieging King Henry's manor at Grosmont when a host of enemy soldiers led by Earl Talbot had fallen upon them. Reinforcements under the leadership of Owain Glyndwr's eldest son Gruffydd were sent to help them.

They withdrew to a hillside outside the town of Usk to rally their forces and tend to their wounded. While there, another army headed by Lord Grey of Codnor attacked them. It was a worse rout than the last. When Howel Vaughan, Eden, and the brothers of the Bay of the White Stones arrived the slaughter was at its height. Riderless horses were galloping their several ways in panic and on every side the dead and dying were lying in heaps. Little Garmon, who had once helped to conceal Griffith Llwyd, the bard, in the haunted mound on the Isle of

Mona fell in the course of this bitter engagement. So too did that fiercest of Cistercians, the Prior of Llantarnam*. Word had it that while dying he admitted that only one thing lay heavy on his spirit, namely: that thereafter he would be unable to raise his voice and sword against God's enemies. Now he too lay quiet on that hillside, with no more cares in this world.

The rest of his fellows had enough and to spare. Even the weather had gone against them, it seemed. Half the day had languished under a dark veil of rain. Now that they could have used it for cover—behold the sun winking out, the sky serene, and the meadowlands around as clear as glass. And yet the ground was as wet and treacherous as before. Down by the river, grey and turbulent and swollen with mud, it was like a swamp. Some of the Welsh soldiers were drowned there, some were trampled into the mire before they could get so far, others were so broken with their wounds and fatigue that they could do little more than raise their hands in a futile effort to protect themselves from the deadly blows that were falling on their heads and shoulders.

"By cock, look at the rascals fall!" one of the enemy riders called out with a high whinnying laugh. Some rebels who were skirmishing in the rear of their foot, covering their retreat, overheard him. Howel Vaughan flew at him like a shot from an arbalest.

"Let's hear you crow now, you son of a bitch!" he yelled as he drove his spear into his face.

Sometimes, Eden thought, it is a blessing to have no English. The men of Nantconway had a troop of enemy horse hanging angrily at their tails for some distance after that as they struck westward into the hills. Happily, their mounts were smaller and swifter than the chargers of their more heavily armed pursuers and they finally escaped them. A while later, they came upon a fir wood, where a group of their countrymen sat silently huddled under the dripping hood of the trees. Among them was Samson Clidro, an itinerant poet of dubious merit whom Eden had first seen in the encampment at Caer Gai. A much dinted steel basinet covered his head to his ears, and over his boiled leather jacket he wore a long patched purple mantle fastened at the shoulder with a tin brooch the size of a child's buckler. Beside him lay one whom Eden recognized as Brochwel of the Spears, an old warrior who had fought under King Sigismund in the Last Crusade at Nicopolis. His broad, bluff leathery

*The Prior of Llantarnam: Ieuan ap Rhys: Called the Welsh Savonarola.

face was white and drawn with pain and one of his legs, wrapped about with bloodstained rags, was propped on a log. In the distance the walls of Usk were glowing with fires and the chill air was shuddering with strange cries.

"They are slaughtering our lads," somebody said. "They are putting them to the sword under those walls, all their captives."

"They have caught our Prince's son," Samson said.

"Will they kill him?"

Howel gave a bitter laugh.

"I doubt it. They will have other uses for our lord Gruffydd."

Rain began falling again. "We had best get going," said Howel. They made a litter of green fir-branches for Brochwel and slung it up between two horses. An hour later they came upon a cluster of shaggy hovels in the crook of a deep grassy glen where a charcoal pit was making a great smoke. Hogs were grunting along the dung-littered ground, and in a field nearby some folk were dibbling beans. A woman, broad in the bone and swarthy, appeared in a doorway.

"God keep you," Howel said in greeting, "and are you Christians here?"

"God's welcome to you, chieftains, what else would we be?"

"I don't know," Howel remarked. "The Lord has mingled us forth such a wild cup in this land it is not always easy to tell. You could be fairies."

She laughed at that, showing them her long white teeth. They were her best feature by far; they winked like bucklers.

"Fairies, ha!"

"Or Saeson,* maybe."

"You are Saeson more like it."

"Before God, woman, don't laugh at us. If it's true Saeson you are wanting to see, however, you may get your wish sooner than you expect," he cautioned. He went on to tell her the story of their misadventures, of the big battle at Usk and the pursuit. "And our friend is hurt, as you can see. He is a brave man. Help him. Help us, my dear," he urged and he fished her some coins out of his saddlebag. "As you tender the good of Wales and your countrymen."

"Come inside," she said, pouching the money promptly.

They helped Brochwel of the Spears inside, and after having washed

* Saeson (W.): English

and dressed his wound, they made him as comfortable as they could on a bed of straw near a pit fire that gave off an acrid odor of burning dung-cakes and gorse. His leg was badly broken; ragged splinters of the big bone had torn through the flesh and his comrades had small hope for him. While they tended to the old warrior's wounds, the woman kept up a constant stream of chatter. Where was their home then? They did not sound like Southerners. Ah, Gwynedd. She should have known. She had always heard tell that the men of Gwynedd were so handsome. No, no, they must not speak to her of their being filthy, she would not hear of it. Dirt, whisht, what was dirt? Away with such tomfoolery. Did she not know a handsome man when she saw one? How their wives dared leave them out of their sight was a wonder to her. And what pretty voices they had. God's truth, she could sit and listen to them talk all day. It was every bit as good as going to Mass.

She brought them some boiled meat for supper—it was black and tough, but the men were so hungry, that tears of relish combed their filthy cheeks into a myriad muddy wrinkles. Eden offered some to Brochwel of the Spears; but he whispered no with a smile, and asked for his psalter.

The islander removed the psalter from the old warrior's wallet and placed it in his hands. "Take it," said Brochwel. "I have a little granddaughter Nest. Give it to her." Eden placed the psalter in his saddlebag, then he took off his belt and sword, lay down in the straw beside the old warrior and fell asleep. Some hours later he woke with the smell of burning in his nostrils. Some red splinters of gorse from the fire had fallen into Brochwel's hair. Eden brushed them away, then looked down into the other's face. His cheeks were still warm but his jaw was hanging and his hands were cold. Samson Clidro raised himself on his elbows, alike staring, then bound up the dead man's jaw with a strip of cloth torn from his threadbare mantle. Silently the others rose and knelt around.

"It's pity of it there was no holy man here to give him the last sacraments," someone said at last.

"I gave them to him," Samson Clidro announced.

His comrades stared at him, yellow faces hovering in the smoke like rings of grease in the soup.

"How can that be? You are not a priest."

"It is said that where no priest is present it is permitted in an exigency for a blade of grass blessed by a comrade to be taken in the mouth of one who is dying."

"Who said that? I have never heard such a thing before."

"Master Walter Brut told it me."

"The Lollard? You believe the babblings of a heretic?"

"I would sooner believe Master Walter than many a shaveling," said Eden.

"Old Brochwel smiled when he took the blade of grass," Samson Clidro told the others. "I know he is in Heaven."

"Then he will need no more of our prayers, will he?" Howel said abruptly.

He rose, poked his head out of the door and sniffed the air.

"Come, lads, get your gear ready. It is time to be on our way."

The weather had cleared when they left the glen of the charcoal pit. A gentle breeze was driving fluffy white clouds across the blue sky and birds were twittering in the willows and birches along the way. In a nearby village they found a dirty crumbling little church dressed with paintings on wood where a bent figure in a shabby cassock was reciting prayers for the dead over corpses plucked away from the battle. They laid the body of Brochwel of the Spears among them and afterwards helped dig the graves. Then they walked into the muddy square, where women were drawing water from a well and old men squinnying and lazily licking the watery sunbeams.

"I have Brochwel's psalter," said Eden. "He wished his granddaughter to have it, a maid called Nest."

"She would be the orphan child who was with him at Caer Gai a while agone," said Samson Clidro. "A funny little woman. A right jili-go-ffrit to run and hide in woods with the wild elves."

"Where would she be now, think you?"

"I daresay at Dreamod, Brochwel's hall near Brecon. I can lead you there."

"Good God, that is miles out of our way," exclaimed Howel. "I am for home, lads. My big Olwen will be hopping on thorns."

"And my she-comrade, too," said Tango.

"God speed then, my friends" said Eden. "I have no wife, so I shall go with Samson."

"I have no wife, either," said Tango's brother, Collwyn.

"No more do I," said Rosier, the youngest sprig of the ancestral bush.

"Curse of my stars," said Tango. "I cannot abandon my brothers. Have it so. I shall bear you company."

"Go with my blessing," said Howel, as he wheeled his horse towards the north.

Led by Samson Clidro, poet and self-proclaimed augur, in his filthy tattered purple mantle, the others made head towards Brecon—a sorry scantling of run-down, beaten-in, haggled-out heroes, who would have liked nothing better in those hours than to have a bellyful of food and a warm and secure snug for the night. They hoped to find them at the hall of Brochwel of the Spears, who in life had been a most kindly and generous chieftain.

Alas, it was a cold welcome that they were fated to receive, although Dreamod was a pretty enough place, all set about with trees, with a little park and heronry and a stream running through flagreeds and watercresses. As they rode into the courtyard, heads popped out of windows and peepholes, goggling and agape. A steward in livery appeared in the doorway of the hall, and stared at them frowningly. Eden saluted him, and told him who they were and the purpose of their coming. The steward disappeared inside and after several minutes returned, bade them place their weapons in lawful rest, and told them that they might enter.

Mallt, the eldest daughter of Brochwel of the Spears and the sister of Nest's late mother, received them in a hall dressed with fine tapestries depicting forest scenes with deer and unicorns. She was a superb blonde of almost angelic beauty. The two men who sat beside her might have been attendant gargoyles. One was her husband, Bleddyn Horty, a baggy fleshed man with two wrinkled-up eyes sunken in his large round face like a greenness in a cheese. The other, a priest, was thin and sallow with a long sharp nose and glittering, close-set eyes. His upper lip vaunted a wart—brave, black and bristling to fascinate the eye. It sat there, Eden soon decided, like a sermon for the parish.

Courtesies were exchanged, whereon Mallt bade her visitors be seated on a bench from which the coverings of velvet had been removed and replaced by a length of sackcloth. Her large blue eyes under their beautifully arched and sweeping brows gazed upon the warriors as they eased their aching limbs upon the bench, as if they beheld creatures who had spent a year in a snail's lodging.

Eden flushed and shifted uneasily

"Forgive our appearance, lady," he said "We are very dirty I know, but we have been in a terrible battle, in which it is my sad duty to tell you that your good father, Brochwel of the Spears, all honor be to his name, has been slain."

"What?" she gasped. "My father is dead?"

She burst into tears. Bleddyn Horty put his arm about her shoulders and murmured soothingly into her ear. The men bowed their heads humbly.

"God have mercy on his soul," said the priest, crossing himself.

"God have mercy on his soul," murmured the others.

"Och, my dear father," Mallt wept, "shall I see you no more in this world then?"

"I could wish to bring you happier tidings, lady," Eden said simply.

"What do you say?" the priest exclaimed at that. "It has pleased our Father in Heaven to remove His child Brochwel from the filth and monstrous evil of this earth and you deem that an unhappy act?" He turned to Mallt. "Come now, my daughter, end the lamentation. Courage."

She uncovered her face to show him her eyes brimming with tears.

"There, there, weep no more," he told her. "Do not forget that it is a blessed thing to die in our Lord and to join the community of His saints and angels."

"I have Brochwel's psalter," Eden said. "He wished it to be given to his granddaughter Nest."

The priest looked at him sharply.

"His psalter?"

"It will be of use to the child where she goes," Bleddyn Horty observed.

"Why? Where does she go then?" Eden asked.

"To the convent."

Mallt dabbed her eyes with a handkerchief and sighed tremulously.

"Oia, these are such hubbub days and our possessions are much diminished," she explained. "We have children of our own to provide for, two sons and a daughter to bestow in marriage. It is a huge expense. And my sister's child is a wayward strange little girl. There are times when I think she is simple of wit. Distract even."

"Nay," said the priest, "she is too wilful for that. She is a cunning little creature, full of tricks and dodges. Some demon has taught her how to run with the foxes, as young as she is."

"How young is she?" asked Tango.

"Seven years."

"And you would put her in a convent?"

"The Evil One is gaining on her. It is for her own good. Why, my sons," the priest said with a harsh laugh, "to look at you one would imagine we were making her dedicate to witches and succubi. These are holy nuns, those purest of maidens who for the term of their lives on this earth have taken the vow to live chaste to God."

"May we see the child?" Eden asked.

Mallt summoned a servant who left at a run, and presently returned with a ewenecked hobbledehoy with a big nose and an undershot chin.

"Morrice," the lady said to him, "be so good as to find your cousin Nest and bring her here."

Moments later a little flaxen-haired girl entered the hall. Her garments were torn and muddy and her pale cheeks scratched and besmutched.

Bleddyn Horty frowned and gave a disgusted cluck.

"Look at her! Where did you find her *this* time?"

"Playing with the ducks again."

"And talking to them, I doubt not," said the priest with a dolorous sigh.

A sad smile shadowed Mallt's face.

"Och, little one," she said, "Taid* has left us and gone to live in Heaven."

The little girl heard none of what was said. All she could see were those five strange men sitting on the bench. Her wondering gaze dwelt upon them, moving slowly over each in turn: the crane-shanked man with the snake-locks in the long, dirty, ragged, purple mantle; the one with the dark sad eyes and the kindly smile, and the two springalds with the wild shocks of yellow hair and the merry winking eyes. It came to rest at last upon one who seemed to her the fairest man she had ever seen. Dirty though he was, his eyes shone out of their wide sockets like two great sapphires. There was the flash of teeth in the curly deeps of his beard as he beckoned to her. Shyly and hesitantly, she moved towards him.

*Taid: Grandfather

"God rest you merry, little Nest," he said as he furtively plucked away the louse that was crawling in her hair and cracked it between his black fingernails. He looked up at Mallt and her husband.

"My lady lost an infant this Advent last past and has been bereft beyond words. It has been a great worry to us. Pray let me take this child home to her. It would be our delight to raise her as one of our own."

Dumbfounded, his brothers lowered their eyes and stared at the floor. The priest's eyes glittered fiercely.

"What is this nonsense now?"

Mallt raised a hand as though in benediction.

"A moment, good Father, I beseech you. Let him speak. What assurance do you give us," she asked Tango, "that you are indeed what you say you are—and not some, some . . . ?"

"Trafficker in the things of the flesh," Bleddyn Horty suggested.

Tango exploded into fury.

"I am the head, shield, and defender of the tribe of Collwyn ap Tango, one of the great houses of this land and God strike me dead and commit me to the pits of perpetual fire if I lie."

"You can be a lord of high renown and yet a toad of depravity." the priest said grimly.

"I will be his avoucher," Eden broke in suddenly. "I know him well. He was a groomsman at my wedding and has always been a true and gallant gentleman." He undid the fastenings at his throat and drew from about his neck a golden cross garnished with rubies. "Take this as surety. My beloved lady gave it to me at the time of our wedding. She had a great love for little children. I know she would be pleased for you to have it."

The three passed it from one to the other, nodding their heads together and whispering.

"It is of some antiquity," Eden remarked.

Mallt pursed her lips and held the cross up to the light, appraising it.

"Aye, and of great value. Why would you wear a thing so precious into battle?"

"Perhaps because it is said to bring its bearer long life and good fortune."

"Or so it has been fabled, I dare say," the priest said, with a covert sneer.

Eden glanced at him with an air of scornful detachment.

"Honor and honesty, however, require me to tell you, lady," he went on drily, "that this blessing only attends those who are honest and honorable themselves."

Mallt glanced at him sharply for a moment, and then smiled.

"What a blessed day this is for little Nest," she said. "For through the death of her brave grandfather it seems that she has gained not only a father but a godfather, too."

"I am glad we have come to a right understanding, lady," Eden said. "And now if it would not disaccommodate you greatly, we would like to wash and have some food and also a place to rest for the night."

"There is a well in the courtyard," she told him, "and a loft above the stables where you can sleep. Meat and drink will be brought to you there."

As soon as they were alone in the loft together, Tango turned upon Eden.

"How could you have given Annes' wedding gift to that greedy vixen?" he exclaimed angrily. "It was St Brychan's cross. It is priceless."

"No, there you are wrong, friend Tango," said Eden. "It has a price."

They left at daybreak. Nest's hair had been washed, combed and braided, and she wore a bright hooded mantle lined with rabbit fur, albeit the dress it covered was the same shabby old one she wore on workdays around the hall. Her aunt hugged her and wept as the time of departure arrived, and she told her niece to remember to recite her prayers and to be a good girl, for even though Taid, God rest him, now dwelt in the realm of the blessed he would believe himself in the domain of the damned if she were naughty. Nest, too, began to cry at that,—she so rarely saw Auntie sad—and then big hands lifted her up and seated her on the crupper of her new father's horse. "Wave goodbye to your kinfolk, Nest," one of the springalds enjoined her as they rode away. She turned about with her hand raised, but her aunt and uncle had already disappeared. Her glance lingered for some moments further on the little oakwood, the heronry, and the pond with its swimming ducks, and then they too were gone. For the rest of that journey, she saw before her only the road, the sky, the birds, the flowers, and the big broad back of the head, shield and defender of the proud tribe of Collwyn ap Tango.

They parted ways at the edge of the great forest that marked the border of the lordship of the religious knights. Tango with Nest and his brothers rode north to the Bay of the White Stones. Samson Clidro, who was eager to see the face of Tango's she-comrade Llio when she found out that she had acquired another daughter to add to those she had already, accompanied them. Eden rode east towards the Marches where he spent the next weeks on the spy.

The troubles that way were coming thick. The men of Shropshire had recently concluded a three month truce with the Welsh, hence all was quiet for the nonce at Shrewsbury. Against this, little if nothing was quiet at Hereford. An army in its thousands was being mustered there during the weeks of May. Sometimes the Welsh lookouts lay so close to the town they could hear the clamor going on within—the sound of trumpets, the noise of anvils, the beat of drums. More and more tents were pitched in the fields as the levies poured in. Once more that most dread and sovereign lord, the King of England designed to advance his banners and standards upon the Welsh. This time he was going to annihilate them once and for all.

And where were their French allies in the meantime? The sixty ships, the crossbowmen, the men-at-arms, the proud chivalry? What a godsend if it was now they would come!

It was June and Eden was catching ponies in the uplands east of Harlech when he received word that Owain Glyndwr wished to see him. It was early morning when he arrived at the castle. A mist lay over earth and sea, presaging a hot day. The Pendragon was aloft on the walk near the chapel tower. He was wearing a long heavy woolen mantle, the hood raised against the chill and he was gazing seaward. At Eden's greeting he turned with a smile.

"Heaven prosper you, Ednyved."

Glyndwr took him by the hand and they walked out along the platform side by side. There was a gentle quiet at that hour, so uncommon up there on those heights, where the winds had their hurly-burly tilting ground. Everything was as peaceful as could be, never a sound to quarrel with the lullabying of the waves and the singing of matins in the chapel below and the ringing of faraway bells among the lonely fisher monks on their isles in the sea.

Eden asked him about his son Gruffydd, taken captive at Usk, and learned that he was a prisoner in the Tower of London and little more. The Prince's voice was calm and thoughtful, more matter-of-fact than sorrowful to his mind. He invited Eden's witness then of the warlike preparations at Hereford, and thinking that it was for this he had been summoned, Eden told him all that he had heard and observed, and Glyndwr listened to him and now and then fingered his lip reflectively, and nothing one way or the other could be read in his face.

At last they went over to the parapet and sat down. The sun was coming up, yawning through the mist. A ripple of light, pale and vagabond as the blush of a wild rose, glanced over the the jagged straggling line of rocks that snarled at the base of the crag, the black anemone pools, the blue and violet fishing nets hanging from the masts of fishing boats, the prows of ghostly ships adrift in the bay.

"I love the sea," said Glyndwr. "You know they say you can sometimes see the Lost Lands of Wales out there when the waters have ebbed."

"It's not the morning for it, my prince. Not with this mist."

"Ah, but that is where you are wrong. That is the best time, one might perhaps even say the only time to see them. It is not Henry of Lancaster we have to be worried about now, kinsman."

Eden stared at him.

"If all goes as planned," Glyndwr went on, "the Earl of Northumberland will soon be launching an attack from the north that is going to draw that army away from our borders. It is from the west that our scourge is coming now. Do you see that dromond down there at the base of the crag? It bears us news from friends in Ireland. It seems that Stephen Scrope, the Lord-lieutenant's deputy, is raising an army in Dublin to set forth against us."

"Mona!"

"Aye, it is not to be doubted that it is there that they will make infall."

"Holy St Cybi!"

"You must get everyone out of the island as soon as possible. These men will show no mercy. Nothing should be left to the use and behoof of the invaders. What you cannot bring with you, burn, destroy. Leave not so much as a dog to bark at Scrope's coming."

Eden left so quickly that he forgot to pay his respects to the Lady.

"Was that Ednyved ap Tudor leaving without as much as a courtesy?" she asked in surprise.

2

The Sheriff of Mona had undergone a surprising change in the course of that year. It had begun in those days when he had lain sick in his house at Rhosyr after the capture of Beaumaris. While he was recovering from the spear wound in his side, he had been stricken by a dangerous and burning ague. He had suffered the extremity of pain and it was thought for a while that he would die of it. He was given the last sacraments. He was delirious for days on end.

One night he dreamt that he was sitting in his warehouse making entries in the big ledger when he raised his eyes to see a dark figure standing in the shadows. It is the Angel of Death come to fetch me, he thought. And he said, quite without fear: "I am ready."

At that the figure came towards him and he saw that it was not an angel at all, for it had no wings. It was a large man—or a presence—big to fill a doorway, not handsome by any means, perhaps even rather ugly. Under the thick pelt of black hair, his face was wind-darkened and deep grooves cut into the flesh of his forehead and about the bearded mouth like scars in a rugged bark. But the eyes were the most marvelous the son of Kenvric had ever seen—as alive and blue as flames they were— you felt as if they could bring light with them into the darkest of places. And his smile was infinitely sweet and lovable.

He bent low over the table where the merchant was sitting until their heads almost touched.

"My dear Meredith ap Kenvric, how is it with you?" he asked in a voice of deep and beautiful timbre.

"Who are you?"

"Courage, my brave one," the mysterious visitor said. "I am St Cybi the Swarthy, who in the life of this world was the son of Solomon, Duke of Cornwall, son of Geraint ab Erbin who was with Arthur the seven Easters and five Christmasses and one Pentecost he held court at Caerleon. Will you be my liegeman and do my work on this island?"

"Aye, that will I, beloved saint. Tell me what I must do," he replied, but scarcely had the words left his lips than his divine visitor disappeared.

After the night of that visitation he began to get better. He continued to improve. When he first walked outside he felt as though he were treading on air. His head seemed to be sweetly aglow; it lit up everything around him. He was happy as he had never been before in his life.

"I bought you as a maid from that scoundrel, your grandfather, the wizard of Mechain," he told his mistress, the stewlady. "I set you free now, woman. You may go when you will."

"I thought I was always free to go," she replied. "But if you say that all these years I have been in your bond, it may be I have grown to like my servitude. Don't talk so foolishly, my dear. Where would I go at my age? Sit down and eat now."

Eating no longer interested him—what is the body more than a wretched sack of dung, he asked himself?—but for her sake he drank a bowl of goat's milk at sunrise and sunset each day. She whipped yolks of egg into it on the sly. With an occasional salt herring and griddle cake this now became his sole nourishment.

Much about this time, on a misty spring evening, the Prior of the monastery on the Holy Head was leaving the chapel of the shrine when he saw a man, long and thin and dressed in dark garments, standing down among the spumy jags and puffins at the water's edge. In the dying light there was a quality almost rootless about him-—an ethereality, as though he were less akin to the things of this earth than to some fantastic seabird that would take wing and fly away. A great black-feathered cormorant suggested itself to the Prior at once.

He hailed him. The man turned his head and then made his way up the slope towards him, treading lightly and springingly on the barnacle-rough rocks with sandaled feet.

Why, it is the Sheriff, the Prior said to himself in surprise—but how changed he is! He looked sadly wasted—a yellow skin drawn over a gaunt scaffolding of bones; but his eyes, that seemed to fill half his face were shining with all the fervor and stubborness of life.

"My dear Meredith ap Kenvric," the Prior said with concern, "How is it with you?"

The man gave a start as though struck.

"That is what he said," he cried. "Yes, those were his very words."

"Who?"

"St Cybi. Yes, yes, I have seen him, dear Father. A month ago. He came to visit me in the dark night of my despond," he breathed ecstatically. "I do not lie. It is true."

"Our Lord God direct all to His glory," said the Prior, and he led the Sheriff away to his cell.

They were there far into the night, their heads bent close together over the wasting stump of a candle, the sea booming around them as though in some cavern of the deep.

"How selfish and misguided my life seems now, good Father," the Sheriff confessed. "How shoddy and contemptible my conceits. I have been blind as a mole, deaf as an adder, daft as a nit."

"The mercy of our Lord is above all praise truly," the Prior agreed. "For it is sure that you have provoked Him greatly. For years you have looked only to your vanities and self-interest. O, my son, when we consider the power of our Lord, what are we? The best of us, what are we? The greatest of men, what is he more than a straw to be blown away at a breath?"

"But I was given back to life. I swore to be St Cybi's liegeman and to do his work. But what that work is I know not."

"Consider where in your vision he appeared to you. In your temple of vanities. It is plain that our precious saint, protector of Mona, spirit of this holy house, means you to begin by parting with your worldly goods."

"But I have already done so. They have been taken from me long since."

"Are you certain?"

The son of Kenvric pondered. On the next day he saddled his piebald nag and rode to Beaumaris. What he found there surprised him. It was not so much that the stuffs in his warehouse were untouched—although that, it is true, was astonishing enough—but that there were so many men lodged in there. Derelicts and prison birds most of them were. Thin, haggard and deathlike, with bones protruding from arms, legs and backs, some looked like nothing human.

"Bless my soul, you are Shoni Gwilt, are you not?" he asked one shriveled-up old man—he had been in the dungeon since the days of the Sheriff's predecessor, Baldwin Radington.

"Begging your pardon, my lord," the ancient said fearfully—for he and his companions still quailed before him as of old, and in spite of the Sheriff's new sweet wild look. "We mean no harm. We are only sojourning here."

The phrase took the son of Kenvric's breath away. Why is it, he wondered, that nowadays the simplest words seem to be invested with the profoundest meanings?

"You have named me your name," he told them. "Henceforward you shall be known as 'The Sojourners'."

With that he flung open his rich albeit dusty and mouldy apartments to them and took them into his ward. Some in the way of things left him in due course, but many of them continued to cleave to him like burrs. They followed him to Rhosyr and slept in the stalls of the byre and stable. The stewlady with some of the goodwives of the neigborhood made them tunics out of cloth of russet. Their breasts gleamed with simple crosses of tin and copper, and from their hempen girdles hung rosaries made out of seashells and chips of shale. Sometimes, on festival days in the summer, the Prior of the Holy Head came to preach to them under the great oak in the churchyard.

And in this way a year passed. Then it was June again and Eden arrived on the island from Harlech.

He rode first to Penmynydd.

"What is to do over at the mill?" he asked Mam Indeg once she had finished washing his face in the salty river of her kisses.

"O, those two silly men are fighting again, my dear."

What had happened was that the Chieftain had been sitting with Father Conan in the fireroom of the priest's house after Mass when they heard that Ianco the swineherd and Pill Hanereg* the miller had fallen to brawling. Nor had the mischief ended there. For upon Meredith's entering the mill, his thundering "What's this?" had caused the swineherd to unhand the miller so abruptly, that Pill Hanereg had stumbled back against the cage of a ferret he kept for ratting. He had grasped the bars to steady himself. There had been a ferocious ripple of movement and in a moment the ferret had bitten through his hand to the bone.

So matters stood when Eden got there. Some five or six men were

*Pill Hanereg: Pill Half-Measure

standing outside, jabbering and laughing. Ianco the swineherd was waving his arms about and working his toothless jaws with a will. "Your husband has fleeced us once too often. He has got his just deserts, the knave!" Eden heard him inform the miller's wife. She, scarlet-cheeked with fury, was trying to glare him down, cradling her bosom on her muscular arms. The miller was half-lying against some sacks of meal along the wall. White and shaken, he was staring as if astonished at the pool of blood on the ground. Father Conan was crouched beside him dressing his hand, while Meredith stood nearby watching with a bored and faintly derisive air.

"Greetings, my chieftain," said Eden. "Do you have your fill of solicitudes?"

Meredith turned towards him with a smile.

"As you see, little brother," he said, embracing him.

Supported by two of his sons, the miller tottered to his feet.

"Father," he said, "the pain is terrible. If only I could have something to dead it."

"I think I have some valerian. Let me go and see."

Father Conan bustled out, giving Eden's arm an affectionate squeeze in passing.

"You look tired," the Chieftain said once the miller had been borne away and they were alone. "Come up to the hall. You can rest there and Marged will give you something to eat and drink."

"There is that I must tell you first."

"Come now, your manners!" he chided, jesting yet uneasy. "Were you never told that a well-bred freeman never states his reason for coming until he is on point of leaving? Can it not wait?"

"No, Meredith," said Eden. "What I have to tell you cannot wait. It has been too long on the anvil already."

The Chieftain turned, the furrow of thought cutting so deep between his brows that they ran together in one brooding ridge.

"Go to then. Strike it."

For a while after Eden had told him there was such a silence that they could hear the flour dust whispering about the walls.

"Holy God," Meredith said at last. "these are tidings." Again he fixed on Eden a gaze of frowning intensity. "You are sure? The world is ringing with such rumors."

"This is no rumor."

"Curse of our stars, no," he growled. "Sure, it wouldn't be."

They walked outside. For some moments the Chieftain leaned back against the doorpost, scowling across the millrace at the garth and sky, his lips stretched back over his teeth in a tight bloodless line. A yellow dog came sniffing along the ground at their heels, drawn by the miller's bloody spoor.

"Begone, you mangy cur!" Meredith snarled with savage suddenness, giving the poor creature a kick that sent it howling halfway down the steps.

Eden observed, "Glyndwr said not to leave as much as a dog behind to bark at Scrope's coming."

"Did he now?" Meredith sneered. "Why does he not cook us up one of his famous weathers, eh? Call up a tempest to drown our enemies, aye, the whole damned pack of them? I love these big lobs, so ready with their advice. Dear Lord, and Rhys and Gwilym out of the land, look you," he grouched. "And those females of theirs, Eva, Eilian— Curse it, why can't a man live on this earth in peace? What is this unholy itch on the great world to put us all in blood? Simple, honest, law-abiding men . . . and what are you smiling about?" He turned on Eden furiously. "You can smile at such a time? Do you find this amusing?"

"Ah, Meredith," his brother replied. "What can I say? We are alive."

The Chieftain stared at him for a few moments, then grudgingly parted his lips in an ungracious grin.

"Aye, that we are," he agreed. "You are right, of course. There is no time to lose. Least of all for repining. Gather up the boys. We shall meet at the Old Hall."

So it befell. From the hour of dusk onward Mona started pouring the leaders of its tribal and religious factions into the first settlement of the fathers. All the islanders of note were there, saving only the Prior of Caer Gybi on the Holy Isle, and those who were away in the service of the rebellion. They had already caught wind of what was afoot. It remained only to confirm it.

"So it's true then?"

"Yes, true."

The youngsters and warriors who were already caught up in the conflict accepted their lot gaily, ready as hitherto to take life lightly and as it came, but some of the older chieftains grumbled.

"Och, and shall the wasp, too, not have her old nest?" sighed one on hearing of the order to fire the island.

The talk grew ever louder and more heated. A few suggested parleying with Scrope, but that idea was laughed to scorn at once. "The only parleying that scoundrel will do will be at swordpoint."

"Listen, my friends," said Meredith, calling for silence, "when Scrope lands, this island will be caught as in a winepress between his army and the enemy garrisons at Caernarvon and Conway. But if the fruit is wanting, where then will be the vintage? And this is still our land, remember. Garrisons devour up men who must be fed, clothed, paid, and kept far from their homes where by and by they will be more needed. Time is in our favor. Be patient and trust in God."

Eden looked at Andras of Dyngannan, and thought of Mererid. The old woman was still alive he had been told, if in no condition to dance in the timbrels. Where would the priest's daughter go? And when, he wondered, had she burrowed her way into his heart? It was as though some wild creature, long dormant, were suddenly awake and stirring in there.

"Why is the Prior of the Holy Head not here?" he heard Meredith asking.

"He refuses to leave," someone replied.

"We'll see about that."

On the following morning the Chieftain and Eden rode to the Holy Head to reason with the Prior, but he would not be persuaded that any Christian force was going to be so black of heart as to attack his house, home as it was of the miraculous shrine of St Cybi, the patron saint of Mona.

"I shall not leave the shrine," he said.

"Then," said Meredith, "we shall take the shrine with us."

"No, you shall not," said the Prior resolutely. "You will have to slay us first."

At last the brothers left, the Chieftain in a thunderous fume. "It is the wise and merciful God who offers us these providences, is it not? Flee, my children, He is as good as telling us. But they will not see it, the fools, no, no, they will not see it."

On the way back, Eden rode to Rhosyr to see his father-in-law. Marged Vaughan—on her knees in the hall at Penmynydd, wrapping her pots and bowls in linen and packing them in hay and straw in the great cauldron, a model of resourcefulness and presence of mind—had urged him to do so.

"The Sheriff's been crazy in his health lately," she told her brother-in-law.

"How do you mean, crazy?"

Choler morbus, distempers of the bowels, the megrims? He did not delay. And all along the way the scenes were the same: excitement and fluster, children bawling, women wailing, men shouting, beast creatures in a stir, horripilated dogs snarling and snapping at their own shadows. What was his surprise then on reaching his father-in-law's house to breathe in an air of nothing but rest and calm. It was like the third watch of the night there in respect of hurry and scurry. That is not to say there was no one about. Some fifteen to twenty men were squatting on their hams along the sunlit walls. They had a rough and beggarly look about them. God knows he had seen better sights than some in coffins. Yet they seemed friendly enough. And it was a chorus of Heaven's greetings from them upon him as soon as he broke on their view. "The power of Holy Cross be with you, brother" —and—"God save you, brother."

"Who are you 'brothering'?" Eden asked them in amazement. "What are you? Lollards?"

"We are 'The Sojourners'," one of them said.

"What is that? Another sect?" it was on his tongue to proffer next, but at that moment a door creaked on its hinge, there was a busy whispering: "It is she, it is she, our sister," and the Sheriff's lovewoman, Gwervyl Mechain, appeared in the opening of the wicket.

"Eden's here," she called back over her shoulder. "Come in, my dear."

She beckoned to him and he followed her through the wall wicket into the orchard where he was greeted anew by the familiar dwarf oak with its knobs and wens and glanders where once he had shared many sweet hours of delight with Annes. Now it was her father who sat there, reading in his breviary.

Eden was unable to master his exasperation.

"What are you about, in-law? Our enemies are designing to invade us, have you not heard? Why are you dawdling like this? Why are you not gathering up your chattels?"

"What chattels?" the Sheriff smiled. "The clothing on my back, my spear, sword and buckler? My piebald bony nag? Let me see, what else? O, yes, one arbalest with tackle; a spinning wheel, a cauldron, a few skins of wine. . . . Come, don't fret, lad. All is taken care of. And, look you, we are so near the love-saint's isle here."

"Is that where you will take your departure? With the monks?"

"So we have been directed. There is a ship off the headland yonder. Come, sit down, It would content me greatly. You have lookouts posted, do you not?"

"On land and sea," Eden replied, and since in truth he had no objection to complying with the Sheriff's request, having slept no more than two hours in as many nights, he sat down on the grass facing the bench where his father-in-law was sitting and told him of the morning's encounter with the Prior of Caer Gybi.

"We could not make head with him at all," he said.

"That is as it should be," the Sheriff said calmly. "The Prior knows where his duty lies. He cannot allow the shrine to be taken from this island. He must guard it with his life."

"I do not follow you, in-law."

"But you must know that after the slaughter of the Holy Druids here by the Romans, Mona was known as an Island of the Dead. King Gwyn, the lord of the fairies and the Underworld had dominion here then. Banhounds, bolols, evil sprites. Pagan burial pits everywhere. Heathens lighted fires to Beal on the Holy Head, think of it. St Cybi it was who converted them and drove out the demons. O, my soul, you can see now, can you not?—that we cannot let those sacred bones be borne away from Mona or this island is doomed anew."

Eden was silent for some moments, staring.

"I hear you have been ill of late," he ventured then.

"I was very sick some while back," the Sheriff nodded, "but to the praise of God and our beloved St Cybi I say it, I am so much better now that I do not think I have felt so well in years."

The stewlady brought Eden a cup of wine. It did not fail to go to his head. And it was no doubt due to this, added to the fatigue and worry and crowd of matters which the tempest-riven wreck of the time had set adrift like so much flotsam through his aching brain, that he did not fully grasp the import of the tale his father-in-law proceeded to tell him now. As in a daze he listened to the Sheriff, watched his shining eyes, a tear tracing its glistening course along the hollow cheek. What has happened to him? What is he talking about? A visitation? God's my life, the fantastic cracks in this universe through which a man's soul can slip! Madness, all is madness.

"Ah, if only I had the tongue of angels," the Sheriff sang out in a soft and joyous voice, "so that I could make you understand, my dear Eden."

"Allow a poor mortal his frailties, in-law."

"But that is what we all are, is it not?" the older man said with a beatific smile. "Poor mortals at the perpetual disposition of Heaven. Each one of us must do what he is given to do. Go with my blessing now."

"Aye," said Eden, rising. "The sunclocks are racing."

The Sheriff's woman pressed his arm.

"Do not worry about us," she said. "All will work to the good, you will see."

"May it be so, Gwervyl."

He turned and looked at the Sheriff who now rose and embraced him.

"Farewell, Sir Siri," he said. "God be with you."

"Likewise, my son," said the Sheriff. "Fair wind and full sea."

At Penmynydd, Meredith's rough organ could be heard ringing across the yards.

"Where have you been?" he shouted as Eden came riding up. "Is this the time to be paying your devoirs?"

"Marged. . . ." Eden began.

"O, Marged!" the Chieftain snorted.

The islanders were convoying their chattels towards Aber Menai. Down at the ferries the ground was packed with a scrambling mass of humans, their creatures and goods. Little boys, as ragged as colts darted in and out of the lanes among the carts herding pigs and goats. Hens pecked and bickered in handcarts under stout cord nettings. And how futile to the eye all of a sudden, how forlorn seemed those red ribbons against misfortune which streamed like bright pennoncels of blood from the manes of donkeys and ponies and the horns of oxen.

Early the next morning the bellows in the forges at Beaumaris were cut. Everything portable was removed from the castle. Emrys of Myvyrian's ship was fastened to the ring at the castle dock waiting to be loaded. Farther out, moored at the tower that fronted the Sheriff's old house, lay the vessel of the Abbey of Aberconway, manned by the monks, and captained by their holy leader, Sulien. His lean, vigorous, thong-chastened body was girt in a coat of mail. A white cross shone out against his crimson surcoat. His long monkish pate was helmeted. Pale his cheek, fierce his eye, and you could tell at a glance that the dangerous lines of those big stubborn jaws had not come there of themselves. The Father Abbot was on Crusade—Bohemund before Antioch.

And then, the loading done, the town was put to the torch—the dilapidated merchants' houses facing on the weedy moat, the abandoned shops, the hovels, and the pothouses. Nor did the burning stop there.

It was midday when Meredith ap Tudor set the torch to the wickers girdling the hayricks at Penmynydd. "Go to," he told the others. "We will build all better when we return."

Men's hearts took fire in proportion as the conflagration was borne to the hall and its houses. Every last qualm was stifled. Hooting with destructive excitement they scampered homeward to their thatched huts. Come, who would not ruin himself? Soon the fires could be seen running up the fields from croft to croft, from the tribal woods to the turbary pools of the fairies at Nant-y-Gath.

Nobody stopped to think unless the Chieftain did. Years ago he had pulled down the old hall and rebuilt it of stone. He had built it to last. He must have known it would not burn well. So much could not be said for the Old Hall. Those ancient timbers, which had provided tenantries down through the generations for successive races of woodworm, burned magnificently. It was enough to walk into the hall with a flaming brand and sneeze across the wind, it seemed, and lo, the flames were flickering across the strawed floor. The dais boards were smoking and the silentiary's post, battered repository of who knows how many forgotten songs, was coming alight like a Paris candle.

"I am glad that Sioned and the women are not here to see this," Gerallt said grimly.

And while his son Gwyn and his fellows shot fire-arrows into the thatch of the roofs, he stood aside from the incendiary work in a sort of speechless homage. Robyn wept unabashedly. Amen, thought Eden, they had loved the Old Hall so much better than he. They recalled warmth and laughter and happy days where he could see only bitterness, sorrow and despair. It was a place of corpses to him, those of hopes and dreams as of the humans who in life had harbored them so unwisely. Why not have done with it? Lay the obscene old monster once and for all? Immolate him in his funeral pyre?

Meanwhile, the wind was rising. On their way back from Rhys Ddu's hall the windmill near Coeten Arthur and the burial mounds was aflame. Its bark wings were whirling crazily against the sky, shooting great tails of sparks far and wide across the moorland among quitchgrass and hay and the bone-dry flinders of dead trees. All the game thereabouts was afoot. Frogs were belching irefully in the marshes and the blue, smoke-scented air was vibrant with the throb of wings, the cluck, chatter and scream of birds. Eden and his companions could hardly hear themselves speak. It was deafening, marvelous—aye, like the end of the world.

It was late afternoon when they finally turned their horses' heads towards the sea-river. They boarded *Morwyn Maenan*, the white monks' vessel and sailed out across the water to Aber of the White Shells where their wives and families awaited them. After they had taken their ease, the Chieftain turned inland with most of the company, following the ancient path of the peregrini eastward through the mountains to the Valley of the Conway, leaving Gerallt and Eden and a few of their comrades to ride down to Bangor to see how matters stood in that quarter and give help where needful.

The town was deserted when they arrived. Strangely huge and silent the Cathedral loomed amidst the night and its shadows. But farther south at the ferries the banks remained populous and rowdy. Andras of Dyngannan with Emrys of Myvyrian and Asa Coedana were standing on a slab of rock down by the water where the slope was gentle enough to be passable for carts, watching a group of islanders sorting their bullocks.

"Are these the last of them?" Eden asked.

"It's not known about those monks on the Holy Isle."

"Mother of God, look after them," a fisherman said, crossing himself.

Eden looked at the opposite shore. The dark waters glassed the flames of the burning hamlet. Flakes of soot flew up about the glowing treetops like rooks. So far as could be seen, all there, too, was empty of life.

"Where is my sister?" Gerallt asked Andras of Dyngannan.

"She has departed with my wife and family. Did not your father, the priest, tell you?"

"We have been busy."

Andras frowned. "You know we shall take good care of your sister, Gerallt ap Conan. After all, it is not as if she is going with these herds to their grazing grounds in the mountains, is it? She will be lodged in one of the great houses of our land, my mother's ancestral home."

"So that is where she is going then?"

"Yes," said Andras. "To Nannau."

It was not until a week later that Eden learned that the Sheriff and Gwervyl Mechain had not left the island. The story of their strange and terrible end baffled and haunted him. In his imagination, he seemed to see the black lines of a large cross swaying against the sky. Two figures in long mantles of sable color strode along below it. Behind them like a flock of red birds hopped The Sojourners. But was it the King of all Lords and his servant, St Cybi, who had put it in the Sheriff's head to go out and meet the invading host? And what had been his purpose? To draw Scrope and his army into a bog as the islanders had done in the past with their enemies or to try to win his heart to mercy?

"I regret now that I did not pay him more heed," Eden said to the Chieftain, "but my wits were far too weary then to set to his riddle. Do you think it is the truth he saw St Cybi?"

"Who am I to say what he saw or did not see?" his brother replied. "Or what is dream and what reality in a world where not even the Holy Sacraments can defend a man from illusion? It was a miracle he lived for sure. I can remember carrying an old nostrum of Marged's family over to him one night when he was raving with fever. A little while after we had given him the medicine, he woke up and looked at me. 'I am ready,' he said. I think he thought I was his death. It gave me an odd feeling at the time. But his health improved after that, so I daresay that nostrum cured him."

Eden shook his head.

"But why?"

"Why indeed?" said the Chieftain. "Now that too must pass in

10
NANNAU (1405)

The journey of Elianor of Dyngannan and her small troop from the island to her native hall of Nannau in the mountains could hardly have been said to be a happy one. The old woman blamed her companions for everything. To hear her talk, you would have thought them responsible for the invasion of Mona, to say nothing of the condition of the road and the weather. The inn where they spent the night was filthy and crowded. Only one bed was available. Elianor, as a matter of course, was given that. Bundles of fresh straw were pitched in for Em, Mererid and the children. The serving folk had to make shift for themselves.

Happy they, the priest's daughter thought.

Elianor's threnody was unceasing. Nothing was right. There were bugs in the bed, the chaff-stuffed mattress was uncomfortable, the food was disgusting, she felt too hot, she felt too cold, and the groans of a carnal engagement on the other side of the threadbare curtain separating her from the guests of lowlier estate so infuriated her that she summoned the innkeeper to her bedside in the middle of the night.

"How is this, you pissant? Is it a swiney house that you are keeping here?"

She threatened him with the curse of the clergy. A ban would be put on his food and drink for a hundred years.

On the next morning they set off again. The road began to climb; the country grew wilder. On her bed of cushions in a covered cart the old woman felt every bump along the stony weather-torn way. She damned her stars and cried up nothing but woe and calamity. She could not suffer her grandchildren to be near her—they pestered her; they snored and kicked, they fouled the air, they brought in the flies with them. Let them ride with their mother and the priest's daughter—the children should be their concern and not hers, an old and ailing woman. Sure, they had no care for her at all.

For two days further they traveled, passing through forsaken rock-strewn glens, and lying out on the one night in an abandoned hermitage and on the next in a mountain croft that boasted a firehole, earthen benches, and the smoke-blackened posts of a cowplace littered with dried dung and branch butts. And then, on the afternoon of the fourth day after they had left the island, they descended into the town of Dolgellau, winding down the falling hills with the twistings of a stream.

Elianor heard a familiar voice, the cloth canopy of her cart was parted and there stood her nephew Howel Sele, the lord of Nannau. He was in dark rich raiment, his eyes were as blue as cornflowers, his curly hair and beard were golden, he carried a white falcon on his wrist— never had she seen a man so fair.

"My dear aunt," he said to her and in the next moment soft lips and fluffy perfumed whiskers brushed her yellow cheek.

Her heart trembled with delight. Here are the true men, here. There are none the likes of the lords of Nannau to be found on the Isle of Mona—those fellows there are dung in comparison. Her own blood— best of the best.

The hall and spacious park of Nannau lay almost a thousand feet above the town. Over the gates stood a large red painted wolf of timber. Beyond that the hall rose, built of huge logs with ornate carvings. The steward's house, allotted to Elianor and her retinue, consisted of a small hall with a bedchamber and a ladder leading to a cockloft with a lattice square that looked out over the valley towards the Cistercian abbey of Cymmer.

Howel Sele carried his aunt inside and laid her down on a couch before a sweet-smelling fire of cherry wood.

"Home," she smiled, her nostrils dilating with pleasure. "It is easy to kindle a fire on an old hearth, Howel."

"We would have lodged you in the main hall," he explained, "but we must keep a chamber there in readiness for our Prince Owain."

"Glyndwr? Are you expecting him here then?"

"He and his army are encamped in the meadowland before the Abbey."

"But I thought he was in Harlech."

"Last week he was in Harlech. This week he is in Dolgellau. I am thinking of holding a hunting drive here in his honor."

Her face clouded but not for long. Her blood was beginning to thrill again to the old music. In spite of her piteous condition and the hardships of the past days she insisted on going to supper with her host and hostess. Em and Mererid labored over her as though they were getting a bride ready to meet her groom. They brushed her hair, washed and scented her, dressed her in her best gown of red brocaded velvet and at her bidding rubbed her cheeks and lips with berry juice. A great ruby red hat was put on her head, bejewelled rings were forced on her bent fingers, thick gold chains were hung about her neck, and then, her toilette complete, her thin crooked body was lifted up by two manservants, carried into the hall and there set down carefully in the high seat between Howel Sele and his wife Gaenor. Propped up stiffly between the two, with her black eyepatch, twisted ossified mouth and painted face, she looked more hideous than ever.

At the table for children and dependents Mererid was dreaming. Aching with nostalgia, she thought of those she loved in far off Nantconway. She stared absently at a broad-shouldered stranger who was sitting on the left side of the lady Gaenor. His hair was cut straight across his forehead and one of his eyes turned inward, giving him a look at once sinister and comical. Meeting her abstracted gaze he grinned and nodded his head. Suddenly her glance flashed like a viper's fang. She reddened and looked down at her platter.

'That fiery young beauty," the stranger asked Gaenor. "Who is she?"

The lady of Nannau looked and shrugged her shoulders indifferently. "A serving maid of my husband's aunt, I believe. A person of no consequence."

"Of a truth?" said the stranger, still grinning at Mererid. "You surprise me."

By my soul, thought the priest's daughter, that man has a worse turn in his eye than Eden's.

His name was Davydd ap Llywelyn; his nickname was Davy Gam.* He was the lord of Castell Einion Sais and other lands in the County of Brecknock. He was also the King of England's squire.

"You can see, can you not?" he told Howel Sele when they were alone together later that same evening, "that our Lord Owain is going to ruin Wales? And for what? A dream, say you? Universities for North and South, a Church independent of Canterbury as in the days of the glory? Well, sure, that is all very fine. But dreams do not build of themselves, do they? They are raised out of the blood and dust of

*Davy Gam: Knighted on the field of Agincourt, he is said to have been the original of Fluellen in Shakespeare's Henry V.

countless poor fools such as you and me. Aye, my friend, first the warshout, and the bloodletting, and the heartache, eh? Then the dream."

Howel Sele was silent. His youngest brother had been killed at the battle of Usk. Two other kinsmen had also died since the rebellion had begun.

"Dreamers frighten me personally," Davy Gam said with sarcasm. "And the greater the dreamer, the greater the fright."

He spoke to Howel Sele about the Tripartite Indenture of the Earl of Northumberland, Sir Edmund Mortimer, and Owain Glyndwr wherein it was agreed that the land of Wales should extend to its ancient boundaries.

"The Ash Trees of Meigion," said the King's squire. "Do you know where they are? Near Worcester. Why do you think Glyndwr selected those as our line of March?"

"Our forebears once enjoyed good inheritances there."

"Aye, and in Edinburgh and London. Once."

He winked his squinting eye and bent forward confidingly.

"Merlin predicted that the Great Eagle would one day muster his host of Welsh warriors at the Ash Trees of Meigion—that is why Glyndwr chose that spot. He fancies himself in the part of the Great Eagle. Why, the man has gone mad with power, do you doubt it? O, he is an eagle, right you, but it is to be doubted he is great. Remember the Eagle of Gwernabwy, eh? He flew so high at the start of his career, but in the end where was he? Sitting on a stone not a handbreadth in height. Only he did not know it, poor deluded bird. Each evening he still thought he was pecking at the stars, when in truth his claws were fixed in the sod and his beak in the clay. Illusion! Illusion!"

Howel Sele smiled. Davy Gam was clever. Devilishly so. But the lord of Nannau saw his cunning.

'Why am I the one who has been chosen?" he asked.

"Owain Glyndwr trusts you."

"What makes you think he has reason not to?"

"The King has his sources. We have been watching you this long while besides that."

"Ah."

"You are harboring the sons of Red Iwan, the former governor of Caernarvon here."

"Pia of Nanmor, their stepmother is my wife's sister. She asked me to give them shelter."

"Why did she not ask the wife of Rhys Ddu of Mona? She is Red Iwan's daughter. Look, Howel Sele, I know it little behooves me to remind you that the rewards to yourself would be dazzling. You are above such base considerations. Why did I even raise the matter? Let us forget it. For your country's sake, I appeal to you."

Leaning his head against the back of his chair, the lord of Nannau pressed his heavily beringed fingers against his temples. The fate of Wales now lies in these hands, he thought. It was a profound moment.

"Where are those two lions, Madoc and Huw?" Davy Gam asked after a while. "Are they near?"

"They are at the Roman Tower a mile from here."

"I should very much like to meet them."

Howel Sele summoned one of his henchmen and sent him on his way. About half an hour later he heard a distant door slamming. Thinking that they had arrived he went into the hall. His wife was standing there talking to one of the maids in Elianor's retinue. When Gaenor saw Howel, she came towards him, frowning.

"Your aunt has collapsed," she said with exasperation. "They think she is dying. This is really too much. She has been here only a few hours—and now this! She should never have come to sup with us tonight, it was utter stupidity!"

Spots came before Howel Sele's eyes, his hands felt suddenly clammy. Holy God, why now?

"What is it?" asked Davy Gam, coming up behind him.

"My aunt. She is dying."

"Merciful heavens!"

The russet-haired young beauty he had marked earlier passed him swiftly, brows fretting. Davy Gam was hard put not to give her a playful pat on her shapely rump, but conscious of the solemnity of the occasion, he mastered himself and tried to look grave and concerned.

On her way out of the hall Mererid almost collided with two men. They stepped aside for her to pass. They seemed familiar to her, especially the taller of the two. He was very handsome, lean-thewed and graceful, with large doe-soft dark eyes and fine-boned features the color of ivory or new-cloven wood. Where have I seen him before? Mererid puzzled.

"Here they are, the sons of thunder!" the squint-eyed man laughed, coming forward to greet them.

Eva, thought Mererid suddenly. He looked like Eva, even down to the waspish wrinkling of the brows and the crooked scornful little smile. Holy Mother, it is Madoc and the other of course is Huw. Red Iwan's sons. And is Howel Sele of their persuasion then? And is it he who is inviting Owain Glyndwr here for a hunt?

At once her quick mind saw all, divined all, and the cunningly woven work of months was unraveled in a moment.

While the sons of Red Iwan spoke with Davy Gam, the lord of Nannau and his lady went to see Elianor. The steward's house, which such a short time before had been merry with laughter and the sweet scents of cherrywood was now filled with the whisperings and odors of death. Unobtrusively, Gaenor withdrew the sachet of lavender she wore between her breasts and held it to her nostrils. Wondering how long it was going to take her to die, Howel Sele stared at his aunt through narrowed eyes. Her face was purple, her one eye was bulging and bloody and she was snoring horribly.

"Have her children been sent for?"

"Only her eldest son Andras, my lord. It's not known where the others are."

"She is the last of my father's people," Howel intoned gravely. "With this great lady there dies an era. The years pass away like smoke, yea, and the generations like the shadows of the morning."

While Em knelt at the bedside, Mererid sat on the bench against the wall with her arms about the two children, watching with dry eyes. Her heart was pounding wildly. There no longer seemed any easy thought she could enter into or rest upon. She was filled with a sudden rush of hatred for these people. They could have been Turks or Tartars-so alien they appeared to her.

She knew she had to get word to Owain Glyndwr? But how?

The old lady lived on for four more days without recovering consciousness. Her long dying lay on Nannau like a nightmare. Howel Sele was driven to the brink of distraction. Glyndwr will be gone and the death still rattling in that stubborn tenacious throat. And Mererid thought: She must die soon and then the wolves will gather for the kill.

At the end of the fourth day Elianor breathed out her soul. The grave women washed and clothed her in her gown of red brocaded velvet and laid her out on a table in the chapel of Nannau with candles burning at her head and feet. Her face was terrible. The skin had turned black and because the women had bound up her lower jaw too tightly her lips were wrenched by a hideous grin, like a grimace carved in an idol of bogwood. Flies clung to her eyes and nose. The air was foul. Already worn out by vigil and fasting, Em, whose health was never of the best, fainted in the chapel before she had been there more than a few minutes.

"Another one now," Gaenor whispered to her husband. "Truly our cup runneth over."

On the following morning Andras arrived. Mouthing the appropriate words in a silky sympathetic voice, Howel Sele grasped his hand warmly between both of his, but his cousin with a perfunctory nod and an ungracious mumbling withdrew it almost at once and went into the chapel. A while later, his morose black eyes red with weeping, he crossed the yard to the steward's house. He kissed his pallid unsmiling children and went up the ladder to the cockloft where Em was lying. He stood with tightened lips and knitted brows and took gloomy stock of the surroundings.

"Is this the best they can do for the lady of Dyngannan?" he muttered angrily.

Em looked up at him with a trembling, timorous smile. "I could have had your mother's chamber, but I was afraid to lie there after. . . ."

"What nonsense!"

He stood at her bedside irresolutely, looking down at her wan grey face. He wanted to kiss her, but Mererid's presence disconcerted him, and this made him more cross-grained than ever. He gave the priest's daughter a dark look.

"And what is wrong with you?" he demanded, running his eyes over her sullenly. "Are you ill too, eh? You look like a ghost."

"You must be hungry," Mererid said. "I will get you something to eat."

"I have some salt herring and cheese in my saddlebag. Bread will serve."

The priest's daughter went to the bakehouse. They were getting ready for the funeral feast. As she was leaving with a loaf of bread, an oddly familiar sound arrested her. A fat woman was rolling out pastry on a board, and as she did so her wedding ring kept knocking against the wood. So Mam Indeg's used to do of old, her daughter now remembered. Suddenly, she was overwhelmed with memories. Choking back a sob she hurried out into the yard. What am I waiting for? And if I am caught, what of it? The welfare of my own beloved people is at stake. More precious to me than my life.

After she had given the bread to Andras she took her brown cloak and without a word to anyone she mounted her horse and rode down the hills to the valley and out along the meadowland to Glyndwr's encampment at the Abbey of Cymmer. As with many daring actions which are taken on an impulse her course was unimpeded. Her absence was marked only by Em, Andras and the children. When upon her return she gave as an explanation her need to break free for a few hours they did not question it. For what reason should they have done so?

In the days following the burial of Elianor of Dyngannan in the family vault at Nannau, the sound of horns and the baying of hounds were to be heard in the countryside around Dolgellau as Howel Sele and his guests with their whippers-in and falconers scattered far and wide along the paths of the forested hills.

The hall and chambers were hung with bright suits of tapestry and the floors strewn with sweet flag. The feast of welcome itself was one of the most memorable held at Nannau. There was wine out of silver, mead out of buffalo horn and ale out of maple, and among the many courses prepared by the cook were salmon bellies, capon bakemeat, venison, and roast boar which Howel Sele, resplendent in an apple-green gown of branched damask wrought with tiny white flowers, ceremoniously carved. Everyone was particularly captivated by a subtlety depicting Glyndwr in the guise of a crusader in armor trampling the neck of a horned and devilishly writhing King of England, all artfully wrought in jelly of brightest vermilion.

"I had thoughts of a subtlety with yourself trampling the neck of the Hewer at first," Howel Sele told his guest of honor.

Glyndwr turned his gaze upon him slowly, his face shadowed with a faint smile.

"So you have heard of the Hewer then?

"Who has not? The tale is on the lips of everyone. Lord, you are the legend made flesh."

"Have pity upon me, my friend," Glyndwr chided him humorously.

"It is a vain world and the flesh is weak. And then," he went on to remind his host, "to give the devil his due, it was Lord Grey who slew the great boar. So had you contrived to have my subtlety crushing the neck of the Hewer underfoot, it would have been artifice indeed."

Howel Sele groaned inwardly. He was in no mood to engage in word play. He suffered from the megrims and feared the onset of one now—that little throb in his right temple, a faint sense of nausea, a slight blurring of the vision. And the thoughts that were teeming in his brain!

"What know I of artifice, my Lord Owain?" he countered lightly. "I am an artless man."

"Truly?" Glyndwr marveled. "So you do not indulge in chimeras then?"

Howel Sele cast an appealing glance at his wife, who was appareled for the occasion in a pali of wine-colored silk and a flowing veil bound at the brow with a chaplet of flowers, after the wont of women in the old time of the princes, a style her table companion, the Abbot of Cymmer, an old fashioned man, found most chaste and becoming.

"The Parthian ladies were used to dress so," he was beginning to tell Gaenor when she caught her husband's eye. She marked his pallor, the reddening about the lids. By the body of the Virgin, another of those headaches! Has he drunk wine, the fool? She nodded to the steward. He clapped his hands. At once a flock of mummers entered, dancing to the music of sackbut, drums and shawms, and the hall was filled with revel and sound.

Under the patriarchal moss of his brows Glyndwr let his eyes range through and past the masks and medley of the mummers to the faces crowded about the tables and benches before him. His searching gaze came to rest briefly on Mererid. Seated amidst the children and dependents of the house of Nannau she was unaware of it. She herself was looking for the squint-eyed man, but he was nowhere to be seen. So he must be known to Glyndwr, she concluded, as are those twins in perfidy, the sons of Red Iwan. Where were they at that hour, she wondered? And what devil's work were they plotting?

Still musing she looked at Em and Andras who were sitting apart from her and the children amidst the kindred. Both felt wretched; Em because she was ill, and Andras, because of all those gathered that night in the lofty hall of Nannau with its dancing and dazzle of lights and mummery, he was the only one who had a thought for the lady who lay quietly rotting away at that hour in the family vault: his own beloved mother, Elianor of Dyngannan.

On the final day the host and his principal guest went out together into the forest with their longbows. Howel Sele was one of the most celebrated bowmen in Wales and he had promised to give Owain Glyndwr a demonstration of his skill.

"If I do not nail you dead a stag with my first arrow, my lord Owain," he said. "I will furnish you forth a war band that will be the pride of your host."

When they had ridden for an hour they dismounted in a glade and leaving their horses in the care of the lord of Nannau's chief huntsman, struck off for Gogan's Well, a pool in a ravine about half a mile away.

Howel Sele quivered like a wolf, thinking of what must be. His companion in the meantime spoke to him affably of one inconsequential after the other. The lord of Nannau laughed more than was necessary to hide his excitement. And if there were no deer that day at Gogan's Well? Away, what of it if there were not? he thought. He was out for bigger game.

The thickets through which they were passing were swarming with squirrels—they ran up the treetrunks and peered at them from the branches. They put Glyndwr in mind of his first hunt. He began to tell his host about it. It had happened on a Christmastide when he was six or seven years old. Snow had fallen and he and his boy cousins and friends had gone out with their slings and holly darts and dogs hunting squirrels in the glen.

"We had bagged a few, when we saw one up on high in the trees. Everyone started hallooing and hurling their stones and missiles at him but to no end. Off he flew like an imp of Satan, leaping from branch to branch, tree to tree. He kept us on the run for half the morning. But in the end he was struck by a holly dart that was hurled by Ifan, the son of Cadifor of Bodfari. We could see him falling through the branches. Off with us, pell mell, boys and dogs as one. But when we came to the spot we thought to find him, he was not there. He had vanished."

"Vanished?"

"Without a trace. Where could he be? we wondered. We searched and searched. High and low and all about. It must have been one of the dogs, we decided. Turco, perhaps. He was the chieftain Cadifor's lead hound, a black mastiff with a giant maw."

"He swallowed the squirrel?"

"All in one gulp, holus-bolus. What else could account for it?"

Howel Sele's thoughts drifted. He could no longer follow the thread of this meandering tale. He nodded and smiled almost without knowing why he was doing so. Other words kept chasing after one another through his brain.

"Dear Mother of God," he seemed to hear himself saying, "there he was lying with an arrow in his back. Think of my horror. The golden-handed Lord of the Vale of the Divine Water, our *pater patriæ*, the hope of our race. But you ask, who could have done it? Aye, so did I. I have now to tell you this. I am sheltering the sons of Red Iwan, the quondam governor of Caernarvon here. My wife is the sister of their stepmother, Pia of Nanmor, a good lady of spotless life. She begged me to give them asylum before she renounced this world to take the mantle and the ring. What could I do? I am a soft-hearted man. Is that a sin? But by my soul, I never dreamed. . . . Och no, not Madoc and Huw. I pray God they are innocent of this most wicked crime!"

It would be simple. He could not see how he could fail. And everything was falling into place so neatly, aye, quite as if Providence had willed it.

"The guilty sees his shadow between himself and the sun," Glyndwr said.

Howel Sele started and stared at him. For a moment he had a sickening sense that all was discovered, but it was only transitory. Glyndwr's humorously reflective eyes expressed nothing but absorption in the childish tale he was telling.

"So the old byword goes, does it not?" he rambled on. "Figure on it, my friend. Within days, nay hours, of that hunt Turco died. The lord Cadifor was put in much perplexity. A healthy hound like that. In his prime. And of no little value, to be sure. A Gascon breed, I believe. What could account for it? Now Cadifor was something of a chirurgeon. He cut the carcass open forthwith and what did he find lodged therein but the fur and divers minute bones of the squirrel as well as the head of the dart that had slain it. He deduced at once from the stench and black putrefaction of the organs that the dart had been envenomed, perhaps with the juice of *atropa belladonna*."

Howel Sele stared at Glyndwr, uncomprehending.

"The boy killed the squirrel with an envenomed dart? Why?"

"Perhaps in order to poison the one he designed to eat it. Ifan's stepmother was a notable shrew. Cadifor had no easy life with her. And she was harsh to the lad. But let that be on the bye. While sleeping one night not long after Turco's death Ifan felt a great weight on his chest, suffocating him. Something black and inhuman that left behind it a wild and acrid odor as of wolf or dog."

"Turco?"

"Or an incubus in the form of Turco. Each night thereafter he was visited by this nightmare. He became distraught and ill. He could scarce breathe. At last he feared to lie down in his bed. He spent his nights sitting on the highbacked settle in the fireroom at Bodfari. It was there that they found him dead one morning, a broken straw at twenty."

"Mercy on us!"

"Aye, my lord Howel," said Glyndwr, "mercy on us."

The path they were taking now became muddier. Fresh deer droppings glistened like black berries in the grass. The two men became silent. They unslung their bows and crept forward cautiously to the head of a small ravine. A magnificent buck with a white blaze on his forehead between his antlers was standing beside the pool nibbling peacefully at the wet grasses. There was no wind. Owain Glyndwr made a face expressive of delighted incredulity. Taking an arrow from his quiver, the lord of Nannau nodded to his companion to move away to another vantage point. Glyndwr took his stand behind an oak some little distance away from the other, with his back turned towards him. Howel Sele calmly fitted the arrow to the string, drew it to its head, took aim, then all at once spun around and shot it at Glyndwr. A moment later he stared in stupefaction and horror. The arrow lay broken in two pieces at the Prince's feet.

But how? His heart felt at point of stopping, his head reeled. The eyes that regarded him, laughing and friendly only a short while before, were now narrowed down into glittering chips of unfeeling ice. He felt a cold as of the tomb in his bones. The forest had suddenly become dark and gloomy.

The guilty sees his shadow between himself and the sun. Had that story been told for a purpose? As a warning perhaps? Too late now. Shadowy forms were emerging from the trees.

"Put him in bolts," Glyndwr said.

Em was lying in her sickbed that July night. Mererid had stretched a hide curtain over the lattice square, but the loft was so stuffy she begged her to withdraw it.

"They are killing Howel Sele out there, Em."

"I am choking. I must have air," she said.

She was drenched in sweat and strengthless. Mererid took away the covering. The red light of torches flickered over the dark timbered walls and there was the sound of crying and moaning. The two of them were silent, listening. In the floor below the two children were bickering shrilly.

"O, tell them to stop," Em pleaded. "I cannot suffer it. I think I shall scream."

Later Andras came. His step was heavy on the stair.

"They have hanged him," he said. "The death of Judas."

Crouched on a stool beside his wife's bed, he sat rubbing his sweaty livid face with trembling hands. He had never liked Howel Sele, but for all that it troubled him that his death should mean less to him than the fact of his betrayal. For that he had been betrayed there was no doubt. Before his execution the would-be assassin had given his kinsmen to know that Glyndwr had been forewarned.

And Andras knew who the informer was. He was sure of it.

The house was to be burned to the ground and those of the men of Nannau not sworn to Glyndwr's sword driven out of the land. But he, Andras of Dyngannan, had been told that he and his family were free to go when and wherever they chose. He found this disturbing. Not so much because he had been told it, perhaps, but because he had been told it in confidence. Only a simpleton would not have sensed a complicity here.

So it was the priest's daughter then. That afternoon she had gone out riding alone—he remembered. She who had seemed to him as good as a child's happiness was no better than a murderess. At first the realization had driven him wild. He had ridden down the hillsides almost all the way to Dolgellau before he could collect his wits. Dark knots of people stood whispering in awe and fear everywhere. He scarcely saw them. If he returned to the steward's house at Nannau then he must certainly have done something irrevocable. He must have killed her or abused her. Either way she would have been lost to him then.

And yet, at the same time, he understood why she had done what she had done. If Glyndwr fell, her faction too would fall. The sons of Tudor would fall.

He knew he could never pledge his allegiance to the cause of Glyndwr now. He had to ride with the men of Nannau. So he told Em and Mererid on his return to the steward's house. His wife's face fell.

"But I thought we could go to my mother's family at Nanhoron," she said softly.

"They are certainly closer," Mererid frowned. "Your wife is a sick woman. Would you subject her to yet another long journey?"

"I have no choice," he told Em, ignoring the priest's daughter. "Your people are supporters of Glyndwr. If I went to Nanhoron now, how would it look to my kinsmen? Would they not be within their rights to believe me the man who betrayed Howel Sele?"

"If your conscience is clear, what of it?" said Mererid.

He glanced at her in astonishment, but her face showed him nothing. Nobody could have looked more guiltless. "Let me decide what is best for my wife," he told her coldly. "For yourself there is no reason for you to stay with us further. You may leave when you will."

"Yes, my dear friend, you must go home to your own now. They will be wanting to see you again," said Em, but at that she broke down and began to weep so helplessly that it wrung Mererid's heart. It was plain that she was in despair. Why in the name of charity could he not take her to her father and mother and kinfolk at Nanhoron, where she would be loved and cared for instead of among strangers? The stupid man would put everything to the hazard in the name of honor.

Ah, what a coil! She knew she could not leave this poor woman and her two children as they now were. If she went to Nantconway she would never rest easily, thinking of them. It would be on her conscience, yes.

"Well, of course, I am going to stay with you," she said to Em. "But only until you are better. Then I will leave."

So she is entrapped, thought Andras. He would have smiled perhaps, if only he had not felt so miserable.

11
THE ASH TREES OF MEIGION (1405)

1

On the first of August the French, led by the Marshal Jean de Rieux and Jean de Hangest, lord of Hugueville and grand master of the arbalestriers, landed at Milford Haven. It was a golden day, not a cloud. The spacious harbor was thick with masts. Men-at-arms, crossbowmen and knights of France thronged the quays. Bucklers, helmets, lances, corselets—there was such a dazzle to all that steel in the summer sunlight that it almost seemed to encroach on the marches of fire.

News of their arrival had brought a crowd of folk down to the shore from the neigboring countryside. Rustics and burghers, friars and bawds, fishermen and goodwives and wide-eyed barefoot urchins, vied with one another in staring at the newcomers, in marveling at the elaborate armor of the knights, their splendid hauberks, their crested helms, their thick studded belts, their jingling, glittering spurs. Robert de la Heuze, in particular, fascinated them. Known from his deformity as Le Borgne, he was a ferocious little man with thick coarse black hair like a horse's mane and one eye dressed with a hideous rag of skin.

"Ou sont les *goddams?*" he bellowed at the onlookers, much to their wonder and amusement.

Flanked by his Chancellor and Bishop Trevor of St Asaph, Owain Glyndwr came down to the strand to greet the French chiefs. Three of his five sons, in handsome cloaks and tunics, walked behind him. The Siri Mawr followed, leading a black plump-haunched charger richly trapped and after him, under great silken banners, came a procession of dignitaries headed by John Hanmer and Philip Scudamore of Troy.

The host and his guests then proceeded to a nearby meadow where tents and a pavilion dressed with tapestries depicting the feats of King Arthur had been pitched for their repose and refreshment. Sweet bread, cheese, capon bakemeat, wafers with hippocras, fruit and wine were furnished forth, while musicians entertained them on the psaltery and the harp, and Patroullart de la Trie played a farandole on the lute.

Then Le Borgne, glowering about him with humorous menace, demanded: "Ou sont les *goddams?*"

"Les *goddams*?" Glyndwr queried with amusement.

"Les *bigods*, seigneur," Le Borgne explained.

They moved without loss of time. As soon as the festivities were over and the goods of the French unloaded, the army marched upon Haverford and took it. On the next day they pushed ahead through Pembroke. Over Cemais and Emlyn they went. Carmarthen, which they had lost and won and lost again, became theirs once more. Throughout the following days they advanced through South Wales, recapturing towns which had been retaken by the King's men since the last campaign, distributing booty among the indigent and returning their liberties and immunities to those from whom they had been withdrawn by Henry of Lancaster.

Hundreds of hooves, thousands of feet—the earth groaned as the captains and their soldiery moved forward under their bright and tossing standards. The summer wind carried the songs and shouts of men, the rumbling of wagons, the thud of hooves, and the creak of harness far and wide over heath and meadowland. And in Glyn Rhondda Owain Glyndwr unloosed his mighty warshout upon the hills:

"Cadwgan, whet your battle-axe!"

And with that (as told by Florimond le Bel, the chronicler appointed by Duke Louis of Orleans to keep an account of the expedition for the delight and instruction of the brainsick King of France and his court) behold rabbits scattering in the fern and squirrels in a panic and birds clamoring skyward and in another moment the woods discharging spearshafts and scores of men leaping and yelling under them. Indeed, wild mountain goats impaled on spits and uttering howls of pain appeared to be bounding down the hillsides as Cadwgan, the lord of Glyn Rhondda and his men rushed to their leader's call.

On the sixteenth day of August they pitched camp at Caerleon, near the ruins of the Roman city and the noble abbey of Arthurian legend. There they were joined by Howel Vaughan and another body of men from Nantconway.

A moon as round and pale as a millstone shone in the heavens that night. The world was drenched in its eerie light. The ruins cast huge shadows, the leafy branches of the trees wove whispering nets in the long grass; in the meadows the campfires winked like lost stars in a milkwhite sea.

"Father Conan's daughter is your foster sister, is she not?" Howel

Vaughan asked Eden.

Eden felt a tremor of alarm.

"Yes," he said quickly. "Has something happened?"

"Her people are upset about her. She did not return to them after the burning of Nannau."

"Where is she then?"

"She has gone with Howel Sele's faction."

Eden laughed incredulously.

"It's true. The story is that she is Andras of Dyngannan's lovewoman."

The words had scarcely left his mouth, when Howel Vaughan staggered back, his nose and lip bleeding from a jarring blow.

"Fool!" he snarled. "You will answer for this."

On the following day Eden was sent back to Glamorgan to help Black Rhys and Henry Don, who were besieging Coety castle. The rest of the army moved northward along the Marches towards Usk. By this time, their numbers totaled some fifteen thousand men.

Meanwhile the men of Nannau had been offered sanctuary at the King's manor at Grosmont in Monmouthshire. They rode slowly at first, suiting their pace to the small train of Dyngannan, with its two young children and their ailing mother, who was now couched if with far more meek forbearance, in the same covered cart in which Elianor had journeyed. And then, some leagues north of Ewyas Harold, they received word from Davy Gam that the French had disembarked and were making their way towards the Marches. A surge of restlessness swept over them, making them put their horses to a faster trot. It tasked Andras to keep up with them. At last he told them to go ahead. They feigned concern, but he was not taken in.

"We will send an escort back from Grosmont to meet you," they told him finally.

"Aye," said Andras. "Thank you kindly."

Em, who had been holding on to the poles of the cart for dear life for she did not know how long, her lips bitten white in the effort to keep herself from screaming, opened her eyes, feeling the wheels rocking slowly to a halt. She gave a sigh of relief and in a little crawled forward and opened the flap of the canopy. Her eyes were gladdened by the sight of a rowan tree in full berry, blazoned brightly against the blue sky.

"O, Meri," she said.

The priest's daughter, following her glance, plucked off a twig and handed it to her.

"Do you believe that the wood of the quicken bush protects one from misfortune?" Em asked, kissing the twig and putting it in the purse at her girdle.

"I would as soon believe it as not," Mererid smiled.

It was not long before her belief was shaken. Troubles never come singly in very truth. They found shelter for the night at an inn outside Ewyas Harold. It stood on the banks of the River Monnow—a wattle-built shoddy with an earthen floor and an oven steaming with cabbage. After the privations of the journey through the wilds of Wales, its dubious comforts were accepted with gratitude by Em, Mererid and the children. But Andras was less easily pleased. Arrogant and surly, he gave only curt replies to the questionings of the innkeeper, a friendly but meddling brothbowl. In justice to the man of Dyngannan he was upset less for himself than for those in his charge. The sight of the rats scampering over the sleeping forms of his children filled him with despair and rage.

"Your place is filthy," he told the innkeeper. "For pity's sake, scour it."

Early the next morning before it was light they were roused out of their beds to find soldiers awaiting them in the common room of the inn. Andras, alarmed now, gave them the story they demanded. He explained to them that they were on their way to the King's manor at Grosmont, but the very idea of that struck the men-at-arms as so ridiculous that they burst out laughing.

"Aye, very like, very like," exclaimed the sergeant, their leader. His grin turned into a ferocious grimace. "You will have to spin us a better yarn than that one, Welshman. Who do you think you are fooling with your lies? You must come with us."

In convoy of ten soldiers they were led to Abergavenny through the Wood of Revenge where of old Morgan ab Owain had slain Richard de Clare. They arrived in the town about noon. Many of the houses were charred ruins and famished-looking dogs slunk along the sooty lanes. Abergavenny had been the center of fighting more than once. Rising out of the dungheaps of its serfs, the castle raised by Hamelin son of Dru de

Baladun on the site of the fastness of the giant Agros, still harbored its ancient menace, however, within its blackened but unbroken walls. Here the prisoners were conducted, Andras carrying his wife in his arms, Mererid leading the children by the hand. They were brought into a gloomy hall that was so cold that a great fire burned there as in the dead days of winter. Awaiting them behind a table was the constable, a grim long-faced man with a grey crop of hair that shot up from his head like bristles of soiled frost. He bade the women and children be seated on a bench along the wall, and then began to question Andras. Once more he recited his story. The constable heard him out in silence and then guffawed scornfully. Weary, dazed and humiliated, the lord of Dyngannan could see no way out of his dilemma. He begged the constable to let the women and children go free at least, but to no avail. The man was inflexible. This was war, he said, and there was no trusting of anyone.

"You know, do you not," he observed darkly, "that at this very hour the villainous Glyndowrdy and his French cronies are marching upon England to the despite of its people and the destruction of the English tongue? And do you wonder that I am harsh?"

The questioning went on for an hour. For an hour Andras swore that he was loyal to the King's allegiance.

"You must tell me the truth," the constable admonished him sternly. "Otherwise, by God, you will answer for it at your utmost peril."

And with a movement of dread and unmistakable import he tapped his neck smartly with the edge of his hand and rolled his eyes upward with lolling tongue to the cobweb-festooned rooftree. Em, who had no English and hence could not follow what was being said, imagined the worst. With an imploring cry she darted out into the middle of the floor, but once there her strength failed her—she clutched at her breast and swayed as though she had been arrested by the blow of a fist. Andras caught her in his arms on the point of collapse and bore her back to the bench. Her face had turned a deathly white and she was gasping for air like a fish in a net. Hushing the children who had begun to wail, Mererid quickly loosened the sick woman's girdle and covered her up with her mantle.

Bending over them his dour ungainly form, Andras looked down at Mererid's bright head hovering over his wife's thin ghastly face and for some reason found himself thinking of the rowan tree beside which they had halted the day before. So she too flourished in this doomed and bitter world, he felt,—vivid, defiant and touched with blessing.

What? A murderess? A tongue-reddener? The enemy of his sect? God help me. He pulled himself together with a start. What ailed him, thinking such thoughts at such a terrible time? And his poor wife lying there in agony? Horrified at his treacherous lapse he seized her limp hand and pressed it fervently to his lips. Rarely had he indulged her with a caress before; his mother's forbidding shadow had lain between them. Now he was overcome with remorse. Tears welled to his eyes and he babbled endearments.

"What are you saying?" the constable demanded. "Speak English so that we can understand."

Andras rose, twitching oddly and his teeth chattered.

"You vermin!" burst from his lips hoarsely and he grabbed the constable's throat. In the next moment he was knocked senseless and amidst the screams of his children dragged from the hall.

"Are they going to kill Dada, Meri?" Iori sobbed, plucking at her sleeve.

"Of course, they are not. People do not kill innocent men. Hisht now, and stop your bawling," Mererid said sternly, trying to master the shake in her voice and collect her straying frightened wits.

"What is wrong with that woman?" the constable asked her, peering down at Em with a frown.

Mererid turned on him fiercely.

"Can you not see, man," she hissed, "that she is in the throes of a pestilential fever?"

The ruse worked. On the following evening they were brought to the hospice of the Knights Hospitallers at Hereford. There it was discovered that Em was not suffering from the pest, but rather from a dangerous debility of the heart. She was put in a dorter with sickly old woman and orphans. One of the lay sisters in attendance was a broad hipped matron whose face was hearty and lined with the marks of much pleasure and pain endured. Alice Brut by name, she and the priest's daughter soon became good friends.

When she had an idle moment Mistress Alice often came to Em's bedside for a chat. The sick woman had little difficulty in understanding her, for she illustrated her speech with many and eloquent gestures. Apart from that, she had a fair amount of Welsh picked up from her husband, a Lollard of Welsh descent now in the service of Glyndwr. In fact, she told Em and Mererid, he had visited their native isle once. The occasion had been an unhappy one. In the brawl and business that had arisen about him as he was preaching at the market cross of one of the island towns, he had barely escaped with his life and the constable of Beaumaris had been slain.

"Dear my fathers!" Mererid said in amazement.

It came back to her. But how long ago it now seemed. That was when Eden had fallen into sin with that feather-brained wanton, Gwennan of Croes Gwion. She remembered how on hearing of it from Sioned she had run out into the churchyard and flung herself down weeping amidst the graves and broom. She had thought of Eden as well-nigh a god then and Annes a goddess. Like sun and moon they had compassed her little world with light. After that she had felt only disdain for Eden for a long while. Looking back upon those days as she rested now in the house of the Knights Hospitallers at Hereford five years later, she saw from the ache of her heart how profoundly her feelings about him had changed.

Em, too, was lost in reverie. She thought of the island and Dyngannan. She thought of Andras. "I am so worried about him," she told Mererid when they were alone. "I wonder where he is now."

"At Grosmont, I'll go bail. When you are better we will go there."

"I am going to get no better, my friend. Deny that I am dying."

"What are you asking me to say?" said Mererid, her eyes filling with tears. "We are all dying, Em, some of us sooner, some later. It may be that you will get better for all I know. For sure we are in the hands of a merciful providence or we would not have been placed here among these kind folk, would we? And as for dying, I remember my father once saying over some words of Taliesin Chief Bard: 'A man is oldest when he is born, and after that younger and younger all the time.' I could not grasp his sense then, but now it seems to me that what he meant is that in death we are reborn."

"Your father is an uncommon priest."

"Aye, that he is," Mererid said with her quick smile. "Or else he would not have married my mother."

Em died on the following day. In the morning of the small hours she was seized by violent heart spasms. After she had received the last sacraments she turned her dilated eyes on her children. She clutched Mererid's hand and worked her mouth for a few moments, trying to speak.

"My little ones . . . look after. . . ."

From afar she heard the voice of the priest's daughter reassuring her and then her ears were filled with a sound as of the roaring of surf that grew fainter and fainter, and so at last she left the pain and hubbub of this world and passed quietly into oblivion.

Later that day Mererid gathered the children to her.

"You must not grieve for your mother. She is at peace above the torments now."

"Shall we see her again?"

"It is not to be doubted. She is in Paradise among the saints, the most loving of your friends. She is your hope, your very best hope of Heaven. She is going to watch over you all your days. Do not vex, you Iori in particular. You are seven now, a big lad. At your age many boys in Wales are put out to foster. While your father is away you must stand in his stead and be his deputy. And do you look after us, aye? Poor silly helpless women such as we are."

"Aye."

"Good boy."

"Where are we going now, Meri?"

"We are going to stay with Mistress Alice Brut for a while."

She lived near the Scalding House, the last of a row of little cottages thatched with straw. The low-roofed hearthroom had an earthen floor and whitewashed walls that rippled like fleece in the firelight. Upon one of them hung a crude black wooden cross. They were bare of all else.

"What did Master Walter preach that was held to be heretical?" Mererid asked her friend.

"For one thing," said Mistress Alice, "that God will not forgive men through confessions of mouth or the assoiling of priests or bulls of pardon. If a sinner has inward sorrow and true contrition for his sins he can be saved without going to shrift."

"Priests would lose dignity so."

"And mass pence and tithes also, my dear child. So many of them have grown covetous. Christ and his apostles did not demand tithes. They were content with but the food and clothing that were their due. For this reason priests should be poor and weak."

"Perhaps so. You live according to the rule, it is plain. All the more reason then that we three should not batten on your board too long. We must come by some way to get back to our people in Wales."

"It is dangerous, lass. A woman alone with two innocents. All this border country is in broils. Ravening wolves and robbers everywhere. You must find companions and armed at that. Until then, stay. I am much alone and your company is a blessing to me."

They remained with her for five days. Although they missed their father and mother and pined after them in their childlike fashion, Iori and his sister Betris had rarely been so happy. An exciting pageant opened upon their eyes by the hour at Mistress Alice Brut's. Here came a woman striding along with two hens hanging from either hand full feather and cackle, and here a gaggle of geese stretching their necks and shrilling. Beyond the Scalding House with its great steam and stench of wet chicken feathers, at the end of an earthen lane bestrewn with fluff and beaks of birds, lay the flesh shambles. Men were fetching off the heads of fowls with bills at chopping blocks there, blood flowed in the gutters and decapitated hens ran around in circles, a sight at which the children marveled greatly.

Once Mererid led them up an alley past a tenter yard to an almshouse and put some eggs on the sill of an open window that was covered with a linen cloth upon which rosary beads were spread.

And one morning Mistress Alice took them to Mass at the great cathedral. The air was dark and filled with jubilant murmurings. Veiled in incense, a shadowy host of men and women knelt about the nave and side aisles, but once in their midst the children barely saw them for staring at the high altar that glowed with so many candles and bejeweled cloths that they almost fancied they saw an enchanted grot in a dusky wind-rocked woodland. Openmouthed and wide-eyed, the little ones were still caught in the spell when the sound of shouting was heard. On that, the doors were thrown open and the worshippers began to pour out. A crowd was milling in the square, talking excitedly and looking at the ramparts of the castle and town walls where soldiers were running and barking orders.

"What has happened?" Mistress Alice asked.

"There is a Welsh army a few leagues away—Glendowrdy and his host."

Throughout the rest of the day the bells of the cathedral and churches rang out through the town. Men came streaming in from the surrounding countryside with their animals. Mistress Alice thought it wise for Mererid and the children to stay indoors, for there was no telling what would happen if their identity became known.

They were sitting down to their supper of bacon and peas when there came three knocks at the door in rapid succession. Mererid's heart turned over and Alice, as a rule such a model of self-possession, all but jumped out of her skin.

"No, no, have no fear," she reassured the priest's daughter promptly in a husky trembling voice. "Three taps—it is Walter!"

She rushed to the door, and pulling her husband inside, held him a full minute in a bone-crushing and wordless embrace.

"Walter Brut! Walter Brut!" she wept, holding his broad, smiling, nutbrown face between her two big, red, toil-chafed hands.

So wrapped up in her husband was she indeed, that Mistress Alice did not realize for some little while that he had brought a companion with him. But Mererid and the children saw him at once—a tall gangling man with black hair in ringlets and a mournful face. He was dressed in a long threadbare mantle, and on his head he wore a large straw hat bearing the badge of the guild of London fishmongers, a sturgeon gilt.

At last Mistress Alice saw him, too, and fell to staring.

"This is my friend, Samson Clidro," said Walter, drawing the man forward by the hand. "He is a poet."

"You live not on a single dish," Samson intoned thereon, "Now beef's preferred, and now 'tis fish. Just so, for all things there's a time, For preaching now, and now to rhyme."

"Yes," said Mistress Alice with a smile. "Did your parents name you Samson after the saint or the strong man in the Bible?"

"People always ask me that for some reason," said Samson. "No, the truth is that I owe my name to Samson Dry-lip, one of Arthur Pendragon's henchmen. Have you never heard of him?"

"There were so many of those fellows."

"The blood-comrade of Sgilti Lightfoot?" Samson looked at her hopefully, shook his head, then went on to say. "Well then, he was also a kinsman of the lord March. Does that name ring a bell? The chieftain with a horse's ears?"

Mererid broke in laughing:

"Who slew his barbers lest they betray his secret?"

"Of a truth," said Samson, casting her an admiring glance. "Where did you hear of him, fair maid?"

"From my mother," Mererid replied. "She has all the tales. Our Chieftain calls her Mam Awen."

"The Mother of Fantasy,*" said Master Walter. "What a beautiful name!"

"Yes," said Mererid. "But I am not sure our Chieftain thinks so."

"But did you know," Samson went on, " that March's descendants still live in the Llyn peninsula? Aye, hardby the old pilgrim's way to the Isle of the Saints. Strange to relate, but many of them, lads and lasses alike, still share their ancestor's deformity. The men have to grow their locks long and bushy like the girls, so they cannot take up soldiering seriously, of course, until their hair starts dropping out with age. Then because of this tribal stigma of theirs they have to wear great bonnets— very like those worn by courtiers in France."

"Chaperons," suggested Mistress Alice.

"Aye, only much bigger. Out to the ridge of their shoulders and down to their jawbones."

"He's off," Master Walter smiled.

"Whisht, why should I lie? That's why they call that tribe the Big Bonnets down in Llyn. They are very touchy about it, mind you. I recall traveling there once to attend an *eisteddfod cler*, a contest of bards as you well know. Quite by chance I came upon the master on a morning pinning back his hair so that he could fit all into the bonnet, and there they were—ears as big as a young donkey's. Heyday, chieftain, I said to him, and where are you burying your barbers these days? Well, he went to ice at that. Nor have I been asked back there since."

"I should think not," said Mistress Alice, her eyes sparkling as merrily as a girl's.

"And that, alas, is why I have been unable to recruit the Big Bonnets in our cause.'Tis pity of it indeed, for I think if our enemies could see those lads, they would all die laughing. Which would be a most merciful way of ridding ourselves of them, I think you will agree."

It was a jolly evening. Later Master Walter revealed that the Welsh

* Also, The Muse.

army was bypassing Hereford and heading for Worcester, twenty-five miles to the east.

"You will come with us, of course," he said to Mererid when he had heard her story. "What else is there for it? Some party or other will be returning homeward one of these days with messages and the wounded. It will be best. Good heavens, aye, the sons of Tudor are in the host, now that I think of it."

Mererid's heart beat fast, but Mistress Alice was troubled.

"You have been at some risk coming to see me, Walter. How will you get out of here?"

"The same way we got in, dear wife. With the rustics and the fugitives. Seeing that the danger is past for the time being, they will be crowding out at cockcrow and the townsfolk will not be for detaining them."

All fell out as he predicted. Early the next morning they left. Mistress Alice came with them almost as far as the town gates. She embraced them one by one. About her husband's neck she hung a medal of St Christopher and they kissed and blessed one another 'ex toto corde meo.' She followed them with her eyes as they mingled with the throng leaving the town. When they had passed out of sight, she turned and with her head lowered as though lost in thought she walked slowly some distance, then with ever quickening pace hastened up the streets to her cottage with her apron crumpled against her mouth.

On the Feast of St Bartholomew the Apostle the Welsh soldiers and their French allies were resting at Woodbury Hill, when it was learned that King Henry was drawing out his forces at the city of Worcester, some eight miles distant. They hastened there and at mid-afternoon they were charging out of the woods and down along the slopes towards the river Severn where their enemies were massed.

The battle raged fiercely until sunset on both sides of the river. Horses were felled, men were riddled with arrows. Then trumpets brayed and the enemy troops began to retreat, running and galloping towards the city on the ridge. After them swarmed their opponents, hurling spears. Thighs and stirrups quivering, Howel Vaughan drew rein beside Rhys Ddu and Gwilym ap Tudor. Nearby a French knight in a pig-faced helmet came to a halt; he raised his vizor to reveal a broken nose and one bright bulging brown eye: Le Borgne.

"*A mort!*"

A boisterous whoop burst from his lips as he let out his horse at full gallop along the turf. In a flash he had left his Welsh comrades far behind. Not only that but he had cut off the head of an enemy horseman with a stroke so sheer that it was still snarling curses as it struck the earth. Meanwhile a shower of stones and arrows rained down from the city walls upon those below. Within moments the English were inside and the curtains and battlements were glittering with their steel caps and spears.

At that such a silence fell that for a moment Howel Vaughan wondered if he had gone deaf. Then someone started crowing. Almost at once thousands of throats broke into a roar across the hillside. A thrill of exhilaration ran through him for a moment only to be succeeded by a feeling of frustration and bewilderment. He and his comrades had been counting on the issue turning upon a field battle. It seemed King Henry had decided otherwise.

"Look!" said Rhys Ddu, pointing at the cathedral tower which could be seen rising like ruddy giant thumb above the grey walls of the city. Something was winking and sparkling up there, the way a gem or chip of rock crystal will when it is caught by the sun.

"King Hal, I'll be bound," said Howel Vaughan. "Overlooking the field. What is he saying, think you? Eh, who would have dreamt that the barefoot knaves could so overbear us with numbers? By St George the dragonslayer, there must be thirty thousand men down there at least."

"No," said Rhys Ddu, "that is not what he is saying. He is saying, only wait until the rest of our army arrives and falls arear of the barefoot knaves. By St George the dragonslayer, what a merry slaughter we shall have then."

"Go home, you rip, I had better thoughts of you."

"Think on it. You were not born yesterday, no more than that begor up yonder. He is bent on playing a waiting game with us, it's plain."

Owain Glyndwr was of a mind with him, as it turned out. In a council of war which he summoned in his tent after the morrow mass he impressed on the captains how little they could afford to trifle out time. Their choice was therefore one of two: either to march away and maybe lure the enemy out of his stronghold thereby or else aim at a speedier resolution by putting the city to a storm. Some of the Welsh chieftains, including the sons of Tudor were for marching away. Jean de Hangest, the grand master of the French crossbowmen and the leader of his compatriots, declared for a storm without reserve. So it was decided. Throughout the day they prepared their batteries. As soon as dark fell they crossed the river. Two hours after midnight, straw was fired at the North Gate as a signal for the attack to begin. Their thought in acting so early was to take their enemies by surprise but the King's men were wakeful cocks. Clarions and bells rang the alarm directly. Soldiers poured along the ramparts. The first of the besiegers had scarcely gained the topmost round of the ladders before they were caught in the thick of it. The fighting waxed so hot and bitter there at first, indeed, that the attackers were forced to recoil. The second attempt was more successful. They even got ground of the defenders for a while, due no doubt to the fact that in the meantime the French had scaled the walls at the gate on the other side of the city. Nobody had been expecting them there, the bastions and curtains being difficult of access. The main body of the besiegers, all the tumult and smoke, were centered around the North Gate. Hence, so soon as ever the alarm had sounded, everyone had rushed in that direction, leaving only a handful of soldiers to guard the other gate.

Le Borgne was the first to gain the summit of the parapet, followed by Howel Vaughan, Jean d'Espagne and six other Frenchmen. As they ran down the steps in their cloth-muffled shoes they came face to face with a guard. Struck dumb with amazement, he had no time to move before he was felled by Le Borgne's axe. There were five other men-at-arms on guard near the gate. At the death cry of their comrade they turned and peered into the darkness, seeing glints of steel moving. Four of them were slain within moments. The other darted away into the dark and narrow gorges of the city.

While the French set to work breaking the gate, Howel gave the fleeing soldier chase. He raced after him through garden plots, unlighted lanes and a tannery. All this part of the city seemed deserted, but as Howel rounded a corner he came upon the marketplace, rats banqueting among the cabbage-stumps under the empty streetstalls. His quarry was talking to a group of townsfolk: goodwives with their hair hanging loose, burghers shivering in their nightshirts. Behind them the cathedral stood out like a ragged mountain peak against the yellow smoke of the fires. The soldier was working his mouth and gesticulating wildly. Howel took one look, and set off once more at a run, save that he was now the one pursued. Soon there was an outcry behind him. Bruit and threat spread through the streets. Torchlight wove in and out of the maze of dwellings, whirling and crackling against the black air. There was the clang of iron as feet pounded along the earth.

"Whip to it, lads!" he cried to his comrades, who were almost at point of breaking the gate. "We have lost the turn. Away!"

A dove-grey dawn was breaking as they and the force of soldiers who had lain hidden in a thicket below the walls reached the clump of willows near the river where their horses were tethered, and soon after this the rest of the besieging army, too, gave up hope of carrying the city by force and expedition. Drawing off their dead and wounded, the allies retired to their camp at Woodbury Hill.

It was there that Master Walter Brut and his small company found them when they arrived on the evening of that day.

The children were mute with astonishment at the sight that awaited them. Set high among woods and the ruins of ancient fortifications, glowing with the smoke of a thousand fires, Woodbury Hill as they first saw it seemed a torchlit realm of elf-folk to the little boy and girl. Master Walter and the long shanked poet Samson Clidro led them upward in tow of Mererid along the grassy trenches of old earthworks and through the crowding tents. All sorts of people were to be seen there, going about their errands in the smoky blue dusk: friars in their heavy grey cassocks; men in warlike array; women gossiping and preparing supper; armorers and potboys; and herds tending to the goats, horses and ponies that wandered through the willow copses and along the slopes. The twilight was noisy with laughter, songs, the barking of dogs, the groans of the wounded and the ring of the hammers of tinker and smith.

Gwilym ap Tudor was sitting in the opening of his tent, lost in reverie, when he saw a small group of people heading towards him.

"Why must they bring small children to a place like this?" he wondered with disapproval.

They came to a halt before him.

"God's blessing upon you, son of Tudor," said the one, a broad short man with a ruddy brown face.

"And upon you also, my friend," said Gwilym.

Blinking his tired eyes, the master of Trecastell shifted his gaze to the face of his greeter's companion—a long man cloaked in imperial if old and weatherworn purple. Who is this? he thought laughingly. Please God it is not another prophet.

"Greetings," the long man said, bowing his head amiably. "Allow me to present ourselves. I am Samson Clidro the poet and this is Master Walter Brut, the heretic."

"I have heard of you," Gwilym said to the Lollard at that. "You used to be a priest at Hereford, did you not?"

"They were gathering up brush to burn him when he escaped," said Samson. "We cannot let this English King overbear us, chieftain. He will kill all our cranks and clowns and we shall die of boredom."

"This lass is one of yours," said Master Walter. "Will you take her into your keeping?"

"Bless my soul, it is Father Conan's daughter," Gwilym exclaimed. "Where are you coming from now?"

The master of Trecastell had always intimidated Mererid in the past, but at this moment his familiar presence and his island-accented Welsh so wrought upon her that before she knew it she was pouring out her heart to him as though they were old and intimate friends. Dignified and reserved as he generally was, Gwilym listened to her and in his turn was touched by her confidence and her story. He looked from her to the two little ones—Andras of Dyngannan's children, so pale and weary and forlorn.

"Are you hungry?" He hunted in his wallet and brought out some raisins and stale bread. "A woman will be bringing us supper soon," he smiled. "And then you shall have some soup."

For the sake of the children, who were sitting in the grass at his feet watching him intently, he did not tell Mererid his thought, that probably their father was still a prisoner in Abergavenny castle.

"The King's strongholds at Grosmont and White Castle have fallen and it is said that the men of Nannau are now in Monmouth," he told her. "I dare say Andras is with his kinsmen there."

What an extraordinary maid this is, he reflected not without a little amusement. No female had ever spoken to him hitherto as she had done this evening.

Later on Rhys Ddu and Howel Vaughan returned. They stood in smiling astonishment when they saw Mererid and the children.

"You have acquired a family since we last saw you, it seems," Rhys

Ddu observed.

Gwilym introduced them.

"So you are this candle of maids I have been hearing so much about," Howel Vaughan said and stared at her so hard that she became confused and averted her gaze.

"It is no use looking around for Eden," he teased her then. "He is not here."

Blushing to the bone she anxiously met his laughing unshifting stare. Gwilym took pity on her.

"Do not worry, Mererid," he said. "He is in South Wales, outside Coety castle."

She glanced at him gratefully. "I bless the day," she said.

As for the days that followed, however, Mererid would have been the first to agree that it would have been pleasant to forget them. Each morning in the grey light the Welsh and their French allies sent out bodies of men to contend with the English in the field on both sides of the river. There were many brave passages of arms and notable feats, particularly by Le Borgne and his comrades.

"Sir Rolando has been put in the shade," Howel jested.

"They live for fame, it is the way of them," said Gwilym.

"O, he who desires fame, let him die," said Rhys Du, citing the old byword.

Inevitably, the toll of dead and wounded mounted. Each evening carts rolled into the encampment laden with the casualties of battle. Then as the bloody thread of those August days began to run out, the weather took a turn for the worse. Rain fell, winds blew. The morning air grew raw and misty. Like dripping shag-haired dogs the trees of the woods shook their heads over the tents where men sat dressing their hurts and riddling the blood-swollen lice from the hair of their heads and bodies. Distempers of the bowels soon became common and the loathsome smell of carrion and excrement was dismaying and inescapable.

Meanwhile, it both amazed and relieved Mererid how swiftly the two children, her charges, became inured to the horrors that were visited upon their eyes. They came with her while she helped Master Brut nurse the sick and wounded. Men writhing in the throes of their death agonies, corpses stretched out on their pallets, terrible maimings—it was all one to those two urchins after a while. They looked on with big, shining, timorous eyes for a space, then they skipped away after something or other—a dog, a bird, a butterfly—and it was as if they had seen nothing, heard nothing. Like the birds of the air they took each moment as it came and as it succeeded to the last. They slid down the grassy banks of the earthworks, picked blackberries, gathered rushes, whistled on reeds and made mud castles.

"You would think you had been bred up in a pig bed," Mererid flung out at them with flashing eyes and tongue when they returned to the tent one evening. "Shame on you! Think what your grandmother would say could she but see you now!"

There indeed was a thought! Angry and fatigued as she was, the priest's daughter could not help laughing at that.

Still, had she ever been so witless and unheeding as those two mites?

"I find it hard to believe," she admitted to Gwilym ap Tudor with a wry half-hearted smile.

"It is as well that they are so," he replied. "God is merciful. They will forget the ugliness with time, and that is as it should be."

Afterwards, as he had foretold, the son and daughter of Em and Andras of Dyngannan remembered only the best of those days—the glowing hillside, the hubbub hours, the bright banners over the tents, the smiles of the soldiers, the songs and stories. As a woman Betris would recall as though they lay under her eyes to see, the crumbling stones of the earthworks upon which she had more than once skinned her knees, the green mosses on the treetrunks, the curly ferntips like elfin rams' horns, and the milky globes of the clover she had sucked. Sure, it almost seemed to her as she remembered Woodbury Hill that she touched upon a magic thing. She completely forgot, as did her brother, that Gwilym ap Tudor had died there, although the two of them lay in the tent with him the night he was dying.

His arm had been broken by a blow from a mace the day before. He had bound it up with the help of Rhys Ddu, then had given it little thought for a while. By evening it had become swollen and inflamed. He felt nauseated and had no stomach for food. A leechwoman bled him, bathed his arm and wrapped it about with wet poultices, and after that he went to lie down in the tent.

Night came on. The air was cool and a rank sweet scent arose from the wet grass. Somewhere in the nameless region across the river a bittern boomed. Across the rain-washed moonlit sky a procession of clouds moved like stately galleons. Gwilym watched them dreamily, letting his thoughts drift along in their foamy wake. He almost felt as though drowning into that heavenly flood. It was distantly that he was aware of the sounds of the encampment: the rough laughter of the soldiery, the occasional jingle of a horse's hoof as it rang against a stone, the music of pibcorn and crowth. Suddenly a wild scrannel shriek split the air.

Gwilym started. A shiver ran down his back.

"Mererid . . . Father Conan's daughter, where is she?" he called out in alarm.

Someone wailed in the shadows at the back of the tent: "Meri . . . where is Meri?"

Ochan, he had clean forgot about the children.

Rhys Ddu bent over him. "Come, don't worry," he said. "She is safe. She is out with the Lollard. Shall I fetch them to you?"

Gwilym shook his head. "There is no need. Let them be."

"Are you sure? What is it, my heart? Are you in pain? Shall I get you a posset maybe? Or some opium?"

Some little time after that the injured man dozed off, an old dog's drowse, dull and fitful. His arm stiffened and throbbed. It felt huge. He thought of one of those monstrous fungi that grow in woods, puffed-up and ghostly. Step on it and it would crumble into dust. Dust—well, is that not what we all are, he thought? Aye, ashes and dust.

By evening, he was burning with fever. He heard the voice of the priest's daughter nearby, felt her strong young hand on his brow, cool and solicitous. He opened his eyes but could not make out her face for the blaze of the morning sun at her back.

"God keep you, chieftain," she said. She looked down at him anxiously. His face was heavily flushed and under the grey-sprinkled brows the dark eyes glittered dully, their glance abstracted and strange.

"Do you know me, Gwilym?" she asked.

"Aye, I know you, Mererid," he answered. He made an effort to smile. "Would that I had known you sooner."

Later that morning he was given a soporific sponge and his arm was hacked off below the elbow by a barber surgeon. In a painful swoon between sleeping and waking he thought of his pitiful devoted wife Eilian whom he had never loved. And then, as clearly as though even now it lay before him, he saw the sea-river at Bangor sparkling under spring sunshine. He and his uncle, Sir Howel, the Archdeacon of Mona, were returning from the islet of St Tysilio with its green cloud of trees and old grey tower speckled with gull-droppings. As the boat ground up along the shingle of the Bangor shore a frisky gust of wind darted past them, snatching gaily at the lappets of the Archdeacon's hood, dancing in the freshets, scurrying through the brine and filling the air with a mist of spray. Sir Howel was laughing and holding onto Gwilym's arm, his short nose was wrinkled up, his eyes were glittering like drops of sea-crystal under the tufty brows, everything was so plain.

Sir Howel's voice was alive in his ear, laughter was breaking over his own lips, even as his opened eyes saw the August sunlight glinting through the curtained entrance of the tent on a heap of armor, heard the sounds of the camp outside.

"Rhys. . . ."

Rhys Ddu leaned over him and grasped his hand.

"Aye, my brother."

"Uncle Howel has come to fetch me home," the dying man said indistinctly.

His brother bit his grey lips and was silent.

"Shall I bring the priest to him?" Mererid whispered huskily, her eyes wet with tears.

"Aye, he will not live out this day."

After Gwilym had been given the last sacraments he spoke to his brother. "Have pity on Eilian, Rhys," he said. He closed his eyes and gave a shuddering sigh. "Bury me in Welsh earth." A faint smile quivered on his parched lips. "I do not think my body would lie easy among the bones that have been whitening in these fields so long."

Rhys Ddu brushed back the hair that was plastered to his brother's brow and kissed him. Soon after that the dying man lost consciousness.

That same evening, in Owain Glyndwr's tent, the captains were put to fresh consultations. He who had been Sheriff of Caernarvonshire under King Richard the Second, that much loved warhorse known throughout the hundreds of Gwynedd as the Siri Mawr, did not scruple in voicing his objections to prolonging the campaign.

"Like enough they are victualled in that fastness of theirs for a twelvemonth or more, my prince. Strong fortifications, seat on a ridge, home ground, good cover from the weathers, the river—no, there is too much in their favor, that is my opinion."

While he spoke Owain Glyndwr sat looking out through half-shut eyes at the far-off waters of the Severn flowing through its meadowland. The noble river glimmering in the last of the light he was seeing in mind as a little stream lying like a silver thread between its rushy banks high up in the bleak wilds of the Pumlumon range far off to the west. Four years earlier he had raised the red dragon banner at its source. The dream that had then taken shape in his mind, of restoring its easternmost running as one of the boundaries of Wales, he now saw fading.

He turned to look at Rhys Ddu.

"And what say you, son of Tudor?"

Rhys Ddu replied: "I have a brother who has asked me to bury him in Welsh earth."

Glyndwr's face showed a sudden tremor of emotion. "Is Gwilym ap Tudor dead then, kinsman?"

"He is at the threshold of the Eternities, Pendragon."

Glyndwr bestirred himself, almost with anger.

"Aye, and too many others with him," he said. "Very well. Be it so. Let us eat grass. We shall go home."

On the following day they were on their way back to Wales. Gwilym ap Tudor was buried at the Abbey of Cwmhir. Mererid and the children returned with Rhys Ddu and Howel Vaughan to Nantconway.

12
STORM AND SIEGE (1405 - 1407)

1

As soon as it was decided that the departure of Glyndwr and his host was a retreat rather than a ruse, the King called a general muster at Hereford and marched upon South Wales at the head of the largest army he had yet set forth against that rebellious land. Stupefied at the size of the invading force, the men of Glamorgan fled into their coverts in the hills with their livestock and possessions. The open country through which the army passed was empty of life. Horns were blown and proclamations shouted in the towns. Under a cloth of state embroidered with the arms of England quartered with those of France, the King sat in castle hall and before market cross to receive the submissions of the people. There were summary executions and punishments.

The siege of Coety castle by a mixed band of Welsh and French under the command of Black Rhys was in its seventh week, and there was reason to believe that the hard-pressed enemy garrison was on point of surrender when the besiegers received the news that the King was only a day's march away.

"You thrice-accursed son of a dog!" Black Rhys furiously bellowed at the bearer of the ill-tidings, and then, among other oaths not to be recited, he ordered the withdrawal of his men. The main body, with the artillery and machines of siege, moved westward towards the Vale of the Towy, while Black Rhys accompanied by his son-in-law Robyn Holland, Henry Don of Kidwelly, Eden and Jean d'Espagne rode into the hills to the north, where the wedding feast of one of Cadwgan of Glyn Rhondda's sons was in its second or third day.

The lord's vills and hall in the valley had been burned during the desolations of a previous invasion, so he now made his home in an upland cwm, in a makeshift settlement of sod huts, roofed with moss and heather, which could be abandoned at a moment's notice.

It was a cloudy evening and heavy with stillness. The grasses rustled mysteriously and the moorland was drenched in the ancient scents of bog and mountain. Rain, thought Eden. It is just as well that we are going to be out of it.

Following a rough and miry track running among peat stacks and gorse brakes, Black Rhys brought his companions at last to a crook in the hills. Shouts and laughter rang out in the dusk, and then when the noise died down for a moment, the strains of a harp could be heard. Red points of light flickered among an assemblage of turf huts dominated by a long house of sods, which lay alongside a heathery hummock like a glowing ridge of black earth. Cadwgan's hulking form and ogre's head, with its red hairy ears, slanting evilly-laughing eyes, big teeth and whitening mane of yellow hair appeared in the lighted doorway.

"Who are these nightriders?"

"I," said their leader, "am Black Rhys, lord of a hundred vills, the great dragon of Penweddig and the stout backbone of Ceredigion."

"If you are a great dragon, Black Rhys, why do you seek lodging here and not in Coety castle?"

"It is easy to answer that. There is no room for a great Welsh dragon and that ranging bear the King of England under the same roof."

"Ah, I catch your meaning," said Cadwgan. "So he is here again? He must like us well, to be visiting us so often. What a pity he has such a terrible temper! But for that I would ask him up here for a vesper bowl of my lady's brew. Enter, my friends, and have welcome of my Castle of Wonders."

In spite of the scented flowers which had been strewn over the floor, the long hall stank of dried dung and peat smoke. Battle harness hung along the walls. A hundred red candles burned along the board and the bowls and platters were of finely chased silver. Half of the men, not to say more than a few of the women, were as uproariously drunk as their host.

"Where is the bride," asked Black Rhys, "so that I may kiss her?"

"I do not know," said Cadwgan, looking about. "Where is she, torch of worlds?" he asked his wife, a corpulent little woman with round black eyes and crimson cheeks.

"Where indeed?" she caroled merrily. "With her groom belike."

"Belike, belike," sang Cadwgan.

The vesper bowl was indeed potent. Achingly tired as he was, Eden's head soon began to reel. Black spots swam before his eyes like frogs' spawn in a yellow pool, and his ears hummed. After a while he and Jean d'Espagne escaped the smoky longhouse to breathe the fresh upland air. There was an excited flurry and whispering under a hawthorn bush a few paces away.

"I think we may have intruded upon the bridal bower, friend Jean," Eden whispered.

They strolled along a path that led to a nearby hill-water. The black cattle stood in the rushes there, tossing their heads and nervously sniffing the air.

"A bad weather-sign," observed the Frenchman.

"Yes," Eden said, "We have that one, too."

Even as they spoke the first drops of rain began to fall. It was nothing you would heed at first, a mere sprinkling. And then, somewhere in the distance, thunder growled. All at once a gust of wind tore through the fern brakes, a green arrow of lightning darted among the crags and within moments the storm broke in earnest. So began a deluge such as few men could remember having fallen in Wales in time of mind.

For days on end the rain fell, setting at naught, as twice before, the King's punitive plans, washing away his army's tents and gear, destroying provisions, and sinking his baggage train. Rivers overflowed their banks; meadowlands were turned into lakes, and hillocks became islands. The wild hills roared like angry giants; their flanks were scored with a thousand swollen veins of water, foaming and twisting downward in milky knots among trees and ragged outcrops of rock. In glen and gorge the forsaken huts of the crofters gave way, and rods, thatch, fencing, and rubbish of all sorts drifted on the breast of the flood or were dashed up among the withies and bushes that were stuck in the mire.

Sick and tired and out of heart, the King's bedraggled squadrons were hard put to find land with their feet as they faced about their dripping banners. Little indeed was wanting, as Cadwgan of Glyn Rhondda put it, but that their enemies would have been better served going home in boats. They had to make their way as best they could, shuffling and limping over slopes, clambering through the debris of broken trees, defiling along spines of earth that rose out of bog and flood like the bulks of sea-cows and river-horses. And as if this were not enough, they were prey all this while to every rebel chieftain or fugitive band ranging through the encircling hills with an anger to vent or a score to settle.

Rage, howl, wail, crash! Sheltered in their coverts, the men of South Wales grinned as they listened to the voices of the tempest. They sang and made merry and blessed the Lord. Nonetheless, for them, too, the day would arrive when the blessing would become a curse.

Far to the north, in the isolation of mountain glens and forests where folk felt they had far less to fear from the vengeful wrath of the King of England, the storm had not been considered a blessing even at the outset. Devils o' the deep, when had there ever been such rain? It was out of all reckoning. The men of Mona had never known the like. They were afraid to go out of their hovels to attend to their chores, it was pouring such torrents.

Disease did not long delay in making its due figure. As September gave way to October men began to fall into decay like the earth itself. Among the first to die was Father Conan, who had been toiling and moiling through the mud and rain against all counsel. Then, within days of his burial, Mam Indeg fell sick with a hot burning fever and shivering fits. She lay in the great bed in Dolwyddelan castle for almost two weeks, breathing hoarsely, her once wide, sunny, freckled face wasted and sallow, the flames in her once splendid hair gone to ash. A smile of the tenderest joy hovered over her bloodless lips as she watched her three children—Gerallt, Mererid and Alun—remembering the days when they had been small. Everything was fading into memory—just now and then, perhaps, a whiff of the present, a wrying of the nostril. . . . "That odd smell . . . ? They are leaching wood-ashes in the hall. . . . O, I see. . . ." And then she would be off again. "You were such a wild one when you were small, Mererid. But there, all my children were so. People used to think me such a foolish, feckless mother. The boys are up in the turbary again, they would shout. Heaven of the little birds, and they with their poor rickety mites. And my lads so big and bonny. Apple cheeks and strong white teeth fit to crunch stones. . . ."

And as the days went on she began to spend less and less time with her grown children at Dolwyddelan—in fact, she barely knew them now—and more and more with her little ones on the island. And at last she could not be coaxed back from there at all. One day she stayed there altogether.

Alas, what profit is there in the things of this world? Not two months later her youngest child Alun was also dead.

It was a terrible time. And all the tokens gave warning that the winter would be no better. Garners were scarce and a great many cattle had to be slaughtered. As early as Martinmas people came knocking at the castle gates, some asking for meal and provender, and others—the old and sickly and the waifs and strays—for shelter and care. From morning till night pots of broth and gruel were kept boiling on the fire, and as the days wore on the smells of smoking touchwood, incense and suffimige became ever more rampant on the air. The women were run ragged seeing to everything; they began to crack under the strain. Soon the Chieftain's sister Enid, the lady of the castle, found that she could no longer stand the sight of him. Only to see him ease his weary limbs down in the straw near the hearthstone seemed to irritate her beyond belief. She said not a word, no—but get you gone, the fierce clucks, the sudden broomwhiskings and potbangings! "What, are you going to loll there again?" they as good as told the Chieftain. "How are we going to find food for all these poor folk if you sit there idling?"

And yet, game, too, was scarce that winter. The best hunt men got up in those parts was after the wolves that were pestering their already diminished flocks and herds. For the rest they were lucky, if as on one long remembered day, they returned to the castle with a bag of rabbits and squirrels, poor shrunk-up creatures barely able in life to raise a hop out of their enfeebled shanks. The look those gracious ladies, his wife and sister, gave him when he laid the carcasses on the table before them would have been his death sentence, the Chieftain thought, in the days of the Matronae* and the Old People.

"Where are all the deer that used to roam our forests of yore?" Marged Vaughan asked him. "All the wild pigs and goats?"

"Who knows, my dear?" he replied. "It may be that they have gone to the Underworld to keep warm."

"You will be wishing yourself there if you cannot bring us better fleshmeat than this," his sister Enid warned him, between scolding and laughing.

And wherever he and the lads were going, the Chieftain thought gloomily, be it the Underworld or the back of the North Wind, would be Heaven beside life in the castle those days, with its line of washing and cooking pots, its bawling babes and jawfallen invalids, its nagging women, and the red-nosed shivering crocks scrambling for a place at the hearth. They rode in quest of the red deer and the wild and tusky boar, he and Gerallt and their band of hunters. Their journeys took them far

*Matronae: the goddess mothers of Ancient Britain.

and in all kinds of weather, through rain, snow, sleet, fog, and even—by the good pleasure of the King of all Lords!—occasional sunshine. They slept where they could: in the halls of chieftains, in the haylofts of crofters, in monastic cells and among the ruined stones of castles as ancient and mysterious as the hippogriff.

During Advent they were resting in a derelict homestead near the border when the Chieftain received word that David ap Jenkin, the outlaw, begged his company in the great forest by a league west of Chirk.

"He says for me to tell you, lord, that you will find it worth your while," said the messenger, a stumpy bristle-pated man with the brand of a felon burned into the flesh of his brow.

"Let us hope so, countryman," Meredith said.

A wintry sun hung low over the horizon as the hunters entered the forest. They had gone only a little way when they saw a figure in wolfskins riding towards them on a fine sorrel. It was Outlaw Jenkin. He saluted his nephew Robyn with a "Hoi mwsh!" and a hearty clap on the back, and exchanged courtesies with the Chieftain.

"Greetings, Meredith ap Tudor."

"Well met, son of Jenkin."

"You are no way as angry now as you were the last time we met, great bull of Mona," the outlaw observed with a laugh.

"Do you say so? When was that?"

"Years ago. At the Old Hall."

The outlaw glanced at his nephew quickly and winked. Robyn felt his cheeks redden.

"My brother Trahern, God rest him, had fathered a child on one of the serving maids yonder, if you recall."

The Chieftain stiffened.

"My memory holds sway over such charnel pits of dead matter, Outlaw Jenkin," he said drily, "that I would fain not recall. What is it that you wish of us?"

"I shall answer your question with a question," the outlaw replied blithely. "Do you have enough for belly and back these days?"

The hunters could but laugh in reply.

"Well and good then," he said. "Follow me."

He led them deep into the forest along a maze of devious and indeterminate tracks. They rode in silence through dense groves of winter-stripped trees and a score of narrow swampy glades. Darkness was closing in about them when they came upon a dingle where folk were sitting and stirring about a large fire. Outlaw Jenkin called out to them in greeting and women's laughter shrilled in the smoke. "Davy's back," someone cried. A wild haired girl darted out of the shadows and kissed him. Laughingly, the outlaw slapped her across her rump, then walked on. At the far side of the dingle another fire burned in the lee of an overhanging rock. Five or six brigandly-looking men were taking their ease there, watching a shaggy red-haired woman stirring wild meat in a pot. As the outlaw and the Chieftain's company approached she looked up. The firelight played over her features, her one eyelid drooping under the weight of a big wart, the other standing open to reveal an eye bright and alive with a gleam of what might have been guile or cupidity or both.

"These are the friends I was telling you about, Mother Mampudding," the outlaw announced to her in the English tongue.

She straightened up and stared at them frowningly.

"How many are there?" she asked in a deep hoarse voice like a man's.

"Ten."

"Ten's not many, Davy. I thought there would be more."

"Ten will serve. And then there's my twelve, eh? And you have another ten."

"I have eight," Mother Mampudding said grimly. "They have caught Jack Yoo and Nick Lofkin."

"Have they, by cock?"

"So that leaves us with thirty all told," she said.

"A good round figure."

"Aye, and one that I still wish could be bigger."

She fell silent, plucking at her chin hairs, calculating.

"I wonder if we can get word to John Astwick and his renegadoes," she said at last.

"What are you talking about?" the outlaw exclaimed abruptly. "No, that's not to be thought of. A crowd of men like that? Fine pickings any of us would have then."

"Davy's right," one of the brigands agreed, spitting copiously. "Too many is as bad as too few."

"Worse," said Outlaw Jenkin. "Come, don't worry. We have a good plenty."

The Chieftain put on a pretense of calm, but inwardly he was angry and troubled. What is this, he wondered? I must have been out of my mind to bring my lambs into this den of wolves. How to win his flock free of it with the least ado, as it were with the ease and craft of a conjurer—this became the first and principal ground of his thought during the moments that followed.

Meanwhile the woman served her guests meat in a huge trencher fashioned out of a hollow log. The Chieftain pricked up a collop on the point of his dagger and stared at her with an unwinking gaze.

"Where do you come from, goodwife?" he asked her at last.

"From Oswestry, lord."

"Ah, so you are a border woman then."

"She used to keep a hostelry there," Outlaw Jenkin explained. "But it has been inhibited by the clergy."

"Aye," the woman said bitterly. "A squire of the Bishop's claimed that one of my serving wenches infected him with the burning."

Professions of anger among the brigands made the air thunderous with growls and curses.

"That sow's get!"

"Devil fetch him, the hag's abortion!"

"May his pizzle rot, the crackhemp!"

"There are young lads here," the Chieftain broke in sternly, albeit he realized that having no English his younger charges would be happily innocent of what was being said. His eyes traveled from the face of Mother Mampudding to that of the outlaw. "Will no one tell me what is transacting here?"

Mother Mampudding nodded.

"You tell him, Davy."

It was now that the outlaw brought up the scheme in which he and his comrades wished to enlist the Chieftain and his company. Less than a week earlier Mother Mampudding had been given to know by informants in her fee along the Marches that the Lord of Misrule would be leaving Ellesmere for Chirk on the Friday next following at the head of a procession of hogs, oxen, sheep, and other creatures fattened against the Feast of Christmas.

"So it was our thought that perhaps you and your lads would like to join us in the venture," said the outlaw. "Half of my men lie sick and dying in the hospice, poor rascals, and it is too good a prize to pass by.

We could split the booty three ways, eh?"

"How say you, my fosterlings?" asked the Chieftain, glancing around at his band. Gerallt's eyes were sparkling and the others were grinning from ear to ear.

Meredith nodded.

"It likes me little to offend against the holy festival," he said, "But need makes men bold."

They clasped hands and laid their plans. Three days later they were lying in their coverts between Ellesmere and Chirk. An hour had scarcely elapsed when they saw the holiday procession unwinding like a multi-colored ribbon along the frosty meadowland that stretched away before their eyes. Astride a mule, and dressed up as a fat and jolly king, the Lord of Misrule rode at its head, followed by maskers in red and white livery and a company of slowly plodding sheep, pigs and oxen decorated with bays and streamers. A baggage train laden, as would be soon discovered, with sacks of corn and malt, firkins of cheese, pickled fish, and carcasses of geese, chickens and pheasants brought up the rear, accompanied by an outguard of soldiers, all of them tipsy and whistling as they walked along to the tunes of the pipes and sackbuts.

Outlaw Jenkin and his men were hidden behind a wooded rise overlooking the path of the procession. It was agreed that as soon as the mummers reached halfway up the hill, his archers would level their bows and strike, while Meredith's men and Mother Mampudding's brigands would attack the baggage train from the rear.

So it happened. As with drawn breath the men in ambush watched their prey ascend the hill, still rollicking and whistling, one of the deadliest arrows that ever parted from a bowstring in this world knocked the Lord of Misrule's mule cold in the middle of the road. At once there was nothing but hubbub and panic. The fat and jovial king was on his back in a ditch, the drunken soldiers were running everywhere but where they ought, Mother Mampudding's comrades-at-arms were driving off the beasts, the outlaw's men were shooting arrows into the tails of the fleeing fools and maskers, and the Chieftain and his band were bearing away the baggage train.

They made with all haste towards the appointed meeting place in the forest west of Chirk. There, amidst much laughter and jesting, they divided the spoils before going their separate ways. The laughter was still warm and living on the lips of the Chieftain's men an hour later. And then, quite without warning, and like some fearful mountain-wave, Death caught them all in its cold and stunning wash, and everything was turned in a moment into agony, madness and tears.

They were still within the bounds of the great forest when it happened. Robyn, Alun ap Conan, and Enid's two youngest sons had ridden ahead on the spy. They had not been long gone when they returned at a gallop, saying that in a nearby ravine they had heard voices speaking English and a man wearing a steel cap and a gambeson had appeared before them.

"Christ! Welshmen!" he had bawled and had fled back into the trees.

"Where is Alun?" Gerallt asked suddenly.

Robyn and his two comrades turned about in alarm. Gerallt and the chieftain tore off through the trees. Others sped after them, swords clattering against stirrups, hearts thumping, breath roaring white against the freezing blue air. They were too late. The first thing they saw was Alun's horse struggling to rise out of the icy hollow of a streamlet athwart their path. The youth was lying nearby. Three soldiers were standing over him. They were running his body through with their lances as if for play. Howling and afire with frenzy, the youth's brother and comrades fell upon them. As in a delirium the Chieftain saw, heard, felt what happened then—the butchery, the wild screams, the burning blood-borne starfires bursting in his brain, whirling before his eyes.

He might have lost consciousness; he could never afterwards be certain. He knew only that sometime later he found himself leaning up against a tree. His horse was standing nearby, bit clanking, nibbling peacefully at the frost-nipped grasses. Did I fall, he wondered? Perhaps he had dismounted. He had no recollection of it. An icy coldness was in his flesh and his limbs were trembling uncontrollably.

Gerallt was sitting among the moldering leaves a few paces away holding his young brother's head in his lap. Others knelt about him with their heads lowered, as motionless as the body of their dead comrade. Beyond them the dark mass of thorn trees and saplings stretched away, mournfully somber and forbidding in the wintry twilight.

How long did they remain so? Five minutes? An hour? The sudden whoosh of birds' wings overhead, like the powerful blast of a bellows, broke the spell. Crows or buzzard hawks flying homeward in the gathering dusk. Gerallt bent over Alun and kissed him, then picked him up in his arms and moved slowly towards the other men who stood with the animals among the trees along the hillside, mutely watching.

Staggering along behind Gerallt on legs that felt as weak as water, the Chieftain could not take his eyes away from the head of the dead youth, hanging back over his brother's arm. It was unbelievable to him. He is gone, he thought; that lovely joyous lad who was alive such a short while ago is gone. Like the rain that falls and the clouds that pass, he has gone to all appearance and time.

"We had best send word ahead, perhaps, Meredith."

"Aye, Gerallt, God help us."

Two days later they were crossing the home meadow at Dolwyddelan when they saw Marged Vaughan and Mererid walking towards them. Suddenly the priest's daughter broke into a run. The men drew rein as she came to a halt before them, panting and distaught.

"Mererid," Gerallt said.

Her wild, dark-shadowed eyes moved upon him for a moment, but it was as though they did not see him. She walked over to the litter and plucked away the cover. She looked down at the dead youth's face for what seemed to the waiting men an age, then kissed the blue cheeks and lips. "Alun, my little one. . . ." Her voice broke. She fell on her knees beside the litter, clutching at the body, her shoulders racked with painful sobs. The Chieftain closed his eyes.

"Ah, let's go," he heard Gerallt say. "It is cold here standing."

How do I live? the Chieftain wondered, and he seemed to feel the grief of the ages crumbling in his bones.

The tragedy would leave its mark upon him. He aged visibly in the weeks that followed. His broad shoulders bent, his hair whitened, his eyes grew more sunken and his cheeks became gaunt. Seeing the action in Chirkeland as one full of shame and dishonor to himself, he was tormented by an anguish that would not let him sleep and often made him difficult to live with. He picked at his food, quarreled with his wife and sister, and interpreting Mererid's glances as accusatory, was cold and gruff with her, sometimes reducing her to tears.

"My heart is like a dried-up saltpit," he told Gerallt.

"For pity's sake, Meredith, why must you punish yourself like this?" the younger man demanded. "There is no blame upon you for what happened."

"I wish I could believe it."

Only one thing soothed him to a degree and that was music. Often of an evening he would ask Robyn to play the harp for him. Then he would sit in his chair with his eyes closed, listening, trying to seek oblivion if only for a short while.

So he was absorbed one night when he fell into a doze. Waking on a sudden, he found himself looking at No Pencaergo, a doddering, dim-eyed, whining, scrag-end of humanity, who could not be got away from his post at the fire for an instant; crouched there at the hearthrock the livelong day, wizened claws held out prayerfully to the blazing logs. The fire its custos and demon. Ancient worm coiled over his ring of gold, squinnying venomously round the hump of his shoulder at anyone so bold as to trespass on his mesnie, be it only to fetch water to scald a hen or flame to singe a coney.

Poor wretch, the Chieftain thought—half-deaf, half-blind, half-witted. What a burden such a life must be, what a misery! Ah, well, that is a burden the boy will never have to bear, will he? That is a misery he will never know.

He turned his head and saw the young harper watching him intently with his sad, searching dark eyes.

"How you are staring!" he said. "What do you see, I wonder, when you look at me so?"

"I see Meredith ap Tudor," Robyn replied simply. "The lord of the Men of Eden."

The Chieftain eyed him dubiously.

"And is that all you see?" he said. "A head of kin? No more than that? Sure, that is hardly worth the staring."

Robyn shook his head.

"I do not know what you want me to tell you, lord," he said humbly.

"Tell me what you see when you look at me," said the Chieftain. "Come, you were once the apprentice of a fine bard. Mabon, aye. Were that old bard here in spirit tonight I know what he would say. 'You are looking old and tired, Meredith ap Tudor. It is high time for you to be confessed and communicated, and come lie beside me amidst the solitude of the graves on the Isle of the Saints.'"

Robyn let his grave eyes rest on the man's face, at the bones of the gaunt cheeks gleaming like sea-washed stones under the rough grey stubble. Yes, it was true that he had aged. The broad shoulders were stooped and fleshless under his brown robe, and the big hands outspread on his knees were leathery and heavily-veined. And yet, for all that, he had presence. He had grandeur. He filled this hall. He was still the Chieftain.

"Very well. How of this then, lord?" Robyn said at last. "When I look at you I seem to see Pwyll, Prince of Dyved, when he came back home after his term in the Underworld and took on his own form and semblance again. Most people did not know that he was any other than the King of the Underworld who had ruled Dyved for a year in his stead. But those who were close to him and loved him said: Something has happened. He is the same. And yet he is different."

The Chieftain fingered his beard, pondering.

"Or," he amended in a little, "he is different. And yet, he is the same."

He began to smile.

"Good, Robyn ap Trahern," he nodded. "I think you show promise."

Even then he heard laughter near at hand and his wife's quick step. He looked up to see Marged's beaming face.

"Sioned has given birth to twins," she said.

"Away!" he said in disbelief. "How can that be?"

"What kind of a question is that?" Marged laughed. "Come and see for yourself."

The Chieftain followed his wife into the bedchamber. The mother was smiling down on everyone from the high remove of her snowy pillows as though she brought them jewels from India the Greater. Meredith looked at the two naked creatures wriggling and bawling furiously in the trough, and blinked his eyes. What brightness! Everything else seemed so dull and colorless beside them. Och, little fledglings, he thought—coming into this great cold terrible world! And at such a time of year!

He signed their infant brows with the figure of the cross.

"And how is it that they are so fat," he laughed, "and everyone else so skinny? But bundle them up quickly now, lest they catch cold. Gerallt," he announced, "we will have a feast."

The happy father grinned but the priest in attendance frowned.

"It is the beginning of Lent," he observed. "This is the time when men should be remembering that they bear bodies of sin and death."

The Chieftain stared at him in amazement.

"What!" he exclaimed. "Do you think we need remembering of that? But our Lord is Love, is he not? He is the Light of the World, from whom all gifts and blessings flow. Come, I think He will forgive us this small delinquency."

From that hour his spirits began to mend. And then, not long after that, warmer weather came. The sun shone, birds sang in the budding thickets, the first dazzlingly white lambs frisked in the water-meadows, and the green mountainsides were covered with flickering streams like the hair of girls running to a wedding.

On one such day Eden arrived. With him he brought Andras of Dyngannan.

Eden entered first.

"God save all here."

"Amen," said Meredith, bright-eyed as a child. "You have kept us waiting."

"I did not know that," said Eden. "Had I known it I would of course have come sooner."

"Aye, so you say, my dear."

The Chieftain turned to look at his brother's companion.

"Andras, have welcome," he said, staring interrogatively and with ill-suppressed amusement at the other's face, now shaven clean like an Englishman's, with the shaggy black hair cut close to the head in a bowlcrop, bringing into prominence the large waxen ears and the sallow expanses of the glum countenance. "Out of prison, eh?"

"King Henry rested at Abergavenny castle on his way back from South Wales," Andras replied, "and I was brought before him for questioning. He has a Welsh squire, Davy Gam. He put in a good word for me."

"Davy Gam?" the Chieftain mused. "Why would they call him that? Does he have a deformity?"

"He is cross-eyed," said Eden.

"But not so cross-eyed that he cannot see straight at times, it appears," the Chieftain smiled. "So the King's squire is an acquaintance of yours then, Andras?"

"He was at Nannau when I arrived there for my mother's burial."

"Ah."

The Chieftain paused reflectively.

"Was he in the plot to kill Owain Glyndwr?"

"I dare say he must have been. Of course he was not to be found when they went looking for him."

"Of course," said Eden.

Andras felt an unpleasant prickling at his tone.

"Your cousins were also there," he hastened to observe. "Red Iwan's sons."

Eden snorted and spat. The Chieftain's features assumed an expression of gravity and calm, almost of indifference.

"It is not unknown to me," he said.

Andras was silent. How could he possibly know? Then it dawned on him.

"Mererid must have told you. . . ."

The name had slipped from his lips all unwittingly. His face burned. He glanced quickly at Eden. The younger of the brothers was still smiling but his eyes had hardened.

"Yes," said the Chieftain, "she saw them there." He paused and surveyed his guest with curious but not unsympathetic eyes. "Where did you go when you were set free?" he asked "To your mother's kinsmen?"

"No, I did not," he said abruptly, and his voice rang with bitterness. "I have a sister who lives on the coast of Gower in South Wales. She is married to a shipowner. They are good people. At Shrovetide I learned that Eden was in Carmarthen and I went there to see him. He told me that my children were here."

A little while later Mererid came. She darted into the hall and stood for a moment at the threshold of the great doors, with her hands clapped against her cheeks, staring.

"It's true, it's true," she cried out in happy amazement. "I can scarce believe my eyes."

"Come up closer then, little sister," Eden laughed, "so that you can see me better."

Calling over her shoulder to the children, she ran towards her foster-brother, stood on tiptoe to kiss him, then turned to Andras with outstretched hands. An indescribable tremor ran through him. The light of the morning sun was on her hair, eyes, cheeks, lips and her face was pure joy.

"You are free and well, Andras," she said. "I am glad."

He clasped her hands fervently in his. During the past months his feelings for her had undergone a change. In the loathing and despite which had been aroused in his breast for the men of Nannau, who had not made a move to find out what had happened to him, let alone help him and his little family, Mererid's betrayal of Howel Sele no longer seemed to him so great a thing. What he remembered now was her steadfast and devoted care for Em and his children. He almost felt that already they were bound to each other by the most indissoluble of ties.

She drew his son and daughter forward by the hand.

"Come, don't be afraid," she told them tenderly. "Here is your father. Are you not going to greet him?"

Andras's eyes grew moist and his lips quivered as he gazed upon them.

"Look at you! How you have grown!" he said, trying to master the shake in his voice. "My lambs. . . ."

He took them into his arms and set them upon his knees. Iori hugged him and fell to chattering at once, but Betris pulled away, shy and frightened, until he plucked out of his purse an Agnus Dei with coral beads and put it in her hand. "Give me a kiss now," he said. She looked up at him quickly and smiled. And then, all at once, she bobbed up and pecked at his yellow jaw. He pressed her head against his breast and buried his lips in her hair.

After a few moments he glanced furtively at Mererid. She was standing hand in hand with her brother, talking to Eden. Her eyes were brimming with tears and Gerallt's lids looked red. They must be telling Tudor's son about the death of their parents and young Alun, he thought, and discreetly held himself aloof.

During the next few days the lord of Dyngannan had no opportunity to see the priest's daughter save in the presence of others, and when they spoke together it was always of Em, the children, his mother, and the old life at Dyngannan. But her voice touched him like a caress, and sometimes when she turned her dark-lashed blue eyes upon him, he thought he could detect in their direct glance a tender gleam. At last, one afternoon he asked the Chieftain and Gerallt if he could speak to them in private. They withdrew to an unoccupied part of the hall. Once there, Andras made his suit for Mererid's hand in marriage.

"She has proved herself a worthy young woman," he said. "I would be pleased to make her the mistress of my bed and board."

He fell silent, searching their faces. The two of them sat staring at him, as though benumbed. He felt the blood rushing to his cheeks. Sensing that his proposal was welcome to neither, he expressed himself with a certain arrogance.

"I shall not have to tell you of my good name," he observed stiffly. "You know that for sure already. But I know what you are thinking. Why should we wed her to a man who is not listed in our cause? A neuter, so to speak, in the conflict. And what does he offer her? Imprimis, security. It is not to be scorned. In the last resort, as I think you will agree, Meredith ap Tudor, all sensible men must put their safety above their liberties."

The Chieftain raised his brows.

"In the last resort," he said, still eyeing the other with astonishment, "that may well be so. But dear my fathers, is this then the last resort? Ah well," he sighed, giving a weary flap to his hand, "I am in no mood to labor the point. I am getting no younger, Andras, and this world will not last always. What say you to this, Gerallt?"

"Is it for me to decide? That is for Mererid to say," her brother replied. "She has a mind of her own, my sister."

"A mind of her own, yes, indeed," the Chieftain agreed.

"Be it so then," said Andras.

They were leaving the parish church after Vespers that same day when the lord of Dyngannan plucked at Mererid's mantle, detaining her under the yews. She looked at him in surprise. He was breathing hard and in the shadows his deepset kestrel eyes gleamed with a wild light. He bent towards her, whispering: "'Blessed is he to whom God grants a bright girl's virgin favour, gentle beauty.'"

"What is it you want of me?" she said in alarm, quietly disengaging her hand.

"Marriage," he said. "You have been as a mother to my children. Be one now in very truth."

She shook her head.

"Your children are dear to me, my friend," she replied softly, "but forgive me, I cannot marry you."

Her refusal so startled him, so affronted him—he who for so many months had seen her in no other guise but that of his lady and mistress—that at first he was unwilling to accept it. He felt that she must be feigning coyness in order to hide from him the true depth of her feelings, or perhaps to further inflame him with desire. But then he met her gaze bent upon him pityingly and an angry spasm seized his throat.

"You say this—to me?" he said hoarsely, staring at her with eyes full of entreaty and rage. "Why, Mererid? Am I so hateful to you?"

"O, no, you must not think it," she hastened to reassure him. "It is only that my heart is engaged to another."

"Who?" he demanded savagely. "Eden?"

She said nothing, afraid to speak. Her silence lashed him.

"And do you think he will marry you, eh?" he sneered. "You? A priest's daughter? And he so cock-a-hoop and fine? Why, he will use you and cast you aside like a drab."

She flamed up.

"A drab?" she retorted with passion. "His betrothed?"

"What?"

Trembling agitatedly, he gripped her arm and stared into her face with an intense and burning gaze.

"You lie!" he snarled.

"Do I?" she flung at him challengingly.

She tore herself away and ran back to the castle without looking around. There, aghast at what she had said, sensing the storm impending, she pleaded a headache and hid herself away in the women's tiring room. In the hall they were sitting down to supper when Andras strode balefully in.

"How is it, lord," he demanded angrily of the Chieftain. "that you send me to propose marriage to yon Mererid when she is already betrothed to your brother sitting there beside you?" There was a clatter of knives on the board and a shocked hush. The Chieftain's dark lids drooped over his peacock-blue eyes as he turned their stare from Andras upon Eden, who alone of all those seated at the board, seemed the least affected, picking at his food and chewing as before, with an unhurried and measured munch.

"What is this, my brother? Have you been keeping secrets from us?"

Eden looked up. He gave a shamefaced smile.

"Oia," he said. "All's out, I see."

The women were astounded.

"What are you saying? You and Mererid are betrothed?"

"We are bound to one another by the sweetest of oaths, aye."

"How can this be?" Marged Vaughan demanded frowningly. "I do not understand. Why did you not tell us? Did you think we would oppose the match?"

Enid pressed her lips together angrily.

"Aye, you might have had the courtesy to consult your kindred," she declared. "I cannot find the words to tell you how hurt I am."

"Then be quiet, good sister," Meredith told her. He looked sadly at the lord of Dyngannan and spread his hands.

"Alas, Andras," he said.

Early next morning Mererid went down to the river to fetch water. It was cool. Forest and mountain were lost in mist and a light rain was falling. She filled her pails and was about to turn back when she saw the figure of a man coming towards her in the grey light. Blood flooded her cheeks as she recognized him. She lowered the yoke from her shoulders and waited for him, her trembling hands tucked into her apron.

"Good morning, Eden," she said as he came up.

A sudden splashing noise in the water made him look away a moment.

"The fish are jumping," he said. "I should have brought my spear and net."

Their eyes met. He smiled.

"You have put me in a very awkward position, little sister," he said. "I do not see how it is possible for me to extricate myself gracefully."

"You have no need to pretend now that Andras is gone," she whispered humbly. "You must know that."

"Ah, but I do not know that. Are you aware that they are making ready for a formal handfasting up there? A feast and so on? It has been announced to the whole parish already and by tonight it will be all over Gwynedd."

"I beg you, Eden, do not tease me," she pleaded. "I could not think what to say to him. If he had thought I had spurned him for himself alone, it seemed to me that the wound would have been much deeper and harder to heal. And I was afraid."

"And that was the only reason you said it?"

He took her hands in his and drew her to him.

"When I saw you standing at the threshold that first day," he breathed happily, "my heart seemed to understand all and it leapt for joy. I love you, my precious life. If I have hesitated to say so before this, it was only because I could have wished you a happier lot."

She kissed him with cool rain-sprinkled lips.

"How happier?" she smiled. "With Andras?"

"It would have been a marriage of some proposition for you, my dear," he said. "Of course," he added slily in a moment or two, "you can do better."

They stayed down on the river bank for a long while. A yellow sun was sparkling in the ground mist over the water-meadows when at last they took their way back to the castle. From the roof of the keep. Sioned and Robyn watched them walking slowly up the hillside. The yoke was now hoisted upon Eden'shoulders and Mererid's arm was about his waist. Every now and then the pails would sway and slop as he stooped to kiss her. Her laughter rang out, merry, full-throated, proud and shameless.

"That is a sight to see, eh, Robyn?" said Sioned. "Eden is under the yoke already."

"So sweet a yoke, however," the youth smiled.

"Aye, sweet indeed," said Sioned. "But have you ever marked, lad, how often and as it were all unwittingly Mererid seems to get her own way in this world?"

The wedding was held at Easter. It was fine weather, fresh and smiling. Crofts, castle and church, newly washed with lime, dazzled the eye with their whiteness, and the path of the bridal procession was strewn with spring flowers.

As for the feast that followed, all were agreed that it was the merriest that had been held in those parts in many a year, with dancing and minstrelsy; and servants staggering under the loads they were carrying on their heads; and an old man with a beard like a waterfall holding a silentiary's staff wreathed in garlands of white lilies and orpine; and what seemed to be half the population of Gwynedd tumbling over tables in the water-meadows.

Among the guests was the traveling poet Samson Clidro. He had arrived at the castle in the cavalcade of Eden's groomsmen, the brothers from the Bay of the White Stones. Robyn, who had met the older poet at Caer Gai while recovering from his wounds, sought to avoid him, but the man was inescapable. Like a murrain, the young bard thought.

"Stay! I know you, do I not?" Samson cried. "What's your name? The boy who was hamstrung at the Battle of Pilleth? The pet of the monks? A boy no more, to be sure. A young man. Aye, now it comes to me! It's Robyn of Mona, is it not? Bowels of Beal, but how changed you are! So lean and sad of countenance! God knows how I spied you out. It must have been the limp."

Samson was robed in velvet of russet color—a gift from a patron perhaps. It was faded here and there—rubbed bare in spots like the back of an old pony. A dragon mounted belt engrailed in gilt was about his waist, and upon his head he wore a red bonnet.

"And you are losing your hair, too. What a tragedy! And you so young. And you used to have such a mop, as I recall. But wait! *Sursum corda*! Do not despair! I have a receipt. Plucked out of the mouth of the wizard of Trillo, a wise man and magician of note A cure for baldness. Listen now. Commit it to mind. Take one part Spanish fly and rub it up with nine parts cold pork fat and any kind of sweet hair—infant, maiden, duckling, civet. Rub it hard in the scalp twice a day, at cocklight and cockshut, for a year."

"A year is a long time," Robyn observed.

"Truer word was never spoken, Robyn ap Trahern," Samson agreed. "A year is a long time. Time, time. And I must furbish an ode for supper. Ah, but is she not fair, our lady Mererid? And he so goodly, too, in spite of that wandering eye. Sure, nothing is wanting but Avalon."

The timeless peace of the immortals, Robyn reflected. Aye, nothing was more certain than that it was wanting during that lively wedding feast. For three days it went on. For three nights the wedded couple went to bed to the glitter of bared swords, to the din of shawms, reeds, horns, fiddles and drums. And then on the morning of the fourth day Eden was summoned to Pennal, near the township of Machynlleth in mid-Wales.

There, before an assembly of Welsh magnates and clerics, the Lord Chancellor, Griffith Young, announced the decision of Owain Glyndwr and his council to transfer the ecclesiastical allegiance of Wales from Rome to Avignon. Eden with Rhys Ddu and John Hanmer left for France at once, in a train that included the Earl of Northumberland and Lord Bardolf, the past Earl Marshal of England.

At first the young bride wept unhappy tears to have her groom so soon wrested from her, but evidently the hand of God was in it. Not two weeks after Eden's departure from the country, there was a monstrous bloody battle on the border in which more than a thousand Welshmen were slain.

"They killed Owain Glyndwr's brother and two of his sons," Mererid told her husband when he came back towards the end of June. "And Master Walter Brut," she murmured, her eyes filling with tears. "Mother Mary and our sweet Lord Jesus take him most tenderly into their keeping, do you remember him, my dear? He came preaching on the island once."

Eden crossed himself. What memories that brought back to him! Yes, he remembered all—the fair at Croes Gwion, the murder of Robert Crossetes, Gwennan and her sheep fells, the midsummer fires. And Annes appeared to him, her grave eyes, her slow melancholy smile, his dear lady of sorrows.

"Peace to his ashes, aye," said Eden. "I do remember Master Walter Brut."

For the rest of that year and much of the next Eden did not stray far from his wife's side. Against this, his sister-in-law Eva saw little of her Rhys Ddu. Among the foremost of Welsh mariners, he kept the seas throughout the winter and the following spring, prowling the waters for English trading vessels bound for Wales with provisions for enemy garrisons, or for a chance argosy sailing for Bristol, Newport or Dublin.

Early in the July of 1407 he put into Aberystwyth, one of the most powerful of coastal castles, with a shipload of supplies for the Welsh garrison. In his wake, also loaded with provisions, sailed two French galleys captained by Jean d'Espagne and Guy de Ferrebouc, a Breton with a bushy brown head a-chuckle in laps of fat and good living. Black Rhys was the castellan of the moment. He was one of the most generous and entertaining of hosts. They spent some merry days together.

They were at mass at first light one morning when a sentry ran into the chapel, wind in fist.

"Lord, there is an army out there!"

Moments later Black Rhys and his company were on the platforms, overlooking the beach and the adjoining heath upon which as though by magic had gathered a warlike host. Ships and galleys were on the water, while in numbers not to be exceeded it seemed by the pebbles of the shore, the forces of their enemies ranged far and wide among the tussocks and the sedge, a vast and glittering array. Disembarking, pitching camp, swarms of English soldiers moved in a constant stir through the grey of the morning. Tents went up as the castellan and his companions watched. Banners and standards were displayed. Horsemen rode here and there, shouting orders. Catching sight of the Welsh on the ramparts, a few of them let spurs to their mounts and circled the walls at a gallop, hooting and jeering. Some of their foot came after them a little way, shaking their fists and howling like infidels.

Black Rhys watched them in silence, fingering his beard reflectively. His captain and son-in-law, Robyn Holland, scanned his face and after a while asked:

"So, old dragon, what is your thought?"

"It's a mercy, lad."

Get you gone, the staring! If they had been living in the days of the Mabinogi, no doubt Black Rhys would have been seeking improbable adventures in the direction of India. Nothing could pull that proud stomach down; the sun was in his face all the way.

"Say you so?"

"A true godsend."

"Oia!"

"Praise God, aye, that we are so well provisioned. Imagine if the knaves had arrived a fortnight ago. What would you call that if not a mercy? It bespeaks the indulgence of Heaven for sure."

"Black Rhys!"

"Aye?"

"You are being summoned."

A herald was at the gates—parti-colored, pouter-breasted and raucous. As they loved their lives he now commanded the defenders to deliver the castle to the use of the Lord Henry, Prince of Wales. Black Rhys bellowed in reply that he could not do that, forasmuch as he was engaged by the Lord Owain, Prince of Wales, to hold the castle against all assaults, aye, even to the bleeding of his last drop.

The herald bawled scornfully: "God have mercy on you then!"

Black Rhys bellowed scornfully: "God will do as God wills, you clownish loon! Get you back home, you ugly geck, and be damned to you!"

The herald rode away. A burst from a bombard, followed by a crash that made the ground tremble under the Welsh feet and dislodged fragments from a nearby bulwark, gave them advertisement how kindly the constable's wishes had been taken. The siege had begun.

It proved a hot one, not to say lengthy. All summer it went on. Chains were laid across the harbor from ship to ship, in order to enclose Aberystwyth from all succors by water. Towering siege engines attended by parties of soldiers rumbled towards the castle through the smoky light, like angry giants goaded by swarms of hornets. For days in succession they hurled rocks and fireballs against the walls. Waves of assault troops piled into the breaches, the defenders drove them back. The gates were fired; the Welsh barricaded them up with stones. The besiegers dug under the walls; the besieged stank them out with smoking salvoes of sulphur and pitch. And so it went on for one month, then two.

By summer's end both sides were equally war-weary. The English soldiers, who had yet to receive a day's pay, were mutinous and consumed with sickness from lying out in the wet and rushy ground so long. Meanwhile, in the castle hall the strawed stones were black with the blood of the wounded ranged along the walls. Groans and curses mingled with prayers in the passageways. Flies droned dismally amidst the filth. Lice swarmed next to the skin, tormenting men with the itch. And still Black Rhys remained constant in his resolution. There was no getting him overset. Bright banderols were flown from the castle towers at his command. And every evening, for an hour at his behest, his men were entertained with harps and song, although less to comfort them, perhaps, than to discomfort their foes.

September came. It was one morning betimes, with a big sea running, when Prince Henry's herald appeared before the castle walls, inviting the defenders to parley. Black Rhys selected a party to accompany him. The wind was in his sails. Only the aspect that was upon some of his companions gave him pause. He was anxious to make a forceful impression on their foes. And his lads had grown lean, there was no getting away from it. Some of them had no more flesh on their bones than almsmen. Others had daubed themselves with pitch to keep away the vermin. Demons rather than human beings they seemed, Black Rhys fulmnated—bogeys decked out in their violets for All Hallow's Eve.

They made shift as best they could. With rain-water gathered in buckets and tubs, they scrubbed themselves until the hair fell off their bodies in scaly tufts. They trimmed their beards; they anointed their limbs with sweet oil, and over their filthy sweat-rotted shirts they wore armor furbished so bright that were it night and dark, as Rhys Ddu of Mona would tell it to his two brothers, you would have thought them moonbeams issuing from a cloud. But he who without question was most splendidly arrayed was Black Rhys himself.

For the occasion he wore a magnificent plum-dark robe embroidered with gold, of five garments, with facings of ermine.

"Go to God," Rhys Ddu marveled when he saw him, "you look like a king."

"And so I should," the castellan told him. "This is the King of England's own robe. You remember that terrible weather we had the summer before last? When our foes had to swim and paddle their way back home? We came by a fine booty then—forty wagon loads in all. Did not Ednyved tell you about it? I have a crown to go with the robe, too."

"A crown even?"

"A jewel in it the size of a baby's fist. A sovereign nostrum for the down at heel, believe you me, son of Tudor. It was in my mind to wear it today, but then I had second thoughts. It might rub a few heels yonder."

"It well might, Sir Constable."

Their way took them through a mob of enemy soldiers. Those to the fore seemed of a stature beyond the common. Black Rhys could not help wondering whether they had been chosen to the end they would scare his lads. Big strapping yeomen they were; their brawny hands, clenched to the wood of bow and poleax, could have been clubs. "Ignore them," Rhys Ddu muttered as their enemies rudely entertained them with their figs and gibes.

"Look mighty and triumphing," said he, as they entered the sainted precincts of Llanbadarn Fawr.

It was there, in a house of stone and timber covered with baked tile, in a chamber dressed with hangings and side of arras, under a cloth of estate embroidered with the arms of England quartered with those of France, and supported between two angels, that they found the lord of the English—a sternbrowed old man of some two and twenty years, with hard thornbright eyes, shaven jaw, monkish bowlcrop and a cheek deeply cleft by an arrow scar. If he recognized the robe Black Rhys wore as his father's he gave no sign of it. His face wore an expression of stony immobility. Only once did a smile pass over his lips, a wind-wrinkle over an icy pond, and that was when the Welsh caught sight of Davy Gam among the Prince's family of wise men and gentles.

Black Rhys was beside himself. Though prior to this he had fully intended, perhaps, to express himself as a great lord, worthy descendant of Brutus and the Trojans, he now lost track of his designs completely.

"No, I will not have it," he exploded. "You must send that dog away. I will not stay in the same room as him. He poisons the air."

He was terrible to behold, grey as ashes in the face, his eyes ablaze; but the worst was when Davy Gam, playing the innocent, advanced towards him, smiling and holding out his hands to him in a gesture of reconciliation. For a moment his comrades feared that Black Rhys would throttle him. Happily he pulled himself together in the nick of time. He stepped back.

"Stand aloof, Judas."

"Come, my lord Rhys, don't be childish."

"Out of my sight, you cock's egg hatched of vipers!" Black Rhys roared at him, stamping out of the chamber. Nor could he be persuaded to re-enter it, until the King's Welsh squire had shown his fellow-countrymen his prettier side, that is to say, his back and blind one.

It was now that the Prince's chief advisor, the Lord Courtenay, Chancellor of Oxford, made the Welsh his proffer: a truce of six weeks during which time Black Rhys and his men might come and go as they pleased, provided that the English might abide where they were without disturbance. At the end of this period Owain Glyndwr was to be given one week in which to raise the siege. If he failed to do so, the defenders were to hand over the castle to the English and do homage to Henry of Monmouth as Prince of Wales in return for free pardon and indemnity. Black Rhys agreed.

He left for Harlech at once to secure the Pendragon's approval to the English propositions. It was a strange time. The Welsh discharged their sick and wounded, repaired their fortifications and laid up fresh stores. Rhys Ddu, Jean d'Espagne and Guy de Ferrebouc had their galleys on the stocks, repairing the damage done to them by their enemies. Not that they were without their diversions. Services were conducted for their ghostly weal by learned divines in the church of St Padarn. At Michaelmas, the men defending the castle ran courses with their enemies along the flood plain of the Rheidol. They were dressing up their camp, the Welsh noticed. Scutcheons and armories were bright and new-painted. Flags and bunting snared the turns of the wind. Lamps of glass with oil burning in them twinkled at night along the ancient lanes of Llanbadarn Fawr. Bonfires blazed in the moorish waste. Trumpeters, drummers and pipers sounded their instruments. The defenders were disturbed and bewildered. Surely the uncertain posture of their enemies did not answer with this. What could be the reason for these festive preparations? Since their enemies were under no obligation to tell them, the Welsh had no other recourse but to draw that conclusion which lay next at hand: The King of England must be heading their way.

He was indeed. And with that state and equipage best befitting the triumphal progress of a conqueror. It was a matter of common fame soon enough. He had already set forth from London, accompanied as far as the town ditch by the lord mayor, the aldermen and the mysteries.

"We have been tricked," said Robyn Holland.

"Aye, so it seems," said Rhys Ddu.

Early one morning in October the men in the castle were awakened by noise and shouting. Rhys Ddu bumped into Robyn Holland.

"What is it?"

"A host coming."

They ran up to the ramparts and gazed. It was damp and cold. A pall of mist hung over the heath where the night's fires lay darkly smoldering, but the sky was clear and brimming with light when they perceived on the hill overlooking Clarach and Geneu'r Glyn what looked at first like streams in flood, flickering and tumbling along the slopes; and then even as they watched, these turned into the glitterings of a warlike array—the steel caps, bucklers and spears of bands of soldiers darting and twisting downhill among the rocks and furze.

"Heaven be praised!" Robyn Holland breathed. "They are ours."

Glyndwr had come. Bugles were soon blowing in the English camp. Knights clapped spurs to their horses; bowmen and billboys chased after them, stretching their limbs across bushes and ditches. By the time Glyndwr's spears had reached the castle mound, their enemies were drawing up along the seashore a hundred yards away. There they stopped. All eyes were on Glyndwr as he approached the castle walls. A low murmur ran through the English ranks. They watched him suspiciously, but with fascination, too. That Egyptian feather, by God!

That gold patterned casque, that sable cloak, that crazy eye, that wind-combed beard! Aye, and the tales! Above all, the tales! Tamburlaine had inspired few more fearsome. So this then was he—the terrible Glendowrdy, the black enchanter, of whose nativity it was said, that on the same night he was born, his father's horses were found standing up to their bellies in blood and the stars had been tumbled from their courses.

"Robyn Holland!"

Those two words were the first and last to be understood by the English in the exchange that followed, the rest being spoken by the Welsh in their own country tongue, that same language styled by the fabulist Geoffrey of Monmouth in former time as crooked Greek.

"May God prosper you, my lord Owain," came the answering shout from the ramparts.

"Good my soul, then let me in!"

"Stop! Treachery!"

Raising a yell so piercing that it was a wonder that the bashful sun did not retreat entirely into its watery bed, a man in the harness of a royal squire came bowling forth from the English ranks. A Welshman, judging by his speech; aye, Davy Gam, snarling and spitting like Paluc's cat.*

"Don't you listen to him!" he yelled. "You are still under truce, remember!"

A deep growl arose among the Welsh spears. Motioning them to be quiet, Glyndwr bent on Davy a grave and pitying gaze: "What truce? I sanctioned no truce."

"You did! You did!" Davy cried, spluttering with rage. "Rhys ap Griffith swore. Your deputy. In your name. He held out his right hand; he swore on the sacred books. Everybody saw him, God in Heaven is our witness. Ask Rhys ap Griffith. Let him say it's a lie. Where is he? Let him answer for it."

Owain Glyndwr deferred mockingly.

"So he shall, little man."

He gave an imperious turn to his hand. Watching his every move like folk at a fair in the toils of a conjurer, the crowd followed the direction of his down-pointing finger. The throng of spears parted to

---

* Paluc's Cat: the most destructive of the curious and magical progeny of Henwen, the Great Sow, hunted by Coll, named in the Welsh Triads as one of the Three Stout Swineherds of the Island of Britain.

make way for a group of soldiers drawing a hurdle upon which a man was mounted. It was the castellan. Stunned as by a thunderclap, a great shuddering gasp passed through the battalions. Black Rhys, proud lord of a hundred vills, the great dragon of Penweddig, the trusty backbone of Ceredigion, was dressed in a fool's coat, a cap of skin adorned with a donkey's ears, and huge beaked shoes hung with tiny tinkling bells.

"God in Heaven!" Robyn Holland breathed.

"What's to do? Interpret, sirra!" the mystified knights shouted at Davy Gam, but the royal squire had his hands full making head on his own behalf. Suddenly he was as stupefied as the rest.

"Bring the jackass here! Let the English see him!" Owain Glyndwr roared.

Several men rushed forward and dragged Black Rhys into the open space that divided the two forces. Like the scum of malefactors they flung him sprawling face down in the wet grass. At a sign a headsman stepped forward and bared the castellan's neck in readiness for the axe.

"Dear God!" Robyn Holland murmured in horror. "No, it cannot be."

"Mercy!"

All at once everyone on the ramparts was yelling:

"Mercy, Lord! Spare him!"

The Pendragon stayed the headsman's axe with a nod of his flamboyant plume and addressed himself once more to the battlements.

"Is it you begging for mercy up yonder?"

"Mercy! Mercy!"

"But sure, it is yours to give. Open the gates."

They hesitated. They were under truce. Or were they? They made mirrors of their eyes to reflect each other's staring. So might have passed five seconds.

"You are laying too much weight on my patience, my children!" Glyndwr thundered. "Obey me!"

What could they do? The world would be so much duller without Black Rhys. They needed the old dragon. They needed his laughter, his great simple heart. They opened the gates. The host poured in. Infuriated by what they interpreted as a breach of faith, their enemies gave them chase. They hurled themselves against the walls, howling for blood. But to no end. All were inside, safe and sound.

"Well met, my brethren," said Glyndwr."

"Well met, supreme chief of kindred!"

"You were magnificent, seigneur," Jean d'Espagne grinned.

"With God's help, my gallant Jean. And then, if a man is to make speed he must set his sails to catch the wind, is that not true?"

"*Grace a Dieu, c'est vrai.*"

"Whisht, but what a fright you gave us!" Robyn Holland sighed.

"Pardon the care. Believe me, I would not have been so bold if your welfare were not as mine. Well, I could not let you be put out of possession, could I?"

His flickering ghost of a smile suddenly took on a livelier gleam of malice and mockery upon hearing an elfin flurry of bells nearby.

"You are chiming most melodiously, Sir Constable. You are making happier music now, it seems to me, than you were a while agone."

"I feel happier, by bodo. The dice turned up well for us this time, did they not?"

"Yes, my pet. This time."

Afterwards they sat alone together. Glyndwr seemed in a genial mood, but Black Rhys was sunk in reflection. Suddenly he felt sad and weary. He knew that he had exceeded his proper bounds, concluding a truce without sanction, and he studied his lord and comrade-at-arms more closely than was his custom. He well understood what their struggle had already cost Glyndwr in blood and suffering—the hard condition of the land; the uncounted numbers who had laid down their lives in his cause, kinsmen more than a few; his beloved brother and two of his sons slain; another, his heir, rotting away in the Tower of London. Aye, the old lion was far from being as affable as he let on, come you. He was grim beyond reckoning under those bristling humorous brows of his. A whole Troytown of woe lay entombed there. True God, it did not bear thinking about.

A sigh escaped Black Rhys at unawares. Glyndwr looked at him.

"There is some trouble on your spirit, my friend. What is it?"

"If I ask you a question," the castellan replied, "will you answer me truly?"

Glyndwr nodded.

"Go to. Ask me."

"If things had taken a less happy ply down there," Black Rhys said at that, "you would have struck off my head without a qualm, would you not, my prince?"

Glyndwr stared at him for a moment or two in silence. Then he leaned forward and most tenderly laid his hand over the hand of his old friend and liegeman.

"You are wrong, my brave heart," he said softly. "I would have had a qualm."

Three mornings later saw the day dawn over a sea empty of shipping. Their enemies had struck their tents in the course of the night. Nothing was left to mark their occupation but their refuse. Soon that too was gone. Before or ever Prince Henry met his father, the King, at Hereford, the scavengers had moved in. Scores of ragged nativi contended with herring gulls and salt wind for an army's leavings: pots, pans, buttons, buckles, tools, fripperies, broken bread, meal, oats, and marrow bones. By the time the English held their Parliament at Gloucester, the seafowl had reclaimed their ancient hereditaments along the flood plain of the Rheidol. They drifted in like blown spray over the moor, filling the air with their passionless cries.

How good it must be, thought Owain Glyndwr, to be spared occupations of mind. Their liberties, because ignorant, were so much more carefree than those of men.

More enduring certainly. A month after the departure of the English from Aberystwyth, the Earl of Northumberland and Lord Bardolf were slain in the battle of Bramham Moor. So, too, in Paris, did Louis of Orleans, that loyal and generous ally of the Welsh, lie dead—struck down by the bravos of the Duke of Burgundy.

The time of the assassins had arrived.

13
THE TIME OF THE ASSASSINS (1407 - 1409)

1

*"Oncques mais on ne perpetra en ce royaume si mauvais ne si traistre meurtre,"** declared the Duke of Burgundy, his voice shaking with emotion, as he sat with the King of Sicily, and the Dukes of Berri and Bourbon at the Hotel d'Anjou on the night of the murder of Louis of Orleans. It was the 23rd day of November, 1407. Three months later, his guilt revealed, he was acclaimed the saviour of France for tyrannicide.

"The Burgundians have taken over Paris," Jean d'Espagne told Eden and Rhys Ddu when he returned to Wales that spring, "and their chief is in the saddle."

So far had the Duke of Burgundy triumphed indeed, Jean informed Tudor's sons, that he had extracted a letter from the French King thanking him for delivering his royal person from the sorceries of Louis, the evil brother who had deprived him of his wits.

"The hour of the wolf is upon us, my friends," Jean said somberly.

"And of the jackal," said Eden.

At Shrovetide, envoys of Henry of Lancaster had appeared in Nantconway, friars Augustine with cunning eyes and smooth tongues. They exerted their eloquence on the King's behalf at pulpit tree and market cross, offering amnesty to all islanders not outlawed in the rebellion. After the privations of exile, the three terrible winters that had condemned them to disease, cold feet, leaky huts, black bread, wild roots and nettle stew, the men of Mona sprang quickly to the lure at first. At night around their fires, patching clothes and mending harness, they looked into the flames with a misty gaze. Their talk ran on the familiar homestead, its small husbandry, the old life. And the air grew heavy with sighs.

But then an impediment loomed. The language held by the King of England turned out to be less generous than was first thought. One day when Howel Vaughan rode into Dolwyddelan, he found a crowd of

*Never in this realm has there been perpetrated such a wicked and traitorous murder.

islanders squawking like rooks around the castle crag.

"Good luck to you, lads," he called out. "What's to do?"

"We shall need that good luck, my dear," one old fellow grumbled, and with that he told the lord of Mathebrud that it had been learned that a fine was to be levied on the heads of all returning islanders by the powers in possession there.

"They say the money is to be used by our enemies to put down the rebellion," he sighed bitterly.

"Don't you worry, daddy," Howel said. "It will take more than groats and silverlings to do that."

Other men were inside the castle with Eden and the Chieftain, filling the air with moaning wind. What simpletons they were! How innocently trusting! To believe that they were to be allowed to get off so easily! Good God, what was to become of them? Was their long run of evil fortune never going to end? It was true that the Chieftain, who had been among the first to urge them to submit to the King's commissioners, had undertaken to furnish them as far as he was able with the necessaries to tide them over the first hard weeks at Penmynydd. But if even that much was to be wrested from them, what was to be done? For without funds how were they to restore a countryside devastated both by an invading soldiery and themselves? How rebuild their crofts laid in ashes? How plough and sow their fields gone to waste? How marry off their unhappy daughters? How buy victuals? How make bread? How indeed live?

Run the hazard, was what the Chieftain told them. Plead poverty, delay, set their case squarely before the King's commissioners at Beaumaris, nothing was to be lost by plain dealing.

There was a fresh outcry at this. Was Meredith ap Tudor really suggesting that they put their necks and pitiful few possessions in the power of a man whose cruelties and oppressions were notorious? God bless him, the Chieftain meant well, but why did he not say: Get up, lads, and suffer death? Ianco the swineherd, as always, was quick to crane up horrors out of the pit. Heave-ho, the rock was shouldered aside, out they came swarming. Their enemies would seize them, pluck away their flesh with fiery tongs, hang them by their purses, flay them alive, draw them by the heels through the streets of Beaumaris at horsetails, sentence them to perpetual imprisonment in the dungeon.

Meredith heard their repinings patiently, attentively, kindly, smiling a little, shaking his head now and again—no, no, these were vain imaginations. Calm down, let them use their wits. He argued that as long as Henry of Lancaster had something to fear from the anger and hatred of the Welsh—and sure he still had a good plenty—it was plainly his interest to act up to the spirit of his word. Wasn't the very fact that he was making overtures to the barefoot knaves sufficient proof of that?

"Figure on it, my friends," he reasoned. "Don't you think he has troubles enough? Tumults everywhere. A powerful faction crossing his designs in his own land. Nothing in the strongbox, or so near nothing a thief would scorn to pick it. Would he be scrabbling about for poor men's pennies otherwise? Malcontents at his every turn. His very name a byword of odium. Well now, I ask you, is this the color of a man who would stir up more people in blood and fury against him? Scare up more bogeys to haunt his days and nights?"

He paused. He fastened his gaze upon them.

"Perhaps the Prophet of Ffinnant has laid a curse on him." Sunk in their pits under the fierce frowning brows, the blue-purple eyes gleamed. "They say he's a sick man. We shall have to go to prayers, eh, my friends?" he suggested, grinning wickedly.

Never a smile, however, greeted him in return. It was hard going trying to gain on those islanders. Miserably dumb they stood there, shuffling their feet, looking at him, looking at one another, their faces twisted up into humps and dumps of worry and unease.

"Chieftain," a voice outburst on a sudden—Wil Sgarthion, the great uncle of Pill Hanereg the miller, and the oldest of his tribe. He farmed the croft nearest the turbary, a thin, bowed, morose, puzzleheaded man. "Chieftain," he pleaded plaintively, "come back with us."

"Alas, Wil."

"We wouldn't be afraid then, son of Tudor," Ianco agreed. "You would know how to deal with these English, you are wise to their tricks, you can speak their language. Your tongue wouldn't get tied up in knots like ours. 'There are lots of feathers on that old bird up at the hall,' my Mali used to say, God rest her. 'He's got something else in his head besides lice.'"

Meredith shook his head.

"Alas, my friends, there's no going back for me now."

"Go back, Meredith!" Howel Vaughan exclaimed suddenly. "Why not?"

"Say if you like," the Chieftain replied drily, "that I am gone too old and stiff in the joint to bend a knee."

"Am I hearing aright?" his brother-in-law hooted derisively. "Leave off your bleating like a boozy Methusalem, my heart? Is it you that is talking of old age?"

"I was talking of honor."

"Honor, pah!"

The Chieftain motioned with his head to the islanders. They were quick to take their leave.

"What is your mind, Howel?" he asked then. A glimmer of irony slipped over Meredith's lips as he glanced at Eden, who was sitting nearby with Mererid, listening in smiling silence "Would you have me grovel before men who have condemned my brothers to death as outlaws?"

"It's a rabble world, Meredith. Dog eat dog. I too am under the ban of outlawry, remember. And I say go back to Mona. You are a man of peace. A justiciar. Why, they will welcome you with open arms yonder. Who can induce the men of Mona to obedience more than you? And isn't that what King Hal wants? A quiet and docile population he can bridle and ride at his pleasure?"

"No, Howel."

"Well, what are you going to do then?" Howel demanded angrily. "Lie down here and rot?" There's work to be done in Mona yet. You could be laboring and scheming to subvert the designs of our enemies there. And what about these poor folk of yours? Will you let them bear their burdens alone?"

"But if a man bear not his own burdens well, how can he another's?"

"Ach, don't preach, Meredith. I'm in no mood for it. Who is to speak for these men? Who will plead their cause before the commissioners? Those are slippery knaves. I would not trust them for the worth of a penny. How can you even consider opposing these rustics to the wiles of such antagonists?"

"I was not. Gerallt will go back with them. He will be their advocate."

"What!"

Now it was the son of Conan's turn to be startled. Across his wheat-brown face spread a ruddy-bright flame. His eyes were full of pain and shock.

"No, Meredith," he said, when he had recovered speech.

"Yes, Gerallt," said the Chieftain. "I lay it to your charge."

It was so determined. It was so carried out. During the following days the islanders prepared to leave. They got their goods and gear together, piled them into wagons and scoured the surrounding countryside for stray animals. At last everything was sorted and settled and they set out homeward.

Eden and Mererid accompanied the departing crowd of islanders on a part of their journey. The weather was changing again. Grey clouds were drifting over the mountain tops. The trunks of the trees gleamed wetly and the hooves of horses sank in the clay of the road. A blustering wind tore through the spinneys and oat-stubble, driving before it like a plague of hissing cockchafers, the sear brown leaves of the winter past.

"More bad weather," said Eden, hunching up in his mantle.

Her eyes glittering with tears, Mererid looked at Gerallt and Sioned with a quivering smile.

"Will you think of us sometimes?"

"Always, my dear one."

Her brother spoke tenderly, watching the twirling leaves and sadly likening their aimless driven course to the haphazard twists and turns of human existence.

They arrived at the ferries three days later. People were crowded along the bank waiting for the tide to ebb, so that they could swim the larger animals over. The opposite shore was like an armed camp. Men-at-arms were in the muddy lanes, in the doorways of the charred hovels, under the trees, and along the sandspits. Near the blackened heap of the tavern where the Sheriff of Mona's lovewoman had once presided, crooning her bawdy ditties and siren songs, a group of soldiers were entertaining a preaching friar rudely, ringing him around with their long spear-pikes like a boar for the baiting. They had his satchel open, emptying out its contents into the mud, peering at parchments frowningly.

A soldier demanded of Gerallt who he was and where he was going. When he replied that he was bound for Penmynydd, his questioner's face went even harder and paler than it was already. He made a sign to some of his comrades, who came hurrying up.

"Are you sure you are not one of the sons of Tudor?"

"As sure as I am that God is in Heaven."

"Do you have an avoucher?"

"All these folk here will bear me witness."

"Your family and partisans? That will not do, Welshman. You must have an avoucher or you will be adjudged to prison until one can be found."

Weary and footsore and not understanding a word, the freemen of Penmynydd stood about, watching Gerallt arguing with the soldiers, and fingering their crosses and amulets. Sioned spread out a horseblanket on the ground and sat down upon it, nestling her twins in her arms. Staring past her husband, she let her eyes wander along the broad shelf of shingle to the royal dower woods where in happier days the natives had run so merrily, hunting the hart and the hind. A corpse was hanging from a branch of a large tree. Every now and then the breeze brought them a dismaying whiff.

Her son Gwyn gave a cry: "Look, Mam, there is the man who wanted to marry Mererid."

"Hush, boy!" she hissed in alarm, herself looking.

A man in black, mounted on a big chestnut was riding towards them. Yes, it was Andras of Dyngannan. He was wearing his old chain of office as the Keeper of the ports and ferries of Mona. His whole being breathed an air of arrogance and stern authority.

"By what right are you detaining this freeman?" he demanded of the soldiers.

"He has no avoucher, sir."

"Now he has one. Release him."

Never hitherto had the priest's son dreamed that he would ever have had reason to be as thankful to that dour man with his dark stone-cut face as he was then. A few minutes later they were on their way.

"It hardly enlarged your interest yonder to say that you were going to Penmynydd, you know," Andras observed as they rode along.

"I could hardly have said anything else," Gerallt smiled, "since it is there that we are going."

"Why is Meredith ap Tudor not with you? The English have not outlawed him."

"He chose not to come."

"Ah. Because of his brothers, I doubt not."

"In great part. He is a man of honor."

"Aye, so he has ever been. What of Ednyved? How is he?"

"He is well. He has fathered a baby daughter this past year."

"I am glad to hear it," said Andras, and then fell silent, staring in front of him with a dark unwinking gaze.

Gerallt looked about him at the land. Several groups of islanders quartered in other districts of North Wales had returned in the previous year, so that some tillage had been resumed. Along the black newly-turned earth of the rain-drenched ploughlands, rooks, gulls and plover were gathering in flocks. The spinneys were putting out their little yellow buds. Hens with chicks were combing dunghills, wild ducks were paddling in the reeds. Sparrows were flying back and forth over the roofs of the crofts, carrying feathers and straws for their nests in the thatch.

"It is said," Gerallt ventured hesitantly, "that a fine is to be levied on our heads."

"According to the magnitude of the misdemeanor committed, aye," Andras nodded. "Are you and the freemen of Penmynydd guilty of any?"

"I know of none."

"No more do I. I will have a word with the King's commissioners."

Gerallt breathed an inward sigh of relief. The lord of Dyngannan was oddly likable today.

"Give you thanks, Andras."

The freemen with throbbing hearts and wet eyes left the road and turned up through the tribal woods towards the granges of the manor. Only Gerallt and Sioned stood hand in hand a while gazing eastward across the waters. Through the mist that veiled them the mountains looked like bursts of black smoke. Even as they watched they were vanishing.

2

It was darkest night. Over the battlements of Conway castle a wild wind blew in shuddering gusts, whistling down the stony throat of the turrets and along passageways where the flames of pitchpine torches tossed and sputtered in their sconces. In the hall the new Constable was stretching his feet before a large fire when he heard the door open and the sound of voices. He rose to his feet as a group of men, cloaked up from foot to head in black, entered the hall. By God, look at it, he thought laughingly. If it is not the Brotherhood of Death itself!

"Your arrival is welcome," he said, "if you are the men I trust you are."

They came forward towards the fire and put back their hoods. One of them, a tall handsome man with a pale skin and large, dark, rather calfish eyes, bowed his head.

"We are Madoc and Huw, the sons of Red Iwan, the late governor of Caernarvon."

"And you?" said the Constable, turning to the others.

"We are the men of Nannau," was the reply.

"And you?" the man called Madoc demanded. "Who would you be then?"

Detecting a note of challenge and mockery in his voice, the Constable stared at him in surprise. And in that moment it seemed to him that he saw a different man. The lips of this one were wrinkled back over the teeth in a sneer, there was a viperish glint in the soft dark eyes.
Ah, you're a killer, my friend, he thought.

"I am Sir Richard Thelwall," he said. "Does that name mean anything to you?"

"It should," Madoc replied with a harsh laugh. "My sister Eva is the wife of Rhys ap Tudor of Mona."

"Who had something to do with the murder of my nephew Simon Thelwall, I believe."

"Who had everything to do with it," said Madoc. "So, you see, sir knight, you have a grudge to pay."

"And it is not the only one," the other added.

Six years earlier the knight had been taken captive with his liege lord and comrade, Lord Grey of Ruthin, and held prisoner for a year at Dolbadarn castle in the wilderness of Eryri under less than happy conditions. Apart from that, the widow of John Massey, the sometime Constable of Conway, was his cousin. Hence the news that the population of the Valley of the Conway had been so greatly reduced by the departure of the men of Mona for their native isle had filled his heart with joy. When, after that, matters had begun to fall into place so fitly he had not hesitated to send a messenger to the King's castle at Monmouth. Red Iwan's sons and the men of Nannau had ridden posthaste along the Marches to Chester and thence taken ship along the northern coast to

Conway.

"Howel Vaughan is holding a hunting drive up the valley two weeks hence. It is not to be doubted that the sons of Tudor will be there. They are much about at the present time, we hear. How many men do you judge they have at their backs?"

"Rhys Ddu has a *gosgordd*," said Madoc. "A warband."

"How many would that be?"

"A hundred and forty men."

"And Howel Vaughan?"

"He has the Men of Ithon. And then there are the mountain men, a potvaliant tribe of ruffians. They are led by Gualo, a giant, a great fighter, but a bombard and a bit of a fool. But sure," he went on, eyeing his questioner with amusement, "you do not imagine that every man-jack of them will be present at Mathebrud, do you? Howel Vaughan is a liberal-handed chieftain, aye, but not as giving as that, I think."

The Constable nodded.

"Still," he remarked, "I wish I could be certain how many men will be there."

"Then my brother and I shall journey there and find out," said Madoc calmly.

"How do you mean?" Sir Richard asked with an astonished stare. "You will go there in person?"

"In propria persona, yes," Madoc smiled. "I think the time has come for us to be reconciled with our Chieftain."

"It is mad!" the Constable exclaimed. "He will suspect."

"Why should he? There will be only the two of us and our servant. Besides," Madoc observed, "it was our father, Red Iwan, who sinned against the Men of Eden. My brother and I have done no wrong. And Meredith ap Tudor, our Chieftain, is nothing if not just."

"Aye, and yet I do not like it," the Constable frowned. "It's a gambler's throw."

"Well then, Sir Richard," Madoc rejoined, "what is life?"

As he was undressing that night in the turret room he shared with Huw, his brother, Madoc withdrew a crucifix from about his neck and set it on the table lighted by a guttering candle. It was of silver and it contained a shred of the shroud of St Beuno. It had belonged to his stepmother, Pia of Nanmor. When she had died last year she had given it to the Dominican friar, Red Iwan's bastard, to give to Madoc at

Monmouth.

"She prays you to make peace with the sons of Tudor," Brother Gwern had said. "As if one can make peace with fiends, poor deluded lady. Christ's curse is upon them, can you doubt it? The islanders have lost the sacred shrine of St Cybi. The Irish bore it away to Dublin with them. Our kinsmen yonder are doomed and damned of Heaven for their mischiefs and cruelties. I shall never forget when I saw Eva last. So cold and pitiless she was. They have poisoned the wells of her very thought, even as our earthly father said."

Eva! Madoc's mind drifted back to his childhood days at the Great Strand. Porpoises were tumbling along the milky horizon, and fishermen, their red and blue tunics bellying on their backs, were trimming frames for coracles with their light axes under whinstone ramparts, and Eva was laughing and squeezing her eyes up tight against the blowing brightness of the sunlight over sand and sea. She could have been no more than ten years of age then—how wondrously sweet and pure she had been!

"What are you thinking about, Madoc?"

"About the Great Strand. When we were children. The rich old life—the life they took away from us!"

The veins on his brow filled with blood. He snatched up his sword, and grating his teeth drove it into the straw mattress time and time again. Then he hurled it ringing against the stones of the floor at the other side of the room and stood with his arms outstretched along the walls on either side of the window slit, staring out into the night.

Huw watched him with pity mixed with love. He did not like this business, but he was caught up in it. There was no way out. He was afraid.

Howel Vaughan, the lord of Mathebrud, was in the toils of a perverse madness that season. His main pleasure in life seemed to be wrangling. Say one thing, he would say the opposite. Call crows black, he would paint them white. Hence his mockery of his countrymen's old French allies. In truth, when they had been guests in the land, no one could have been a more generous or delightful host than Howel. Le Borgne could scarcely be drawn away from Mathebrud, it had been such fun. Never since he had lost his eye had he laughed so much. He had feared for the sight of the other, bellowing. Sire Howel was certainly a lively and amusing person! What a naughty wit he had!

How it would have astonished that gallant knight to hear that same naughty wit now turned against him and his confederates. Not that Howel meant it, as his wife and kinsmen well knew. He had wicked moods. It was the way of him. He was only doing it to vex. He knew where his victims were sore; he could not resist rubbing away: The Duke of Burgundy, now there was a fellow of mark for you! Say what you like, these last ages had seen no one to surpass that prince in sheer knavery. Getting himself acclaimed the savior of France for murdering the King's brother—why the man was extraordinary! What an intelligence! It was he the Welsh ought to have had on their side, not Louis.

"What bad luck for us then that he's already in the King of England's camp," Rhys Ddu observed drily.

Eden snorted with disgust.

"Ach, why do I sit here listening to this? Don't you want such men about you as make some conscience of what they do? You could be thankful towards them, at least."

"But I am. Who says I'm not thankful? They are setting up on their own score now. God above, why should I not be thankful? Their neglects of us, why, it's a mercy, fellow my boy! We shall not be cajoled into attempting another Ronsifal now, shall we? I must say I was in terror of that for a while. Worcester now. Do you remember Worcester, Rhys Ddu? Every morning a tilt? Horns blowing for Oliver? The lads scared me like the devil, I don't mind telling you. Worse, by Brute, being more palpable."

Even worse and more palpable where Olwen, Howel's wife, was concerned, was the matter of the marriage of their son Elise and Cristin, the daughter of Morys Wynn of Lloran. The two fathers had agreed to the match over a pot of ale on the youth's seventeenth birthday, and since that time had done nothing but argue. The wedding, for instance. Since Morys Wynn and his wife Luned wanted the ceremony to be held at the cathedral church of St Deiniol in Bangor, it seemed to them but right and fitting that he who officiated there should be the Bishop.

Howel feigned ignorance.

"Who would that be then, Morys Wynn? I did not know we had one."

"Sure you know we have one. Our Lord Griffith Young. He has been provided to the see by the Holy Father himself."

"Which Holy Father are we talking about, say you?"

"Why, Pope Benedict of Avignon, of course."

"Pedro de Luna you mean? The Anti-Pope?" Howel laughed scornfully. "I would as soon my son be married by the potbellied little wizard of Merthevin," he declared on that, "with the singing birds doing service as a choir, than by that Spaniard's lackey, Griffith Young."

The Master of Lloran drew a deep breath, striving to be calm.

"And yet," he said, "I think our Lord Griffith did you a good service once."

"When was that?"

"The time you were in Conway. Under siege."

"Where did you unearth this figment?"

"Rhys Ddu of Mona said so."

"And you believed that fellow?" Howel Vaughan scoffed. "An excommunicate?"

"Excommunicate no more," Morys Wynn said. "The ban is now raised."

"By the Anti-Pope, sure. What's incest to him?"

"And what is incest to you, Howel Vaughan?" the lord of Lloran exclaimed hotly. "Your mother's parents were second cousins. Are you so free of corruption?"

"And what of you, Morys Wynn? Was not your own mother, the daughter of your grandfather's lovewoman, born out of wedlock?"

"Enough!"

Was that the last word? It certainly seemed so. Morys Wynn was in such a fury that everybody was ready to put the fiddle in the roof—everybody, that is to say, save the young couple most closely concerned. Little Cristin of Lloran fell into a despond directly and would not eat. For his part, Elise, one of the most good-natured and mild-tempered of youths, became on a sudden surly and rebellious. Howel bullied and badgered him to no end. One day they even came to blows. "He cursed me, his own father!" he shouted at Olwen, as Elise ran into the hall, frothing at the mouth, his nose dripping blood.

Olwen was beside herself. She appealed to the Chieftain to mediate between her husband and the lord of Lloran,—"You know what Howel is like, Meredith. Speak to him. He will listen to you,"—but he was so disgusted with the affair that at the outset he begged his excuses. He would put in a special supplication for the estranged parties in his prayers, he said with sarcasm. Eden was engaged to speak to Howel in his turn. In his turn he was heard to no purpose. "Elise is only a lad, he will get over it. There are better matches. Plenty more fish in the sea, as the saying is. God knows, yon Morys Wynn is such a pompous ass! I cannot suffer the man. And so unclean! The last time I saw him he was stinking like an old goat."

Eden could not resist a grim smile—environed about as they were at the time by Gualo and his company, rough-hewn beauties from the wilds in fee to Howel. Flakes of last summer's tar still clung like lichen to their tough hides. They were at Ostro Bodo, a hostelry some miles east of Mathebrud. An autumn day in the forest—wild, red and windy. The air within was so thick and crackling that you could have sworn their enemies were firing the door with heaps of straw.

"Can you do nothing about this smoke, my sweet?" Howel asked the stewlady Siwan, with the tender honey smile he reserved for women.

Sitting across the table from his host, Eden asked:

"You are not jealous of him, are you?"

Howel knit his brows, staring.

"Jealous of whom? Morys Wynn?"

"No," Eden replied. "Of Elise."

"What?"

The cry that burst from Howel's throat was startling in its vehemence.

"Jealous? Me? Of my own son?"

Eden eyed him shrewdly for a moment or two, and then nodded.

"Aye, jealous of Elise. Your own fair son. Jealous of his youth. Why else would you seek to come between him and his happiness? Because of Morys Wynn? Come now, fellow my boy," he mocked, "the hawk of the bower is in moult, and would devour his fledgling. Plenty more fish in the sea, you say. What fine fish do you have in mind for your bonny son, I wonder? Some great chieftain's big, fat daughter whose couch Elise will desert at every chance for the bed of a whore or a tumble in the hay? Like his. . . ."

Eden hesitated.

"Like his who?" Howel asked, very coldly.

White in the face, the lord of Mathebrud rose. He kicked back his chair with a leather booted foot. Alepots went flying before the savage sweep of his hand.

"Like his who?" he demanded again. "Like his father? Say it, bastard! And who is this great chieftain's big, fat daughter you are talking about? Can it be my Olwen? That dear, good woman who has been like a mother to you all these years? A very saint! You can slight her so, damn you!" he snarled, raising his fist in threat.

"I would not do that, if I were you, kinsman," Eden warned—calm, despicable.

Howel paused, fist poised to strike. So he stood for a moment or two, glaring down at him through the coiling smoke with mad eyes. Finally he uncurled his fingers. He let fall his hand to his side and grinned. Eden did not like that grin. He knew it of old.

Screwing up a wicked eye, Howel outthrust his hand towards him.

"Your wager!" he demanded.

"What wager?"

"Ach, get you gone, son of Tudor! The one you staked on Orleans winning the supremacy over Burgundy."

"Good God!"

"Have you so soon forgot? You put your ring in gage."

"I did no such thing. And then, who says the Orleanais are done for?"

"Well, by the Lord, where have you been living? It's all the talk around here, is it not, lads? The rout and ruin of the house of Orleans is total. Tell him, Gualo."

"Howel Vaughan says true, son of Tudor," that honest spirit nodded gravely. "What's-his-name has walloped the Dolphin."

"What's-his-name go fiddle, you buffoon!" Eden jeered. " You whistle-headed lump, don't play your fool's games with me!"

"I am deadly serious, Eden," said Howel. "Give me your ring!"

"No will I."

"We'll see about that," he said. He nodded at his ruffians. "Get it."

With that they were upon him. It was useless to struggle. Half of them had him pinned down, while the other half tugged at his ring. But over the course of the years it must have grown into the habit of his finger, for pull and twist as they might they could not win it loose. He laughed at them tauntingly. That enraged Howel anew. All of a sudden he grabbed Eden's hand and brought it open with a flattening blow against the board. Then he snatched up a billhook from the woodpile.

He bared his teeth coldly. "I'll have the finger off your hand then, shall I?"

Eden's backbone froze.

"For pity's sake!"

"Och, poor wretch, I've no pity left," Howel sighed in mock lament. "Things were different once. When I was young and in my prime. But as you say I'm old now. I'm a cranky hard old codger gone."

"In God's name, Howel, you know I did not speak in earnest."

"No, kinsman, you dealt with me plain and true. I thank you for your honesty. Avarice is a sign of old age, is it not? No doubt that's why I covet your jewel so."

"Faith, if you want it so badly, you can have it."

"Give it me then."

"But look, I can't get it off my finger."

Thump! His hand was fastened to the board again.

"Wait!" Eden flung at him desperately. "Think of the consequences."

Another stay of execution was won the threatened finger. The steel crescent danced away to scratch his tormentor's tufty beard.

"The blood fine, you mean? Let's see. How much would that be, Gualo? You are up on the laws."

"The wedding finger? Oh, I would say, a cow and twenty pence."

"Oia, a mic! A mere trifle. What's a cow and twenty pence?"

"Be sure, it will cost you far more than that, Howel Vaughan," Eden gritted bitterly.

Howel raised his brows in mock alarm.

"*Libera nos*! The fellow's a cracker."

"God save all here!"

Another voice sounded in the doorway. It was Howel's cousin, Meurig Vaughan, a kindly—and at this moment—a most welcome presence.

"What's to do?"

Grinning from ear to ear, Howel returned Eden his hand and his courage.

"Just a little sport, kinsman."

Eden gave a harsh laugh.

"Sport? Get back to hell, you son of a bitch!"

"By the mass, son of Tudor," Meurig said, staring at him in blank amazement. "What do these words mean?"

"Ask him," Eden said, jutting the box of his chin at the lord of Mathebrud. "Ask your cousin and his louts what they mean. I am going."

"Stay, kinsman!" Meurig cried. "Don't tear off like this! Why are you so angry?"

"Bah, let him go!" Howel prattled. "He's in the grip of a frenzy, poor lad. There's no reasoning with him. It's hopeless. He's gone quite mad. Do you know what? He's taken it into his head that I'm after his wedding ring—have you ever heard the like? Sure, he's been visited with the mentality of a miser. As if I had not rings and baubles enough of my own! No, leave him be. He will cool off by and by."

"Don't count on it!" Eden hurled back at him in parting.

"God keep you, chieftain!" the woman Siwan shouted after him.

Riding away through the trees, Eden turned at her cry to see her standing there at the horseblock, straining her voice against the wind crashing like surf, and the figure of a man some paces behind her, crouched over himself as though doubled up with laughter—a dark blur in the uncertain light. Like enough it was Howel, but it could just as well have been his demon, or the genius loci of that unholy place.

Eden rode up the valley to the hall of Trellan, where his brother, the Chieftain, was a guest at the time. His hosts were Robert and Lelo, cousins of Red Iwan's, loyal to Glyndwr, who were known throughout the region as the Widowers. Meredith was in the forge with the old lords and two cowmen when Eden arrived. They were tanning hide in there; the stink was fearsome. If the castle had not been so full of womenfolk in those days Eden would have been tempted to ride on.

"You are back early," said Meredith.

"I have quarreled with your brother-in-law."

"You too?"

Meredith was inclined to shrug it off. "Away, these were drunken pratings. He was just having some fun at your expense. He would never have done it."

"Wouldn't he, by the Lord!"

"I am of opinion with Ednyved," Robert put in gravely. "Howel Vaughan's bad these days. This business with Lloran, for instance. They say the little she's in a decline yonder. Holy Mary keep her, I saw her mother and father the other day in church. How's little Cristin? Nothing out of the Old Hand to be sure but a sniff and a frown. Ochan, it's a pity for her. Such a pretty girl, all dimples and blushes. Dainty as a pin. Never used to miss her Mass, did she, Lelo? Always a smile and a greeting."

"God give you goodday, sir. The greetings of Heaven, sir. A lovely maid, aye."

"And Elise is a good lad, too."

"O, a fine lad. Well, it's a concernment to us all. Olwen is so worried about him—he has become so angry and sullen. Tell me, Meredith, what demon gets into these fathers? Watching over their innocent lambs as though wolves?"

"How fondly you descant, Lelo. You are so tender grown I marvel the two of you did not get yourselves wives again."

The gap of a missing tooth to which the Chieftain could never get accustomed broke the pointed design of Lelo's face.

"After Marged Vaughan and Tudor's daughter Enid were spoken for, who was left for us?"

"You have engaged my heart," Meredith smiled.

Two days later, much to the delight of Olwen, who had arrived at the castle earlier in the week, he left to cure what he described as the puerility between Howel Vaughan and Morys Wynn of Lloran. He would have liked Eden to accompany him, but his younger brother refused outright.

"Blessed are the peacemakers, remember, little brother," Meredith told him with a smile.

So it was that the Chieftain rode to Mathebrud and Eden stayed on at the castle at Dolwyddelan and the best and the worst befell.

The best for Eden was the week that followed, when he referred the world with its pains and troublings to the providence of high Heaven and studied his delight alone. Long would he cherish the memory of those October days. Days of his birth. The last sheaf of corn, reapers dancing the Old Hag* home. The silvery track of the straw running over the brow of the stubble-field into the luminous twilight. Wind-bent tussock grass. Bryn Bronwala and kisses among the gravestones. The shippon, more

*The Old Hag was made out of the last cut of standing corn.

kisses remembered among the frothing milkpails. Cakes and honey at the beadhouse beside a monstrous oak hung with wild mosses. Bracken on mountain, glittering skeletons of cow-parsley in the water-meadows. White mist in the heather, white starlings arriving in flocks, wild ducks and snipe making stir in the sedge. Horns blowing, owls hooting, stags belling.

One day they rode to a christening ale at Pennant Machno. Staying on their return to watch an otter bitch playing slide with her young in a gorge of the river, they got separated from the rest of the party. Following as they thought the path the others had taken they were soon lost, magically so. Deeper and deeper into the forest they strayed. Over the thud of the horses' hooves, soft in moss, loud in brush, the greatest sound to be heard was that of the crows cawing in the high trees. Not a living soul did they see anywhere. She did not know, the priest's daughter, whether to laugh or tremble.

"Are you sure you know where we are going, Ednyved?"

Clumps of ghostly fungi puffed into view like fantastic mushrooms and squat fat oaks stood out as somber blurs among the drifting vapors. Torn-up roots of dead trees like the bared stumps of Yspaddaden Chief Giant's teeth yawned foul and ragged out of the mighty flinders of the forest. "Come, confess. We are lost. You have no idea where we are, do you?"

"Yes, I do, Mererid mine. We are in the lordship of the religious knights. This is the great sanctuary."

"God help us."

Finally they came upon a glade, green and open to the sky "No, don't move, manon. Stay where you are!" St Cybi, there was a sight for you! She was tangled in gossamer threads. They were everywhere about—there must have been thousands of them, harnessing the grass, swinging from bush to bush, tree to tree; miraculous webs, pearled with dewdrops, diamonded with sunlight. He could not stare his fill. It was sorcery plainly. Gwyn ap Nudd was near.

"Eden. . . ."

"Hush, hush.

"What do you mean, hushing? Uch, look at all these horrible cobwebs sticking to me!"

"Hush, lady. Stay. Not a word. You are in mortal peril."

She stood still, wide-eyed and unbreathing as he plucked away the threads fron the stuff of her mantle, her hair, her cheeks and throat.

"There, it's done. You are free."

"Free from what?"

"Why, the fairies of course. They almost had you snared in their nets there for a while."

"Fool!" she laughed, but gave him the kiss he claimed for all that, and for overplus, a garland of scarlet briony berries.

A little while after, some homely pigs came snorting and snuffling among the bushes. They led them in due course to a forester's hut, where before a great fire of branches they feasted on blochta* and oatcakes that left seeds in their teeth for hours, long after they had reached home indeed.

It was late by then. In the water-green sky above the castle towers, the young moon was sitting on the winking crescent of its backside and men were in tree-tops looking for them. Enid was almost witless with worry. She felt herself entitled to fortify her battered emotions by giving Eden the stern edge of her tongue for an hour. Where had they been? How could they be so thoughtless? Did they know what a sweat she had been in, running up and down the steps of the keep as if she were getting paid for it? Where was Eden's head, going off alone with Mererid into the wildest heart of the forest? And at such a time of year? The unholy powers everywhere on the prowl, raising mists in every dingle, lighting candles in every bog? Black Satan leering in his ambush, werewolves, fairies, hobgoblins, bolols, and mercy on us, the Wild Hunt!

Nothing from Marged Vaughan the while. Whatever she did not know, she knew those two. She scanned them in silence as Enid spoke, and smiled, a wise and secret little smile.

All were in the castle hall—the women weaving, Robyn playing the harp, the men mending gear—the day a small group of riders rode into the home meadow from the north. They were led by Elise, the heir of Howel Vaughan of Mathebrud, and Owain, the Chieftain's son, the delight and flower of his family, a boy of fourteen with the sooty black hair of his father's tribe and the radiant grey eyes of the Vaughans.

"Welcome, my boys," smiled Olwen at the sight of their grinning faces, "I trust you are merry for good reason."

*blochta; whey cheese, curd.

"Aye, mother, things are sorting out as well as could be wished." said Elise. "Father goes to Lloran after the hunt. But as it fortunes it is another errand that brings us here today. The fact is that Madoc and Huw, Red Iwan's sons, are at Mathebrud and Meredith wants Eden to go there to meet them."

Everyone fell silent, astounded. Something began to hum in Mererid's head like a wasp in a bottle. She drew a deep breath and looked at her husband, who had been playing with their baby daughter Angharad in the straw nearby. Eden's face had paled and hardened.

"How long have they been there?" he asked.

"Since the night before last," the youth replied.

They had come knocking at the doors, he said, like pilgrims, in rough coarse garments, and Joseph's shoes, with staves in their hands, and a brown-faced little serving man dragging in the heels of them. On entering the hall they had gone down on their knees before the Chieftain and humbly placed themselves at his mercy.

"Madoc showed him a crucifix he had from his stepmother, Pia of Nanmor, when she died," Elise went on. "A reliquary. Some saint's bone in it or the like. It was her dying wish, he said, that he and Huw make peace with their kindred."

Eden rose, picking up his baby daughter, and set her down on her mother's lap. He turned to Elise with a troubled frown.

"Where did they come from?"

"From the hospice, they said," the youth replied. "At Dolgynwal. Huw had lain there sick for several days, and indeed, he still looked ill and beaten down."

"And they had no weapons with them?"

"Only their knives. When they offered to deliver them up as if swords to be placed in lawful rest after the custom, everybody had to laugh. Jesus save you, keep them, Father told Madoc and Huw. You will need them to eat the fatted calf."

Brows fretting, Marged Vaughan drew her son aside.

"How did your father look through all this, Owain?" she asked.

"A little taken aback," he said, "but not unfriendly. Don't worry, mother. All is well."

"Has Rhys Ddu been sent for?" Eden asked Elise.

"Aye. And Gualo's sons have gone to fetch the Widowers."

Without another word Eden beckoned to the sergeant-at-arms and led him aside. They spoke together a while and then went into the armory. Pale and anxious, Mererid followed them. She saw that her husband and the men of the castle were arming themselves.

"You do not trust them, do you?"

Eden stroked her face gently.

"Sure you know that a man's weapons are the call on all events in our land these days, Mererid."

"And yet," she said, "Madoc and Huw came to Mathebrud unarmed."

"And out of the wilderness, aye," said Eden. "I too have thought of that. Yet it is not out of credibility that they have had a change of heart. It can happen." He glanced at her with a sly smile. "Look at Andras."

They set out, an armed band of fifteen men, a few minutes later, following a path that led them northward through woods and rocky river gorges. A misty dawn was breaking as they overtook the Widowers and a small party of riders moving at a walking pace along the valley road to the village of Llanrwst. Robert, the younger of the brothers, raised his voice in thanksgiving as soon as he saw Eden.

"What a manifest witnessing of God, son of Tudor. Our nephews have come home. Sure, it's bitter living on the bread of strangers. Home is always best, eh, among one's own kith and kin?"

"Home is best," echoed Lelo.

While they prattled on, Eden cast an eye over the Widowers' party. It was made up of three grizzled retainers and Siarlo Marc, the steward of Trellan, a live coal, full of warmth and genial light. They wore sheepskin coats and axes swung from their saddlebows. Where were Gualo's sons? he wondered. Ah well, like enough they had been left behind at Trellan to look after things. Then it occurred to him: the Chieftain has sent all the boys away.

An hour later they rode into Llanrwst. The freemen's huts, stripped of their summer coat of lime, stood out along their path like mounds of brown hay. Swart and shaggy, the cattle were bellowing in the yellow muck outside the tribal shippon. Hens squawked and scattered at the horsemen's approach. Pigs and goats wandered in and out of open doors at will. Eden and the Widowers dismounted at the dung-bailiff's hut and went inside. The ashes of the fire were cold and an old boar hound lay cradling his bone next to the woodpile. He watched them warily as they entered, the red eyes gleaming back in his skull beneath the sparse mesh of coarse hair.

"Where is everyone?" Robert asked.

"They are at Mass, sure," said Lelo.

"I have heard no bells."

"There has been no priest here," said Eden, "since Father Mathau died."

They mounted their horses and went on. Llanrwst was like a village abandoned in the path of a rampaging giant or pestilence.

A long cold shudder of dread flowed down Eden's back. All at once he put his horse to a fast trot, then lashed it to a gallop through the woods that lay between the village and Mathebrud, drawing rein only when he had reached the head of the rise looking down the long field at the hall. He did not know what he had expected to find, a smoking ruin perhaps, so at first sight he felt something akin to relief. Outwardly nothing seemed different. The shaggy grey thatch of the roofs gleamed peacefully in the early morning light. Rooks were hopping about in the stackyard and settling in flocks among the glistening black clods of a nearby oatfield. A brown nag grazed lazily in the pasture; ducks were paddling in the pond under the willows: a homely scene. If only, here as elsewhere, the cows had not been lowing so miserably.

Something caught his attention. He might not have noticed it if it had not moved. It was like a flash at the corner of his eye. Turning his head swiftly, he saw whatever it was scuffling into the hazel wood at the end of the meadow, as if trying to lose itself there.

"Someone in russet. A crofter perhaps," said the sergeant-at-arms as he came to a halt beside Eden with his troop.

Moments later the Widowers rode puffing up, staring like goats in thunder.

"Mercy on us, kinsman," Robert gasped. "I thought you would break your neck riding along so."

"There are others in the trees there," the sergeant-at-arms began to say, and then he gave a start, and his face took on a grey ashen color as he stared past the company at the hall.

"Jesus, Maria," he murmured.

The gates were creaking open. A cow with a distended udder was rubbing her flanks against the log posts. But it was not that. It was what was over the gates, some dark and lumpish adornment. A small round mass standing out against the silver-grey peak of the thatch behind it,

like a bell in a clochiard. Deathly pale, Eden rode down the slope in
front of the others, and reining in his horse stared up at the head impaled
on the stake above him. He could hear the throbbing of his heart, the
blood pounding in his throat and ears. Someone was crying.
"Och, Eden, whom have they murdered? Ow, where shall we turn?
Look, Lelo, look what they have done. They have butchered our
Chieftain, curse them! Our noble old eagle."
Like the stab of a knife the cry pierced Eden's brain. His head
seemed to be bursting. Faces, things, swam in and out of the edges of his
vision like chimeras, dim and monstrous. All he could see was
Meredith. He could not take his eyes off his face. His lips and skin were
as grey as clay. The blood-clotted beard was parted in a cold and
dreadful grimace over the bared teeth. Buried in their sockets under the
heavy ridge of the brows, his eyes glared over and past them at clouds
and mountains they did not see, pits of blackest oblivion.
"We are finished. Give us over to the priests and sineaters. Let them
dig us graves. We are done for, it is the end. Galanas,* galanastra! Ah,
that they are not all of them dead in there. . . !"
Robert's plea summoned Eden back from the depths. He stared at
the old man with wild eyes.
"I'm afraid to go in there, Eden, lad. I'm afraid to think of it. And
what if it's a trap? Do you think the killers are still around here
somewhere, lying in wait? What shall we do?"
A harsh strangling cry was torn from Eden's throat. Tearing open
the fastenings at his neck so that he could breathe, he swiftly crossed the
empty courtyard. The doors of the hall were ajar. A few hens were
pecking about on the threshold. Beyond them, nothing else seemed to
have been left alive. Men lay wallowing in their blood the length and
breadth of the hall. Benches were overturned, casks and firkins
shattered, costers were half-torn off the walls. Open mouths, staring
eyes, slashed limbs—the bodies lay twisted in all manner of postures,
grotesque, obscene, pitiful. Eden had thought himself hardened to such
sights, but for a moment he was gripped by such a fit of trembling and
nausea that he thought he would swoon. Where did one begin? Plainly
the thing not to do was to stand idle. Besides, as soon became apparent,
some of the bodies still had life in them. Seeing that friends had arrived,
they started moaning and crying: "In the name of charity, help us!"

*Galanas: massacre.

They set to work, agitatedly sorting out the dead from the wounded, stanching wounds, filling water-bougets, ransacking coffers for salves, potions and linen for bandages. Eden went into Howel's sleeping chamber. His headless corpse lay sprawling on the ground, the arm stretched out along the stones, the rigid fingers curled like a claw about the hilt of his sword. "God's one Son, what have they done with the head?" he wondered in loathing and horror. As he was stripping the sheets from the bed, he heard someone cough. Looking about he found an old man crouched under the cloths of the table that served as an altar. He pulled him out by the wools of his tunic and twisting the liripipe around his hand, half-throttled him. The old man looked at him with prayerful eyes and a quivering little smile.

"No, no, have mercy, son of Tudor, don't you see who it is?"

Eden released him so abruptly that the ancient stumbled and all but fell.

"Cado, forgive me!" he said with an anguished sigh.

The old man began to beat his breast and wail.

"O, my little Howel, what have they done to you? My little dear, my darling. . . ."

"Never mind that now," Eden said hoarsely. "Where are the other serving folk?"

Some had run away into the woods, some had gone down into the cellar underneath the hall. They had broken down the ladder after them, so that the killers would be unable to follow them there. They were helped out and put to work. Cows were herded to the doors and milk brought hot from them to the wounded. Water was heated to wash the dead, while the serving folk bustled around cleaning the blood from the floor and laying it with new-gathered rushes. Gradually Eden lost all sense of time. His hands and feet seemed to move by themselves. They had nothing to do with the rest of him, with his ghostly part, which was as though suspended in space, looking on everything that was outside itself with a bloodless indifference, with eyes as cold and insensate as the stones.

Later in the morning Rhys Ddu and Eva arrived. Indescribable the look on those two faces as their eyes first swept the hall. Outlaw Jenkin was in their company along with several of his henchmen. They walked up and down, staring at the victims of the massacre with curiosity and astonishment.

"There must be hi-jinks in Hell today for sure," said Rhys Ddu with a harsh laugh. "The murderers came up the valley from Conway, of course."

"Yes," said Eden. "Where Sir Richard Thelwall is now Constable."

They had come in the dead hours of the night while everybody was asleep, the brains of many bemused by ale and metheglin. No one could arrive at any clear account as to how many armed men there were, only that there had been a great many. They had come swarming out of the darkness with weapons and torches. They had swept through the hall like a deadly whirlwind. Within minutes the place was running with blood like a flesh-market. Only a few had a chance to dare the killers to their teeth, yet fewer to do more than that. Gualo, the mountain man, had been one. Coming awake with a roar, he had laid about him with his axe, scattering several and killing two, before being himself cut down.

"Have you sent for the women?" Rhys Ddu asked.

"Yes," said Eden, "not an hour since."

They arrived the next morning, before daybreak. Black-hooded, mantles bellying about them, they seemed shades hastening towards the hall through the dark forest and the mist - priestesses come to attend the festival of death. They reeled into the hall, half-crazed with grief. Eden drew Mererid into his arms, and then she shuddered away from him; his garments were soaked in blood—now it was on her, too. Clinging to her white-faced son, Marged Vaughan looked through her husband's brothers as though they were not there. Olwen was distraught beyond recognition. As though possessed by demons, she flung herself on the mutilated corpse of her husband and fell to clawing it and dabbling her fingers in the blood.

"Ah, where's his head? Christ, what have they done to you, my lovely old boy?" she screamed. "What have they done with my Howel's head?"

She kept saying it over and over, she showered kisses on the livid blackening hands, she tore off her hood and pulled out her hair in bunches. Her son Elise and her kinsmen took her by the arms to restrain her, but she turned on them, shrieking and scratching with a ferocity more animal than human. She wrenched herself free and spun around to dodge them. Something winked in her hand and she was out through the door.

"After her! She has a knife."

Rhys Ddu, Eden and Elise were the first off the mark, the outlaw and his band hard in their heels. In the grey light of the breaking dawn they could see the dark line of Olwen's kirtle darting through the gates and along the hillside beyond the willows. She turned and watched them, her rough tangle of grey hair hanging loose and ragged to her shoulders like undressed wool. They saw her arms raised as though she were calling down malediction, but when they came close she set off again like a wild mare. By a wallow where the mud was churned up by the beasts, she finally stumbled and lost her footing. The knife slipped from her fingers. Outlaw Jenkin with one huge leap and as prodigious a slither, was at her side to catch her as she fell. "Help!" he panted. "The lady's a ton. She is asking more arms than I have."

They helped him lift her up. She showed no more desire to come to a grapple with them. Moaning and ever and anon hiccuping, she let them half-carry, half-drag her back to the hall. Once there, however, the outlaw in his unthinking way asked her: "What can we do for you now, Olwen? Maybe you would like us to slaughter some swine against the wake," and that set her off again.

"Aye, slaughter them!" she shrieked. "Kill the swine that have killed our men."

"Their deaths will be avenged a hundredfold, Olwen," Rhys Ddu assured her. "We will not rest until Red Iwan's sons and everybody under the guilt are brought to account for their crimes."

"And the woman, what of her?" she demanded. "Alison Massey, will you slay her, too?"

They stared at her in dumb horror.

"It's she who has Howel's head, the whore," she said. "What will she do with it, I wonder? Garnish it with flowers to sit at her bedside? Or hang it over the jakes when she takes a shit."

"Stop it, Olwen!" Rhys Ddu frowned. "God help us, you are blabbing nothing but foolishness."

"Foolishness, is it?" she cried, her big full-bosomed body reeling. "No, it's not foolishness," she declared wildly She tore open her dress and began to beat her breast, "By this blood that runs about my heart, I know it. Howel made her lose her head, ha, ha, and damn the whore to Hell if she has not made him lose his!"

"I can do nothing with her," said Rhys Ddu.

"Leave her be," said Marged Vaughan.

Her eyes red and swollen from weeping, the Chieftain's widow nodded the men away, and taking Olwen in her arms, cradled her swooning head against her shoulder.

"Alison Massey," Eden mused in a while, "isn't she a Thelwall?"

"God in Heaven, lad," Rhys Ddu said with a grim laugh, "how could it be that silly woman? Howel's head hangs over the gates of Conway at this hour, I'll wager you."

"Let's have no more wagers," said Eden.

Another day was beginning, another lifetime. He lay down for a space on a bench next the wall and stuffed straw in his ears to shut out the groans and cries of the wounded and bereaved. He closed his eyes and tried to empty his mind of thought, but to no avail. People kept arriving through the hours. Chieftains and tribesmen thronged the gates; the courtyard was a press of glittering spears and swaying mantles. Among them came the Abbot of Aberconway and a group of monks. His tall austere figure halted a moment at the threshold as he made a sweeping sign of the Cross in the air.

"God have mercy on all in this house," he said.

"God?" Olwen was up and at him with her unnerving shriek at once. "Is it you who are calling upon Him to have mercy upon us? But He is our enemy, can't you see that? Look about you, old man. A handsome set of corpses, are they not? Deny God's in hostility against us. He has let my dear man and his comrades be butchered in cold blood by the scum of this earth. Our Father in Heaven, indeed! No, leave off your hushing!" she cried, angrily brushing aside the folk who were trying to restrain her. "What's in my heart must come out. Do what you will with me after, I don't care. Shout anathema at me. Stop up the doors and windows with thorns, it's nothing to me."

"I think you do not mean so!" the Abbot broke in sternly. "No, no, you do not mean so!" he declared roughly and obdurately when she began to shout again. "Enough now, Olwen, listen to me. Haven't I known you all these years for a Christian woman? A loving minister of the Queen of the Angels? Come now, my child, is it you that is presuming to lay the weight of man's random and brutish acts on the back of Almighty God? Sure you know better than that. His ways and works are above you to speak."

"I am in misery, dear Father."

"Do not turn from God, Olwen. He is your refuge and your strength.

Put yourself in His healing hands. He will not forsake you. Aye, weep, that's it!" he urged gently. "That is good. Tears are balm. They are cleansing."

Anima Christi, sanctifica me, Corpus Christi, salve me, Passio Christi, conforta me. O bone Iesu, exaudi me. Prayers and hymns were now sung; candles of wax and rush were lighted, and torches blazed along the walls among hangings of crimson and gold. Wisps of incense uncurled from the mouths of censers. Green fir branches and hazel rods were cut and brought in. Salt was sprinkled over the desolately silent and broken heaps. It was more than Eden could bear. Later in the morning he rode out into the woods.

Near a butt of earth used for the slinging of javelins he dismounted and rested for a while. The day had begun with rain and now it drifted in a soft pale mist among the trees so that the mountains were to be seen only as masses of shadow where the river flowed. A mournful stillness reigned. Only now and then a breath of cool air would brush his cheek, bringing with it the faint creaking of branches like the sound of a ship afloat on a lazy sea. He thought of the dead, friends and kin, but he could no longer hold them close. Already they were beginning to slip away from him. Even their voices were fading out. Och, did the air hold the voices of the dead, he wondered, as the earth held their bones? He found himself straining his ears, listening, as if to penetrate and surpass the limits of sense. Howel's merry, malicious cackle, Meredith's rich, deep, ringing bell, did they still have their life out there, just out of earshot, in the heart of the great silence?

He heard a footfall and turned. Mererid was stumbling towards him through the trees; tears were streaming down her face. Pale and beautiful, her body one black against the misty air, she seemed to breathe the very soul of grief. He caught her to him swiftly, or she would have fallen at his feet.

"The men of Nannau were here. They must have come because of me," she cried wildly. "Eden, I betrayed Howel Sele."

"How does one betray a traitor? Hush, hush, my Mererid, you must not think such things."

He stood in quiet, holding her fast in his embrace, listening to her heart-rending sobs, aware as never before of the God-abandoned fiends that prowl the dark bourns of human life, denizens of the farthest smoke.

Blessed are the peacemakers, he thought suddenly.

Only then did he, too, begin to weep.

3

One hot September afternoon the next year, Gerallt was taking his way homeward with a load of peat across the untended sequestered fields of the Old Hall when he came across Emrys, the white-haired lord of Myvyrian staring at the blackened hearthrock, which was all that was left of the dwelling place.

Emrys looked up with a smile.

"It stands," he said.

"Yes. That alone," said Gerallt, looking about at the yard overgrown with nettles, rushes and thistles—the mossy well-shaft and the fallen holly tree rotting among docks.

"I was passing and had the oddest feeling," the old lord said. "Why, there it is, I said to myself, the old hearthrock of the Ottadini. It has outlived the ages like the blessing of friends. What do you hear of those good people?"

"They were all at Lloran for the big wedding some time back. Marged Vaughan, too."

"Marged, God bless her. It's here she should be. We would take care of her."

"Give her time. She will come. How are your sons, my lord Emrys?"

"Still alive, God willing. Still in the fray. They were at Harlech a month ago, but they got out in time. You have heard that the castle has fallen."

"Aye, it came about most suddenly."

"A matter of days," said the old man, crossing himself.

They spoke a little while further and then went their separate ways. Dusk was coming on when Gerallt reached Penmynydd. He loved this hour of the day when the earth as he seemed to take one long last breath into its breast of the wild island air that smelt of sun-warmed turf and wind and sea, when in that afterglow all things stood out more sharply and clearly against the sky as if they had something great to make of themselves before the coming of the dark.

It had been a rarely fine harvest they had had on the island that year. The stackyards and garners were full to bursting. Meredith ap Tudor would have been well pleased.

His Chieftain. For weeks after Gerallt had heard of his murder, a dreary pain had gripped his vitals, but then one day Sioned had said:

"It is not to excuse those wicked men and what they did. But in a way I think a part of Meredith died when he left this island. He was never the same after. This was his heart's home. The air here is full of him, don't you feel it? I feel him very close to me at times. Look how he built this place. That day when we came back I thought for sure it would be a ruin. But see, here it is!"

Years ago Meredith had rebuilt it of stone by the labor of the masons of Rhosyr. White with a snow of dust from the stonecutter's adz, the priest's son could still see the Chieftain in his mind's eye, standing in the court, watching wasps fly into a crack in the wall. "Hm," he had said, "a storm is brewing." Gerallt and Eden, only boys then, had known what that clever head had not known—*he* was the storm. The Man who Came the crofters round about had called him when he had first settled at Penmynydd. Even now Gerallt could not help smiling at that name, because to hear it you would think that here strode some shaggy—bearded settler out of ancientry, all brawn and muscle, to set his seal on virgin soil with hoe and mattock—Hu the Mighty in his guise as ploughman no less. And yet, to tell truth, they had called him so not without reason. "That man up yonder must think he is going to live forever," the women of the vill had tattled. "He is putting tiles down on the floors and quarry stone in the roofs."

Driving the horses slowly across the darkening meadows, Gerallt stared with an unshifting gaze at the hall of Penmynydd with its houses whitely gleaming along its slope. Seagulls were wheeling and circling over the roofs. The longhorned black cows were coming from the byre. Moving lazily through the high swaying grass, they looked like coracles afloat on the swells of a gentle sea. Gwyn and the farm dogs leapt and yapped alongside. There was the tinkle of goatbells. Sioned was walking with the twins along the narrow way between the houses, her headlinen palely gleaming. Somewhere in the distance, men were whistling and calling.

And Gerallt's heart was lapped about with old wine. How peaceful and safe it all looked! Everything was informed with such happy care. The odors of byre and stable, mixed with the dried scents of clover and mint, came to him out of the homely air that kissed his nostrils, and it was most good and sweet to him as he clung to it then, rich and princely and intoxicating in that moment beyond words, as though it would make nothing of the great world beyond the waters. Nothing of the cruelties and injustices of conquest, of the magnificence of causes, ideals and dreams, of blood, war, tyrants, heroes, and deeds of high emprize. Nothing of the pilgrimage of men in search of a fitter destiny. No, nothing at all.

Damn the castles, Gerallt thought.

As it was the pestilence that had once brought about the capture of Harlech by the Welsh, so now it was disease that delivered up the castle once more into the hands of their enemies. Dark and doomed on its sea-girt crag, Bran the Blessed's ancient seat was a charnel house. The bodies of Sir Edmund Mortimer and John Hanmer lay among the dead in the chapel awaiting burial. The stench was fearful. Lice swarmed over the garments of the sick people gathered in a banqueting hall thick with the smoke of purging fires. Only a few escaped the disease. Among them were the indomitable Margaret Hanmer, her three little granddaughters and their mother, Lady Mortimer.

When Earl Talbot and his men entered the courtyard, the Lady went to her chamber. She sank down on her knees at the prie-dieu and prayed for several minutes. Then she doffed her rough grey working dress that was acrid with the smells of sweat and smoke, put on a dark blue gown with a gold girdle and a black mantle. For headgear she wore no more than a wimple of fine white linen.

Hearing bells ring from afar, among the fisher monks on St Tudwal's Isles, she glanced out of the window. The sea was incredibly blue. Fleecy clouds floated in serene tranquillity beyond a clearness of rain-washed air. Why are they ringing those bells at this hour? It is not yet nones. Is it for us that they are being rung, she wondered? Tears prickled her eyes and she feelingly crossed herself.

In the audience chamber her daughter, pale and sunken of cheek and arrayed completely in black, awaited her with the three little girls. Master Howel Deget held one of them on his lap. His ashen face, still streaked with sweat from the sick hall, showed his exhaustion. A few minutes later Earl Talbot entered with a band of soldiers. He was a handsome man with a courtly bearing, but not finding at Harlech the great prize he had looked for had angered him.

"Madame," he said, bowing before her sternly, "I have orders to convey you and Lady Mortimer to the Tower of London."

"And you must obey them naturally," said the Lady. "Well, God be praised that we shall not be alone there. A beloved son of mine, my first born, has been imprisoned in that fortress these past few years. My heart rejoices to think I shall meet him so soon again."

She looked at Howel Deget. Tears were flowing down his lean, haggard cheeks, but his face was rigid, the lips pressed together in a hard thin line.

"I pray you spare this young man's life," she said. "He is Master Howel Deget, the secretary of my lord husband, our Prince, whom our God in Heaven comfort and preserve. Master Howel is not a soldier. He is a scholar and a gentle man. He has been a great stay and comfort to all of us here during these last terrible days. Have mercy upon him."

The Earl bowed his head gravely.

Owain Glyndwr's secretary now took his leave of the ladies with whose fortunes his own had been entangled so long. He kissed their hands, and stroking the heads of the fatherless little maids in blessing, looked for a moment into the eyes of Lady Mortimer, mournfully dimmed now by the tears of memory. Something snapped inside him, but by a supreme effort of will he mastered himself.

"The Holy Trinity watch over you in all your ways and days," he said in a quivering voice.

At Vespers, a few hours after they had left, he was led out with the remaining soldiers of the garrison, to the hillside on the eastern side of the castle and put to the sword. His body like theirs was cast into a common grave.

14
MERERID (1409 - 1410)

1

Several years had now passed since tillage had been suspended throughout the Welsh districts bordering on England. The tribes had long since retreated with their flocks and herds, their harps, distaffs and cauldrons—those immemorial marks of the freeman—into the mountains. They were no longer as they once had been. The shifts of a vagrant and predatory existence had changed them, and yet so imperceptibly had this come about, that they seemed scarcely aware of it themselves. Going about their daily business—hunting, toiling, making love, eating, sleeping, praying, playing, exercising their wasters and bucklers—they moved amidst the ebb and flow of their great struggles as though this was the only way of life they had ever known, as simply and naturally as petrels riding the waves of a stormy sea.

The spring and summer of 1409 were not unkind to them. The weather was of unprecedented kindness and beauty. The oats that were sown on the stony hillsides came to heavy milky ear, and their raids on the border lordships brought them a good booty.

Although all but the native fortresses in the mountains had now been retaken, Owain Glyndwr still ranged far and wide through the open country outside the walls of the garrison towns. His army was now swollen by warbands from Scotland and France. In the spring, Jean d'Espagne and Guy de Ferrebouc arrived from Brittany with a force of men. The supporters of the House of Orleans had lately discarded Duke Louis' device of the gnarled staff with its arrogant motto: *Je l'ennuie*. On their banners now was embroidered one word alone: *Justice*.

"That is what we all seek in very truth," Glyndwr agreed. "There is the grand seigneur whose smile is coveted by even the basest of hearts."

Each interpreted the ideal after his own fashion. Aflame with revenge, the Men of Eden and the Men of Ithon drew a draft on the heads of those responsible for the massacre at Mathebrud. They sent out scouts on the spy everywhere and had their informers in the garrison towns and the halls of the border. One of the murderers was tricked into their hands by the luring love-play of a woman in their fee; another by the false news of a mother's death. Another time a band of their partisans came within a hair of ambushing a hunting party led by the brother of Howel Sele's widow Gaenor as they were gutting deer in a wood near White Castle, but they got wind of it and fled in a panic, leaving game and gear behind them. And then, on a day in August, in the space of one tumultuous hour, the three children of Red Iwan by his first wife were slain.

There had been heavy fighting near Overton and Tudor's sons with Philip Scudamore and their men were returning home with their wounded. They had stopped awhile to rest and water their horses at a stream near Capel Collen, an old church inside the Welsh border. The day was drawing on to dusk when they saw the cloaked figure of a woman riding towards them. It was Eva. She told them that at the hall of Pencoppy near Corwen where she had been awaiting their return, she had been unable to sleep the night before for a dog howling.

"I was certain something terrible must have happened," she said.

"And so you had to come all the way to Capel Collen to find out," her husband smiled. "Come, confess, you were simply tired of sitting and spinning among those old ladies at Pencoppy."

"Well, as you know, I was never much for sitting and spinning, my dear. Let me look my fill at you," she said, pressing herself against him and caressing his face. "I bless the Lord that you are alive."

An hour or so afterwards they descended into the Glens of Dee. Night had fallen and the moon was shining bright when they came to a bridge spanning the torrent, swollen and turbulent after the recent rains. It looked unsafe, so Rhys Ddu told some of the men to take the horses and cross them further downstream. Meanwhile the wounded were cautiously carried and helped across the bridge. As this was being done, Rhys Ddu's eyes turned for a moment to the dark bulk of a hut on the opposite bank, where more than once he had shared a meal with the owner, an old forester whose pastime it was on sunny days to sit in his doorway feeding the sparrows on the crumbs of bread he planted in his long beard. Not a spark of candleshine or firelight was to be seen in the windowhole, and the door was inhospitably closed. Where has the old lad got himself off to this night, Rhys wondered?

Eva and the last of the wounded had crossed to the other bank and the rest of the soldiers were making ready to follow them when they heard shouts from the men down below. Eva's shriek rang out in the same moment and Rhys Ddu and his comrades whirled around. The hooves of their mounts muffled by the roar of wind and torrent, a company of armed horsemen had burst out of the woods above and behind them. Red Iwan's sons, Madoc and Huw, were at their head. Whooping and jeering, swords in hand, they came charging down the sloping ground with the whole ride at their heels. Rhys had barely time to dodge the swinging stroke of Madoc's sword. Eva, darting back like a lightning across the bridge and clutching wildly at the mane of her brother's horse, got the blow that was meant for her husband.

In the flash of that one shattering moment both men were so stricken that life and death were equal to them. A wild primitive cry was wrenched out of the throat of Madoc—"Eva!" At that his horse reared and stumbled, throwing him forward. The wooden handrail, then the whole bridge gave way, plunging him into the torrent, dashing him half-dead among the rocks below, where the men hacked him to pieces, so great was their hatred of him and their fury.

Oblivious to all, Rhys Ddu flung himself on his knees at Eva's side. Eden bestrode him, swinging his sword in both hands, while their comrades made a wall with their shields and weapons. The onset of their enemies was so fierce at first, that they could barely withstand it, but soon the rest of the company came riding up from the fording place, to be joined within moments by partisans who lived nearby. Their assailants broke away and began to scatter in disorder. Eden snatched up a spear, sighted Madoc's brother Huw, and hurled it at him, pinning his thigh to the side of his horse. As the wounded man fought to control his screaming mount, Philip Scudamore swept down on him and swung at him with his axe, splitting his head down to the jawbone.

Rhys Ddu had in the meantime borne Eva to the edge of the river. He had torn off his mantle and was trying to stanch the flow of blood from her half-severed neck. But there was far too much of it—it was even trickling from her ears and bubbling from her mouth. Her face looked as white as snow in the moonlight; her eyes had a glassy gleam under the half-closed lids. Rhys raised her head in his arms and cradled it against his breast, kissing her and murmuring endearments, but he was talking for his ears only. Eva could not hear him. Other voices, other presences were claiming her now.

They bore her body that night to the Abbey in the Valley of the Cross and buried her in the graveyard there. For long Rhys Ddu knelt beside the grave of his wife, his eyes closed, his hands held close to his breast with the palms touching. He remembered her as she had been when, a young widow of seventeen, he had come to ship her homeward to the Great Strand from the nunnery on the western shores of Mona.

"Come away with me," he had said. "If you dare."

"Curse you, you rogue, how not?" she had breathed laughingly. "You are in my blood."

So many years had passed since then, yet he remembered it as vividly as though it were yesterday. They had set sail in the twilight of the early morning. She had stood hand in hand with him on the deck, looking out across the waters with shining eyes, smiling and unafraid. It was hard for him to believe that it was she indeed who lay under this pile of soft damp earth this gracious autumn morning, in that dark pit, in her grey shroud, blackening, rotting—his Eva, fair as the dawn breaking over a desert sea.

Five weeks after Eva's death Marged Vaughan left Dolwyddelan and returned to the island. Early in the summer Gerallt had visited her upon the pledge of Andras of Dyngannan and urged her to come home. Afraid of her own grief, she had shrunk from the idea then, but over the course of the months, as if Gerallt's plea had served to arouse in her longings which she had thought dead when they were only sleeping, the conviction had grown in her that it was the best thing she could do. Late in October she sent for her son Owain, who had been living with his eldest sister and her husband Steffan Bodda of Derwen, to bear her company homeward.

"Steffan saw your husband a while ago," he told Mererid with youthful blitheness. "He had been cut about a little, but he told Steffan that if he or any of us saw you we were to tell you not to worry and to greet you warmly and to tell you he would be home one of these days."

As pale as death, Mererid said: "Cut about?" and demanded to know more. The youth told her as much as he had heard. It had happened at the garrison town of Ruthin at Michaelmas. Flanked by the Sheriff and his men, Davy Gam, the King of England's Welsh squire, had been addressing the populace at the market cross, exhorting them to support their divinely appointed lord and monarch Henry of Lancaster when a band of rebels, disguised as artisans and rustics, had set a bull on the gathering and borne the orator captive away. It was in the midst of the turmoil that had ensued that Eden had caught a glancing blow from a spear in his thigh as he was falling back skirmishing towards the gates. There, the Welsh, having laid their prisoner fast and fired up piles of straw to hinder pursuit, had ridden away southward towards Mathraval, where Glyndwr was then quartered with much of his power. But a few leagues south of Ruthin Eden had been obliged to stop. His wound had not been dressed properly and had begun to fester. His comrades had left him at Derwen in the care of one of Steffan Bodda's brothers. Two days later the outlaw David ap Jenkin and a few of his men had arrived from a raid on the border and he had gone with them into the mountains.

"Where have they taken him?" Mererid asked.

"I cannot tell you that, for I do not know," Owain replied. "Somewhere safe wherever it is. Oia, Mererid, how you take on! It's only a cut in the thigh. One or two inches deep, maybe. Nothing serious. Enough to make him unserviceable for a while, that's all. Ach, what's that to him? That bull of battles! It will take more than that to lay Ednyved ap Tudor in the dust."

A bitter little smile flickered over her lips.

"You hold encouraging language, lad. I wish I could believe you."

"God's truth. And if you do not believe me go ask Outlaw Jenkin. He will tell you."

"Well, I should like to. Where is he?"

Marged Vaughan flew at her son on the instant.

"What madness! Owain, where are your wits? You are turned of fifteen years, and still bear you like a weanling. Mererid," she said, "if you are thinking of sorting forth into the mountains among those ruffians, put it out of your mind this moment. I will not countenance it."

"You might as well rip the heart out of my body then," Mererid declared stubbornly.

"Do not defy me!" Marged exclaimed sternly. "You are committed to my care. Have I not promised your brother and your husband? After what happened to Eva, do you think Eden would ever forgive us if we let you go? No, it cannot be. Swear."

Mererid began to weep. Marged Vaughan closed her eyes and shook her head sadly, wearily.

"I love you with my heart. You are like my own child. If you do not give me your word, your solemn oath, then I cannot leave this castle. I shall have to remain here."

With her lips bitten pale, Mererid at last assented, but all the while her heart beat fast as she inwardly planned her course of action. She had spent so many days, weeks, months, in the expectation that Eden would return that she no longer believed that he would come. Weary of waiting, burning with longing, troubled by the news, what could she do? If she wished to see him she would have to seek him out. She was left with no other choice.

The bells were ringing for vespers that same day when Mererid whispered to her old comrade Robyn: "Walk with me later."

The young bard sighed, sensing at once what it was that she had to say to him. For some reason he remembered that day years ago when she had coaxed him into going along with her and Alun to the commorthy on the island. She was as dear to him as his own heart. Touched by the memory, he knew that now, just as upon that earlier occasion, he would be helpless to resist her.

He walked back slowly from the church, across the darkening meadows. Above the castle the sky was ashen, there was a faint sprinkling of stars, a skin of a moon. He heard her footfall, the rustle of her skirts in the high grass. She came with an air of breathless haste, as though she had been running.

"Can you guess what I want of you?"

"Aye. You would like me to take you to my uncle, the outlaw, in the Grey Rock Woods."

"Will you, my friend?"

"But how are you going to approve yourself to God and your conscience?" he asked her, half in sadness, half in jest. "You gave your sacred word to Marged Vaughan and the lady Enid, remember?"

"God and the ladies will understand," said Mererid. "You can see how it is, dear Robyn. The moments we share with those we love are all too few."

Suddenly their ears were arrested by a strange sound coming from the north. "It is the wild geese," said Robyn, and as they watched they could see the flocks moving towards them, distancing the sky over the forests. Theirs was a far-away chattering at first, as of the chatter of worshippers reciting their responses at Mass, but as they drew nearer their voices grew ever louder and shriller until at last when they were passing overhead, their necks outstretched and their glistening wings beating the air, there was nothing else to be heard but their weird unearthly cries, so like the baying of hounds that Robyn found it easy to understand why so many people called them 'The Hounds of Heaven'. The two of them watched their passage across the sky until their cries faded out over the high passes. There, Mererid thought, out in those wilds somewhere, Eden lay at that hour, perhaps, listening to the wild geese trailing their high belling cries southward through the night. Thither now, too, flew all her yearning thoughts.

Marged Vaughan, her son Owain and their troop left early the next day. Leaving her little daughter Angharad in Enid's keeping, Mererid accompanied them on a part of their journey. Robyn rode beside her. Their saddlebags were stuffed to bursting, but the Chieftain's widow was too haunted by sorrowful reminiscence to notice.

When they had ridden a league Marged Vaughan took her leave of them. She embraced Robyn and signed his brow with the figure of the Cross.

"Be steadfast, Robyn."

"Always, my lady."

"Mererid," she said softly, her eyes filling with tears, "my dear, dear Mererid." She kissed her and held her to her bosom fervently. "May the Queen of Heaven guard you and protect you."

Tearfully the two watched the little troop until it had passed out of sight, but then instead of turning back along the road upon which they had come, they took the path leading into the river valley of the Machno and the lordship of the religious knights. The forests ranging about the hospice were the wildest in Wales, and Robyn, who was in no haste to enter them, suggested to Mererid that they spend the night with the Widowers at the hall of Trellan.

"What are you saying?" she exclaimed. "Robert and Lelo would have us back at the castle by daybreak."

He started arguing with her, but he fairly well knew that all he was doing was trifling out time. Spinning out his precious breath beyond necessity. She had made her mind up, nothing he could say would unmake it. Murderers, thieves, robbers, fiends, wild beasts—she showed not the least terror or timidity at the thought of the dangers and hazards of the way.

And in truth, the journey was not as terrible as his fears had imaged forth. They were not overtaken by a storm of rain; they were not set upon by desperate men and savage beasts. Still, terrors are no less present for not being seen. The ghostly mist in swamp and gully, the way the wind was sighing and breathing cold in the gorges, the sinewy witchlike tangle of thorn and thicket, the sound of pheasants and squirrels scampering in the underbrush, the cries of the young deer in some lonely ravine, were enough alone to give play to fancy in its most hideous and unnerving forms.

And then again—no light consideration—were they really on the right path for Outlaw Jenkin's lair in the Grey Rock Woods? Robyn could have sworn that he knew—his uncle had described it to him in the past—but now he was no longer certain. "It is a crag, that rises above the trees," he told Mererid. "It is called Carreg-y-Walch*. My uncle says it is well known throughout the lordship."

As it fortuned there was no missing the path to the hospice of the Knights Hospitallers, it was so well-trodden in those days. They decided to go there in search of more definite information. Robyn reckoned that they were halfway there, when they saw some men coming towards them. "Talk of the devil," he murmured to Mererid. But was it possible they had been watched and followed this while? Had word of their coming run ahead of them? Like enough, he thought.

"Heyday, if it is not the right cockalorum!" the outlaw called out in greeting. "As jolly as ever I see. And where might you be going?"

"We were coming to look for you."

"But you are heading in the wrong direction. This road leads to the hospice. Don't go there. They're all dying of the plague there, och, it's pitiful to see them. Foot to head, head to foot. Masses all day long, poor lobs," he said, but that was so much talk to tickle the ribs of hags and hobgoblins, for his eyes were on Mererid as he spoke and he was grinning.

"Who is this lovely child? Something tells me I ought to know her. That face."

She gazed at the outlaw with a grave and tremulous smile.

"You saw me at Mathebrud, perhaps, son of Jenkin," she said.

"God prosper you, lass, perhaps so," he said, "although there are

* Carreg-y-Walch: Hawk's Rock.

times when I think I saw nothing but wrecks and death there."

"She is Mererid," said Robyn, "the wife of my foster father, Eden."

The outlaw stared at him with astonished eyes.

"Dammo, blewyn, you don't say so! She's your foster-mother then? Small wonder they can't find wives to please you. Would that I had such a mother! I swear I'd give up drabs. By God, that Eden! What an eye for the women! First that sainted sister Agnus Dei and now this luscious armful!"

Ignoring his chaff, she looked at him with troubled serious eyes and told him the nature of their errand.

"It is said you know where my husband is."

"Ochan, Mererid, what can I say?"

The smile died on his lips. Pulling a gloomy face he looked past her, sighing.

"Must I tell her? Alas, the news is very bad, my dear. Eden is dead."

She watched him silently, with a long probing gaze, her features wearing a pale and smiling defiance against the outlaw's cruelly searching eyes, only her mouth showing a tremor of what might have been anxiety, a fugitive terror.

"Aye, God rest his soul, I was with him when he died. A precious dear man. His last words to me were, 'Take care of my widow.'"

She shook her head.

"Good you, son of Jenkin, don't tease me for the love of Christ. There is such a heaviness on my heart. Only tell me where he is and I will bless you till the day I die."

"Why will you not believe me when I say that Eden is dead.?"

"I cannot believe our Holy Mother has brought me this far to no purpose."

"But of course she has a purpose, lass. She has brought you here to help me, don't you see? I have lived a sinful life too long. She has seen my folly and wicked ways. Save me, good sister. It's Heaven that has called you to this charitable work."

"I will pray for you, I promise."

"It's not your prayers I an wanting, fair witch. Rest here with me. I will look after you."

Robyn felt the skin tremble and tighten around his mouth. The way he was looking at her. Those evilly gleaming green eyes. Toads winking in slime. He began to speak, but Mererid checked him with a glance and a nudge of her foot.

"And my child?" she said. "Will you look after him, too?"

He laughed.

"Who? Robyn?"

"No," she said. "The child I am carrying."

"Fo!"

Robyn was startled no less than his uncle. He thought: How can this be? So sudden it was, he could not fathom it.

"Go to God, you are never breeding?"

"Praise be, but I am, son of Jenkin," she replied gravely, and she gently patted the heavy folds of the black mantle and robe about her belly. "I'm six months gone or near. Well, do you see now? Sure, it's not comely before God's angels and saints to torment one so soon to become a mother."

"Ach, but it can't be true." He shook his head and eyed her suspiciously. "You look in great, good health for one so far along with child."

"God be thanked for it. It's a providence I share with the women of my house. The mother of Lewis Trevor, my grandfather. . . ."

"Stay!"

He stared at her, as one stunned.

"Lewis Trevor was your grandfather? Him who dwelt in the vale of the Alun of old and was killed by a bull?"

"Aye," she replied. "The very same."

"Lewis Trevor was my mother's cousin in the third degree."

"Truly?"

"Unfeignedly."

He drew breath, smiling.

"By God, Mererid," he exclaimed, "can it be that we have blood in common?"

He was amazed. As well he might be, thought Robyn. As might a wolf on finding out that he was related to a doe; or a crow to a swan. Howbeit, this intelligence marked the beginning of a long discourse that went on, more or less, through the rest of the day and much of the night that followed. In the meantime they were brought to Carreg-y-Walch. Mid-afternoon and already it was getting dark, a batlight glimmering in the face of the crag like a bloodshot eye sunk in the head of a giant. "My fastness. My Noah's Ark," the outlaw announced blithely, and a dark and shuddering unease came upon Robyn's spirit. He and Mererid exchanged glances—if this was what was fated to survive the tempest of their times, God help them. Such filth and mire everywhere. And the folk who came popping out of bushes and hovels to ogle them! Urchins as naked as worms, horrible shacks with the faces of wild beasts, women like men.

Mind you, once it was seen that they were guests and not captives they became friendly enough. A nod from their robber chief and there was nothing but noise and frolic. They sang and danced to the music of the fiddle and the pipes. Wild meat was added to the nettles and onions simmering in the big cauldron. Heaps of rushes were brought into the cave for them to sleep on, while for Mererid there was the addition of a cushion of brocaded silk and a coverlid of red velvet, not to speak of bunches of tussilago to defend her from the suffocating smells of smoke and unwashed feet.

But what if they were captives no less than guests? Robyn was not long in riddling this new worry out of the dreary whirl in his head. Supposing the black-hearted knave had decided to hold them for ransom. Once this thought occurred to him he knew that sleep was out of the question.

Not that he would have been allowed to sleep in any event. His uncle was too busy talking, lying across the fire from them, drinking strong liquor from a jug. "Are you sure you will not have some, fair cousin? It's fine bragget. Don't ask me where I came upon it. But it was brewed for the wedding feast of the daughter of a very considerable swine, I will tell you that much."

He told them more. He must have told them the whole story of his life, jabbering there. The cock-and-bull stories came thick. It was a wonder to Robyn that Mererid could believe them. Yet there she lay, with her cheek on her hand, her eyes shining in the firelight, as one enrapt: "Yes, and what happened then, son of Jenkin?" Or: "Dear my fathers!" she'd cry out and start laughing.

Her laughter bruised Robyn's heart. He, who knew his uncle so much better than she did, hated to see her so taken in. She put him in mind of a wild goose, seduced by the call-birds and cheating play of a master fowler into his circling nets. Traps, aye, he saw them everywhere around David ap Jenkin. It was, in truth, not without a sense of relief that he bade farewell to him on the following day, as he was quick to admit to Mererid.

"Why do you say that, Robyn? He does not seem such a bad man."

"But he is. I know him well. He is a scoundrel. You did not believe those stories he told us last night, did you?"

"Fibs and figments, were they?"

"In large part."

"Hm. Ah well, they made good listening, did they not? They took my mind off my woes for a while for sure. And there, as to telling fibs, how many of us can claim to be entirely guiltless? After all," she confessed then, "I'm not pregnant, either."

"I had thoughts about that."

She sent him a humorous glance, quick and glancing.

"Aye, Robyn," she said. "I had a notion you were doing your sums back there."

They were well on their way now, high up among the grazing lands, on the path to the havoty* beyond Marsli's Dishes where Eden lay. Outlaw Jenkin had brought them as far as the bounds of the wilderness, but had begged the leisure to accompany them farther.

"And then, you know what day this is, don't you?" he said.

"Winter's Eve," Mererid told him.

"The dead will be leaving their graves tonight," the outlaw warned them. "Don't grudge your horses the whip."

"Don't worry, kinsman," the priest's daughter assured him. "The power of the Cross will guard us."

"I'm sure it will. All the same, what is to be lost in looking lively, eh? Get indoors by nightfall."

It made good sense from his uncle's point of view, thought Robyn— so many of the dead had scores to settle with him. He could not pretend that he felt all that easy on his own account. The weather in the uplands was bleak and daunting. A rack of tattered clouds drifted across the face of the mountains and the cold cut to the bone. No less dismal to the eye was the light that was dying to the sight as the day advanced, a stormy light that was full of eerie shadows and whisperings. Gusts of bitter air whipped their mantles and packs of grey wind-wolves raced through the bent grass and over the stone heaps. A hundred will o' the wisps vexed Robyn's sore and peering eyes.

* havoty—havotai: summer hut, huts

Little afflicted Mererid's vision, however. Late that afternoon they were coming down among rocks, following a track that was beaten into the black-tipped heather by the tiny hooves of goats, when she gave a cry.

"Look, Robyn. There it is."

Before them lay a great expanse, as it were half-grassland, half-peatbog, and in the midst of it the two tarns that were called Marsli's Dishes, black and silvering in their rushy beds. And beyond that again, where a mountain was beginning to slope upward to meet a thin curtain of mist, a brown patch of mud and stones was smoking.

"Faith, he's found himself a desolate place, has he not? Oia, is that him?" she breathed, her voice quivering with happy agitation. "Yes, it's him."

Robyn failed to make out anything at first, but as they drew nearer a small bunched darkness showed up against the lighter smudge of wall. It could have been a bush; but no, she was not mistaken. It was Eden. He was standing on the steprock, hugging his spear, and he was staring in their direction. Mererid waved, but he did not return her salute. His carriage did not change. He stood as before, leaning on the shaft of his spear, unmoving and watchful.

"Och, Robyn, he's looking rough."

Nor was she mistaken in that as they discovered moments later when they entered the croft. In truth, both were so shocked at first sight of him that they could not speak. Every last drop of blood left Mererid's face, and her limbs were seized by a sudden trembling. Eden had let the hair of his head and face grow wild, and he was noticeably thinner, his cheeks haggard and sunken, the big bones of his shoulders sticking out like a stretching frame for his hide.

"O, Eden, my love. . . ."

"God above, what are you doing here?"

"We have come to find out how you are faring."

"Who told you to come? Not Marged nor Enid for sure. Those wise ladies would never have sanctioned such a folly."

"Don't be angry, my dear. We heard you were hurt. My heart. . . ."

"Aye, your heart," he broke in sternly. "It would have to be from your heart. It's not from your head, that's plain. Holy Mother, those women down below must be out of their minds with worry." He turned on Robyn. "And you? Why did you not stop her? Are you as witless as she?"

"There is no blame on Robyn," she said. "The sin is all mine. If it is a sin to bring you our love and blessings and a lump of bacon for your larder."

"Larder, ha!"

His glance sped to the bulging saddlebags. "Stole that away, too, did you? Along with yourselves?"

"And some cheese, and venison. Brrh, but it's cold. For the love of the saints, man, let us come in and warm ourselves at least."

"But it's dirty in there," he protested furiously, hobbling back into the havoty. "You are going to fuss and carry on—the dear knows, I am not equal to it." Spear in hand, he tried to set the place in order at that—pitching orts, old husks and black straw like derelict birds' nests through the holly bars that divided the fireroom from the stable, as if Robyn and Mererid were not in the doorway watching him. "Everything is upside down, as you see. Why did you have to come here like this? No time to wash and put myself tidy. Shave, trim beard."

"You say true, my lord," said Mererid, smilingly running her eyes around the fireroom. "Your lodge is in a pretty state."

"Mind your own errands! Who asked you to come here, you headstrong filly? You are not wanting in crust, I'll say that much for you. What are you hunting around for now?"

"A broom."

"What broom?" he scoffed. "I have no broom."

Taking off her mantle and rolling up her sleeves, she went into the stable and came back with an ox goad and a bunch of heather and gorse sticks.

"Fetch me some water, Robyn."

"What are you doing with those sticks?" Eden asked.

"You have no broom. I purpose to make one."

"O, Lord, give them me."

When Robyn returned, the broom was finished and Eden was leaning back on one elbow on a couch of bracken, watching her sweep. Weary though she was, her gaiety was as sparkling as a spring freshet. Eden glanced at his foster son and let his eyelids drop briefly over his slily smiling dark eyes, as if to say: "What's the use, eh, lad?"

Suddenly a surge of almost unbearable joy overwhelmed him.

"Mererid, my dream, my life!"

He grabbed out at her.

"Enough! Come here! Stop it!" he said, pulling her down beside him.

With unabashed delight Mererid clasped her arms around his neck. Laughing and crying by turns, and heedless of Robyn's presence, she planted fierce little kisses all over his face, his bristling dark cheeks, his nose, his lips, his eyes, his throat. At last with a boundlessly tender and foolish smile, he gasped. "Hai-how, well, it's clear I shall have to put up with you. O, heaven of the little birds, the crazy romp has made me hungry. Where is that bacon you were talking about?"

Later he drew his foster-son aside.

"You will have to sleep in with the horses tonight, Robyn. You will not take it unkindly, I trust. You could have colder company on a night such as this."

Robyn agreed. It was not to be questioned that the exhalations from the bodies of the horses did keep the cold at bay. For all that, warm as his bed was that night, he doubted that it was as warm as Eden's.

They were alone together for almost four months. Four months together in that great solitude. A breathing space, an hour of quiet, their summer's home in the heart of the winter wilderness.

They had few visitors. The first was David ap Jenkin, the outlaw. He came at Martinmas.

"So you have decided against the hermit's life, chieftain. I thought you did not have the stuff in you."

"What tidings from the world, Deio?"

"The same shitton dreary jig. Stay where you are, my friends. By the bye, Rome has provided another Bishop to the see of Bangor. To keep company belike with him the French Pope has given us."

"Sanctum sanctorum," Eden laughed, "now that is what I call being too generous. An overplus of grace."

"An Englishman I hear."

"To be sure. Ah well, the more the merrier as we say in Mona."

"We have that byword in the Grey Rock Woods, too, son of Tudor. Though I dare avow," he added, winking wickedly over at Mererid, "that it is not all of us who have the same happy knack for putting it to the proof as you do."

Be it remarked that he did not come to the havoty empty-handed. Towards their belly cheer he had brought them the meat of a slaughtered goat and a bag of oatmeal. Still less did he leave empty-handed, since upon his departure Eden asked him on the score of favor and old fellowship to return Robyn and Mererid's horses to the castle at Dolwyddelan, where they would have better care through the hard days of the winter than high in the mountains.

"We have my horse and the nag Ystec here if needs be," Eden said. "And my sister, the lady yonder, must be troubling about us and thinking that our little Angharad has lost her parents. Tell her how our affairs stand, Deio, and ask her to send one of the horses back up to us in the spring. I am in hope that we shall see her then."

"You have my hand and honor," swore the outlaw.

Honor, aye. Hide nor hair of those beasts was ever seen in the river valley where the castle stood. They had been eaten, his uncle told Robyn when the bard asked about them in afterdays. Snow everywhere, up to their knees, up to their backsides, up to their chins—Outlaw Jenkin's lads and lasses had been unable to beat a path out of the lordship until the Feast of St David, long before which time their victuals were spent, and they themselves so famished for want of food that they looked like new-hatched crows. What wonder if they had slaughtered, flayed and roasted the horses! As far as their robber chief was concerned it would have been a good thrift if they had killed them sooner; the brutes had consumed such a store of horsebeans and fodder which could have been better used to the behoof of the poor starving people and their children.

So he claimed, his honorable uncle. He had sold them if the truth of the matter were known, his nephew concluded.

Later that month came Edlym and Gwynno, two herds of the tribe whose summer pasture lay nearby, bringing with them a store of meat and flour. Flannel, too, with needles and thread. And a hair-comb prettily ornamented with crystal stones. It was clear that word of Mererid's presence had reached the ears of folk in the valleys below. It was Eden's thought that Brother Septentinus might have told them. The Cistercian monk had visited them earlier on, accompanied by a rustic leading a sumpter horse laden with wax candles, lease-records, manuscripts, bottles of ink, rolls of unused parchment, and a quantity of rough paper, of which scholars and calligraphs were already beginning to be in some want. According to the monk their enemies designed to stop the inflow of paper altogether. Wherever they could they were plundering the monasteries of vellum and parchment. Books and chronicles relating to the history of the land were being piled up and burnt. Hence the monks were making haste to secrete their treasures in various hiding-holes throughout the mountains and wildernesses, in remote grots, hermitages, havotai and monastic cells.

"The thirsty papyrus, aye," Brother Septentinus intoned gravely. "It will be a great rarity here one of these days."

"Brother Aymon was saying the same thing when he was up here a while back," said Eden.

"More precious than jewels of India. Or gold of Ophir."

"Good my father," said Mererid, "don't worry. We will guard them well."

"God multiply his blessings upon you, my little ones."

"Aye, never you fret," said Eden. "I will keep an eye on your things."

Nor did he lie, as his companions were quick to observe. They kept his eye in some exercise subsequently. And his hand. And his wit.

No later than the next day and there he was, bent over a table raised out of black peat-blocks, eyes squinting down at his moving hand, an edge of tongue licking the hairs of his beard—inkhorn, goosefeather, scratching away.

"You will ruin your eyesight, chieftain," Mererid told him.

Off with her straightway to the ironbound coffer in the corner. She drew out a tall Paris candle, lit it and set it before him. Stood she then a space, looking down, knitting her brows, considering.

"What are you writing?"

"I am transcribing a copy of 'Historia Pontius Pilatus'."

"No, be serious. Is that the paper from the Abbey?"

"It is."

"The paper you were engaged to preserve? O, Eden!"

"What of it?"

"So precious as it is. And look at you, wasting it on your chaff."

"Chaff? A moment now. Before you judge, go to the strongbox yonder and let your eyes glance over some of those calendars of ancient correspondence, then tell me if I am not preserving this paper to a better purpose than did ever those shavelings at the Valley of the Cross? And since when has sauce for the goose ceased to be sauce for the gander, say you? Where did you get this candle to light my page? And what about that corporal you are using for a towel?"

"It's not the same."

"And there, it's been said I have the brand of the devil on me."

"Who said so?"

"Someone a long time ago."

"No, tell me. That was a terrible thing to say. I want to know."

"Caradoc of Penhesgin, for one. That time he came back from the Jubilee in Rome."

"Did he say that to you? Why did you not ask him whether he was in fee to the devil," she demanded, "seeing that he was so familiar with his brand?"

"I did not have your quick wit and tongue, my dear And then," he added slily, "I did not have the pretense to it then."

Mererid thought for a moment or two, then wried her lips scornfully.

"Ah. Gwennan of Croes Gwion," she said.

"Blossoms of old roses. . . ."

"Do they still smell as sweet?"

"The scent is keener, I think. You knew of that affair then? Who told you?"

"Sioned I daresay. It's not who told me that sticks with me, as it happens, but how upset I was. I can remember running out into the churchyard where Alun and Mam could not see me, bawling and yammering amidst the flowers and the crosses."

"A pretty picture."

"I did not feel pretty, I assure you. I felt hateful. You were my good angels, you and Annes. I worshipped you. I could not understand how you could betray your lady with that silly goose. Others prayed for grace for you. I cursed you for a promise breaker and a fool."

Eden burst out laughing at that.

"I am glad to hear it," he said "I bless the Lord for that kind dispensation."

"Kind?" she smiled. "Do you bless my curses then?"

"If they stopped you worshipping me, Mererid mine."

A truce for reverie now, Robyn thought. Out with care. Enough of broils and politics. To the devil with the power and the princes. Peace be our mandate. And they had their wish as near as not. Only Time did not heed them. Time ran over and past them as before. Flocks of crows blackened the grey moor and filled the air with their harsh jargoning. The days grew shorter, the nights set in early. They got in rushes and moss, they angled for char and bream in the mud at the bottom of Marsli's Dishes, and they gathered clay from the shores to plug up the cracks in the walls of their dwelling.

And then the snow came. One morning they looked out and there it was—a long lulling vista of snow falling like blossoms through the windless cold, creating harmony where harmony looked least to be: in the rebellious upreachings of the earth, the black still fantasy of the shrub, the crags like thunder fastened in stone. Sound was hushed away, while here a line became dim and there dissolved, giving place to forms mysterious and unknown.

The air waxed dim and they settled in. Robyn played the crowth*, Mererid sang ballads, and Eden paid them with tales of his youthful adventures and misadventures—of merry pranks and ancient disports. The darkness came softly, throwing great wings of shadow around them where they sat. Their mountain den, spelled with winter sleep. They might have been the only folk alive. Everything else seemed so far away and unreal. No bell was rung for them at eight o' clock. No one told them to put out fire and candle and go to bed. They talked and talked and talked. Halfway through the night and Eden's tongue was still running on.

Robyn loved listening to his stories. They carried a breath of the old life; they bore him back in mind to their island home with its crofts and vills, its lowlying cornhills and flat sea-country. As for Mererid it was not certain that she cared at bottom what her husband was talking about so long as he kept on talking. When the stories ran out so would he. It was like a game to her. Eden was the Lord of Misrule and from Winter's Eve till Shrovetide they were tasked to go with him a-mumming. Fine and subtle disguisings he used at that. So for that matter did Mererid, but hers were not as durable as his by half. Her mask kept on slipping. Especially as time went on she grew negligent. Her eyes were often red and not from the fire; she found it harder to check in her voice a rising note of concern.

For the winter was passing. The icicles along the eaves broke and

*crowth: an ancient Welsh instrument of the viol class.

fell to the ground in little tinkling pools. Spring was approaching; the wind blew from the south. By little and little the earth was laid bare under the early rains, and in the evening there was a great rush over the moorland as if everything stood poised and expectant with the desire for new life. The mists rose from the grass and titmice and pipits were busy.

One afternoon Robyn and Eden returned to the havoty and she was not there. They found her at last sitting among the rocks at the spring hardby. She had her back to them and she was staring away across the moor.

"Fair lady of the fountain," Eden called out, "who loved you when you walked this earth formerly?"

She gave a start and looked around. Her eyes were far off and strange, like the eyes of one shaken out of a deep slumber.

"Why are you here?" she asked harshly. "Go away. Let me be."

"Mererid, Mererid. . . ."

She hooded her face in her hands. Eden sat down beside her and touched her shoulder.

"What is it, my dear?" he asked.

She shook her head. Fiercely then, she rubbed her knuckles into her eyes, gave a shuddering sob and glared away through the glitter of her tears.

"Forgive me," she said huskily. "It was not my thought to snap at you like that. Only you should not have surprised me as you did. Have I upset you? You are not angry with me, are you?"

His eyes creased up.

"You see me," he smiled. "How am I?"

He laid his arm about her shoulders and drew her to him, cradling her head against his breast and pressing his lips against her brow. Her voice crumbled into a whisper.

"Christ save us, Eden, what can we do?"

"What others do, I dare say, Mererid mine. Live out our day," he said and his dreamy black pupils stared straight before him into the distance with a peculiar expression of weariness and vacancy for a few moments.

And then, all of a sudden, she roused herself, seized his hands in hers, pressed one of them against her wet cheek and as fervently kissed it.

"Mary and Joseph, what's wrong with me? Making everyone so

miserable. Curse me for a shrew!"

"Never!"

"When I think of the promises I offered up!" she sang out in a clear, passionate voice. "I was going to make you so happy, true God! I was going to seize happiness tight, tight, with both hands and never let go. I wanted only to forget myself in your pleasure."

Eden laughed.

"Well, if that's all that you want, far be it from me to gainsay you. Forget, forget!" he enjoined her merrily. "Forget everything but one thing. Never forget that I have loved loving you."

They could have been his parting words, although it was Candlemas then and he did not leave until three weeks later. It's not that he told them that he was leaving; that was not the way of him. In fact had Robyn been asked to describe the last night they spent together, he would have been hard put to do so. All those nights were so alike—dreaming, talking, reading pictures in the fire—that his memories of the last could as well have been his memories of many another.

One day a man in a hide coat passed by. He stood awhile talking to Eden at the gate and then went on his way. When Mererid asked what his errand was in these parts and why he had not come inside, Eden told her that he was a herd who was in a hurry to get to his summer croft higher up before dark. The fable that had been set on foot to mislead them was that deer had been seen in the corries beyond Marsli's Dishes.

"I think tomorrow Robyn and I will go hunting," he said.

Early the next morning he saddled his horse, put on his heavy mantle, took his axe, sword and longbow and set forth.

"You will not go wandering too far afield, will you?"

"No, mistress mine."

"The weather is treacherous. You would not want to get caught out there in the bogs and a storm blowing up."

"Indeed not. Don't worry. All will be well."

"God keep you then," she said, kissing him.

"God keep you, little sister," he said.

Furtively wiping the tears from his eyes with the back of his hand, Eden rode down as far as Marsli's Dishes before looking back. She was still standing at the gate—her hair and skirts fluttering in the fresh morning breeze. He waved his hand to her and then with Robyn seated behind him he rode beside the lakes and climbed into the rocky defiles beyond. His heart throbbed painfully. He spoke little to his foster-son, but Robyn did not wonder at it. His mind and purpose like his own, he fancied, were intent on tracking their quarry.

Around midday they halted and sat down in a sheltered hollow and ate the griddle cakes and fish that Mererid had packed for them. The weather set in colder. The sky grew misty among the crags and dark cloud-shadows drifted along the great bare shoulders of the hills. The wind became sharper. It hissed through the flowing mounds of grass like spray.

"So, Robyn," Eden said at last, straightening up and narrowing his eyes against the wind and the wan glare of the day. "What is your mind? Would you like to turn back?"

"And the deer?" Robyn asked. "Have you given up hope of running them to ground?"

"Faith, that I gave up or ever we got started," Eden said, and when Robyn looked at him questioningly explained: "I am not returning with you, lad."

The youth looked at him in dismay. And yet it was fated, he had known it. Night after night he had said to himself—tomorrow he must leave. And now that the morrow had arrived it was as if he had not known it. His mind clung to Eden's words as he stared at him and he began to feel colder and more fearful as the moments passed and as he became more keenly aware that in a short space he would be gone. It flashed on him then that he was seeing his beloved foster-father for the last time—the greying black tumble of hair, the melancholy dark eyes set in their web of kindly creases, the lean hard brown face, the sad settled smiling mouth, and it was almost more than he could bear.

"You are leaving?" he said in a small strained voice. "Right now? You will not be coming back to see her again even?"

He shook his head.

"It is better so. She would only hinder me with her tears. And I have dallied too long as it is. She would hold me there. Chaffering and wheedling the way she does, aye. She would entrap me before I knew it. And she would not have to strive too hard, God knows."

The youth could no longer restrain his tears, the trembling of his mouth. Eden pressed his shoulder hard.

"By our duty we must go in this world, Robyn," he said. "Mererid knows it well."

"But what shall I say to her?"

"What indeed? I don't know. I wonder if it will make much difference. It will hear ill to her however it comes. And after that, if I know her, she will not be listening. Take her back to Mona, Robyn. I rely on you to do your part as a friend between friends. Bring her and our little one to Penmynydd. Marged, Gerallt and Sioned are there. They will look after them. It would be a content to me. My dreams would have a haven then."

"Shall we be seeing you soon again?"

"So may the Lord provide. I will get word to you somehow. I am sorry to leave you with but that nag Ystec at the havoty," he said with a rueful smile. "I was hoping Outlaw Jenkin your uncle would have brought you a better mount by this time."

"It's no matter," said Robyn. "We shall manage."

"Can you find your way back alone, think you? There," said Eden, pointing to the dense stones crowning a ridge some way off, "do you see that cairn? Make head towards it and follow the course of the stream beyond it, you will not go wrong."

They embraced, wished one another a blessing and parted. Robyn stood watching his foster-father for a while as he set out across the bleak waste, then faced about in his turn and started out across the moor for the cairn. Halfway up the slope he paused to catch his breath. He looked out across the silver miles of blowing grass, tossing and wimpling in the raw mountain sunlight, and the black boglands veined with webs of white water-threads and studded with mossy knolls thrusting upwards like green shields out of dark belts of shadow and could not find him. Had he gone? So swiftly? But no, in a little he saw something move, far off to the east, in the direction of the plain of Edeyrnion, and it was he, Eden, a lone horseman moving through the wilderness. It was the last Robyn saw of him. He turned once more when he reached the ridge, but by that time he had gone out of sight altogether.

Soon after that he had an accident. Hastening downhill as best he could with his game leg, he slipped and wrenched his ankle. It soon proved so painful and he had so to nurse it in the mean space that when at last he reached the croft it was dark and Mererid was out among the firs beside the lake waiting. She held a small iron lamp in her hand which made bright color against the black lines of her robe and she was almost witless with worry.

"Holy Mother, where have you been?" she cried.

And then:

"Where's Eden?"

"He's gone."

"What do you mean, gone?"

"Gone," he said. "Gone away."

Here it was, the very calamity she had foreseen. She had known it was preparing no less than Robyn. And yet, now that it had come, she refused to believe it. She stood staring at him as at something vague and unintelligible, then shook her head and gave a beseeching little smile.

"Ach, you. Don't jest."

"God's truth."

She held the lamp close to him and scanned his face anxiously. A nail ran into her heart. With an anguished cry she thrust out her hand and laid the youth fast by the horse blanket he had put about him to keep warm. Her fingers dug into the flesh of his shoulder like the talons of a hawk. "Where? Where did he go?" The flame in the lamp tossed and flared up, lighting up the bones of her face. Her eyes looked black, preternaturally huge and brilliant, her lips were parted over the gleam of teeth. A pythoness.

"You are keeping something from me," she raged. "You know he would not have left me like this. Without a word of farewell."

"For the love of Christ, Mererid, forbear. Let me go. I've hurt my foot."

"Your foot?" she cried with a vicious sneer. "Your foot? What care I for your dumb-deaf stupid foot? Where has he gone? Tell me. I must go after him."

"There is no use your doing that," Robyn said and went on to tell her what Eden had told him in parting. But it was as his foster-father had said, she was not listening. She would not listen. On and on she railed. Where had he gone? Why had he not tried to stop him?

"How could I have stopped him?" Robyn shouted. "Talk sense!"

Finally he tore himself free from her grasp, leaving the blanket in her hand. He hurried stumbling back into the havoty, his foot shot through with pain at every step. Once inside he removed his leather buskin. His foot was puffed up to double its size and had turned blue.

Mererid came in after him. Her fury had abated. She dropped down on her knees before the firepit, covered her face with her hands and began to rock back and forth on her heels. Her whole body was racked with sobs. Minutes on end she wept and then she fell silent. She wiped her face with her wet hands and sighed.

"I am sorry, Robyn."

"It's no matter."

"It's only that I'm in such torment," she said then. "Which way did he go? You must have seen, you are not blind. My dear old knave, he's no new-come fool to be running about the world adventuring and fighting. Up trees and in and out of ditches. Lying out in the cold and wet, no, they've coursed him enough, my Eden. Time for him to rest now."

"Och."

"He's done his part, God knows. Be kind, my friend. I love him so much. He's my very life. You must help me. Which way did he go?"

"Penllyn Hundred," he lied.

"Caer Gai?"

"As like as not."

"Do you know how to get there?"

"Yes, I think so, but I doubt I can go."

"Why do you say that?"

He tendered his foot to her view. She leaned forward, peering. Her eyes widened; something dawned there, a gleam of returning intelligence.

"Why you poor Robyn, you were not lying were you? You have truly hurt your foot."

"I think my ankle is broken."

She took his foot in her lap and ran her hand over it, inspecting skin and bone with practised fingers. "Oia, no, it's a sprain more like." Quick to kindness as to wrath she was off and in a moment was back with a firkin of rainwater.

"There, put your foot in that."

"Lordamercy, it's freezing!"

"Do as I say. If that foot is to carry you tomorrow."

"If it is to what? Mererid, I cannot walk on this foot tomorrow."

"You shall ride then."

"What shall I ride?" Robyn laughed bitterly. "Ystec? And who will carry yourself and the gear? That same spavined nag?"

"Ystec has no spavin. He is a serviceable beast who has been an idle fellow too long. He as we must needs press on now."

When all sensation had left his foot she fetched it nerveless as a stone out of the water and clothed it with flannel. She made him to lie down in the straw. She hoisted his foot on a cushion of moss, prepared him a hot posset and once he had drunk it she blessed his eyelids and brow thrice with the figure of the Cross after the habit of the islanders.

"Sleep now," she said and went over to sit down by the fire.

She sat with her knees drawn up to her breast, gazing into the glowing nest of embers. Her eyes glimmered with a soft liquid glow in the firelight, her hair hanging down loose at her flank burned ruddily like frost-nipped bullrushes. Robyn watched her with sadness mingled with delight from the cover of the shadows. She was dressed as simply as a rustic and the heavy marks of fatigue and sorrow were on her lovely face and yet one felt, as in a fairy-tale, that magic hovered close. Another moment and a wonder would befall. Spray-white trefoils would be flowering in her footprints, the homespun garments would be flame red silks, and pearls and rubies would be at her throat.

Perhaps the true wonder of that night was that he succeeded in sleeping. How he did so and for how long he could not tell, but he woke at earliest light to find her shaking him and bidding him rise. Matins and already my lady was all business. Prayers first, then a mess of porridge to break their fast. She slit his buskin down one side with a deer-knife, packed his foot about with bog moss, crutched him with a forked blackthorn stick, saddled and led the nag Ystec out of his stall, laid a sod of turf on the fire and so they set forth.

The journey was hellish as he had feared. No sooner had they gained the ancient path of the peregrini through the wilds when a storm overtook them. Black cloud-shadows came sweeping down along the mountainsides like giant birds of prey. Darkness grew in the grass and stones, a cold wind rose howling out of the channeled rocks, and the skies opened up. Before long the whole boggy plain between them and Penllyn became a catchment for the rain. Robyn was afraid for a while that the streams would so overflow their banks that they would be all on a sea. It slackened off in due course, however; the sun even shone a little. And still, what was wet on them was running off their mantles and the coverture of their heads in rivulets when at last they reached Caer

Gai.

It was very late by then. It could have been midnight or past, pitch-black and drizzling. The storied castle was like a tomb. Black turrets looming, gates creaking loose on broken hinges, desolate court. They beat on the big doors, once, twice, no answer. They looked at one another, they beat for a third time. Well met, someone was coming, shuffle of feet. The bolts were slid back, an old monk appeared holding a flaming pine-root, peered at them uneasily out of his smoky cocoon of yellow light.

"*In nomine patris et filii et spiritus sancti. . . .*"

"Good you, let us in," Mererid cried. "We are soaked."

When he had admitted them she told him who they were and explained her errand. But he seemed not to understand. He kept on staring at them as if they were lunatic folk.

Then came the beloved Sion, the Father Abbot of Valle Crucis, wagging his hands.

"Good heavens, children, what a state you are in!"

Mererid fell on her knees before him directly, gasping with agitation.

"Eden . . . where is he?. . . my husband. . . ?"

"Get up, my dear. All in good time. Dry first, talk later," he broke in gruffly, at which they were led off their separate ways where they might divest themselves of their wet garments and have refreshment. Robed in a flannel blanket, Robyn then repaired to the big old hall, which was in darkness but for the fire burning on the long hearth. Many people were there, how many he could not well make out. Human forms lay heaped about like bags of meal—fugitives, sick folk and aged persons in decay he surmised. He sat down near the fire. Every now and then someone would come to ply the bellows or pile on more fuel. Drifts of sparks shot upward out of the red heart of the crackling logs, spangling the air with the likeness of a myriad stars gilt before disappearing into the black wells of the high timbers.

Mererid appeared in the doorway and stood there, staring about. Robyn signaled to her. Barefoot, clad in a cassock bound at the waist with a rope, her hair covered with a woolen cloth, she moved towards him.

"You lied to me, did you not? He's not here, he never was here. . . ."

He opened his lips to speak.

"No, there is no need to say anything," she murmured, squeezing his shoulder. "Much boots it."

"You're not of a mind to go on, are you?" he ventured slyly.

"Och, Robyn."

She gave a pitiable little laugh and sat down beside him.

"If you only knew how I felt. I could go no farther now if I heard Tudor's son was over the next hill."

"Whisht, you would be off there this minute, if it meant putting your soul in pawn to the mountain hag for the loan of her broomstick."

"No, truly, I'm deaded." she said, running her eyes upon the bodies moaning and snoring about them. "Where are all these poor folk coming from, say you?"

Suddenly she rubbed her hands along her arms and shuddered.

"What is it? Have you caught cold?" Robyn asked, with concern.

"Away, it's this horrible gown that is making me itch. Aye, they have put me in haircloth for my sins, come you," she lamented humorously, although there was more rue than laughter in her jesting and a strain was pulling at her lips as she smiled.

For the truth was that she had indeed caught cold. The sickness grew upon her in the course of the night. By the next day she was stretched out on her pallet in the toils of a raging fever. Robyn would have hastened to her side, except that he was in almost as sorry sort himself. Not only did his ankle give him pain, but he had fallen prey to a severe colic. Such spasms griped him as he thought at times that the end had come. The monks bled him, doctored him with physic and drugged him with sleepy drinks.

And then at last the darkness was lifted from his eyes. Weak as smoke he came awake to find himself looking up into the sweet and kindly face of Enid, the lady of Dolwyddelan castle.

"So you are with us once more, madyn."

"Madyn, lady? Fox you call me? O, I hope not."

"What shall I call you then? Young sheep?" she smiled. "You broke faith with us, Robyn of Mona."

"I am sorry about that truly."

"We were near distract yonder. And then this! Bringing that gentle lass to Caer Gai through such a tempest of wind and rain. God bless you, lad, but where was your judgment? And in her condition!"

Robyn was silent, puzzling.

"You seem surprised."

"Pardon me, lady, if I am thus dumb."

"Mererid is with child, did she not tell you?"

Robyn smiled.

"Oia, that old tale! Aye, I have heard her say so, sure."

Enid looked at him with a long wondering gaze.

"You speak strangely, Robyn ap Trahern. What is this now? Are you accusing that pure soul of making up tales? Do you not believe what she tells you out of her own mouth?"

He shook his head.

"Lady," he sighed, not without bitterness, "Mererid says I know not what these days and I am tired and in such confusion. What am I to believe?"

"But," she said slowly and reflectively, looking him full in the eyes with her own that were so blue and astonished, "why would she want to lie about such a thing? And what would be the point? It's not as if we were without proofs."

It was his turn to stare.

"It is true then? Mererid is going to have a child?"

"O my," said the lady in a dying voice. "Well, I don't know indeed. I have borne five living children and attended more births I dare say than you have years, and according to my reckoning, yes, I would judge that God willing and provided she go no more a-roaming and putting her health on the hazard she should be a mother before we see another winter."

She glanced away from him and began to laugh.

"Dear Abbot Sion," she observed, "this is an extraordinary knave you have here. I think you had better admit him into orders."

What were his feelings? None of the best, that was certain. There, he thought, she has made a fool of me again. Angry and hurt by turns at this most recent example of her deceit, crushed with shame at having been made a laughing-stock, so soon as ever he was strong enough to hobble to the room in the turret where she was lodged, he quit his sickbed with every intention of pouring his scathe upon her. Once there, however, all his resolutions were dissipated like straws on the wind. She looked so frail and exhausted. Dark blue rings circled her eyes and her skin was as pale as lilies.

From her bed she watched him come with eyes that were misty with tears.

"Robyn, my dear Robyn," she breathed huskily and stretched out both hands towards him.

He clasped them in his and his heart melted.

"How are you? Are you still so lame? Your legs, are they hurting you badly?" she burst forth, all in a rush, solicitous.

"They got me here, as you see." He sat down on her bed and looked at her and then he asked. "Why did you not tell me how it was with you?"

She smiled a little, then said simply:

"You would have told him and then he would have sent me away."

"Sent you away, Mererid? O, no. Not with your mulish will."

"Mules can be mastered, my friend. Yes, he would have," she nodded. "And now," she went on slowly and sighingly, "he has gone and does not know."

Her face was tender and grave, almost dreamy as she spoke; but there was a dark burning glow in her eyes that unnerved him, because as soon as he marked it, so quick and fierce a little light, it seemed to him that he realized right then and there that the spirit in her was yet untamed, that the old fires were still kindling below, as bright and lively as ever, that she had some broth cooking there, some madcap design, some new mischief. She stared at him with a gaze that was wordless and sad, her lips moved, her fingers trembled upon his.

"And it is only right that he should know, is it not? He must know that I am bearing his son. O, my friend, will you do me this favor? Oblige me, Robyn."

A feeling of utter defenselessness came over him. He opened his hands miserably.

"How can I, Mererid? Look at me."

She was all aflame on the instant.

"But I *am* looking at you! I am thinking how lucky you are. I would change places with you this moment if I could. I would take your aches and scars, your sprained ankle, your crazy hocks, what care? I would crawl to him on my knees if I had to."

"It is easy to talk."

"You ought to rejoice, Robyn."

"Heaven help us, why?"

"To be a man!" she cried in a passion. "To be the gossoon of such a great and gallant chieftain. To be able to be with him day in and day out. Sit with him, serve him, aye, live and die with him. Not to be a woman Heaven help us. Not to be reduced to your needle and thread, your washtub and cooking pots. Not to have babies growing under your girdle from one year to the next."

"The age of the Matronae is over, my dear."

It was Enid who spoke from the shadows, where she had been a while listening. Now she came forward and stood before the other two in the light. Her face was stern and set, yet not unkind.

"You lay too much on the backs of your poor donkeys, Mererid," she said firmly. "We are going home now. And there is nothing you can do about it."

15
THE STONE CAULDRON (1410)

Ah, the dream was so noble and splendid—what became of it? It was on Eden's tongue to ask, but then he never did. Earlier on in his life, when he was still capable of being disillusioned, he might well have done so. And in the plainness and simplicity of his heart, what is more, entertained every expectation of receiving an answer. What bitter lessons Time reserves for us! Now that his was an awakening to days whose meanings ran ever deeper and more remote from his vision, he had put away his old pretensions. His dreams did not go much higher now, it seemed to him, than a pot of coals to warm his feet, a bowl of broth to warm his belly, and his beloved to warm his bed. Liberty? Let others do so if they chose; for himself he often felt as if he no longer had either the will or the desire to ride that old nag home.

And then again, Eden told himself, maybe it was home they had ridden the brute at that, if all unknowingly. Maybe this was where all the great shining coursers of their youth were put out to grass in the end. A waft of something like the Chieftain's black laughter passed upon him at the thought. For the spectacle they afforded at the time was really rather comic. Caparisoned in hides of goat and furs of sheep, there they were— some four or five thousand fools, knaves, jesters, and madmen serviceable to the wars, lying out in Epynt, among mountains that had never been described by the draft of a plough.

The days were mild for spring. But the nights were bitter cold. Old wounds ached. Turf smoke hacked men's throats, blackened their chops, and raked red tears out of their eye-sockets. They stank like wolves. One look at them, Eden decided, and any woman not cursed with the burning would hurry to take up the veil, never suspecting their essential civility, their bond as Christians. Goodnight, who would dream that such dreadful forms, such monsters of filth could serve God, the Author of all purity and cleanness?

Hostages of the Doleful Mound, some might call them. Oracles of wail and woe. Not one, it seemed, but what he had lost his home and half his tribe. The Pendragon, as was only meet, led them even in that. Save for his daughter Lady Scudamore and his youngest son Maredudd no one was left him now. All were dead or prisoners in a foreign fastness.

It's not that he told of his grief. Perhaps there had been too much of it—too many daggers had gone into his heart. Perhaps the thought that his beloved dead were serene above the pain and tumult drank up his sorrow. Whenever he mentioned wife and children in the course of his conversation, he spoke of them lovingly, it was true—but as one might do in reminiscing about the long dead, playmates of one's childhood.

Well, he was a strange mixture, there was no getting away from it— sometimes so icy and remote; sometimes so tender and jocular. And yet, a wonderful man with it all, a quite beguiling fellow in his way—now teasing, now wheedling, now bullying, never the same from one hour to the next, crying down the brash and chicken-hearted alike with a word, a glance, a jest.

Always some fresh enterprise at hand. Always on the move. Dislodging garrisons, cleaving cornlands, weaving hoops of fire around isolated vills, storming gates and towers, waylaying baggage trains, stirring up a panic. In those days, for instance, he and his men were awaiting the arrival of Black Rhys with more levies before attempting the manors and lands of the Earl of Arundel. They took almost two weeks coming, and the days dragged for Eden. He dreamed of what it would be like to be home again, the fighting over, and he dreamed of his priestess. He recalled her gestures, her quick soft footfall, the gentle touch of her healing fingers, the way she had of talking and laughing and looking at him, and he was tormented with a passionate yearning that seared his heart. The gaiety of his fellows grated on his nerves. He began to crave solitude, and whenever he could he went off by himself into the wilderness, to the frontiers of the sky, a place of great silences, pauseless and profound, where the shadows of the great clouds drifted as blue as wine grapes across the mountainsides, and wild goats and ponies browsed under the black scaurs.

So it was that day. It was noon, and spear in hand, he had climbed a great stoneshot above the camp when he came across a form stretched out along the ground. It was Glyndwr. With his hands resting on the hilt of St Eliseg's sword, he was lying in the grass with his eyes closed and his legs crossed in the attitude of effigies of crusaders vowed to the Holy Land. He must have been sorting through his treasures, for scattered about him were a wallet spilling forth gold florences; illuminated vellums and manuscripts rescued from the wreckage of Strata Marcella Abbey, a bunch of green linnet feathers, and a crust of wheaten bread sprinkled over with black ants. His roundlet of black sheep's wool had fallen back from his head, and his hair and beard, teased by the wind, were spread out around his broad bony face in a tangled mass of grey tendrils, like claws and curls of ashen deadwood.

Was he asleep or lost in meditation? Whether the one or the other, a man is close to his God in such moments. Shy to intrude, Eden was about to steal away when he saw that the older man's eyes were open and staring at him.

"Where are you off to, kinsman?"

"My prince," Eden said to him, "you ought not to come up here like this. All alone. There are men feed by our enemies to kill you. You ought to study your security more."

"Ought I?"

A quick smile and two black points of light winked at him through the lacings of Glyndwr's fingers.

"And is that what you were studying when you were about to tiptoe off and leave me just now? Begone, Ednyved, I know my mind and heart, they are engaged to our Lord. I have lived by the faith, let that be my security."

Glyndwr sat up and cleared a space for him at his side and they chatted for a while. They spoke of friends and kinfolk, of Glyndwr's son Maredudd, who was now married to Elliw, the youngest daughter of Black Rhys; and of Mererid.

"She came riding into our camp at Cymmer some years ago to warn us about Howel Sele, I recall," Glyndwr reminisced. "Alone and fearless. We did not know whether to believe her at first. But she was as true as the Rood. She is a kinswoman of the Trevors, is she not?"

"Her mother Indeg was the daughter of Lewis Trevor of Alun."

"The Bishop's half-brother? The one who was killed wrestling a bull?"

"After some immoderate quaffing, I'm told," Eden said. "So it was that he could not wed his betrothed."

"And so it was that Indeg lacked a father."

"Until," Eden observed, "Conan ap Gurgeny, the wandering scholar she married was ordained a priest by my uncle, Sir Howel."

Glyndwr burst out laughing. An instant after, both men felt a shadow pass over them. Glancing upward, they saw a large bird high overhead, its wings glistening darkly against the glare of the sun. For a while they gazed at it lilting up and down, rocking undulant with the gentle unseen motion of the air, as with the rise and fall of the waves of the sea.

"A red kite perhaps," said Glyndwr. "What do you think?"

"Or an eagle," Eden replied, squinting hard against the light. "It is hard to tell. Especially with my poor eyes. And so high as it is flying. What is the secret that lies at the root of a bird's wing, I wonder?"

It came to him like that. Out of nowhere. It was an inspired moment.

"O, a wonder indeed!" Glyndwr exclaimed. "The *os coccygis*. The immortal essence."

It was theme after his heart. Kindled, he began to tell Eden then about Gwenaby, a bard who had once lived at Trevgarn in South Wales, at the ancestral hall of their mothers.

"Once he rode with a party of us to the Abbey of Strata Florida. There was a monk there tending geese. 'Why,' Gwenaby asked him, 'is the soft flesh under the ribs of a goose called its soul by our people?' That's no small question, you'll allow. The good brother stared at him as if he beheld a calf with two heads. 'What are you talking about, my son?' he asked. 'Speak plainly.' 'Very well,' said Gwenaby. 'Do you believe that the ashes of a body contain the seed of another?' The monk was all astir at that, crying up heresy. 'Bah,' said the bard, 'yours is the heresy. For if the Primal Intelligence did not intend man to think and ask questions, why did he give him wits?'"

"I think I have heard of Gwenaby," Eden said. "My sister Enid spoke of him once. Was he a hunchback?"

"Aye, and a most singular one," Glyndwr nodded. "He claimed descent from Beli ap Manogan, the Emperor of the Sun."

"Soi-disant," Eden smiled.

"As you will. We youths—cruel, scapegrace knaves such as we were—thought it a merry jest, too. We teased him unmercifully. 'Hoi, Gwenaby, if your ancestor was a sungod, how is it that you look like a goat?' . . . 'Where did you get that hump on your back, Gwenaby? Was it a gift from the Emperor of the Sun or the Man in the Moon?' One day the old bard could take no more. He turned on us. 'I am as golden and immortal as any sungod,' he declared. Sure, there was great laughter at that. 'If you are so golden, why do you not dazzle us, Gwenaby?' 'I do not dazzle you, young blind fools that you are,' he replied with pitying contempt, 'because, alas, you are but dwellers in the flesh.' And with that, all at once, without warning, he flung up his arms heavenward and began to sing the Song of Taliesyn: 'Primary chief bard am I to Elphin, and my original country is the region of the summer stars. I was with our Lord in the highest sphere, on the fall of Lucifer into the depths of Hell. I have borne a banner before Alexander. I know the names of the stars from north to south. I have been on the Galaxy at the throne of the Distributor. . . .'

"I can see it still. We had been salmon fishing. We were couched under St Llawddog's rock at Cenarth Mawr, above the river. It is a holy and haunted place. Echoes dwell there, marvelous and unearthly. Gwenaby's voice roused them. It swallowed up the roar of the cataract. We were robbed of speech, listening. Everything flew out of our heads like chaff. We could see nothing, hear nothing—only old Gwenaby shouting and exulting and waving his arms like wild Merlin in his cups: 'I have been winged with the genius of the silver crozier. I have been in Asia with Noah in the Ark. I have been chief director of the Tower of Nimrod. . . .'

"I was a student at the Inns of Court then. I had sat at the feet of men who had devoted a lifetime to exposing falsities and tracing out the truth. Cunning sophists and learned masters. What did *they* know? What did *I* know? Feathers and fluff. I was spellbound. Call it an epiphany, if you like. Or a rebirth. Even as Little Gwion's, do you remember? He was in the service of the sorceress Ceridwen, but he tasted the magical brew in her stone cauldron and learnt so much of her arts thereby that he became the object of her hatred. He changed himself into a hare; she changed herself into a greyhound. He ran to the river and became a fish; she ran after him and became an otter. He turned himself into a bird of the air; she became a hawk. He turned himself into a grain of winnowed wheat at the bottom of the mow; she turned herself into a high-crested black hen. She found him, swallowed him, and carried him in her womb nine months. At his birth she could not find it in herself to kill him, so she wrapped him in a leathern bag and cast him into the sea. There, he was washed up in a fishing weir of the Lowland Hundred, where he was found and adopted by Prince Elphin and grew up to be the one he was."

"Taliesin Chief Bard," said Eden.

"Even he. The Shining Brow. Who sang the song without beginning or end."

They fell silent then. Some little space, they sat there, reflecting.

Once again Eden became aware of the din of the camp: rough voices of men, yap of dogs and curs, and from the stretch of down that served as a practice ground, the clash of bucklers and the sound of arrows whistling from bows. Beating on hammer stones in forge, splitting of wood in thicket. A youth was playing a crowth on the side of the hill, others were singing. Somewhere, in the near distance, horns were blowing.

God be thanked, Eden thought, Black Rhys is here.

A great cry split the air—suddenly, stunningly, thunderous.

"'I have been in India when Rome was built. . . .'"

Eden all but leapt out of his skin. What on earth! Glyndwr was on his feet, arms upraised to Heaven, shouting ringingly, jubilantly:

"'I have been with my Lord in the manger of the ass. I strengthened Moses through the waters of the Red Sea. I have been fostered in the land of the Deity. I have been teacher of all intelligences. I am able to instruct the whole universe. I am a wonder whose origin is not known. I shall be until the Day of Doom upon the face of this earth.'"

Sitting where he was, Eden stared up at him, entranced. So Glyndwr stood a few moments further, then he lowered his arms and slowly turned this head to look at his cousin, the old demonic gleam in his sea-grey eye.

"We and Little Gwion, eh, kinsman?" he said. "Like him, we, too, have put our fingers into the stone cauldron of the destinies."

Aye, and licked them all too well, thought Eden with rueful humor.

He rose and helped Glyndwr gather up his belongings.

"By my faith, I had almost forgot," the Prince said suddenly. And with that, much to the younger man's astonishment, he plucked out of his wallet a golden cross garnished with rubies and handed it to him.

"A woman died of a wasting sickness in the house of nuns outside Brecon a while ago," he explained. "A daughter of that old warrior Brochwel of the Spears, it seems. She gave this cross into the keeping of the Lady Abbess yonder, asking that it be returned to the man who had given it to her as a surety for her niece after the Battle of Usk. She did not know his name, only that he was a dark chieftain of Mona, that he was a widower, and that he had a strange turn in his eye."

Stunned, Eden held the cross in the cup of his hands and stared down at it. Moments passed before he raised it to his trembling lips. At last, he looked up at Glyndwr.

"Who can she be, my lord?" he asked hesitantly. "The Lady Abbess?"

"An old friend of mine," Glyndwr replied. He bent a fierce glance on Eden, before adding slily: "And of yours too, I believe."

Eden fell silent, reflecting. In a little, his face lit up with a far-off and tender smile.

"Angharad Trevor," he said.

Shouts and cheers rang out nearby. All at once the encampment was buzzing like a hive. Men were riding along the hillside below. Glyndwr squared his shoulders.

"It is time, son of Tudor," he said briskly. "Let us go down now and join hands with those of our friends who are still dwellers in the flesh."

2

It was Whitmonday. Through the buzzard dimness of the early morning twilight the array marched out of the gates of Oswestry. Sir Richard Thelwall, in a raven-figured surcoat over his traveling armor, rode at its head, accompanied by the sergeant-at-arms of the Welshpool garrison. Outside their milking pens, a herd of cattle stared at the men with mournful astonished eyes as they trudged along the rolling meadowland, leaving a smoky trail behind them in the dew-grey grass. The cool air was rich with the scents of the damp earth, of wet woods, and the heady scent of the milk-white thorn. Far away, bells were ringing for matins.

The men-at-arms whistled and chatted as they strode along, but the horsemen were silent, their faces tense and watchful, knowing what their foot-soldiers did not. When Sir Richard had arrived at Oswestry the previous day, he had learned that a forerider he had sent from Chirk to Oswestry to arrange for quarters had been found dead in a thicket near the town.

"He must have run into the Welsh," the Constable of Oswestry told the knight.

"So they are close."

"Yes, my friend. I think they must be after you."

"That may well be so," said the other, "but what makes you think it?"

"We have made a six months truce with Glendower and there is still a month to elapse, so how can we be the object of their interest at this time?"

"A truce, eh?" the knight smiled coldly. "I wonder what the Earl of Arundel has to say to that?"

"If the Earl abode constantly in his lordships as the King has charged him to do, perhaps we would not have been put in such strait," the Constable retorted hotly. "This town has been invaded and burnt to the ground twice in the course of the past ten years. Our people are wool merchants and weavers for the most part. They want only to live and go about their errands in peace."

"The scoundrels!" exclaimed his fellow Constable. "We will pay them."

Word had been sent at once to the Constables of Whittington, Welshpool and Montgomery and plans set afoot. The sergeant-at-arms of the Welshpool garrison had reached Oswestry during the night. He knew the territory well; his task was to lead Sir Richard towards that place south of the town where the forces had arranged to meet.

After they had gone some little distance, they fell in with the road to Shrewsbury, a broad rutted track as worn as a river-bed. It crossed a rolling grassland covered with spinneys and intersected by numerous small valleys and gullies. It was excellent country for ambush to the knight's mind, and he looked about him uneasily as they passed by derelict hovels and the charred heaps of crofts long since given over to weed and bramble. The sun was beginning to rise in the sky. Along the road, the puddles of water that had formed in the holes made by the trampling hooves of horses and cattle, paled and shimmered in the light of the dawn. The air grew clearer. Thelwall's eyes were drawn to what he had taken earlier for a low-lying, blackish pile of cloud. Now, as they approached it, he saw that in reality it was a round wooded hill. The faintest of hazes hung about the trees, and large grey birds wheeled over the summit, with flapping wings and strange cries.

And all at once it occurred to the knight that were he Welsh it was there he would lie in ambush for his enemies. The road he and his company were following ran close by its foot, and at its back lay the wild forests, glens and mountains of Wales. And as soon as this thought entered his mind, the more convinced did he become that there were shadowy figures rustling about among the bushes and trees on that hillside, or lying on their bellies in the undergrowth watching his troops with intent, sinister and murderous eyes.

Aye, and they were there, too, curse them!—those hellcats, the sons of Tudor. The Avengers of the Blood. An unpleasant chill pinched the nape of his neck. Everything now was ominous to him. The crackling of twigs or underbrush was enough to make him start. Even the silky rustling of the leaves in the light breeze seemed fraught with menace. He stared at the hillside so hard that tears sprang to his eyes. Among the trees near the summit, stones were winking in the glow of the sunrise? Or were they stones?

"They are there," he said quickly.

"Nay," said the sergeant in unbelief.

"Yes, they are, I tell you."

"So near Oswestry? Why would they do that?"

"Because the men of Oswestry will not fight them," the knight replied in a jarring tone. "They are under truce."

"Again?"

Sir Richard was not disposed to explain.

"How far is it to the meeting place?" he asked.

"A mile or so."

"We must turn off the road. Draw them out," the knight said curtly.

"Which way shall we go?"

"There," said the sergeant, nodding his head at a cluster of trees crowning a hillock to the southeast.

"Quick. Follow me," shouted Sir Richard, and gave his horse the spur.

The other riders swung away in pursuit and the footsoldiers thudded after them in a bewildered herd. Suddenly there was an outcry to the rear.

"The Welsh!"

The footsoldiers scattered as Sir Richard and his companions put their mounts to a gallop over the hilly ground. Behind them full tilt rode a band of Welsh horsemen led by Black Rhys and Robyn Holland. Farther back by the length of a field galloped Tudor's sons and Jean d'Espagne. Through woodland and down into misty hollow and gully they made their way, the rough shod horses kicking up clods with their hooves as they tore along. As they came over the hilltop indicated by the sergeant-at-arms, and dropped down into the shallow valley beyond, Sir Richard gave an exuberant laugh. Sheep to the slaughter, his heart jubilated. The English were swarming out of the dingles and bushy hollows all around. The Welsh rode straight into the trap.

In the first few moments Robert Puleston's horse went down under

him. An enemy soldier lunged at him with a spear. Black Rhys bore
down on him and struck off his head with an axe, then was himself
lashed with a sword across his hams and tumbled from his horse. Sure
of their death the two men fought side by side with a wild careless
terrible abandon that laid three of their enemies low in the bloody grass
before they themselves were penned in, bleeding and exhausted, the
weapons struck from their hands.

"I claim these two as my prisoners," declared the Constable of
Welshpool as Sir Richard came riding up.

"Be it so," the knight told him coldly. "I have no interest in them.
I am looking for the sons of Tudor."

"What ails you, Sir Chough?" Black Rhys jeered. "Don't you love
life?"

Without a word in reply, Thelwall rode off in search of his prey.
They were fighting on the slope of a hill to the north of the main battle.
The pressure on the Welsh was not as heavy there, but the brothers knew
that it would only be a matter of time before the rest of their enemies
rallied to their comrades' aid, so they put all their strength behind their
weapons, trying to clear themselves a path. Every limb ached and after
a while it seemed to Eden that he saw everything through a swimming
mist—writhing horses, snarling faces, the deadly glitter of ringing iron.

Rhys Ddu fought alongside his younger brother. Standing in the
stirrups as he laid about him, his eye was drawn as though by a lightning
flash to a body of armed men moving towards them from the direction of
Montgomery. Dear Christ, what a disaster, he thought. But the great
joyous shout that was torn from his throat instantaneously, like a trumpet
blowing a victory was : "Hurrah, Glendower!"

The press of adversaries broke in alarm and confusion at the name.
In that moment Rhys Ddu saw his chance and took it. "Away, boys!" he
yelled, and spurring his horse let it out at a full gallop down the other
side of the hill. Eden, Jean d'Espagne and three others raced after him.
In that first impetuous rush, as irresistible as the flight of an arrow, a
swathe was cut through the advancing line of enemy foot-soldiers and
they went beating along the grassland beyond.

Jesus Maria, we have won free, Eden thought. An exulting cry
broke from his lips as he laid his body almost flat along the neck of his
horse. Trees shot past, great swords parrying and thrusting along the
green rush of the earth, and the wind of his speed sang in his head like

the sea. Even then a ray of sun broke through the clouds. A golden-yellow track of light traveled with unearthly swiftness across the shadowy grassland before him. He felt himself drawn along it as though by the force of magic. And for the breath of time it lasted, he too was touched with fire. The surrounding fields, strewn with the dismal refuse of war, might not have existed. There was only himself, his galloping steed and the beckoning light of the morning.

And then, Rhys Ddu's warning shout rent the air.

"Watch out!"

Eden swung away to the left as a black-helmeted horseman wearing the device of a raven on his blue surcoat, overtook him and passed him on the right flank. "It's Thelwall!" he shouted. The knight wheeled about and with his spear crouched, came charging back towards Rhys Ddu. The older of the brothers swerved not a moment too soon. The spear-pike on Thelwall's chafron ran through the flesh of his horse's neck to the depth of an inch and tore into the nostril. While Rhys Ddu was trying to master the rearing frightened animal, Sir Richard, without reining in his mount, made a half-circle and came riding back. Eden whirled around and swooped past him on the other side. He swung his axe, and turning quickly in the saddle, brought it down with all his might on the other's helmet. Glancing back, he saw the knight slumping over and then crashing to the ground in a torrent of blood. Behind him, by a great stoneshot, some fifteen men were riding.

They had almost come as far as the hill of ambush when Rhys Ddu's horse suddenly collapsed under him, hurling his rider among rocks. Feeling the hot searing pain, the rending of flesh and bone, the older of the brothers tried to harden himself against what he now realized lay in store for him.

"I think I have broken my hip," he grimaced as his brother dismounted and knelt beside him.

Jean d'Espagne swung back.

"What is it?"

"Ride, ride, Jean!" Eden cried out. "Go! God be with you!"

In that one last anguished glance he cast upon those two stirring brothers, the one sitting with his arm about the other, calmly, gallantly awaiting their fate, an image was impressed on the Frenchman's mind that he was to bear with him until his own death on the field of Agincourt five years later.

A faint smile pinched the corners of Rhys Ddu's lips.

"It is done, little brother."

Eden kissed him and turned his face away. There were wild hyacinths in the grass; a fiery little cloud was afloat in the blue over the walls and towers of Oswestry; high in the sky a hawk was careening and drifting, the sweep of its wings catching silver in the sunlight.

3

Early in June, Jean d'Espagne rode into Dolwyddelan with a few companions. They stayed at the castle for a day and a night before continuing on their way.

"How is my husband?" Mererid asked.

The French captain replied that he had been alive and well when he had last seen him, that there had been a great raid on the Shropshire border and they had come away with a fine booty. And after that no more was heard for a while. Mererid's mind was haunted by a trouble, half-comprehended, half-vague. She watched those about her curiously—the lady of the castle, Robyn, the grizzled rough-faced soldiers-and wondered why, in spite of the good tidings, they should seem so joyless, why when they smiled and laughed their eyes should gleam with such a somber miserable glitter.

She shrank from admitting her own suspicion to herself, that they were concealing something from her. She decided that her condition was making her overly tender. She was far gone with child then.

At midsummer her brother and sister-in-law arrived from Mona with Marged Vaughan. Sioned looked older—she had grown thinner and more sparrowlike—but Gerallt was much the same. Perhaps there was more grey in his hair and beard, but he still had a vigorous youthful look about him, brawny yet graceful, his face bronzed and lined with work and weather. Mererid was cheered by his presence. She felt she could confide in him.

One afternoon it began to rain. He came with her to the roof of the keep to help her gather up some washing that had been hung out there to dry.

"Would that Eden could be here when his child is born," she said. "It would content me so. Is there no way word can be got to him?"

He hesitated a little before replying.

"In sober heart, my dear sister," he said, "you must know that this cannot be. Where Eden is at this hour I cannot tell. They are hawks and wolves, our lads, always on the move. I'll tell you where not to look for him, and that will be along the pleasantest and most frequented roads, No, go look for him in the wildest places. Where the henbane blows and the witches ride. The abode of unclean spirits. Ah, no!"—he saw her begin to smile—"I ease you of that charge." Laughingly he put his arms about her and hugged her fiercely. "Mererid, who do you think you are? The Lady of Feats? It was a great mercy of God and Mary Virgin to bring you back here safe and sound, when you could be dead at the bottom of a bog. Have a thankful remembrance of that. Have you thought of a name for your child?"

"If the baby is a maid, I shall call her Annes," Mererid said. "And if a knave, he shall be Rhodri."

"A brave and kingly name. Rhodri Mawr. Who drove back the Vikings."

"Do you remember the name of his queen?"

"Angharad. . . ."

Gerallt fell silent, smiling. Mererid leaned towards him and tapped his cheek.

"What were you thinking then? That I would name my daughter after my kinswoman, Eden's old flame?"

"It's not that I was thinking at all," he retorted with tender joy, "but what a beautiful bonny girl your daughter is and what a fine brave boy you are soon to bring us. Do you know what that means, my sister? We shall have another Rhodri and Angharad in our land and they will keep the barbarians at bay. But not this rain I fear," he grinned, swiftly gathering up the wash. "Come quckly before you get wet."

She did not follow him straightway for all that. She stood in the well of the stairway, watching the rain—the sky full of rain; rain like light set whispering along the silver darkness of the river, the misty forests, the cloudy hills. Her mind was full of Eden, and as she stood there, her thoughts went out after him along the tortuous paths through the glens and mountains of the ancient hundreds. They roamed in search of him about a many hundred hiding-holes—halls, crofts, caves, turf castles— that were sealed against her need of knowing in which one of them at the moment her beloved might be lodged; and how he was, and what talk might be going on in his hearing of the exploits of Glyndwr and his followers, and what new enterprise might be hatching, and where he designed to be on the morrow or the day after that. . . .

He had been dead for almost three weeks then.

Early in July Mererid gave birth to her child. It was a son as she had hoped. Only then did they tell her that Rhys Ddu and Eden had been beheaded at Chester.

Driven from the castle by her terrible outpouring of grief, Gerallt and Robyn wandered the countryside for most of the day. Afterwards neither of them could well remember how they spent those hours. They followed the paths of the forest, letting them lead them where they would—down sun-dappled slopes among age-old oaks hung with green mosses, through wallows trampled and fouled by wild beasts, across glades red with foxgloves as tall as a man.

They spent the night at the hall of the Widowers at Trellan. It was a melancholy visit altogether. Where was the pleasant snug of days gone by? Dirt and neglect were evident everywhere and there was a sour moldy smell in the hall. Robert was ill and he lay in the straw near the fire, wrapped up in bandages of flannel, wheezing and sweating. Shrunken and yellow, nibbling at his cheeks without cease like a rabbit, it was painful to see him. Besides that, he had gone quite feeble of wit and failed to recognize them at first.

"Who did you say they were?"

"Eden's foster brother Gerallt and his foster son Robyn."

"Eden?"

"Tudor's son."

"Was he the one we buried with our pride and flower at Maenan?"

"No, that was Meredith."

"Did we not bury Eden there too?"

"No."

"Are you sure?"

"As sure as God."

"Strange, I had it in my thoughts that he was dead. I could have sworn we buried him with the others."

"No, my heart. It is true that Eden is dead, but he is not buried at Maenan."

Robert shook his head.

"Alas."

He sighed and peered into the smoky dimness.

"Oia, it's gone so unreal somehow," he breathed in a little; upon which, quite without warning, he began to weep, snuffling and screwing up his face like a little child.

Jesus help us, Robyn thought, he felt like weeping himself. If destiny had willed that they come here to find some solace in their misery, then she had sorely misled them. The hall was a sink of despond. Other than one slovenly serving man who crept apart as dismally as a mangy sheep for the flies to blow on, he saw nobody around to fetch and carry for the old lads. They were all alone there.

In the grey of the morning Gerallt and Robyn were getting ready to leave when Lelo brought them a thick fascicle of papers bound within stout, if shabby, leathern covers.

"A monk hospitaller left these lease records here a while ago, saying they were for the castle," he told them. "He was in some haste—and you see how it is with us here. It was vexing me, wondering how to get them into your hands. God be thanked for leading you hither yestereven."

Gerallt laughed a little as he asked:

"Can they be of such value then, Lelo? Lease records?"

Robyn could not forbear laughing himself, but as they rode on their way homeward both of them soon fell silent again, dreading what awaited them at the castle. To their relief and no little wonder, a comforting air of calm prevailed when they arrived. The flagstones of the hall were strewn with fresh rushes, and the lady midwives were seated about having a talking time and drinking goblets of water sweetened with honey.

"We thought you two run off to sea," said Marged Vaughan. "Did we frighten you away?"

Gerallt made no answer, but a chalky pallor stole over his face and his eyes reddened. Awkwardly, by reason of his stiff leg, Robyn sank on his knees before the Chieftain's widow and humbly kissed her hand.

"What are you about now?" she asked kindly, raising him up by the elbows. "By the good pleasure of God, you have been spared that rickety stalk of yours for a better purpose I hope, Robyn, than bending it before an old woman. Do not worry about us, lads," said she with a wry glance at her fellow midwives—the lady Enid, Olwen of Mathebrud and Tango's she-comrade Llio, all of them widows. "We have had the practice here. We shall not sink. Be off now and see mother and child."

After they had presented a surprised Enid with the fascicle of papers they had brought back with them from Trellan, and explained to her what they were, Gerallt and Robyn went to the bedchamber. Sitting up in the great bed, dressed in a silken gown of cream color, with her pale gleaming face and a beatific smile, Mererid could have been mistaken for an ivory saint, but for her torrent of russet hair and her eyes still red and swollen from weeping. She greeted both of them lovingly and bade them journey to a cradle tressed with red ribbons to make due obeisance to her baby son. Gerallt made a joyful noise upon sight of his nephew, but to Robyn he seemed much like any other baby; quite ordinary in fact—a pink and wrinkled little manchild, peevish of mien, with fingers no greater than the fingers of mice, and those not of the granary sort. Sure enough, as soon as he saw Robyn, never a fellow of light fiber, he began to wail.

"King Rhodri has great lungs," Gerallt declared laughingly.

"Bring him here," said Mererid. "It is time for his feed."

Gerallt remained in attendance. Robyn begged his excuses and returned to the hall where Rosier, Tango's brother, was romping about with Angharad athwart his shoulders, her hand deepthrust into his curls— a little girl with auburn hair, a short freckled nose and bright clever eyes. Beside them skipped a larger maid with silky flaxen hair and laughing teeth as small and white as nuts of acorn.

"Where is she coming from then?" Robyn asked Sioned.

"Don't you know? That is Nest," she told him. "Have you never heard of her? She is the granddaughter of Brochwel of the Spears. Tango brought her back to the Bay of the White Stones after the Battle of Usk."

"Nest?" Robyn mused. His face broke into a smile. "Aye, now I remember. I met her at Caer Gai. Years ago. A little girl who said that she would grow up but never old."

"Long life to her then. You must be hungry, Robyn. I'll get you some food. While you are waiting, the lady Enid would like you to look through these lease records. Her eyes are weak, she says, and the patience is wanting."

Sighing but dutiful, Robyn retired to a quiet corner and undid the fastenings on the leather coverings of the scrolls. Lease records, aye. So far as he could tell. They were all but indecipherable. As soon interpret the ancient Ogham of the weathers on tree and stone for sure. Smoke and wet had done their do; the pages were yellow and smutched; the characters inscibed thereon so faint and distorted you might think them contrived for the perusal of such as could see a fly rise in the morning with the sun.

He was about to set them aside, when something caught his eye. Some rough pages unlike the rest. Tucked into the heart of the bundle. Carefully and hesitantly, he drew them forth, unwrapped them and smoothed them out. Something hard and glittering slipped through his fingers and fell ringing against the flagstones. God's my life! He sat there staring at it: a golden cross garnished with rubies. For a spell, it seemed to set the very blood shivering about his heart. He looked up at Sioned's voice and it was as if he did not know her.

"Good heavens!" she said. "It is the cross Annes gave Eden when they were wed."

She set down the trencher of food and drink she was carrying. Wiping her hands in her apron, she picked up the cross, pressed it against her lips, and took it to the people gathered about the hearth. All fell silent at once, startled and moved, as they passed the cross from one to the other. Each in turn kissed it reverently, before leaving it at last in the hands of Marged Vaughan, whose eyes were suddenly blind with tears Then Enid said:

"Mererid. It is hers. Let us take it to her."

Marged shook her head wearily

"O, no, not now, dear sister," she sighed. "As the Preacher tells us in Holy Writ, there is a time for everything under the sun. Och, but this is not the time."

The last light of day guttered out. Night came on. The women retired to their sleeping chamber. The men lay down on beds of straw near the hearth. Everything became quiet at last. A wild goose cried far away, from beyond the forest. Some hours later the baby began to wail. There was the sound of a voice crooning, then silence again.

Robyn could not sleep and he could tell from the way Gerallt was breathing that he was awake, too—thinking, remembering, listening.

The young bard spoke low, not to disturb the others

"Who do you think sent the cross to us, Gerallt?" he asked. "Was it our Lord Owain?"

It was not Gerallt, however, who answered. It was Rosier.

"It brought us our Nest, Robyn," he said. "It was the Lord God who sent it."

EPILOGUE

For three to four years after the heads of Tudor's sons and Black Rhys of Ceredigion had fallen under the axe, Owain Glyndwr continue to fight with stubborn if diminished force. And then he too was gone—vanished into the ringing silences of the eternal.

The mystery of his passing haunted Robyn of Mona as it did his countrymen. Long after his reason told him, indeed, that the great enchanter must be dead, his heart went with the common folk in believing that he continued to abide in their midst and in invoking Heaven for his protection. The bards prophesied his triumphant return and he became the subject of popular legend. One of the tales most often told of him relates that one morning before daybreak he was out walking when he met his old friend, the Abbot of Valle Crucis.

"You are up betimes, Father Abbot," he said.

"No, it is you who are up betimes, my friend," the other replied. "By a many hundred years."

The more immediate consequences of his rebellion were less happy. For generations afterwards, Welshmen were denied the ordinary privileges of citizenship: they could not acquire property in land within or near the boroughs; they could not bear arms; they could not serve on juries; intermarriage between them and the English was forbidden; they could not hold office under the Crown; no Englishman could be convicted on the word of a Welshman.

Emancipation from this civil thraldom was possible only through enlistment in the foreign wars of the King of England.

There hangs by this another tale.

In the summer of 1416 Robyn of Mona went on pilgrimage to the shrine of St David at Glyn Rhosin. He saw the heremetical cell of the beloved saint and passed over Lechlavar, the talking bridge of marble. He drank from the Pipe of David, and on a day of misty rain that made his wretched leg ache woefully, he knelt before the miraculous shrine, praying: "Great and good Saint David, all glory be to thy name, keep my beloved people safe. Guard them, comfort them, heal them. Guide, I beseech thee, my poor limping footsteps home to a warm and peaceful haven. Grant there be music there and loving friends."

In July Robyn turned homeward. One day it happened that he was passing through a valley where reapers were at work, the muttering of their feet coming harshly across the cry of the scythes in the grain. When they heard that he had some skill with music, they brought him a crowth and asked him to play. He was thus engaged when someone else arrived. The harvesting party made a respectful path for a woman, small but of noble girth, trapped in billowing garments, wearing a large straw sunhat. She looked at him for a small space in a puzzle, then clapped her hands to her cheeks and shouted:

"Robyn of Mona!"

He, with amazement, recognized in this portly apple-cheeked matron that slender laughing brown-eyed maid, Elin of Brynhodla, with whom several years ago at Caer Gai he had served as a love messenger between Owain Glyndwr's daughter Catrin and Master Howel Deget.

"Enough, leave off your fiddling now!" she cried, as delighted as he to renew an old acquaintance. "You must come back to the hall and meet my husband,"

His name was Llywelyn of Glyn Cothi. Big-bellied and scant of hair, the laps of fat hanging down from his chin like a cow's purse, his was far from being the sort of face which maidens dream of seeing reflected peering over their shoulders in a moonlit pool on midsummer night, but he was the kindest of souls for all that, and was possessed as it fortuned by a boundless appetite for variety. The women of the hall, who pampered and adored him, were certain they had a man of genius in their midst. Why, he could lie down in the grass for hours on end studying the tiny life of the ants, or he could stay up half the night watching the revolution of the stars in the heavens. He dabbled in alchemy and the magic arts, had translated the Penitential Psalms into Welsh, written a treatise on Taliesyn's 'Consolations of Elphin' and indeed had himself strewn upon the green altars of bardism a few flowers of poesy, among which figured a song of praise to his bride, Elin of Brynhodla: "Miraculous-footed. The burning breeze will sooner bruise the grasses than will her light step. . . ."

This extraordinary man took an instant liking to the friend of his wife's youth. Robyn was invited to stay on at the hall through the rest of the summer. By the end of that time, the lord of Glyn Cothi had discovered that his guest was an expert musician and delightful storyteller. The welcome was extended. The days passed as pleasantly as a song, and the nights went up in a dream of harps and the smoke of fires.

Autumn came to an end in the valley, cold winds blew. Stay a little longer, Robyn was urged. He could not go jaunting forth with the winter coming on. Advent, Christmas, Epiphany, Candlemas, the Feast of St David, the months rolled by. Spring arrived in storms of rain. Then the lord Llywelyn fell sick with the yellow sweats and debility, and it was thought he would die, and the priest came with the viaticum and Elin was bereft. "Stay with him, Robyn. You cannot leave us now, he is so fond of you. Play for him, my dear. He seems to brighten up a little when you play."

And that crisis was surmounted. And the lord was another year recovering on porridge, pap, and the first milk of cows and nanny goats. Numbers and magnitude were the master's next obsession—how far ripe was Robyn in knowledge of these matters? But why go on? Almost before Robyn knew it, so to speak, nine years had passed.

It was another time of harvest and the reapers were dancing the Old Hag home when some horsemen rode into the valley: the head of the house of Trevor and some friends. Among them was a man in a plain dark traveling habit. Robyn did not mark him until the stranger called him by name; after that, it might be said, the dark poet of Mona saw no one else. The sight of him almost took his breath away, he looked so much like Eden in his prime—the same soot-black hair and tallow pale skin. Only the eyes were different. The eyes of the master of the Old Hall had been as black as night; the eyes of this man were grey—the great, clear, darklashed grey eyes of Marged and Howel Vaughan of Mathebrud.

"Bless my soul!" Robyn exclaimed.

"So you know me now, eh?"

"Save the mark, aye! Owain ap Meredith! How long has it been since last we met?"

"Since I fled the land. Is it possible that you have forgotten?"

"Forgotten?"

Robyn gave a grim laugh. How indeed forget that year of grace 1415 when peace (God's one Son, what a peace!) had been concluded between the Earl Talbot on the part of the new English King, Henry the Fifth, and Owain Glyndwr's only surviving son Maredudd? Outside castles and towns garrisoned anew with foreign soldiers, the land was torn by broils and feuds. Men of brutish spirit were everywhere in the saddle. Ignored and hence in a manner of speaking, countenanced by the powers in possession, gangs of ruffians in fee to those houses which had supported the King during the uprising roamed the countryside exacting their toll of revenge. Many with drafts sworn on their heads took ship for Ireland and Brittany, the Chieftain's son Owain being one.

More to be remembered: two wedding feasts; the one celebrating the marriage of Nest, the granddaughter of Brochwel of the Spears, to Rosier, the head of the tribe of Collwyn ap Tango; the other of Mererid to Andras, the lord of Dyngannan and the Keeper of the ports and ferries of Mona. The first was held in the birthplace of Tango's widow Llio at Mynytho in the land of the Long Spearmen—for the great hall at the Bay of the White Stones had been sequestered long since—and the second was held at Dyngannan, in a hall gay with flowering branches of thorn and apple, and bright with the lights of a crowd of candles the women had been busy for weeks gathering up goat-wax and vermilion to make. Mererid looked all shining lady, too, sitting up there at the high table beside her dour blackbearded lord and master, but so proud and queenly somehow, so self-possessed and aloof that Robyn felt he scarce knew her. Nor when she came down from the flower strewn dais boards later on to thank Robyn for his songs did she seem any the closer, although he saw that Eden's cross was at her breast; and she kissed him, and her face gave back his smile, and her words were friendly.

They no longer had anything to say to one another, that was the truth. Something had come between them—the ghost of Eden, his own gaucherie, who could tell? He saw very little of her after that, perhaps no more than three times. It seemed as if he were never to meet her but it felt as if someone were running a knife into his heart, so he made it his care to avoid her whenever possible.

"Ten years. So long ago even," Robyn marveled. He looked at his fellow islander and said: "God knows I never looked to see you again. What happy chance has brought you back to our land?"

"None so happy a chance, my friend," said Owain gravely. "You have not heard, I see—but there, how could you have? My mother died not a month since."

"Och. . . ."

Tears sprang to the poet's eyes. He was put sadly on his memory for a while.

"God knows she was dear to my heart," he said then, "I had a deep reverence for her."

Her son nodded.

"So did we all I think She was a great lady."

Under the name of Owen Tudor,* the Chieftain's son now lived in London, an officer at the English court. Robyn almost thought he had heard someone say as much in his hearing some time ago, but had put it out of his mind then as a fable without color of proof. Yet it was true enough. In 1417 Owain had enlisted in the army of the Lord-lieutenant of Ireland and gone into France. There, for eminent services which he did not particularize he had been made a squire of the royal body. After King Henry's death of fever in 1422 at Senlis Owain had entered the household of the widowed Queen, Catherine of France, whom he now served as Chamberlain.

"She is a charming, kind-hearted lady," he said, "and a lonely one. A stranger in the land."

"As are you," the other observed.

"As am I," he smilingly agreed. "But tell me something about yourself now, Robyn. How is it that you did not return to Mona after your pilgrimage to Glyn Rhosin? Folk yonder have been wondering. Sioned thinks my mother was at the root of the trouble, trying to get your feet fastened down."

There was more than a little truth to that, as Robyn had to admit. When he had returned to Mona with Mererid and her little ones after Eden's death, there had been such a dearth of marriageable men on the island—so many having been slain or maimed, and others out of necessity, having adopted the livery of felons and outlaws—that Marged Vaughan said that the women were wearing their eyes down into their sockets looking.

"The convent yonder is full of the unfortunate creatures. How are the nuns to support them all? It is not a rich house."

"Bards do not marry, lady."

"Since when?"

"It seems to be the will of Heaven that they lead a single life."

"Why? Are they monks? Do they take vows of chastity?"

"No."

*See Note 5

"Well then. . . ."

"You can call it an unspoken rule if you like."

"I call it nonsense," said Marged Vaughan abruptly and firmly. "We will amend it."

It had been bootless to tell her how uncongenial marriage was to him. All men were bees at heart, happy only in the hive. Bring us our children, we need our little ones, was her refrain. She had even gone so far as to pick out his wife: the widow of the pastor of Pentraeth. Sian Offeiriad was a proper bonny little woman of perhaps thirty years of age, plump and red-cheeked, who had a young son and a farm and messuage of some antiquity, with a herbary and a water-pump, and she must have made someone a good wife except it was him. Marged Vaughan, to be sure, did not promote her design directly, for if she was an exact woman she was not without guile; but the widow's resorts to the hall of Penmynydd were so frequent, and she cut upon his path at such untoward moments, and the looks that she cast upon him were so melting, not to mention the winks and nudges and sniggers that were general elsewhere, that he was left in no doubt as to what was going on.

Still, that was all over and done with now. Like so much else.

It was a warm night. After supper the two islanders had gone to sit and take their ease away from the rest of the company in the garden They were drowning the harvest in the glen. The stars hung like golden cherries in the heavens and the meadow outside the walls was alive with fires and merriment.

"Gerallt and Sioned, how are they?" asked Robyn.

"Hearty and thriving as the proverbial grain of oats. The twins are both married with children now, imagine! Eden's son Rhodri is a fine lump of a lad with dreams of going to sea like his Uncle Rhys. And little Angharad is the mistress of Myvyrian."

"Old Emrys died then?"

"Four or five years ago. Geraint, his youngest son, is master there now."

Robyn was silent a moment, then asked:

"And Rhodri and Angharad's mother, how is she?"

"She is the queen of the isle," Owain laughed. "Andras may rule others, but it is she who rules Andras. Much as his mother used to do in the past, I believe. Sure, our Mererid is far more comely than old Elianor ever was. And God be thanked, more caring. She nursed my mother most tenderly and devotedly to the last, you know. In truth so many of us are in her keeping. By the way, there is a harp at Penmynydd that awaits you."

"A harp? What harp?"

"It was brought from Dolwyddelan castle a few years back. When my aunt Enid went to work among the lepers in Llyn. That is Robyn ap Trahern's harp, my mother told Sioned. She said my father wanted you to have it. You lightened many a dark hour for him, I'm told, especially in that time after Alun was killed, if you remember."

Robyn swallowed painfully, then nodded.

"I remember it well."

He hesitated a moment, before asking, almost without breath.

"This harp you are talking about? Would that be the Silver Harp?"

"It is known to you then?"

"Known?" Robyn cried out. "Known? It has been a part of my life since ever I was. Mabon won it at Caerhun in your grandfather Tudor's time. In the days of the glory. Everything is there—all the songs, all the magic, all the dreams. The children of the wind and flame are there. Many a night I played it for the Chieftain in the castle hall at Dolwyddelan—aye, you can be sure, the Silver Harp is known to me."

"There you are then," Owain smiled. "That is why it is yours, Robyn. That is why your Chieftain made you a gift of it. Mind you," he added, "you will have to go home to claim it."

Touched and overwhelmed, Robyn could not speak. Sensing that he wished to be left alone, Owain rose at last, laid his hand on the other's shoulder and returned to join the others in the hall. Robyn was scarcely aware that he had left. All he could think about was Mabon's harp. Overcome with emotion, he felt the years falling away from his heart like the leaves from a tree that is forever reborn. A tide of memories was bearing him back, happy and resistless, to an island he now realized that he had never truly left.

Come, his heart sang, let us create that world anew. Let it be spring, that sweetest of times. Crofts, halls, mills, cots and churches have been newly washed with lime. All dwellings on this earth are white. White, too, are the great moving clouds and like blossoms of ocean the gleaming gulls dip and circle in the air, white, all white, and dancing on the wind.

NOTES

P.1 1. Ednyved Vychan
More precisely the name is Ednyfed Fychan—Welsh f's are English v's. The name Vaughan is an Anglicized version of Fychan. It is equivalent in meaning to Junior in English. Eden, the familiar form of the name, is not pronounced like the Garden. It is EDDenn.
The coat-of-arms of Ednyved Vychan-gules, a chevron between three Englishmen's heads proper couped, is still to be seen at the hall of Penmynydd in Anglesey.
The Lord Llywelyn he served was Llywelyn ap Iorwerth, known as Llywelyn Fawr or Vawr—Llywelyn the Great, the Prince of Gwynedd. At his death in 1240 he had extended his sway over most of Wales.

P.10 2. Owain Glyndwr
Glendower, Glyndowrdy, Glendour, Glyndowr, are all English variants of Glyndyfrdwy—glinnDUVRdoi—a literal rendering of which gives us the Glen or Vale of the Dee or Divine Water (Latin *Diva*). It was a lordship in the possession of Owain ap Griffith Vychan and the one so closely associated with him that he became known by its name. The most popular English form is Glendower. In Wales this is always Glyndwr or Glyn Dwr.
His mother Helen and her sister Margaret, the wife of Sir Tudor ap Grono of Mona or Anglesey, were said to be in their day the last surviving lineal descendants of Llywelyn ap Griffith, the last independent prince of Wales. Owain Glyndwr based his claim to the Welsh throne on his mother's ancestry. So in a later time the Tudors of England were to trace their descent through Sir Tudor ap Grono's wife Margaret from the kings of Ancient Britain.

P .51 3. A.D 1400-Griffith ap Davydd writes to Lord Grey de Ruthin:
With owten doute as many men that ye slay and as many houses that ye burn for my sake, as many wil I burn and slay for your sake and doute not I wil have both bredde and ale of the best that is in your lordship.

Written in grete haste at the parke of Bryn Cyffo, the xj day of June
Lord Grey replies:
We hope we shall do thee a pryvy thing; a rope, a ladder and a ring,
high on gallowes for to hinge. And thus shall be your endyng. And he
that made thee be there to helpyng and we on our behalf shall be welle
willying. For thy letter is knowlechynge. *Written, etc.*

P.120 4. The Abbey of Llanvaes.
It was finally rebuilt during the following reign, that of Henry V,
with the proviso that no more than two of the monks be Welsh.

P.186 5. The Battle of Shrewsbury. (The outbreak of the Percies.)
Sir Henry Percy (Hotspur) declared himself at Chester on July 10th,
1403. During the following days he was joined by his uncle, the earl of
Worcester and by great numbers of Cheshire men and Welshmen of the
Marches, who were duped by the story that Richard the Second was still
alive. King Henry the Fourth was on his way north to Scotland when he
heard that Hotspur was moving south, designing to reach Shrewsbury
and seize the young prince, Henry of Monmouth. The King moved with
dispatch, entering Shrewsbury just in time to close the gates against his
enemies.
The battle took place some three miles outside Shrewsbury, at a site
still known as Battlefield, on July 21st. The early moon, we are told by
the chroniclers, was eclipsed that night and the slaughter was
tremendous. "The king's bold initiative," writes the eminent Welsh
historian, Sir John Lloyd, "destroyed the rebels' plan of campaign."
Neither Hotspur's father, the Earl of Northumberland, nor Owain
Glyndwr were near at the time. "It maybe that thus," Sir John suggests,
"a great opportunity was let slip; the overthrow of the House of Lancaster
would certainly have brought with it immediate advantages for Glyndwr
of the most dazzling order. But confederacies of this type are well known
to be unstable and fruitful of discord. The Mortmers and the Percies were
likely in the long run to take the English point of view; for enduring
success the Welsh had none on whom they could reckon but themselves."

P. 417   6. Owain ap Meredith (Owen Tudor).

All the chroniclers of the Tudor era assert confidently that the marriage of Queen Catherine and Owen Tudor was at least tacitly acknowledged in the sixth year of her son's reign. Thus Rymer (i 204): "Catherine, who being young and lusty, following more her own appetite than friendly counsel and regarding more her private affection than her open honour took to husband privily (in 1428) a goodly gentleman and a beautiful person garniged with many godly gifts both of nature and of grace called Owen Tudor, a man brought forth and come of the noble lignage and ancient line of Cadwalladr, the last kynge of the Britons."

Four children were born to Owen and Catherine—Edmund, the father of the future Henry VII, Jasper, Thomas and Margaret—'unwetyng the common people tyl that she were dead and buried.' When the liaison became known to the young King's guardians around 1436, Queen Catherine was sent under restraint to the Abbey of Bermondsey by her brother-in-law, the Duke of Gloucester. This event is supposed to have occurred just after the birth of her little daughter Margaret who lived but a few days. Anxiety of mind threw the queen into declining health and she remained very ill at Bermondsey during the autumn. The children to whom she had previously given birth in secret were torn from her by orders of the council and consigned to the keeping of a sister of the earl of Suffolk. This cruelty undoubtedly hastened her end.

While the queen was sent to Bermondsey, her husband Owen Tudor was thrown into Newgate prison. He was still there when his royal wife and lover died in the following February. In July of that year he escaped and took refuge in Wales. He was pursued there by the forces of his enemy, the Duke of Gloucester, recaptured and thrown once more into Newgate prison, from which he once more escaped 'in the night at searching time, through the help of his priest and hurting foul his keeper." Many more years were to pass before he was exonerated and fully accepted into court circles.

What happened to this gallant fellow finally? At the age of seventy-six he led a royalist army against the Yorkists. He was defeated at Mortimer's Cross. His aged head fell to the headman's axe in Hereford Market Place.

"And he was beheaded in the market-place and his head set upon the highest grise of the market cross; and a mad woman combed his hair and washed away the blood of his face. And she got candles and set about him burning, more than a hundred." (Ellis Griffith-*The Welsh Tudor Chronicles.*)

CHRONOLOGICAL TABLE

1399

King Richard the Second at Conway. Ambushed and taken captive by the forces of Henry Bolingbroke, Duke of Lancaster.

1400

February. Richard the Second dies at Pontefract castle. Henry of Lancaster ascends throne as Henry the Fourth. Hotspur (Sir Henry Percy) appointed Warden of the Welsh Marches and Justice of North Wales. Lord Grey of Ruthin becomes Chief Lord Marcher.

Spring. Glyndwr in London. His landsuit against Lord Grey fails. King Henry marches on Scotland. Glyndwr does not receive his call to arms. Lord Grey raids Glyndwr's property and seizes the disputed land upon the orders of the King. Imprisons Griffith ap Davydd, the Keeper and Master Forester of Chirkeland among others.

St Matthew's Day (Sept. 21st) Glyndwr's rebellion begins. King Henry with army in North Wales. Executes rebels in prisons. The Abbey of Llanvaes in Mona (Anglesey) is attacked and gutted by the royal forces.

1401

Rhys and Gwilym ap Tudor, Howel Vaughan and their partisans burn the town of Conway and seize the castle on Good Friday morning (April 1st). Prince Henry and Hotspur in charge of siege. Glyndwr victory at Hyddgen in Pumlumon range. Tudors and Howel Vaughan come to terms with King Henry around the beginning of July and leave castle.

King attacks South Wales and sacks the Cistercian abbey of Strata Florida.

1402

Comet appears in February. Lord Grey ambushed and taken captive by Glyndwr forces.

Battle of Pilleth. Sir Edmund Mortimer captured. South Wales rises behind Glyndwr. Henry IV invades South Wales, but a train of disaster marks his retreat.

1403

Prince Henry burns Glyndwr's hall of Sycharth, executes Griffith ap Davydd, and ravages surrounding countryside. Popular proclamation of Owain Glyndwr as Prince of Wales at Dryslwyn castle in Vale of Towy. Lunar eclipse. Battle of Shrewsbury. Hotspur slain. Town and castle of Caernarvon besieged by Jean d'Espagne and French auxiliaries.

1404

1st Welsh Parliament at Machynlleth. Coronation of Owain Glyndwr. Formal alliance between Welsh and French in Paris on July 14th. Harlech and Aberystwyth fall to Glyndwr forces. Glyndwr now de facto ruler of Wales.

1405

Tripartite Indenture of Northumberland, Mortimer and Glyndwr at Bangor. Welsh defeated at Battle of Usk (Pwll Melyn.)

June: Stephen Scrope, deputy Lord-lieutenant of Ireland invades the Isle of Mona with army raised in Dublin. Islanders retreat into mountains of Snowdonia with flocks and herds. Attempted assassination of Owain Glyndwr by Howel Sele, lord of Nannau. Howel Sele executed. Nannau burned to the ground.

August 1st: 2nd Welsh parliament at Harlech. French land at Milford Haven. Met by Glyndwr, they make their way through South Wales to Woodbury Hill, eight miles from the city of Worcester. King Henry in city. Issue in balance. Glyndwr, penetrated too far into hostile country, retreats. King Henry invades South Wales. Tempestuous weather destroys his baggage train. Forced to retreat.

1406

St George's Day. (April 23rd). Welsh defeated in border battle. Glyndwr's brother, two of his sons and Master Walter Brut among slain.

1407

Siege of Aberystwyth, held by Black Rhys of Ceredigion. Raised by Glyndwr. Duke of Orleans murdered by henchmen of Jean Sans Peur, the Duke of Burgundy. Earl of Northumberland and Lord Bardolf killed in the Battle of Bramham Moor.

1408

Aberystwyth and Harlech fall. Mortimer dies during siege. Glyndwr's wife, two daughters, three granddaughters carried off and imprisoned in Tower of London.

1410

Welsh raid on border. Ednyved ap Tudor and his brother Rhys Ddu captured. Beheaded in Chester. Black Rhys of Ceredigion captured. Beheaded in London.

1415

Glyndwr disappears.

Other books by Farolito Press

Musings of a Bario Sack Boy, poetry by L. Luis López
A Painting of Sand, poetry by L. Luis López
No Lack of Lonesome, a novel by Albino Gonzales

Farolito Press
P.O. Box 60003
Grand Junction, CO 81506

Telephone: (970) 243-5940
e-mail: melop2@aol.com